T0274290

CLEAN
POINT

CLEAN POINT

A Novel

MEG JONES

AVON

An Imprint of HarperCollins Publishers

CLEAN POINT. Copyright © 2024 by Meg Jones. All rights reserved. Printed in the United States of America. No part of this book may be used or reproduced in any manner whatsoever without written permission except in the case of brief quotations embodied in critical articles and reviews. For information, address HarperCollins Publishers, 195 Broadway, New York, NY 10007.

HarperCollins books may be purchased for educational, business, or sales promotional use. For information, please email the Special Markets Department at SPsales@harpercollins.com.

Avon, Avon & logo, and Avon Books & logo are registered trademarks of HarperCollins Publishers in the United States of America and other countries.

FIRST EDITION

Interior text design by Diahann Sturge-Campbell
Tennis ball illustration © djvstock/Stock.Adobe.com
Tennis racket and ball © Zdenek Sasek/Stock.Adobe.com

Library of Congress Cataloging-in-Publication Data has been applied for.

ISBN 978-0-06-342972-7

24 25 26 27 28 LBC 5 4 3 2 1

For anyone whose first exposure to a sport they love was through pop culture. Be it a TV show, film, smutty romance novel, or even Taylor Swift's boyfriend. Your journey of finding your team is just as legitimate as any other.

GO SPORTS!!!!

Content Warning

Please note that the following subjects/topics are touched upon within this novel:

- Explicit content throughout with open-door scenes (Dicktionary available at the back of the book)
- Abusive father/coach
- Mentions of intentional and secret drugging/medical misuse
- Mentions of disordered eating due to training
- Alcohol consumption
- Sexual harassment
- Verbal abuse/slut shaming

I hope I have written these topics with the care they deserve.

Dear American Reader,

Please note that this book has been written in UK English.

Do not be alarmed by the use of *s* where you are used to seeing a *z*, our (correctly) spelt words that include a *u* (colour vs color) or use of double *ll* (travelling vs traveling).

I understand you chucked all your tea in the water, but please abstain from throwing this book in there too.

Enjoy!
Meg Jones

Playlist

Vampire – Olivia Rodrigo
Coming of Age – Maisie Peters
Burn Alive – The Last Dinner Party
Body And Mind – girl in red
Lisbon – Wolf Alice
You're Just A Boy (And I'm Kinda The Man) – Maisie Peters
Breakfast – Dove Cameron
Not Strong Enough – boygenius
Will We Talk – Sam Fender
$20 – boygenius
Crystal Clear – Hayley Williams
Shatter – Maggie Rogers
Norgaad – The Vaccines
NDA – Billie Eilish
ballad of a homeschooled girl – Olivia Rodrigo
Meltdown – Niall Horan
Brazil – Declan McKenna
Wildest Dreams (Taylor's Version) – Taylor Swift
The Walls Are Way Too Thin – Holly Humberstone
Family Friend – The Vaccines

Final Girl – CHVRCHES

Could've Would've Should've – Taylor Swift

Easier Than Lying – Halsey

Dream Girl Evil – Florence + the Machine

True Blue – boygenius

How Not To Drown – CHVRCHES

Hoax – Taylor Swift

Don't Delete The Kisses – Wolf Alice

Superbloodmoon (feat. d4vd) – Holly Humberstone

Lullabies – CHVRCHES

Eat Your Young – Hozier

Slut! – Taylor Swift

bet u wanna – Sabrina Carpenter

History Of Man – Maisie Peters

Tennis Court – Lorde

You First – Paramore

Peace – Taylor Swift

Call Me Lover – Sam Fender

I Like You – Harry Strange

The Lady of Mercy – The Last Dinner Party

Castles Crumbling – Taylor Swift

Play God – Sam Fender

i don't want to watch the world end with someone else – Clinton Kane

Green Light – LORDE

I Know Places (Taylor's Version) – Taylor Swift

The Great War – Taylor Swift

Karma – Taylor Swift

I Know The End – Phoebe Bridgers

The Alchemy – Taylor Swift

Clean – Taylor Swift

CLEAN POINT

Prologue

Scottie
Vampire – Olivia Rodrigo

A lifetime of living and breathing and bleeding this sport had led to this. A hot summer's day in mid-July, Wimbledon's Centre Court, the Women's Singles Final. First set was hers. The second mine. And the third and final was so close, so within grasp that my hands practically ached to feel the heavy weight of the winner's dish.

Gripping the racket tightly, I rhythmically bounced the small green ball against the grass surface. Tiny thumps echoed around the vast, hushed arena as I counted.

One. Two. Three. Just like Dad used to do.

With a quick glance at the packed, overheated crowd, I found the family box and locked onto him instantly. A former tennis pro himself, he had retired in his late thirties and turned his eye to nurturing my talent. Now, eagerly leaning forward, his arms rested on his knees, his hands clasped together in anticipation as he followed my every move across the court.

I bet he counted too.

With a satisfied nod and a small smile, I focused ahead, finding my opponent, Dylan Bailey, shifting from side to side, ready and impatient for my serve.

I waited for the gust of eastern wind to die before finally tossing the ball into the air. Exhaling, I unleashed my racket, colliding with the ball and firing it across the court like a missile.

With that, the final battle had begun.

Dylan returned my shot, swiftly whipping her racket through the air with a short cut of her backhand. I lunged across the court, extending my arm to strike back. The rally continued, stroke after stroke, as she effortlessly returned each shot.

My opponent was deadly. One mistake and she'd catch it, exploit it, and triumph. Like me, she was hunting for her first Grand Slam title. And today, one of us would walk away. I couldn't afford a single misstep, not if I wanted to end this and win. *Finally* win. I pushed aside the frantic beats of my racing heart, disregarded the piercing gazes from nearly fifteen thousand pairs of eyes fixed upon me. My focus narrowed solely on the one goal I'd trained relentlessly for my entire life.

Return that damn ball.

The hot air grew heavy with the weight of tension as the crowd waited for one of us to falter. The strain was palpable, suffocating and claustrophobic. Her grunts grew tired as she returned another volley, catching me out. Her strings carved down the back of the ball. It spun backward, hit the grass, barely bounced.

My heart stumbled, a surge of adrenaline propelling me from one side of the court to the other. Stretching my arms to their limits, I loosened my grip on the racket as I exerted every ounce of strength to close the distance between the top edge of my racket and the ball. In that moment, milliseconds felt like an eternity.

Years of training, of bloodied blisters on my palms and playing on anyway, of travelling to all the tournaments I could get into, every training session where I hit ball after ball after ball after ball until the strings on my racket broke and I was yelled at to restring the damn thing and start again. It had taken me here, led me onto this court, given my body the strength and resilience it needed to run across the grass in a split second and make this damn return.

My wrist flicked, the top edge of my racket connecting with the ball, striking it back. The ball jumped over the net, launching into the empty space on the other side, before shooting off court and . . . she'd missed. The roar of the crowd erupted, the noise deafening as always, toe-curling shrieks rang out as I looked around and realised that it was all for me.

"Game, set, match—Rossi—"

I had won. This was mine. Earned with bruises and strained, aching muscles. With early mornings and missed parties with friends and all the parts of me that had been taken up with training and practice and recovery. It was for this. I was a Grand Slam champion.

Finally, I had done it.

I tried to catch my breath as I choked back emotion, relief hitting me like a tidal wave. Stumbling, I made my way to the net, extending my arm out to take Dylan's. Her hand met mine, the palm sweaty as her fingers tightened painfully around my already sore hand. I winced in pain, but her gaze only narrowed on me.

She yanked my hand forward, pulling my body close to hers. From the crowd, it might have looked like a hug, yet it was anything but, her reserve of strength much greater than mine after the tiring match.

Amid the deafening cheers, her words were almost lost, but with her lips at my ear, she sneered, "Remember this feeling, Scottie. It won't last forever."

She turned away, releasing me to the crowd as the officials reached me in congratulations. The moment apparently went unnoticed as Dylan gave her speech, receiving the runner-up plate and thanking all the usual people with an expected look of defeat. Her words continued to play around my head, and despite my victory, discomfort lodged itself in my gut.

When my fingers met the cold, polished silver of the Venus Rosewater Dish, the moment fully enveloped me. Relief surged as I remembered every time I'd considered quitting, even as recently as a few months ago, after I'd suffered an injury to my knee and my training came to a grinding halt. I was sure I'd be out for months.

Holding the dish high as the flash of cameras went off around me, I looked to the player's box again, finding my father. His eyes were on me, a warm smile on his lips, his hands wiping at his eyes. I could feel his pride radiating down on me, finally claiming my own title to sit alongside his. Continuing his legacy, training me to pick up his mantle, had been his focus for the last decade, and now it had all paid off.

All of this success, the glory of this win, was intertwined with his support and legacy. From the age of five, when my training first started, he woke at four in the morning, preparing breakfast and setting up drills. He assembled a team of experts, ensuring that I had the best resources at my disposal. His dedication matched, if not surpassed, my own, and he worked tirelessly, sharing my dreams of victory and pouring his heart into every step of our journey.

The rest of the ceremony slipped away in a blissful haze of champagne and celebration. The crowd buzzed as I lifted the dish above my head, walked around the court, and soaked in the reality of it all. The oppressive summer heat had melted away with a cool wind when we finally made our way inside, surrounded by my team and excited press.

By the time the sun set on the warm summer evening, I was beat from weeks of tireless competition. I headed home early, to the house I still lived in with my father. Boundaries would be nice, but since we trained together every morning, it didn't make sense to live apart.

Since I turned twenty-two last year, I moved out to the pool house, giving me some independence and a space to call my own, but I still had to walk through the main house for access.

As I wandered through the halls, aiming for the garden, a noise echoed from the kitchen. I stopped for a moment, before a familiar voice grew loud.

"We need to tell her," my father's right-hand man, Jon, said. He joined our team a few years ago and would often fill in for my dad at practice.

I was careful with my footsteps, silently treading closer to the kitchen, suspicion growing in the pit of my stomach. When my father replied, the suspicion grew into full-blown fear.

"She doesn't need to know."

The apprehension coursed through my veins as Jon's dissenting voice echoed. "I don't agree with you doing this. It's her body, and you're risking everything she's worked for."

"Risking it would have been to do nothing. Everything I've done over the last thirteen years has been for her career. I wasn't going to sit back and watch her miss her shot."

Realisation hit as the weight of their conversation hung in the air, leaving me on edge, overwhelmed by anxiety and fear. Questions flooded my mind as I tried to unravel the cryptic meaning hidden in their words. Me. They had to be talking about me, right?

I wasn't sure if it was the few glasses of champagne I'd consumed on a more or less empty stomach, or if I was hearing this right. I crept closer, keeping to the shadows as I peered into the kitchen.

Jon and my father were locked in a tense confrontation, the

expanse of the wide marble island separating them. My father's back was to me, while I could see the lines of stress etched into Jon's face. Dad's voice sliced through the air once more, laced with threat. "I am very aware of what is at stake. It's my name, my legacy, she's continuing. I've got as much at risk as she does."

Jon's voice trembled with a mixture of regret and urgency as he attempted to interject, his words caught in his throat. "Matteo, I—"

All at once, I'd had enough. Desperation clawed at my skin as I stepped forward, entering the kitchen with a newfound resolve. Jon's hazy eyes widened in surprise as they met mine. His body recoiled, inching away from the counter.

"What are you talking about?" I asked.

My father gradually turned to face me. His gaze, obscured by darkness, carried an unsettling intensity. With a calculated calmness, he said, "It's nothing. You should go to bed. You've had quite a lot to drink."

His words, mixed with a subtle dismissal, only fuelled the resolve burning within me.

"Dad, what is it?" I pressed once more, my voice quavering, certain it couldn't be anything as big as it felt. But as the air in the room grew heavy with unspoken truths, I stood my ground. Desperate for answers, I turned to Jon, my gaze fixed on him, silently pleading for clarity. "Jon, tell me."

Jon's expression shifted, a pained remorse etched upon his face. He shook his head, his eyes unable to meet mine as he uttered his apology. "I'm sorry, kid."

Panic seized my chest, threatening to overwhelm me. I fiercely clenched my hands, nails digging into my palms, fighting to maintain some semblance of control. My notoriously short temper was well-known within the confines of the Rossi household.

"We can talk about this in the morning," Dad started again, his expression betraying no hint of the truth. His demeanour was so calm, so convincing. Momentarily, it swayed me to believe him. Maybe at that point, I *wanted* to believe him. But my gaze fell upon the bottle of pills resting on the counter, a crushed white powder beside my familiar green morning smoothie.

And when my father deliberately shifted in front of it, as if to shield it from my view with his imposing figure, it became clear—it was too late to conceal the truth.

"Is that what I think it is?" I managed to utter. My voice strained as each word was forced. The tension in the room escalated, every passing second exacerbating the brewing storm.

My father's expression faltered, a flicker of apprehension dancing in his eyes before he attempted to regain his composure. His voice wavered ever so slightly, a crack in his carefully crafted facade.

"You don't understand."

"You're right. I don't," I admitted, shaking my head. My voice grew icy and hard. "Explain it to me."

"You were too slow. Months of no improvement. You were ready to throw in the towel. You remember, don't you?" His voice trembled, a hint of regret seeping through his words. But I was learning not to trust it. "I couldn't watch you struggle anymore. You were beating yourself up, I could see it. So, we came up with a plan."

"You came up with a plan," Jon interjected, brows furrowed before his attention turned to me. "Scottie, I found out tonight."

Dad ignored Jon's interjection, and instead took a step closer, his arms wide as if to show he was truly not dangerous, that he was still my dad. "Do you think Dylan Bailey is not doing this too? Everyone's doing it. There's no way to avoid it."

My heart sank, betrayal settling upon my shoulders. The enormity of the situation threatened to crush me as I asked the question that had to be answered, no matter how much it hurt.

"Did you . . ." I paused, almost unable to finish the thought as I considered his words.

Everyone's doing it.

I swallowed, trying to find my resolve as my world crashed down around me. The portrait of the man who had raised me, put a tennis racket in my hand and taught me everything I knew, changing in the space of minutes.

"Did you cheat?" I finally managed.

The room fell into a stifling silence. The truth, now laid bare, awaited its verdict. The revelations had shattered the image I held of my father, leaving me to grapple with the ramifications. The bond between us, once unbreakable, now stood at the precipice, teetering on an abyss.

"Yes." His answer echoed around the kitchen, and the tear between us was physical. A shifted fault line that could never be repaired.

I didn't move an inch as I spoke again. "And me?"

"You needed it." He pleaded, "I couldn't watch my daughter lose again."

I shook my head, tearing my gaze from him. Tears clouded my vision as one word echoed around my mind. One name I'd be called if they all found out, whispered in corridors and locker rooms when I dared to pass by. What I'd be branded as, even if I could prove I had nothing to do with it. What I was.

Cheat.

"How long?"

Cheat.

"Scottie." I hated the way he said my name. Hated the betrayal. Hated he thought he did this for me, that I was weak without it. Hated what he stole from me.

Cheat.

"How long?" My voice trembled as my control began to slacken, my feet growing weak from under me.

Finally, he answered, "Two months."

My mind raced, but I already knew why. My knee injury. Sure, I had been behind on training, recovering, yes, but slowly, too slow to make a real impact this year, but there was always next year. Or the year after. This . . . this could steal everything from me.

Fear flooded my mind as I remembered the federation had stopped by for at least two random drug tests since then, and there was sure to be another visit now I'd won.

"I've done tests since then."

He shook his head. "They won't find it. Not unless they look for it."

I wasn't sure if that was good news, knowing I could get away with this, keep my victory if I kept the truth to myself. I looked to Jon, trying to calculate if he'd report me. We'd worked together for years. He was like an uncle to me, training me day after day, but were we close enough to ask this of him? To keep this secret?

"I . . . I cheated." The words seemed so foreign to me, it felt like somebody else had said them.

"No," Dad said, his voice stern and resolute. He took another step forward, but I clambered backward. "You won."

When I finally managed to look at him again, I swore it would be for the last time. The last time he would have any control over my life. The last time I'd ever think of him as my "Dad."

"I had every chance of winning, but you stole this from me. You didn't believe in me." I spat the words at him, my body growing heated with anger, with shame I'd let this happen. That anyone had owned this power over me where they could steal the one thing I'd been working towards my entire life.

My career, all my training, it had been for him. Matteo Rossi's daughter is what I was. A tool to further his success. That's what my life was reduced to.

Well, fuck that.

I wanted to burn it all to the ground. Free myself from his grip. And if it meant decimating my career, then so be it.

I left the room, left without another word, running to the pool house to grab only the essentials: passport, phone charger, not even a change of clothes, before disappearing into the night, swearing never to return.

Former Grand Slam Champion Stripped of Victory as Doping Scandal Rocks Tennis World

Today the International Tennis Integrity Agency (ITIA) announced that Scottie Sinclair (formerly Rossi) will be stripped of her recent Wimbledon victory.

The agency confirmed the "presence of a prohibited substance in a player's sample," sending shockwaves throughout the sport.

Despite the Brit's voluntary admission to her illicit actions, her failure to provide a plausible explanation for her use of the restricted substance caused the agency to hand down a two-year ban.

Adding fuel to the fire, reports suggest a rift between Sinclair and her father and mentor, Matteo Rossi. At the time of publication, neither party was available for a statement.

Fallen Wimbledon Queen's Wild Night Exposed!

Scottie Sinclair spent a steamy night with two Formula 1 heartthrobs! The golden-haired siren, who has been gallivanting across the European playground ever since her two-year tennis ban twelve months ago, was seen cosying up to the racing duo at an exclusive club before retiring with the two at the famous Hotel de Paris Monte-Carlo.

Despite tantalising eyewitness accounts bolstered by a grainy photograph, this columnist dares not speculate on the juicy details.

This is the latest in a series of scandals for the British beauty. Remember when she had to be dramatically rescued off the sun-kissed Amalfi Coast, after an extravagant champagne-induced escapade caused her to sink an A-lister's luxury yacht, stranding them both in a sea of embarrassment?

Oh, the drama never ceases to follow the irresistible Scottie.

OTHER STORIES: Gut-Wrenching Blow for Tennis Star Nico Kotas as Knee Injury Forces Him Under the Knife!

First Set

CHAPTER ONE

Scottie

Coming of Age – Maisie Peters

(Almost) Two Years Later

I never much cared what the newspapers and gossip rags wrote about me, but the article exposing the threesome with the F1 drivers in Monaco . . . yeah, I cut that one out and framed it.

Monaco had been fun. All of Europe had been fun. Everywhere I went was sun-soaked and carb heavy, with late nights and later mornings. But when that second winter in exile rolled in, I found myself longing for London again. I had ended up crashing at my mum's house.

Kit Sinclair was a supermodel in the '90s, accidentally left knocked up after a one-night stand with Matteo. Barely eighteen, she was on her own, and at the start of a promising career. So, after a brief holiday to Switzerland, a baby, and an intensive version of the cabbage soup diet, she returned triumphant to the runway, leaving all parental rights in the hands of the oh so trustworthy Matteo.

"Good morning, love." Mum yawned, tucking her short blonde hair behind her ear as she walked into the kitchen. "What's making headlines today?"

I glanced at the iPad resting in front of me, featuring a photo of last night's escapade: me being escorted out of a trendy Soho night-club, tightly linked with a Dutch prince. Or wait, was he Swedish?

"Nothing new, really. Not worth looking at."

"I'm sure I'll catch up later." She slid into the chair across from me, a luxurious silk dressing gown draped around her slender frame. Leaning forward, she delicately pinched a slice of toast from my plate, taking a minuscule bite akin to that of a bird, before placing it back.

I arched a brow at her. "I can make you your own if you'd like?"

"No need." She dismissed me with a wave of her hand. "I'm heading out to Bellamy's for lunch. Don't want to spoil my appetite."

I shrugged, not bothering to argue with her, before finishing up my own piece. It had been a spur-of-the-moment decision to reach out to her six months ago, when I discovered we were both in Paris for Fashion Week, courtesy of Page Six. Despite the absence of a relationship between us, I had always assumed it was her who didn't want a connection.

But after tracking her down, and two bottles of French wine later, she'd finally told me the truth. Matteo had forced her to sign over parental rights, threatening to leak stories about her to the press. Her career was only beginning to heat up at that point, and the press was an entirely different beast in the '90s.

Mum had allowed him to take me away, still a teenager herself, believing it was best for her to disappear from my life. I had never felt the absence of a mum until these past few months, and now, I wondered how different my life might have been if she had been a part of it.

"Oh, I forgot to say, a friend stopped by for you last night," she said casually, taking a sip of tea. My eyebrows furrowed as I tried to remember if I was expecting a visitor. I had never brought anyone here, always meeting in hotels or bars. Somewhere public where I could be seen in case I got up to something.

"Who was it?" I asked, curiosity tinged with a hint of caution.

She squinted for a moment as she seemingly racked her brain for a name. "Jonathan?"

My heart clenched as the name hit me like a lightning bolt, throwing me back to that dark night almost two years ago. The last time I'd seen him. He'd called, but I'd blocked his number and tried to forget. He'd claimed to be innocent, but since he had been my coach, I didn't know who I could trust.

"Jon was here?"

Mum nodded, a mischievous twinkle in her eyes. "Tall guy? Handsome? Could do with some Botox around here?" She pointed to the side of her eye. "Only a little, of course, don't want to lose that hunky, weathered look altogether."

I wasn't sure about the wrinkles, but the rest sounded like him. "What did he want?"

"To talk, I think? I told him he could stay. I certainly wouldn't have minded. But I also didn't know when you'd be back."

"Do you know if he's . . ."

"Coming back? I think so. He didn't want to wait around, but he was eager to chat."

I swore under my breath. I had no intentions of "catching up" with anyone from my old life, especially if they had a connection to Matteo. The only news he'd have of me would come from gossip rags. I swiftly carried my dishes to the sink, my mother's eyes tracking my every move.

"I'm going out of town," I said. "I have a Danish prince who offered to show me around Copenhagen."

My mother responded with an exasperated eye roll. "Darling,

been there and done that. Trust me, there's not much excitement in Copenhagen, even with a prince by your side."

I shot her a confused look before resolving. "Fine," I declared, my mind already racing. "I'm sure there's plenty to do in Paris. I'll catch the next train."

Rushing out of the kitchen and up the grand staircase, I made my way to the guest bedroom I'd been calling my own and grabbed an empty duffel bag. I grabbed what clothes I could, not bothering to think of outfits as I went. It was Paris, after all. I could shop.

"Scottie, what are you doing?" My mum lazily appeared in the doorframe, cup of tea in hand.

I didn't bother to even look at her as I answered. "Packing."

"No, I mean you packed my Dior dress," she exclaimed, a small hint of annoyance in her voice. "I love that we are the same size, but I told you—no taking the vintage out of the country."

Without uttering a word, I tossed the dress back to her, my determination undeterred. I continued my packing mission, locating my passport on the dresser and throwing it in the bag.

"I'm not sure why you're in such a rush," my mother remarked, her tone teasing. "He was quite handsome. I wouldn't be so quick to escape if a man like that was searching for me."

"If you knew who his boss was, you'd be running too," I replied cryptically.

"Maybe . . ." She trailed off. "Or . . ."

"Or?"

"Or you could not run and listen to what he has to say," she proposed, her voice gentle yet persuasive. Sounding, dare I say it, motherly?

"And why would I do that?" Scepticism laced my words as I finally spared her a glance.

"Because he left a message begging you to not run and to listen to what he had to say. It's almost like he knows you well."

I hesitated, thinking over the situation. We'd been friends, Jon and I. Sure, he'd worked me to the bone during training. But we'd joke around, he'd listen to me if I was complaining, and would take my aches and pains seriously, an ice pack and some aspirin at the ready.

"You never said he left a message."

"You didn't let me get very far before you stormed up here and started stealing"—she let out a sharp dramatic gasp—"the black Chanel dress from '93. Pass it here." She pointed a thin finger at my bag. I turned, the dress falling out.

Damn, I'd been hoping to get that one past her.

Reluctantly, I pulled the dress out and handed it to her. She clutched the delicate material to her chest before her gaze softened once again, voice tangled with concern. "I think you should hear what he has to say."

"Why? You know what they did to me."

"Wasn't it your father—" I cut her off with a scowl before she corrected herself, "Matteo?"

I shook my head, glancing around the messy room, clothes thrown all over the floor. "I can't be sure," I admitted, a wave of nausea rolling through my stomach at the mere thought. The memory of finding out someone who claimed to love me had drugged and violated me for months was still vivid in my mind. My autonomy stripped away, my body no longer my own. I had spent countless hours in therapy trying to heal from the trauma, but I was still grappling with the aftermath. I was still unsure if I wanted all the details. Sometimes, ignorance was safest.

Silently, Mum moved farther inside the room, settling herself on my bed. With a tender gesture, she patted the spot next to her, and I surrendered, easing myself down onto the mattress. A wave of weariness washed over me as I leaned against her on instinct, breathing in her expensive perfume. Chanel, no doubt.

"You don't need to run, you know," she said. "Your dad isn't chasing you."

I lifted my head, shooting her the "we don't call him that" look, but she brushed it off nonchalantly before continuing. "It's been almost two years. I think you've made it clear by now with all your gallivanting around Europe and throwing your career into the fire that you want nothing to do with him."

"I feel like I'm waiting for him to show up on the doorstep and order me back into a cage." The words were barely louder than a whisper, but they hurt all the same. I hadn't realised how restrictive my life had been until I'd left. How much there was of the world to enjoy. What it was like to have more than one glass of wine and eat both the burger and chips and not feel guilty after. Now I was free, the thought of going back was an enormous monster hiding in the dark, taunting me with only its presence.

"He doesn't make the rules anymore, Scottie. You call the shots, you make the decisions." She raised a hand and gave my blonde hair a gentle, comforting stroke before wrapping her arm around me and pulling me close. "If you want to run to Paris, give me five minutes and I'll pack a bag. Girls' weekend in the City of Lights. The two of us together? We'll tear it to pieces."

I laughed lightly, thinking somebody better pre-warn France. "What about your lunch at Bellamy's?"

She waved a hand, dismissing the thought. "My friends are used to my last-minute cancellations. And besides, who wants to lunch with a group of former models? They hardly touch the food they order."

"We should discuss your eating habits sometime. I'm amazed at how you manage."

She smirked, a mischievous glint in her blue eyes. Deep ocean blue, lined with black. The same as mine. "Oh, I do eat. I just ensure it's worth every single calorie."

Before I could roll my eyes at her playful remark, the sound of the doorbell pierced the air, and my heart skipped a beat. I inhaled deeply, remembering my mother's words.

I was done running.

CHAPTER TWO

Scottie

Burn Alive – The Last Dinner Party

Jon Anderson settled himself into my mother's plush couch, positioned directly across from me. Two steaming cups of tea sat on the coffee table divide, forced upon the American by my mother's good English nature.

"It's good to see you, Scottie. You look well," Jon said, a warm smile forming faint lines on his face. He looked almost the same as he had two years ago, with the same friendly, thin-lipped smile and sharp eyes, his skin now slightly weathered and darkened by countless hours standing outside watching players running across a court.

"Thanks" was all I managed. From the moment I'd opened the door to my mum's townhouse and found him standing on the quiet London street, my mind had been a rush of panicked questions, overwhelming me into an unusual silence.

"Have you been in London long?" my mother asked as she entered the stylishly decorated living room, placing a delicate plate of chocolate-covered biscuits between us, before sitting to my left.

"A week or so. I've been working in Spain for a while."

"Oh, that explains the tan," she remarked with a warm smile. "Was it more coaching work?"

He leaned forward, perching himself on the edge of the sofa as he picked up a sugar cube and plopped it into the brewing liquid. "Yes, I've been working with Inés Costa since—" He paused, as if realising his words. When he continued, his revelation caught me off guard. "Since I was fired."

"Matteo fired you?" I asked, my voice still quiet.

He nodded, his grim expression reflecting the gravity of the situation. "Just after you left."

"I'm sorry."

A smile broke his stony demure. "Don't be. I was about to quit when he did it. And because he terminated my contract early, I got full payment."

I let out a brief, awkward laugh, feeling the tension in the room grow as the conversation settled upon us. The unease in my stomach intensified.

"Listen, I know I said it before, but I promise, I didn't know. I walked in on him crushing the pills for your smoothie, and I knew better than to trust that they were just supplements. I never would've done that without your permission. Hell, I would've quit if your training plan included a banned substance. All that hard work lost because of a blood test?"

I raised an eyebrow at Jon, just as he realised his wording. "Sorry, I . . . I was proud of you for stepping forward. It wasn't you who cheated, but you paid the consequences, anyway."

"I figured the best way for payback was to make it all for nothing."

"It cost you everything, Scottie."

My gaze fixed on my steaming cup of tea as I moved to pick it up, feeling a mix of emotions swirling within me. His words sank in, and a sense of bitterness and regret crept into my voice.

"It is what it is," I muttered, taking a long sip. Nothing like a strong brew to wash away the trauma.

Jon leaned forward, his fingers intertwining. "I don't quite agree there . . ."

"What do you mean?"

"You know your ban is up in a few weeks?"

"So?"

"So"—his voice is light, full of a hope I feel so unfamiliar with—"now is the time to start training again."

I couldn't help the laugh that escaped me, the disbelief I had at the idea. I placed the mug back on the table, barely able to get the words out fast enough. "I have no intention of training ever again."

I was exhausted at the thought alone. That lifestyle was a million miles from my life now. Sure, I'd kept up my fitness with near daily gym visits and the odd escapade running through the streets of Rome with the Italian police at my back. I was a certain male pop star's running companion for a while until I realised he couldn't keep up. However, his short shorts did make up for it.

But that was nothing compared to training professionally. That took body, mind, and soul. I'd been able to commit to it before, but now I'd tasted freedom, and my soul wasn't so sure it wanted to return.

Jon lowered his head, his eyes wide with shock. "What?" The word stumbled out of his slackened mouth.

My back stiffened as I tapped into that white hot rage that lived inside of me. "I have no intention of ever stepping onto a tennis court again, unless Matteo Rossi is trapped inside, and I have a tank of fuel in one hand and a lit match in the other."

He took another sip of his tea as he made me wait for his response. "Well." He shrugged. "I think that's a waste."

I laughed. "Of what? Human organs?"

"Of talent."

"I only won because I cheated," I reminded him, and beside me, my mother stiffened, her reaction reminding me of her presence. I looked over at her and found her brows crinkled with worry. When she noticed my gaze, she smiled weakly, a hand coming over to rest on mine and giving it a tight squeeze of comfort.

Jon coughed to clear his throat. "I can assure you, Scottie, you can absolutely win without cheating. You could be one of the greatest in this sport, but somebody robbed you of the chance to see it. To prove that to yourself."

While I was quiet, he continued. "I've been watching the others. Emilia, Inés—you must've seen she won the French Open. Even Dylan Bailey. They haven't changed tactics in the last two years. All of your competitors, playing the same way, the same old tricks. You were the one who caught them out, saw their plays before they could take advantage of you. You knew how to wear them down. How to trap them. That's how you got to the finals, and I know, with training—good, honest training—you could do it again."

I closed my eyes, shielding myself from his praise. I didn't need to hear how good I once was. It all counted for nothing. "I-I can't go back."

"Why not?"

"Nobody will trust me." *Cheat.* "They'll say it's all drugs." *Cheat.*

All I could think of was how they would look at me with whispered snide remarks, judging for what had happened *to* me, thinking I was the culprit instead of the victim. They'd think I'd brought it on myself.

Cheat.

He shook his head, eyes filled with determination. "We will prove them wrong. The ITIA will test you to within an inch of your life, anyway."

He was right. They'd suck me dry like a vampire.

"I'm too out of practice; there's no way I can catch up."

Jon shrugged my concerns away. "All the more reason to start as soon as we can. It's a challenge, but people have come back from worse."

I rubbed my clammy palms along the denim of my jeans, trying to soothe the rising nerves. I hadn't dared let myself wonder what I'd do when my ban was up. Part of me thought nobody would care anymore. They all had me labelled as a cheat. Besides, with the way the tabloids had reported on my every single move the past few months, my reputation was in near tatters. That was what I'd wanted, what I'd needed for revenge. To reclaim everything from the person who had stolen it.

"I-I can't win. Matteo . . . he will—" I stuttered, the chaos of my mind erupting out of my mouth. Mum's hand squeezed around mine once again.

I hadn't realised Jon had gotten up until he sat down next to me, the couch dipping under his weight. Even sitting down, he towered over me. I was tall myself, long-legged like my mum, but closing in at six-foot-eight, Jon was a certified giant.

"Matteo thought you couldn't win on your own. Prove him wrong. Prove yourself better than he ever was," Jon said, his arm wrapped around the back of the couch to face me. I could see fire and resolve burning in his eyes, the very same that I used to have.

That was what it took to win. You had to be prepared to fight for every strike. Meanwhile, I still felt the weariness in my bones, the fear of losing it all again. If I was going to do this, I had to turn fear into fight. Turn anger into ambition.

And it had to be enough to fuel me.

Jon's smile turned crooked as he changed tactics. "And if it's revenge you're looking for . . ."

I hesitated, something flickering inside. The strike of a match. "Yes?"

A wide grin stretched across his lips, like a hunter realising its prey had fallen into a perfectly laid trap. "Then I have the perfect doubles partner in mind for you."

CHAPTER THREE

Nico
Body And Mind – girl in red

Smashing the tennis racket against the ground did nothing to alleviate the throbbing pain in my right knee, but it sure was cheaper than anger management classes.

The metallic arch of the rim bent like rubber against the floor of the indoor court, before giving in to the force and shattering into bits. Even the string bed crumpled against the ground and lost any structure it once had. The sharp snaps and cracks bounced off the bare walls, ringing loudly in my ears, barely managing to drown out the voice inside my head repeating over and over.

Failure.

In mere seconds, the racket had fallen to pieces in the same way I'd been doing for months.

"Are you done yet?" Jon snipped, appearing at the edge of the court, his tall stature taking up the doorway. He walked over, an unusually light tone to his gruff voice. "Or would you like another racket to beat to death? Perhaps you could throw some balls toward the sun and launch them into outer space?"

I turned away, seething anger and frustration still coursing through my veins. I needed a moment to breathe. Struggling not to limp under the fiery ache in my leg, I stretched for my water bottle, taking a deliberate, prolonged sip, wishing I could perform some kind of miracle and turn the drink into whisky.

"I'm fine," I ground out, tossing the bottle into my racket bag. I needed to massage my knee, work through the pain like the physio had shown me, but I wasn't ready to surrender to that kind of vulnerability. Work through the pain. Pretend it doesn't exist. It's all in my head.

Ever since the accident, a simple slip during a match, my knee wasn't the same. The fatigue of playing professionally had already taken its toll, but after the injury, the pain got worse until it was nearly unbearable to walk for days after competitions.

"The racket begs to differ."

I looked plainly at him, but he only shrugged me off. "How long have you been here?"

A quick glance at a clock on the opposite wall had me realising how much time had passed. Hours in the gym used to be nothing to me. I couldn't let it be any different now.

"Couple hours," I lied easily. I'd had a restless night, pain waking me up at five in the morning despite the pre-bed ice pack. I'd learned the hard way there was no point in trying to get back to sleep, so I'd figured I'd try to train off the pain instead.

I was almost six months post-op—or, more accurately, six months post the *first* surgery—and the recovery process was still too slow. I spent weeks trying to distract myself from all the wasted time lying around. From watching old matches, studying opponents and gameplay, to letting my older brother drag me along to his weekly Dungeons & Dragons group.

At least that wasn't a complete waste. I got my half-orc barbarian to level twenty.

When the physio finally allowed me back to regular training, I had thought this would be it. This would be what my body had been begging me for, my feet on the court and a racket in my hand. Feed the hunger that had been building. And get me away from spending the rest of my orc life fighting imaginary goblins and kobolds.

The destroyed racket was evidence of how wrong I'd been.

"Your physio said you're allowed back with *rest*," Jon reminded me. His tone was soft, yet his words pricked my skin like tiny needles.

I shook my head. "I've rested enough." Reaching down, I grabbed another racket from my bag before looking back at Jon. "Can you just let me practise my returns?"

He didn't move from his spot, his arms folded. "I think you've done plenty for today. Hit the ice bath, take a breather. Get out of the house."

"I go out," I argued back. "I'm here, aren't I?"

"I meant somewhere other than the gym. When did you last go anywhere other than home, here, and the physio?" he interrogated. I didn't answer. There wasn't anything for me elsewhere. This was all that existed. Well, this and my brother's basement, but I wasn't telling Jon anything about game night.

Jon reappeared in my life three months back, sent by my previous trainer when my recovery became too complicated. Jon and I shared a history—buddies from way back when he used to coach me. We'd parted ways after he was poached by another player, but we'd managed to stay in touch, catching up over drinks in hotel bars wherever our paths crossed at tournaments. He'd been helping with the recovery, putting me in contact with his team of doctors and physios. Checking in every few days, he'd blend his analysis into the gameplay I was glued to, insisting on diversifying my watchlist. He forced me through the first *Rocky* film before I gave in, letting him queue up the entire series and the numerous spin-offs without much protest.

I shook my head and pressed a button on a remote. The machine set up on the opposite side of the net began to shoot balls in my direction. Grinding my teeth, I unleashed a barrage of returns, knocking each ball to the other side. I focused my attention on the fluidity of my movements, attempting to find the rhythm that once came so effortlessly. The familiar sound of the ball meeting the strings and the whip of the racket echoed in the air, and for a moment, I felt a glimmer of the joy this used to bring me. The sun's heat on my neck, sweat rolling down; the echo of the umpire's decisions, the relief when it went my way; and the true focus on the win, on my opponent. But every swing carried a reminder of the setback I'd endured, the months of frustration and slow progress. A pang of frustration gripped me, threatening to overshadow my determination. I fought it down, channelling my energy into each stroke, each return.

"Stop favouring your left leg!" Jon shouted as he stood on the sidelines. I swore under my breath. I knew I'd been doing it, but the weariness was returning, creeping into my vision. Pushing on, I took his advice and shifted my weight over to my right leg.

I ran back to return the ball, when my right leg shifted unexpectedly from under me. Falling forward, my leg collided with the ground. Groaning in pain, all the air left my body at once as I held my knee in my hands, lying defeated on the ground. Pain seared from the injury. I could feel the ugly scar, the freshly healed skin below my fingertips.

"Are you going to listen to me now?" Jon's head popped into view, his body leaning over me as I lay useless. Deep ragged breaths escaped me as I tried to pull myself together.

"Probably not," I managed, the sound escaping me on a wheeze.

"Then I guess I'll leave you here to limp home."

"Jon," I called out. He'd already disappeared from view, his footsteps echoing farther and farther away from me. Finally, I relented, frustration getting the better of me. "Wait. Fine. You're right."

There was a pause, as if he was revelling in the satisfaction of being so goddamn right before he reappeared in my view, a friendly smile and a hand offered my way.

"Glad you could admit it," he said with a strain as he hoisted me up from the ground.

I grumbled a thank you before attempting to walk across the hall. Hissing with pain, I tried to stand on my right leg. The pain was still too much, forcing me to limp. Jon let out a sigh before catching up to me, offering me a shoulder to lean on. I fought against the help, but one look at the far-off bench and I was forced to accept the support.

"Thanks," I said yet again as we reached the sidelines, feeling increasingly sorrier for myself. I lowered and took a seat, reaching for my water bottle for some relief.

"When was the last time you let off some steam?"

"Didn't you see the racket from earlier?"

Jon let out a huff of disappointment. "I mean like, what was the last thing you did for fun?"

"Last week. You came over and we watched *Bring It On*."

Jon shook his head. "Something that's not with me. Or your family, for that matter. When's the last time you went out on a date?"

"I don't see the relevance." I turned away from him, my attention focused on throwing items in my bag for a quick exit from this conversation. Truth was, it had been a while since anything more than casual had even stood a chance. It was easier on tour, every few weeks a new city, a new bar, a new selection on the dating apps. Lying at home feeling sorry for myself didn't scream "single and ready to mingle."

"My point is, since the accident, you're not the same player you were before," he said as he sat down beside me, his words carefully chosen.

"Gee, thanks. Glad you're on my team."

He raised an eyebrow at me as if to say "are you done?" before continuing, "But it doesn't mean you can't become better."

I stared at him like he'd lost more than a couple marbles, but the serious look remained on his face. "I have a plan. But you aren't going to like it."

I eyed him for a moment, trying to read his expression, but the lines of his wrinkles and dark brows gave nothing away.

"What is it?"

"You've played doubles before, right?"

"A few times."

"Ever won?" he asked. I shrugged before nodding. Doubles had never been my favourite way to play. I didn't really mind playing that style, but finding the right partner was the biggest struggle. I was fast. I knew how to read the ball, but it was hard to read another player, hard to learn their style and adapt. I knew how to command a court all by myself, so why did I need another person?

Then he told me his plan, and he was right. I hated it.

CHAPTER FOUR

Scottie
Lisbon – Wolf Alice

Three Days Later

I'd considered not showing up at Jon's. My bag was still packed for Paris, and I'd managed to sneak some of Mum's vintage Dior, but the name Nico Kotas kept me curious enough to remain in London. I pressed the doorbell of Jon's rented apartment. My racing heart had barely a moment to settle before a visibly frustrated Jon swung the door open.

"Scottie!" he sang loudly, before his voice dipped into an angry whisper. "You're forty-five minutes late."

"Lovely to see you, Jon." I pushed forward, ignoring his comment, before stepping past him into the hallway. "The tube was busy."

It had taken a lot of convincing to leave the house. Some more to catch the train. I kept thinking of the last few years, of all the freedom I'd had, all the fun. But there was something Jon had said to me when he visited that had played on my mind and kept me wondering.

Could I really win?

I remembered how it felt to raise that Wimbledon plate. The glory of it all, the relief that years of work had led to. The feeling had been stolen from me. But I wanted to feel it again, to earn it, to fight for it. I was still so hungry for that win.

Jon grumbled as he closed the door behind me, and I slipped off my raincoat before hanging it up. I hadn't bothered dressing up, only wearing some comfy leggings and an old designer jumper, but now that I was inside, doubts crept in, and I began to wonder if I should have tried to make a better impression.

Jon led me through to the front room, and there I found him, Nico Kotas. He was only slightly taller than I was, but large. Even his presence was dominating.

Born in the US to Greek immigrants, Nico's backhand had been the thing of legend for fifteen years. The very backhand that destroyed Matteo's career.

Closing the space, I stuck out my hand. "Nico, good to meet you."

He paused, his expression fixed on me, as if he were a tiger deliberating whether I would be its prey. He used the extra inches of height and wide-set shoulders to his advantage, staring me down with storm grey eyes.

With what could only resemble a gruff noise of disapproval, he shifted his gaze to Jon, completely ignoring my outstretched hand.

"Let's get this done with, shall we?" he said, backing away.

What a dick.

I began to feel stupid, cast aside by this man who clearly thought he was better than me. Deflated, I lowered my hand to my side and rubbed my palm against my leggings, trying to soothe my growing frustration.

Summoning my courage, I decided to make an effort and try again.

"I saw some of your quarter-final match with Oliver Anderson last year, at the US Open," I said, his annoyed attention sliding back over his shoulder. "That was a great match. I couldn't believe the fifth set."

In truth, I hadn't missed a single moment of that match. Tucked in a corner cafe, on a rare rainy day in Paris, I had found myself captivated by the way he managed to read his opponent, the way he dominated the court. Suddenly, I'd understood why Matteo had treated him like such a threat.

Fifteen years ago, Matteo had been number one when unseeded Nico Kotas stood opposite him during the Australian Open final. At the top of his game, his skill was unmatched with an almost cruel guarantee he would destroy whoever dared to meet him across a court. Meanwhile, nobody had expected fresh-faced, eighteen-year-old Nico to make it to the quarter finals, let alone the finals.

I'd been in the crowd, ten years old and already deep into my own training. I still remember the shock on my father's face when, against all the odds, Nico took the final set and walked off the court champion.

"Oliver always knows how to put on a show," he finally ground out, although he made it seem like even looking at me was hard work.

"Nico's been recovering from a knee replacement," Jon informed, lingering in the doorway. I suppressed a grimace, acutely aware of the toll tennis took on our bodies. How old was Nico now? Thirty-two? Thirty-three? The wear and tear was more than evident. "There've been a couple of setbacks, but he's ready to get back to training."

I nodded, my gaze fixed on Nico, who stood safely on the opposite side of the room, his strong arms folded as he maintained an unnerving silence. Correction, *almost* complete silence.

"How's your dad?" he asked, a snide grin pulling on the corner of his lips as he spoke. His words took direct aim at my most sensitive nerve.

"I wouldn't know." I shrugged, masking my annoyance with practised ease. "We're not exactly on speaking terms."

Nico rolled his eyes, turning to my former trainer. "Why am I here, Jon?"

I tried to stop myself from grinding my teeth, my hands tightening into fists to restrain my anger. *Was he always this rude?* I'd always heard good things about Nico, that he was friendly and nice, a professional to work with. But this was the opposite.

"You need a partner," Jon interjected.

"I can find somebody else." His unspoken words were clear: *anyone but her.* I was so overwhelmed with irritation that Jon was able to respond to him before I could.

"You won't find anyone as good."

"She hasn't played competitively in years; she can't be that good."

This time, Jon wasn't fast enough to speak, and I seized the opportunity instead. "And you in six months, but you still remember how to pick up a racket and hit a ball, don't you?"

"Still know how to play clean, do you?" he fired back, a cocky smirk on his lips. He looked at me, and I found nothing but judgement held in his eyes. That look was exactly how they would all see me, what they would think about me.

Cheat.

I shook it off, shook him off, and with my own sly smile, I shot back, "Still think you can keep up, old man?"

He laughed, the noise cruel. "Old man? I could wipe the court with you."

Standing tall, my eyes swept across his broad shoulders before locking with his challenging gaze. I'd love to see him on the other side of the net, curious to see how fast his body could move, would love to watch him unravel.

"I'd like to see you try," I challenged, a spark of anticipation igniting within me. He was still across the room, but it might as well have been inches, the tension closing the walls in on us.

Nico's jaw opened as if to deliver a sharp retort, but Jon interjected instead, "See, this is what we want to see, but on the same side."

Nico's attention was torn from me, his dark brows pressing together. "Mixed doubles? With her? Are you insane? You know the single's title is what matters."

"You'd both take part in the singles and the mixed competition." Jon tilted his head, undeterred. "Besides, ever heard 'the enemy of my enemy is my friend'?"

"He's her dad, not her enemy." He pointed an accusatory finger at me, and I fought the urge not to slap it away.

"He's not my dad," I corrected him. "Not anymore."

Jon stepped farther into the room, hands out as if to try to ease the mounting pressure. "It's not that, Nico. You have a brilliant tactical mind, but your speed is still lacking. Your recovery will only take you so far."

I scoffed. "So I'm supposed to carry him?"

"You're supposed to learn from him." Jon shook his head, his eyes soft on me. "You play with him, learn his style, and you'll be unstoppable in the women's competition." I didn't react, instead analysing his plan. Nico had been one of the top tennis players for the last decade. Clearly, even while trying to launch a comeback after his surgery, there was a lot to learn from him. I'd be rusty from my time away, but I still kept my speed and relative fitness. Guidance was precisely what I needed.

Jon continued, looking to Nico, "Meanwhile, she's the perfect training partner for you. She's fast enough to be a challenge and in the mixed, she can compensate if your injury acts up."

I wanted to shout about how unfair it was for me to be expected to compensate for him, especially in a sport that constantly sidelined women, overlooking and underappreciating our accomplish-ments. Where people contest the simple fact we have some of the greatest sportspeople of all time because they were misogynistic or racist or, hell, even both.

But deep down, I understood Jon wasn't suggesting anything of the sort. This was a pact with the devil, and it was as difficult for Nico as it was for me. One look at Nico, and I could tell he was con-templating quitting just to avoid working alongside me.

Yet, Jon had a knack for persuasion. "Play together. Win together. Piss off Matteo together. "

The room fell into a tense silence, Jon's words lingering in the air. I could sense the internal struggle within Nico, his conflicting emotions warring against each other. The prospect of teaming up with me, the daughter of his former rival, was undoubtedly a bitter pill to swallow. But there was something in Jon's proposition that chipped away at his resistance. I weighed my decision too. I could see what Jon was offering, but I'd never played mixed, never trained alongside anyone else. How much of a change would it be?

But without Nico, I couldn't return to tennis. Couldn't allow Mat-teo the satisfaction. I'd be giving in to what he wanted—a tennis prodigy to carry on his mantle. A different surname would never take away the fact that I was his daughter. I needed a way to twist the knife. To come back on my own would prove to him and myself I could do it without cheating, but it wasn't enough.

Teaming up with his rival, however, could be the perfect revenge I've been craving.

Nico let out a frustrated sigh, his gaze darting between Jon and me. "Fine," he muttered begrudgingly, as he ran a hand through his hair, longer strands escaping to fall around his face. Nico's gaze landed on me, a mix of scepticism and curiosity in his eyes. "But don't expect me to go easy on you."

A small smile tugged at the corners of my lips as he extended his hand to me. I took a moment, remembering from before how he'd dismissed mine. I returned the gesture, his calloused fingers rubbing against my own and sealed my fate.

And just like that, the enemy of my enemy was my new teammate.

CHAPTER FIVE

Scottie

You're Just A Boy (And I'm Kinda
The Man) – Maisie Peters

Jon laid out the plan. Within a few days, we'd ship out to a training program he'd set up at a private complex in Rhodes. There were already a few different pros at the camp, which would give us the opportunity to play against varied competitors and would offer shared access to some of the top trainers and professionals in the sport. Then six weeks later, we'd make our anticipated comeback at Wimbledon. It would have been ideal to have a warm-up tournament to attend first, allowing me to ease back into that world, but since this was the first event after my ban expired, it was the only option Jon proposed.

Not to mention, Nico seemed to make it clear this was the only event he was interested in.

After I left Jon's, I heard nothing from my new mixed partner. Not surprising, given he barely looked at me while Jon had laid out the plan, going over the names of personal trainers and nutritionists he'd involve in our training. All of them were new to me. I'd asked Jon only to use people he trusted, and more importantly, people with no connection to Matteo.

I still wasn't sure about the plan when the travel itinerary for the trip to Greece landed in my inbox, still half-convincing myself as I stuffed all my belongings back into the two large suitcases I lived out of.

I stopped at the row listed on my ticket. Ignoring my assigned aisle seat, I slid into the window spot instead. I'd never enjoyed flying. Something about being sealed into a metal container that hurled itself 33,000 feet or so in the air had always left my stomach twisting into knots. The window made it slightly better when motion sickness kicked in, and so I always tried to reserve it. Hopefully the rightful owner wouldn't mind. If they did, I'd grab the barf bag and warn them out of the splash zone.

Getting comfortable, I continued to weigh up the pros and cons of agreeing to become mixed partners with Nico Kotas. I'd been left with sleepless nights ever since Jon appeared on my mum's doorstep, so I had resolved to use the four-hour flight time to sleep it off. Once we landed, there wouldn't be much time for rest. We had a lot of ground to cover if we were going to get into shape in time. Placing a silk sleep mask on before propping my head against the window, I closed my eyes and tried to relax, surrendering to the weariness and allowing sleep to wash over me.

"You're in my seat." I was almost sure I'd dreamt up the voice, but one peep from under the eye mask and I discovered Nico staring down at me, donning a cap and a face contorted with irritation.

Casting a glance at the exasperated passengers forming a line behind him, I suggested quickly, "Can you take the aisle? I'm a nervous flyer."

His grim expression didn't waver, eyes fixed to me.

"No."

His sharp retort hung in the air for a moment, causing me to pause and process it. His hand rested on the headrest in front, fingers tapping impatiently. Somehow, I managed a polite smile

at the growing queue behind him, answering Nico through gritted teeth.

"I'm sure we could swap."

My stomach began to twist, my mouth watering at the memory
of jittery takeoffs, violent spells of turbulence, and that one time I'd
watched *Cast Away*.

He shook his head, his stony, unrelenting reaction not giving me
any further reason to admit weakness to him. "If the plane crashes,
we need to be in our assigned place."

I stared up at him with a blank expression of disbelief, my lips
parting in shock. What kind of sick mind brings up a plane crash
while boarding? I was already beginning to wish I'd accepted that
Valium from Mum. Sighing, I decided to relent, knowing when to
pick my battles, and sparing myself from delving deeper into the
twisted mind of Nico Kotas. Besides, from his insistence, it didn't
seem like he'd be understanding of a fear of flying. He'd probably
call it exposure therapy as he relaxed into his comfortable window
seat.

We'd soon all pay the price if I spent the flight throwing my guts
up into a paper bag.

"What a cheery thought," I grumbled, pushing myself to stand.
I shuffled out of the row and into the aisle. Nico moved, removing
his backpack and beginning to place it in the overhead locker. I had
to lean backward to avoid contact with his large body, the space between us disappearing into millimetres as his thick arms stretched
upward. I twisted my neck, averting my eyes from the distracting
curve of biceps.

As he stepped in front of me, the air filled with an overwhelming scent of clean soap and sharp mint. It felt like forever, but he
finally passed, and I slid down next to him.

Being forced to sit next to him in economy was entirely on Jon.
"Team building," he'd call it.

Pulling the eye mask back down, I tried to settle again, attempting to find some semblance of comfort in the less desirable aisle seat, his knee already bumping against mine as we both tried to stretch out our long legs. Leaning back, I attempted to rest my arms on the shared armrest, only to have my arm abruptly pushed off the side. I pulled away the mask and turned to find Nico settled in his seat, his tree trunk arm occupying the entire middle armrest. My eyes lingered on the intricate black design of the tattoo wrapped around his arm, following the straight geometric ink that started under the cap of his sleeve.

"Excuse me." My voice sliced through the air, my narrowed eyes fixed on him.

He begrudgingly looked my way. "What?"

"You're taking up the entire armrest."

He sighed, exasperated. "So?"

"So?" I repeated, a little louder than I should have in such close quarters. "Everyone knows the aisle gets the middle armrest."

He stared at me for a moment, confusion furrowing his brows. "You've made that up."

My head tilted as I tried to figure out if he was deliberately being obtuse or if he was just an idiot. A smirk curled onto his lips, and I got my answer. A crackling voice filled the cabin, interrupting the growing tension between us, as the flight attendant made an announcement.

"Ladies and gentlemen, I apologise on behalf of the airline, but we are being held up by the luggage loading. We are looking at a forty-five-minute delay and will update you when we have more information."

"This just keeps getting better," Nico muttered, his voice tinged with sarcasm. He relaxed back, his arm remaining on the armrest.

"I don't know why you're complaining; you've got the window *and* the armrest," I grumbled back.

"Yeah, but I've got to sit next to you."

I stifled a laugh, deciding I'd had quite enough.

"I'm not looking at a much better situation here, buddy." I lifted my arm, sharply nudging my elbow into his, forcibly removing it from the coveted armrest and claiming it as my own.

"I am not your buddy," he snapped back, shoving his arm, trying to push mine off.

I spoke back through gritted teeth. "Old man, then."

We struggled, our arms battling against each other like children. Neither of us willing to back down. All the while, our bodies inadvertently pressed closer together with each passing moment. I couldn't help but notice the stiffness of his muscles as he fought my grip, his strong forearm flexed with determination. I felt the heat emanating from his body, the subtle smell of his clean scent mingling with the cabin air.

Was this really the person Jon wanted me to train with? Mixed partners have an unspoken understanding, an ability to anticipate the other's movement, and either compensate or get the hell out of the way, perfectly in sync. So far, all we were in sync over was the need for a window and the occupation of the middle armrest. The flight attendant's cheery voice broke through the tension, announcing the issue with takeoff had been resolved early.

"Fine. Take the damn armrest," he finally relented.

It was impossible not to feel smug as my arm reclaimed the space. It was hardly the comfort of the window seat, but a win was a win.

The feeling was short-lived. As the plane began to taxi, I tried to imagine the jolted movements as gentle waves rocking my imaginary boat, lulling me to sleep. Instead, the anxiety continued to build, the cabin getting smaller and smaller.

"Do you have to do that?" Nico blurted.

My full lips parted inquisitively, the anxiety tightening in my chest. "What?"

He motioned a hand toward my leg. "Shake your leg like a chihua-hua in a thunderstorm?"

I looked to my legs, noticing the shaking I'd been doing, before gazing across to his still, tanned skin, thick thighs exposed by shorts. Did he ever wear full-length trousers? The question faded when I noticed the dark reddish scar running down the centre of his right knee—a visible reminder of his recent operation.

"Sorry," I apologised, willing my legs to still as I grounded my trainers onto the floor, all the while trying to remember the box breathing technique I had learned in yoga class. Was it one breath in, three out? That felt like a recipe for asphyxiation.

"Does Jon normally do this?" Nico asked as I strangled out my sixth exhale. I looked at him for a moment, trying to figure him out, at least a little.

"I guess it's supposed to be team building."

He paused for a moment. "I meant, make us fly coach."

I couldn't be sure, but judging by the raised eyebrow and slight smirk combo, it was supposed to be some sort of joke. I hummed in quiet agreement, a fragile truce settling between us. The plane movement changed to a gradual turn as we reached the start of the runway. With my hand on the armrest, I tried to relax. This was the worst part, and I doubted many people were fans of takeoff. But with deep calming breaths, I focused my mind on the serene stony beaches of Rhodes, imagining the way waves crash against the shore, envisioning the vibrant hues of a sunset as the engines roared and the plane began to pick up speed.

The aircraft jolted upward with a violent bump, causing the en-tire cabin to shake. Panic gripped my body, my heart pounding fiercely in my chest. Instinctively, I clung onto the armrest, seeking any sense of stability.

The cabin emitted two beeps, and the seatbelt sign flashed, reminding us of its crucial importance. The plane shuddered once more, intensifying the anxiety coursing through my veins.

"Scottie?" Nico's voice pierced through my anxiety as the shaking of the plane began to subside. I looked up at him, my heart still in a frenzy.

I responded hesitantly, my voice betraying my apprehension. "Yes?"

For a moment, there was something about him. Maybe it was the panic of the moment, but I took a second to look at him. My gaze trailed around his face, tracing along his sharp cheekbones, across the line of his strong jaw. I was briefly hypnotised as I watched him swallow, the pronounced ball of his Adam's apple bobbing.

Then he spoke, and his words hung in the air, slowly registering in my mind, their impact sinking in.

"That's not the armrest you're holding on to," he stated matter-of-factly.

My gaze dropped involuntarily to his lap, and my horror intensified. The turbulence during takeoff had bumped my arm from the armrest and, instead, it had landed on his crotch. My hand held on to the very top of his thigh, fingers almost grazing what I could assume were not tennis balls stuffed in his pocket.

Mortified, I yanked my hand away, recoiling as if I had burned myself. Even without a mirror, I knew my cheeks were stained a deep shade of crimson. I attempted to form an apology, but the words tumbled out in an incoherent jumble. I was unable to bring myself to glance at him; the thought of looking at him and seeing his no doubt obnoxious face was too much.

I didn't dare to touch the armrest again.

CHAPTER SIX

Scottie
Breakfast – Dove Cameron

The weight of embarrassment threatened to swallow me whole. As soon as the seatbelt sign flickered off, I couldn't control my reflexes. My hand darted up to hit the "call assistance" button. A familiar noise rang around the plane as I straightened, anxiously looking back and forth for an available attendant.

"What are you doing?" Nico asked, but I couldn't bear to face him. Ignoring him was the only option, or else I'd die of sheer mortification. "Scottie? Are you okay?"

"I'm requesting a new seat."

I could hear the question in his voice. His body shifted, bringing his torso closer to mine. When he spoke again, his voice was low and quiet. "Why?"

"I need to move," I hissed.

"Scottie, it was a graze, it's fine." My brain tried to linger on the way he said my name, his American accent sounding heavier, but I shook it off. I knew for a fact it was more than a graze. I had felt . . . things. Things that moved. If I had to stay here for a single moment longer, I was going to get up, find the nearest exit, and throw myself out of this plane.

Relief clenched at my chest as the flight attendant wandered over, her face collected and calm. She reached me with a smile, her hand going to the button to turn it off.

"Hi, how can I help?"

I tried my best to contain my absolute joy at seeing her, the anticipation of being free overwhelming. "Hi. I can't sit here. I need to move. Is there another row I can go to?"

"I'm sorry you and your husband—"

I shook my head furiously, cutting her off before it went too far. "Not husband. Stranger. Just need to move."

He let out a laugh. "I'm offended you'd still describe us as strangers. I thought we had something more."

I tried my best to resist the temptation to give him a dirty look, and instead, with a calming deep breath, I refocused on the flight attendant, whose expression was turning more concerned with every second that passed.

"Is there somewhere else I can sit?" I asked again, keeping my tone matter-of-fact.

Her eyes glanced between us before she lowered them, coming closer to me. "Is he making you feel unsafe?"

I shook my head. "No, no, nothing like that." There were a million other things going on between us, but feeling unsafe wasn't one of them.

He huffed, clearly a little offended. "If anything, I should be the one feeling unsafe."

I closed my eyes, tried to imagine the relaxing beach we were flying toward, trying to find calm before I threw him out of the plane instead. I looked up at the flight attendant and found her eyes narrowed between us. "I'm sorry, but it's not procedure to let people move, in case of an emergency—"

"Told you," Nico murmured, and my fingers clenched into a frustrated fist.

"Is there something else I can help you with?"

I shook my head at her, disappointment growing. "Nope, I guess not."

"Wonderful," she said, the polite smile returning to her lips. "Have a great flight."

She turned, leaving Nico and me alone. I sat straight ahead again before slumping down and closing my eyes. This didn't have to be so bad. I'd touched a penis before. I had done a lot with many penises. I was a certified expert—one quick Google search would tell you that well enough—but for some reason, I could not get past this. Maybe it was because of the way his whispered words sent my skin into goose bumps.

Or maybe it was that knowing, cocky smirk burning itself into my memory.

"Are you going to look at me now?" he asked.

I didn't dare to glance his way. "I can look at you whenever I want."

"Sure, *katsarída*, whatever you say." His whispered accent rang again. On instinct, I turned to look at him.

Well, that lasted long.

His face was a sunshine glow of smugness, his eyes fixed on me. Satisfaction washed over his features as his lips curled upward.

"*Ka-Kat?*" I attempted to repeat, the pronunciation already lost to me.

"It's Greek."

"I assumed. What does it mean?"

"Wouldn't you like to know?"

I rolled my eyes at him before pulling my phone out of my pocket to google the term. "How do you spell it?"

"Good luck getting a signal." He smirked, and I officially gave up. Letting out a frustrated breath, I looked around the cabin, searching for a vacant place, only to find all the seats in the nearby vicinity occupied.

"Did you really burn down a boat in Italy?" he asked, pulling my attention back to him.

"First off, it was a yacht," I corrected. "Second, just because I was on board doesn't mean I set the fire."

"I'm not hearing a denial."

"I was cleared of any wrongdoing."

"By who? Judge Judy?" The way he said her name almost made me giggle, but instead, it raised questions.

"Why are you being so weird? You storm in here, going on about plane crashes and banishing me to the high possibility of midflight motion sickness." I didn't dare mention the armrest fiasco. "And now you're sitting here making jokes."

He shrugged, slinking back. "Just trying to get to know my new partner."

I paused for a moment, trying to decide if I trusted him. I didn't have any reason not to, but I also wasn't sure yet. Jon obviously trusted him, and I'd decided to trust Jon. Was it enough?

It was one of the things I'd gone over and over in therapy. I didn't know how to trust anyone after Matteo's betrayal. I'd been so carefree before, so easily led. Enough that the one person I thought I could rely on took advantage and stole everything from me. That could never happen again; I didn't think I could survive it.

I decided to steer the conversation away from me. "How did you meet Jon?"

"He used to train me."

"Really?" I'd never asked for backgrounds on the team Matteo had put together. I knew he'd only pick the best. Jon and I had grown close while working together, but I'd never asked about his previous clients.

"Yep."

"Why did he stop?"

He turned his head to me, raising an eyebrow with a hint of

mischief in his eyes. "He was poached by a certain tennis pro for his daughter."

"Oh," I responded, my mouth forming a circle, my heart plummeting in my chest at the mere insinuation of him.

"What happened there? With your dad." His tone was relaxed, as he was so obviously unaware of the emotional landmine he had stepped on.

I tried to swallow, but my throat had turned dry at the simple mention of him. It wasn't his business. It wasn't anyone's business. I'd never told anyone, apart from my mum, what had happened.

I'd gone to the ITIA and told them to test my blood again, to double-check every sample because I had used something that strictly was not allowed. I made an educated guess at the drug name, told them it was something they didn't normally test for, and they found it. If I'd given them a reason, placed the blame on my team, my ban could've been shorter. They were always going to strip me of the win, but I could've had six months instead of twenty-four.

But I didn't want six. I didn't want the two years. I wanted forever. I wanted to burn the house down, and his legacy alongside it. I wanted everything he'd ever dreamed of to be impossible, even if it meant I wouldn't be able to play the sport I loved ever again.

"I don't want to talk about it." My answer was a simple shrug, but it wasn't enough to shake him off.

"If we're going to be partners, don't you think I should know?" Nico pressed on, with his eyebrows raised and lips pursed with curiosity. I could hear the cogs ticking in his head. All the rumours over the last few years about what happened to the great Scottie Sinclair for her to go so far off the wagon. What drove her wild?

"I don't see the relevance," I snapped a little too aggressively, desperately trying to put up a defence. I wanted to plead with him to drop the topic, willing to do anything to avoid explaining myself. So, I did what I could to divert the conversation, to steer it away from my own troubled past. "You don't see me asking about your knee," I continued, my tone biting. "How's that going? What complications did you have? Aren't you worried you'll never play again, that you'll need to rely on somebody younger and faster if you want a chance in hell of coming near another title?"

Nico blinked at me, a stormy look brewing across his features. His eyes glanced around my face, reading my own stony, resolute expression. I could feel the pressure growing in the air, like a thunderstorm building in the atmosphere.

"You know what, Rossi—or is it Sinclair?" he began, every word laced with poisonous venom. "I can't wait to get you on that court. You're so cocky, you think you're unbeatable—even after almost two years. But you couldn't win a Grand Slam without cheating. Jon thinks you can do it clean, but he also knows you can't do it without the help of this 'old man' and his fucked knee." Nico kept his voice so low, so quiet, but every bit as aggressive, as if he was screaming the words at me. And all I could do was sit and take it.

"First day of training. You versus me," he challenged, eyes darkened with rage. "Don't forget, *katsarída*, you quit. You gave up, ran away," he continued with a sneer. "But all I've done is train, and fight, and get stronger. We'll play, and we can see who's most worried about never winning again."

My teeth clenched tightly as I tried to hold back my emotions, gritting out a forced response. "Fine."

I stared into his eyes, seeing the anger swirling within them. Without daring to look back, I pushed myself up and out of the row, my heart pounding in my chest, before going in search of another flight attendant.

I'd bribe somebody out of their seat if that's what it took, but I wasn't sitting next to him for another second.

Tweets

OMG! Was that @ScottieSinclair & @NicoKotas I saw TOGETHER getting into a car leaving Rhodes airport? @thedailytea

CAUGHT TOGETHER: Tennis's banned bad girl @ScottieSinclair and two-time Olympic gold winner and five-time Grand Slam champ @NicoKotas seen together leaving a Greek airport for a romantic trip away. READ MORE HERE —The Daily Tea

Me and Daddy Nico Kotas are on the same Greek island. No, I'm not okay.

Imagine the gorgeous tennis nepo baby those two would make? @Elite you should sponsor them.

CHAPTER SEVEN

Scottie
Not Strong Enough – boygenius

didn't make it a habit to google myself. I had my automated daily news roundup for that.

Scrolling through the social media mentions while hanging off the edge of my comfy bed in an upside-down sprawl, I tried to ignore the comments. Sneakily taken photos from last night caught my eye instead—Nico and me, clutching our suitcases, navigating a foreign airport while hungry and exhausted. In every photo, we were barely looking at each other, his baseball cap pulled low as we kept a solid arm's length between us, all while maintaining a strong policy of absolute minimal communication with each other after our fight on the plane.

I tried not to feel betrayed by the human race.

Paparazzi, I'd gotten used to as much as I would. Over the last few years, I had become good at spotting them from afar, even if they were hiding. I'd learned if they were about, whatever I was up to was about to be splashed over the digital pages of a catty tabloid with whatever clever nickname they'd decided to christen me with.

At least I normally had some warning. This, I hadn't expected at all.

Taking a sneaky mobile photo of somebody post-flight in that lighting? Was nothing private anymore? At least Nico looked good. My attention caught on the glimpse of his muscled left thigh, analysing the red scar that ran across his opposite knee.

I scrutinised the photo once more, eyes narrowing on my unwashed blonde hair that had been hastily pulled back into a messy bun, and comfortably baggy joggers and jumper I now regretted not changing out of on the plane.

We had gotten to the villa so late, nobody else except the housekeeper, Elena, was up to greet us, and after a quick snack, we were quickly ushered off to our bedrooms.

Now, ten hours and one refreshingly deep sleep later, I felt like a child trapped in their room. Out there was Nico, the asshole who'd sneered at me on the plane.

My phone vibrated in my hand, my mum's contact photo, a selfie of us both on a road trip to visit Jane Austen's house, covering up the badly taken photos. With no reluctance, I pressed answer, putting the call on loudspeaker.

Her voice boomed from the speaker, the tone accusatory. "Did you take my dress from the Versace '98 runway?"

I sat up straight, my eyes darting to the overflowing suitcase sat in the corner of the room. Mostly stuffed with comfy training clothes, the black dress stood out in a sea of white, the material spilling over the edge. "I'm not sure I've ever seen it."

She hummed in response. "Really? Because I'm looking at a picture of you from last week and it looks like my dress. And I can't find it in my wardrobe."

I could see her perfectly in my mind, sitting in the middle of her kitchen, looking as glamorous as ever, the tabloids from last week thrown open all over the table as she tried to track down all the clothes I'd stolen from her.

"Maybe the maid has it," I tried to reply, but if my shaky response didn't give it away, the fact her first port of call would've been to check with her maid of ten years immediately would've sealed the guilty verdict.

She sighed, and I was sure I heard her taking an angry sip of tea. "Dry clean only and check their Google reviews first. It's vintage."

I grinned as I pushed myself up from the bed and pulled the short dress from the suitcase. Holding the dress up, I replied, "It's something to remember you by."

"I'm not going anywhere," she said. "I've already emailed a dozen times to make sure I'm in the *family* box."

"Stop harassing Jon," I stressed as I hung the dress up, placing it on the outside of the wardrobe. I said a silent apology to the dress for stuffing it in my suitcase and kidnapping it from its owner. "I've not started training yet. We don't even know if I'll make it to Wimbledon."

"Of course you will."

"A hundred things could go wrong before then."

"Like?" she asked, and I let the question hang in the air for a moment.

Like, I could grab my new mixed partner's dick mid-flight after we fought over the armrest. He could call me a strange name I would be up half the night trying to translate on Google, and then we could ignore each other for the rest of the flight and camp, eventually dooming us to fail as a partnership, resulting in either of us barely making it past the first round on the grass courts.

"Injury," I answered, taking back my place on the bed next to my phone.

There was another long pause on the other side, as if she knew it was pointless to argue. "I was researching this new partner of yours, you know."

"Nico?"

I could hear the smirk in her voice. "You mean the six-five hunk?"

I side-eyed the phone with a slight distaste. "Is this a conversation I'm seriously having?"

"I swear, every single photo of that man makes him look like a snack."

"I'm hanging up now!"

I was inches from the red button when she spoke again. "I saw you in the airport. The pictures, I mean."

I sighed at the reminder, my interest in the conversation renewed. It was hard to find people who understood what it was like to see your name in fake headlines. Thankfully, Mum was one of those people.

"I'm not dating him," I began to yammer. "I met him barely a week ago. I can't even be spotted with another tennis player without them assuming the worst."

"Darling, is being tied to that man something we would describe as 'the worst'?"

"You know what I mean."

"I do, but at the end of the day, you know it's outside your control what they write about you. You can't fixate and you certainly shouldn't be googling yourself."

"I wasn't!"

"Turn off the notification and then I'll believe you. You're in training now, and I know you want to take it seriously. Whatever they are or aren't saying about you, it's all a distraction from what matters at the moment."

I grumbled, knowing she was right. I picked up the phone, swiping away from the call to my browser, the horrible photos attacking me all over again. Finding the settings, I disabled the notifications, knowing that not checking for a while, even a few days, would do me a world of good.

Let this all die down and focus on tennis. Show them what they should be talking about.

"Done," I said before returning to the call, the article replaced with my mum's face pressed close to the screen. Two of the same blue eyes stared back at me, and for a moment, I wished to go back to that day when we decided London was too much for us both and we needed to run away to the countryside.

"Good. I'm proud of you for doing this, you know? It's not easy, but if it was, it wouldn't be worth all the fight I know you've still got." I wanted to argue, to ask "what fight?" But instead, I closed my eyes and remembered those words.

I'm proud of you.

"Thanks, Mum."

As we said our goodbyes, my eyes found her dress again, hanging on the wardrobe. Despite her irritation at my sleight of hand, I was glad I had a piece of her with me.

When the call cut out, I was still half-tempted to look up flight times back to Heathrow, if only just to see her again, but instead the persistent grumbling of my empty stomach won, and I made my way out of the room.

I crept out into the upstairs hallway, trying not to make any more noise than was necessary against the marble floor. The villa was huge, consisting of three floors, two of which were bedrooms for guests, and no more furnishings than was necessary. It was luxurious, but the owners had chosen the minimal aesthetic that only the truly rich could achieve: white perfect walls, hallways so empty they echoed like a quiet cathedral.

I hadn't gotten far when the sound of footsteps rose up the hall, chatting voices, and the shriek of laughter. Like a coward, I hid, running into the nearest room and leaving the door slightly ajar, allowing me a sneaky view of the others.

Jon had told us there would be others staying at the villa. It made sense to have a few other pros here. And while we'd mostly be staying out of each other's way, it gave us somebody to play against.

Training sessions would still be private, with scheduled time at the gym and on the court.

The dark glossy black hair of Inés Costa came into view. I knew her well. Back in the day, we'd been on opposite sides of the court more than a couple times. We'd been friendly, despite the fact that during matches, I had the habit of wiping the floor with her. She was smiling at Henrik, a Czech player new on the scene, and one I hadn't met yet, as they turned the corner into the hall.

Nothing to worry about, I told myself. Friendly faces. Then *she* turned the corner.

Dylan Bailey.

"I'm just saying, I don't know why she's here," Dylan started, and my heart fell into my stomach. I hadn't seen her since that day. Her face in perfect view, us walking toward each other to meet at the net, her refusing to take my hand. "She's a cheat. Jon's making a fool of us by having her here."

"She made a mistake." Henrik shrugged. "He must believe in second chances."

I huddled behind the partially open door, straining to hear the conversation.

Dylan's tone was icy. "She cheated, plain and simple. How he can ever trust her again, I'll never understand."

My fingers clenched the edge of the door, knuckles turning white. I could just hear them over the thumping of my heart, the air feeling thin and my head woozy. I'd told myself this was going to happen. I was a cheat to them. I was a cheat to the entire world. For them, I'd crossed that threshold, tried to steal a title for myself, when in fact everything had been stolen from me.

Henrik's voice cut in, a touch of annoyance in his words. "Look, she paid her dues for the mistake. We've all moved on. It's water under the bridge."

Dylan's response was sharp. "Has she, though? You've seen

her on Instagram. The Daily Tea has a shortcut for her on their homepage."

"And why do you care so much?" Inés sighed, her voice carrying a hint of exasperation. "If Jon said it's fine, then it's fine."

"You won't be saying that when she's back on court, and it's your title she's snatching away," Dylan retorted.

I watched as Inés's dark eyes narrowed, her back stiffening. "I can beat her."

"You haven't before." Inés's attention immediately pulled to the Czech.

"She wasn't clean before." A sharp laugh follows Dylan's words. "And now her daddy isn't here to help her win."

All the air had been sucked out of the room. My chest tightened and my lungs burned for a simple breath. This was it, the fear becoming a real, palpable thing. I knew these people, how they thought, and they all had counted me out. Believed I was nothing without cheating, easy prey ripe for the picking. They didn't know the truth, and wouldn't believe it if they did.

I leaned back against the wall, closing my eyes as I pictured that day again. My last day on the court at Wimbledon, finally achieving everything I'd ever dreamed of, only for it to all be tainted without my consent. I had to be better than I was. Had to be clean and vicious and a goddamn animal on the court so there would be no question I'd earned every title I took home. I needed to come back from this stronger, or they'd eat me alive.

CHAPTER EIGHT

Nico

Will We Talk – Sam Fender

The cool water glided down my back as my left arm extended in front of me, pulling my body forward through the villa pool. Tilting my head, I took a quick breath of fresh air before resubmerging under the surface. The movement was second nature, my mind preoccupied with the words of a certain blonde she-devil.

Aren't you worried you'll never play again, that you'll need to rely on somebody younger and faster if you want a chance in hell of coming near another title?

What did she know?

Whatever had gone down to split Matteo Rossi from his golden child prodigy, I knew it could only spell trouble. I'd been a teenager when I first faced him on the court. Nobody had expected me to make it out of the qualifying rounds, let alone the finals. But there I had been, at Flushing Meadows, standing across the net from him.

When I'd won, it felt like a dream. The months after, a nightmare.

I was a kid who found himself at the top of the tennis world and enemy number one to its most successful player. For that first year, hardly anyone would touch me. Coaches would quit overnight, sponsorship deals would be on the table one day and disappear the next, with Matteo suspiciously promoting the brand instead.

And the media. They loved the story of the young underdog taking down a legend until they realised I could do it. An eighteen-year-old against the world's media, nobody reliable to back him up. I couldn't have a life outside of tennis without them reporting on it, barely talking to another person without photos appearing.

Then, when a car crash sealed the fate of Matteo's career, he disappeared to train her.

Matteo Rossi 2.0.

Emerging for a breath of fresh air, I broke the surface but immediately considered sinking to the bottom when I saw who was there.

Speak of the devil, and there she stood—Scottie. With her hand on her hip, wearing a white oversized T-shirt and shorts that accentuated the entire length of her long legs. Her sunshine blonde hair was tied up and tucked under a familiar-looking baseball cap, a few tendrils of her hair playfully escaping around the edges.

To make matters worse, there it was—the infuriating smirk on her face, as if she had been waiting for this moment.

"Well, well, look who's decided to come up for air." She stood there, a mug in hand, clearly revelling in this opportunity to provoke me. "Thought you'd hide at the bottom of the pool forever, huh?"

My jaw clenched, and I forced myself not to let her get under my skin as I swam to the edge of the pool. My feet found the tiled bottom, water dripping from my body as I stood.

"Bet you were hoping I'd drown."

While Scottie Sinclair had been no overnight success, you could see her father's influence giving her a clear advantage in her early days. He'd use his connections, again stealing away people from my team, but this time to her benefit. She certainly had talent. You don't get far in this sport without it. But she also had her father's name and money, and that opened doors. That alone, however, didn't win championships. For that, you had to earn it.

Instead, she'd tried to take the easy way.

There was no sign of our fight from yesterday on her face, and apart from dark circles under her eyes, the usual mask of smug confidence was well intact. She scoffed before rolling her eyes with an unmatched aggression. "Elena sent me to get you. Breakfast is ready." She took a sip from her mug, slurping the liquid and ending with a satisfied sigh.

My eyes narrowed on her, my suspicions rising as I focused on the mug, and more importantly, the liquid inside. "Is that coffee?"

She lowered the mug a little, a mischievous glint in her eyes. "Maybe."

"Decaf?" I asked, but her head shook in denial. "Jon banned caffeine."

"He did," she chirped, enjoying the fact she was breaking the rules. One day. We were one single day into training, and she already wasn't sticking with the training. Why was I surprised?

Irritation burned under my skin, her pleasure in my annoyance only serving to feed the feeling. I was exhausted from travelling and having to deal with her yesterday, and all I'd had this morning to battle any of that was a decaf green tea.

With a sharp movement, I pushed myself out of the pool, sending water cascading down my body as I stood bare-chested before her. Not bothering to grab my towel to dry off, I stood face-to-face with her, the cap atop her head coming into view and I realised . . . it was my hat she had stolen.

For a single moment, I would've sworn her eyes roamed every inch of my tattooed torso, following up my left arm and across my chest. The intensity of her gaze locked with mine, but it didn't last long. My eyes narrowed in response as I broke the silence. "Where did you find the hat?"

Trying to maintain an intimidating stare, I struggled not to be distracted by her height, only a few inches shorter than mine. And I was reminded to ignore her long legs, to forget how soft they looked, to stop thinking about how they'd feel wrapped around my waist.

Her smile was a little devilish thing. "That, old man, is a secret."

It was as if she already knew how much that nickname got under my skin. Unluckily for her, I'd thought of one that was perfect for her.

Katsaría. I had to stop myself from grinning at the memory of my mom beating the little black disgusting bug away with a broom, yelling their name in her native Greek.

Cockroach.

I exhaled in frustration, trying not to let her antics get to me. Despite the shared animosity, I knew we had to find a way to co-exist during our time here. But as Scottie continued to smirk, I couldn't help but wonder how difficult she might make that. Maybe she wanted me to quit, get Jon's time all to herself.

"Tell me where you found the hat," I pressed, but she seemed to revel in delight.

"Why?" Arching an eyebrow in question, she slowly lifted the mug to her mouth, her pink lips parting before she took a long sip. Her eyes fixed on me as if she wanted me to watch her every move. Her challenge hung in the air, and I was left to make the next serve in this game.

"It's mine," I grumbled, taking in the cap's faded blue material, the edges beginning to fray from age.

If she could enjoy this little power play between us, so could I. With a swift, determined motion, I reached for the hat, ready to reclaim what was rightfully mine. But as I tugged it free, Scottie's hand flew upward to stop me and in reaction, I accidentally bashed her hand holding the mug. She yelped as the coffee poured over her. I grimaced, watching the scene unfold, the hat held in between my fingers, paused in mid-air. She took a step backward, and I watched a renewed look of panic quickly wash over her face before she plunged into the pool with a splash, landing in the water behind her. Resurfacing with a gasp, she blinked a few times before her eyes focused with an unmatched fury on me. Strands of golden hair clung to her wet face, and for a fleeting instant, I forgot to pretend she wasn't a goddamn work of art.

"Are you insane?" she yelled, her voice echoing across the pool area.

"I didn't do anything," I said, shaking my head at her. Of course she thought this was my fault. For a moment, I decided to revel in the sight of her in the pool. After the hat and the coffee, it felt good to watch her cool off for a moment. With a smug smile, I placed the hat on my head and crossed my arms.

"You did this over a stupid hat?"

If possible, my smirk grew as I continued, fighting hard not to enjoy the chaos before me. "First off, I did nothing. You did this to yourself."

A loud, shrill noise escaped her as she shrieked in annoyance.

"Second, this is my favourite hat, and you stole it."

The noise she was making increased to a pitch only dogs could hear. I took that as my cue to leave. *Immediately.* Turning, I grabbed my towel from the sunbed, threw it over my shoulder, and slipped my shoes back on.

"Enjoy the rest of your coffee," I said, not bothering to give her a second look. Walking down the path back to the villa and making sure to avoid the gang of stray cats that hung out around the grounds, I quickly used the towel to dry off. Heading through the kitchen, I was greeted with the smell of breakfast, three egg white omelettes plated up beside each other on the counter. Hungrily, I dived in, grabbing a fork and leaning against the counter for support.

"You could have at least put on a T-shirt," Elena, the housekeeper, tsked as she shuffled out from the pantry. Despite her petite height, she exuded an air of authority and wisdom, which was exactly why Jon had hired her in the first place.

"I was hungry," I said between bites. "It's good, though."

She smiled, although her eyes, while kind, held a sharpness that made me think twice about crossing her. It was as if she could see right through me, and with one stern glance and a slight waggle of her finger, I'd feel the same level of guilt as if I'd wronged my own mother.

"Where's Scottie?" she asked as I swallowed another mouthful of food.

As if summoned, Scottie appeared at the kitchen door, hand outstretched and pointed right at me as water dripped from her clothes, a demonic expression on her face.

"You!"

Elena turned to me, wooden spoon in hand. "What did you do?"

"He pushed me into the pool," Scottie called from outside.

"Why would you do that?" Elena asked.

I ignored Scottie as she shouted from the door again, "Because he's a child!"

"She fell in." I shrugged before forking another slice of the delicious omelette into my mouth.

"I did not."

"And she had coffee."

"So?" Elena still had the wooden spoon in her hands, ready to be used as a weapon if necessary.

"We aren't supposed to have it."

"He's an asshole," Scottie added, before taking a single step inside.

Elena spun again, the spoon now pointed in her direction. "No! You stay out there until you dry off."

"What?"

"I just cleaned these floors. You are not dripping pool water everywhere."

Scottie let out a sound of annoyance, but remained in the doorway. Smugness washed over me as I grinned, delighted, at her, her blue eyes full of anger, a sneer on her lips. I knew then I'd started a new battle between us. Whether it was something I could finish, I wasn't quite sure. She wasn't anything to be afraid of, right? Elena, on the other hand . . .

The housekeeper turned to me. "You. Go get her a towel." I paused for a moment, a refusal playing on my lips. But one look at her stern face and the spoon she was still wielding as a weapon, and I swallowed the words. I put the fork down and stepped away from the breakfast bar. "There are fresh towels in the downstairs bathroom."

Without argument, I did what she said, grumbling my way through the villa. When I returned to the kitchen, bath towel in hand, Elena was nowhere to be seen.

"Hello? Elena?" I shouted, looking around for her.

"She went to clean up. Just pass the towel over," Scottie said, appearing in the doorway. She was still soaked, but she'd tied her blonde hair back in some sort of complicated braid. As my eyes wandered down, I noticed her white T-shirt sticking to her, showing off every curve of her body . . . and since the water had made it translucent, the pink lacy bra she was wearing underneath.

The image of Scottie Sinclair in pink lacy underwear plagued my brain, temporarily knocking me out of reality.

"What?" Scottie pulled my attention back to her. "Scared of what I'll do to you if you step outside?"

I gulped, her eyes narrowing on me.

"No, I don't want to get wet again," I lied, edging toward the villa entrance, trying to avoid thinking about the pesky pink bra that was staring right at me, begging my eyes to wander south again.

"Maybe you should be worried."

I stretched out the towel to her. "I don't know what you think you could do."

"A swift kick to the balls?" she joked, placing a hand on her hip.

I pressed my lips together, taking a mental note to keep at least a leg's length of space between us at all times. That girl looked like she had a sharp, strong knee. I gave the towel a little shake. "Do you want this or not?"

She leaned forward, water dripping from her arm to grab the towel, but I moved backward on my heels, taking my turn to smirk at her.

"Say please."

"Really?" she said on an exhale. "This is a game children play."

"Alternatively, you could tell me where you got the coffee."

Her answer was quick and solemn, delivered over crossed arms and with a straightened back. "Never."

"Who's acting like a child now?"

"You threw me in the pool," Scottie cried, looking at me like I'd lost my mind. I almost did as she unwrapped her arms, and the pink bra was revealed once again. It used up all my control not to steal another look.

"I barely touched you."

"And why on earth would I tell you my source now?"

I hummed for a moment. "Call it team building."

"Call it 'I know where you sleep, and I won't hesitate to smother you with a pillow.'"

Stepping away from the doorway, she gave up, the distance between us feeling strained with every step she took. I knew I was being immature, leaving her in the pool and now, with the towel; she didn't deserve it. But everything she'd said on the plane, it cut deeper than she could've known. In the limited time we'd spent together, she'd managed to read me perfectly, and knew how and where to twist the knife. But I also knew I'd evened the playing field. With a shake of my head, I relented.

"Here," I said, stepping out of the kitchen and reaching to pass her the towel. She eyed it with suspicion, calculating the risk. "I promise it's fresh."

It took her another moment before she gave in, taking the towel and wrapping it around her damp body. I tried to look at anything else other than her patting the cotton material across her pale, freckled arms and long legs, ignoring the flash of lace I could still see. Forced myself to fix my gaze on the wall, on the vines of green wrapping their way around the brick of the whitewashed villa. "We need to find a way to get along."

"Maybe if you stop pushing me in pools, that would be a start."

"You know"—I pressed my lips together, trying to let any irritation simmer away—"I didn't push you in." *As much as I wish I had.*

Scottie sighed, throwing the towel over her shoulder. "Let's assume it was an accident."

I saw her words for what they were: an opportunity to meet me in the middle and let the matter go. It was better than spending weeks arguing against each other.

A little more relaxed at her words, I joked, "And you still won't tell me where to get coffee?"

She cracked a smile at my response, her eyes connecting with mine. "And I probably never will."

Her head dipped, and she looked back over through the lush garden again, a long pause filling the space between us.

"But you're right," she continued. "I'm serious about all of this, everything you said on the plane—"

I cut her off. "That was mean of me. I . . . I was mad."

"That's not the problem."

My brows pushed together in confusion as I watched her bite

her lip in a move I could've sworn was nerves—that was, if she was even capable of feeling them.

"It was all true," she added.

"I swear, I was just mad. I didn't mean it," I found myself arguing back for some reason, trying to soothe her.

"You did." She called me out on the lie as a calm look settled across her features. "And so did I. It's not the point. I meant what I said about you, but it doesn't mean it's true. You know yourself, people come back from those surgeries all the time."

She was right. They did. But my situation was different. A heavy knot pulled in my chest, the fear making the air feel tighter. I sat down to the right of her, avoiding the skinny grey cat that was perched at the end of the wall, watching our every move with its big eyes. There were dozens on the grounds of the villa, no doubt acting as a deterrent for mice and insects, but that didn't mean I had to like them.

"There were . . . complications," I admitted. "It wasn't straightforward. The surgeon botched the job, and that's why the rehab took so long."

I didn't want to go into the details, the pain still seared in my memory. It was supposed to be simple, a few weeks of recovery, followed by intensive therapy. Instead, weeks had turned into months and corrective surgeries that never should've been needed, and suddenly I was staring down the barrel of losing everything. I'd never been in that position before, where everything balanced so precariously.

One wrong move, and it was over.

"Jon was right when he said I'm too slow. I lost my speed, and I'm tired too quickly to last a game, never mind an entire tournament. Wimbledon . . . It's always been the dream. The singles title there, it's what got me into tennis."

"Really?"

"I've won the other Slams. Never that one."

She let out a single laugh, side-eyeing me as the air lightened for a moment. "Rub it in, why don't you?"

I scoffed, nudging my shoulder against hers as I hung my head. To say the words out loud made me feel a little too raw, too vulnerable. But I'd known what I've been working toward my entire life. I knew it when I spent two weeks every summer glued to the television, getting up early and watching every match I could. I knew it on the hard blue ground at Rod Laver in Melbourne, on the clay French courts at Paris, on the turf at Flushing Meadows in Queens. I knew it with two gold Olympic medals hanging around my neck.

"I want the Wimbledon title," I admitted. "Then I can retire."

I looked at her, trying to see that she understood what this truly meant to me. I'd spent weeks lying in bed, waiting for my knee to heal, convincing myself I'd lost the chance. That it had slipped through my fingers. But I realised, as I took in the understanding and resolve held in her eyes, that she might be the only person who understood what I had on the line.

After all, regardless of the fact it was her fault, she already had lost everything. And this was her chance at getting it back.

"I know how it feels. Having that goal." Her voice was so fucking hopeful, it almost cracked me wide open. "That's why I'm here too."

I pushed the emotion back down where it belonged, before asking the thing I've been dying to know. "Why are you here?"

"Because Jon convinced me?"

I shook my head, getting to the point. "That's not what I mean. What's this revenge plot you've got against your dad?"

She stiffened, inhaling sharply as she did. Her head tilted down to her lap, where her fingers were rubbing against each other.

"Nico." Her voice cut like a knife's edge. "I know it may not make sense to you, but I need you to stop calling him my dad."

I was about to ask why when she spoke again. "I don't want to talk about it, but believe me, I have my reasons. If I'm going to stay here, if we are going to work together, you've got to stop. Or I'll get back on the plane to London tonight, and we can be done with each other already."

I was itching to know more, but a single look at her stiff posture and darkened eyes told me enough. Instead, I noted the request and nodded. "I won't call him that anymore."

"Thank you." Her voice cracked as she spoke, before sending me a small smile. I watched her for a moment, seeing a different side to her than I'd ever expected.

Professional athletes weren't supposed to show weakness. We were taught to be strong, to carry on through the pain, to risk our bodies and mind and soul for a single trophy. And get up and do it again. We rip our palms and knees and soles of our feet to shreds and thank everyone for supporting us while we did.

But in that moment, she was a raw nerve. Exposed and unprotected. I grew desperate to wrap my arms around her and make sure, whatever she was thinking about, she knew nothing could hold us back.

However reluctantly, she was my teammate. Which meant as much as she was my problem, I was hers too.

I tried to crack the tension with a joke. "And in return, you'll tell me where the coffee is?"

All evidence of our serious conversation disappeared when she looked at me, a glimpse of the playful, annoying sparkle returning to her blue eyes.

"You wish."

CHAPTER NINE

Nico

$20 – boygenius

N o." My firm denial had an immediate effect on Jon, whose shoulders slumped with disappointment. He sat across the desk from us, the chair of his makeshift office creaking as he leaned back. His face was a crumpled mixture of disbelief and hopelessness. I shook my head, lips pressed together as I doubled down. "Absolutely not."

I couldn't believe what he'd proposed. He knew me well enough, knew my career, and understood the kind of respected standing and solid reputation I had in this community. There was no way I could agree to it.

I looked at Scottie for some unspoken solidarity; she was also not on board with his plan. Her frame slouched in the leather chair beside me, her body language mirroring my own. However, her attention remained fixed on Jon, an intensity in her gaze I couldn't read.

"Why not?" he asked, his irritation clear in the gruffness of his tone.

"I don't date." The words were sharp—maybe a little too sharp—but nonetheless true. It had been . . . a while. For years, there was no room in my life for anything more than a couple of nights.

Then, with my knee and the surgery, there was no room at all. It was taken up by appointments, rehab, and anxiety.

"I wasn't suggesting you *actually* date."

"And I wouldn't date her," I added hastily, only realising what I had said when Scottie piped up with an annoyed "Hey!"

Her eyes were narrowed angrily at me, lips pressed into a thin, disapproving line. "Like you'd have a chance."

I fought the urge to pick at her words, to smirk and tease. While I didn't date, it wasn't like I didn't know how to. Like I didn't think about it or her, no matter how much I'd tried not to. Her, with the long legs and the blonde hair I could see tangled up in my fist. Knowing she was only down the hall.

And that's exactly why we couldn't date.

"Again, not the suggestion," Jon said, shaking his head.

"Maybe you better explain, so I understand. Because from here, it seemed like you were proposing I date my mixed partner for money and publicity."

He took a breath to clear his irritation before he spoke again. "Not date," he tried to explain, his voice clear. "Be seen together. Allow the brand to share images of the two of you training and using their products. Let the press and public put two and two together. They think you both can raise the brand's awareness, and I agree."

"This is insane. You're insane," I cried, exasperated, hands flying into the air because I didn't know what else to do with them, except perhaps strangle my coach. My palms landed on the soft material of my navy baseball cap, and I was reminded of the leftover vanilla-and-orange scent Scottie's shampoo had left behind.

"And not for money and publicity. For a brand partnership. They are only interested in the two of you together after you were spotted landing at the airport—"

"You mean after people sneakily took our photos and posted them all over the web?" I corrected. I had only found out about them after Henrik, one of the other players training here, showed me the pictures all over social media. I'd had some paparazzi presence before, usually around tournaments, but it had been years since I'd had any real press interest after learning how to avoid them.

"Gee. Could you sound more like a granddad?" Scottie remarked, sounding too casual with it all.

I narrowed my eyes at her, and her eyes met mine. "You're on board with this?"

She shrugged her shoulders, her face remaining suspiciously neutral as she spoke. "This happens either way to me. At least this time, I'd have a say. Control the narrative."

She didn't mind? She didn't think it was a risk to her career, her image, to let everyone think she was shacking up with her tennis partner? That allowing a brand to manipulate her image to sell rackets and shorts was "controlling the narrative"? Maybe it was because she wanted to see me suffer after the pool incident. Questions were on the tip of my tongue when Jon interrupted again.

"You need sponsors. ELITE is willing to fund everything single-handedly if you both agree to a little extra publicity and play into rumours that have already begun to crop up online." He placed an iPad on his desk, facing it towards us. The homepage of the Daily Tea was open. Something shifted in my gut, a twist as I read the words.

Is Slutty Scottie cleaning up her court? Spotted landing in Rhodes with none other than fellow tennis legend Nico Kotas!

My gaze involuntarily moved to Scottie, the headline burning into my brain like a hot brand. They called her that? Even when things had been bad in the media for me, when I first took off, they had never called me anything like that. Her eyes moved from the iPad to Jon, her expression stony and impossible to read. I thought again about how she'd looked earlier. The memory of the soft request about her father had me seeing the vulnerable side of Scottie for the first time. What was it about her that tempted me to reach out, uncurl her clenched hand, and intertwine her fingers with mine?

Reading the headline back stirred something dark and violent inside of me that made me want to find every bastard who had ever dared to call her that and make them regret it. Yet another reason this was a terrible idea.

Jon's voice cut through the horror. "I wouldn't suggest it if I didn't think it was a good idea. You need funding, and ELITE is willing. And despite what you think, it could be good for you."

"How on earth could this be good for me?"

Jon shifted uncomfortably between us before swallowing. "You have no publicity."

I smiled, trying to recall if I still knew the passwords to my social media. "That's how I like it."

"But because you have no publicity, all people can talk about is your career. Your knee. How they've not seen you in a competition, even as a friendly, in half a year. Longer, if we want to talk about competitions you performed well in."

I gulped at the thought. Had they counted me out? To them, was I another dinosaur trying to keep their career fresh long after the sell-by date? My performance in my last few matches felt like the ugly scar across my knee: red, swollen, and sensitive. In the last one, I'd barely managed to be competitive—spending hours icing my knee at night and praying the painkillers would be effective enough to get me through at least the first set. In the end, I'd had to pull out completely.

"If they're talking about you and Scottie, that's something else," Jon pointed out before turning to her, his head tilted forward. "And you. You have too much publicity. If you do this, we can control it a little and get them talking about you and Nico. Maybe we can protect you."

"I don't need protection. I'm used to this." She said it so easily, but the words replaying over and over in my brain said otherwise. What else had they written about her?

Jon eyed her, clearly as convinced as I was. "That may be, but this gives us an opportunity for some good press. None of this name-calling." He motioned at the iPad as he lifted it from its place and locked the screen. I watched his eyes read the words as they disappeared, hurt flashing there for a moment, and I found myself wondering if this was the best headline he could find. The least offensive.

"It's nice you think that, Jon," she said with a smile so weak it vanished almost as quickly as it appeared. Silence fell over the room as she shifted in her seat. "What are the details? What do they need?"

"They'd send somebody from marketing over here, who would need time to take photos during training to create content or what-ever for social media. You'd switch to their rackets and equipment for the rest of the contract. They'd like a few outings around the island for more 'content,' and then they'd be gone."

I rolled my eyes, crossing my arms. This was ridiculous. "So, essentially, we'd be taking up modelling?"

Jon looked grimly at me before continuing. "They'd want fea-tures of you together on both of your social media accounts." He raised an eyebrow. "No matter how defunct the account may seem. And any time you go out, you have to wear their clothing."

"And I can't do it alone?" Scottie asked.

Jon shook his head. "They want you both. Together or not at all."

"But we don't have to do anything . . ." Scottie trailed off as I shifted in my seat at the thought. "Like, other than being seen to-gether, the implication we might be dating is enough to fulfil the contract. Right?"

"Correct, that's all they need. They don't expect you to confirm anything, only play into it a little."

Indecision buzzed in my brain. I could see the advantages of why Jon felt like this entire charade was necessary. But . . . with her? Scottie looked over at me, her blue eyes meeting mine, giving nothing away.

"It's up to you," she said with a simple rise of her shoulders. I'd known better than to think this was an easy transaction. This company, offering to fund everything we needed, wasn't giving a handout. It wouldn't just be some photos of us together used to sell cheap leggings. It never was. We had opened ourselves up to something we didn't understand, and at a time when the focus should be on our training. I was still slow, and she'd been out of the game even longer. Dedication was normal for an athlete, but we needed to go beyond that. Blood, sweat, and tears wouldn't be enough. I realised Jon knew that and could see what lay ahead of us.

I looked over at Jon, almost apprehensive to ask, "Is this necessary? Is there even a choice?"

Scottie's head had turned, her blonde hair up in a messy bun, as the room fell deadly quiet.

"Honestly?" His throat cleared as he moved in his chair, the hinges creaking again. "You don't have any other funding options. This gives us more choice, access to better training and physios."

"I could pay it out of pocket," I offered.

"Do you want to put it all on the line like that?" he replied. "The added pressure. I've seen it crack more prepared athletes."

Scottie was silent, her head down as if she was already defeated. Maybe I should never have asked the question. Maybe it was better to feel like we had a choice in the matter, pretending like we had any control.

With a deep breath, I let go of the pretence. No wash of relief followed the decision. If anything, the walls of the small office crept in tighter. "Tell them we'll do it."

CHAPTER TEN

Scottie
Crystal Clear – Hayley Williams

The International Tennis Integrity Agency must've heard I was back on the scene because it wasn't long before the vampires were knocking on the door of the villa, bloodsucking syringes in hand.

I was sitting outside the medical room where they'd set up their nest, awaiting my appointment time, when Inés appeared from around the corner, her long black hair pulled out of her round face and into a ponytail. She paused as she saw me sat in the plastic chair outside, before cautiously taking a seat next to me.

There was an awkward, empty silence. A void created by the two years of no communication. We'd been friendly before; dare I push it to friends? Always ending up in the same hotel, and on the nights I could sneak away, meeting up for a drink paired with some friendly competitive chat, hanging out in the warm-up area, supporting each other when we lost with a quick, comforting hug.

But after Wimbledon? Radio silence.

"They called you in too?" I asked, her hazel eyes wide as they met mine. I dug my hand under my thigh, sitting on it as I jigged my leg.

She swallowed. "I think they are taking samples from everyone while they're here."

I nodded, not sure what else to say, and went back to staring at the opposite wall, waiting to be called in. I'd kept up my AITA passport, a sampling regime that was designed to catch changes in a player's profile, while on ban. But every test since Wimbledon left me feeling more anxious. I'd always been confident in the knowledge I was playing fair. That there wasn't anything I was taking I should be worried about. But I'd been wrong.

"Are you okay?" Inés's accent cut through my anxiety.

I forced a smile, admitting, "Just nervous."

She pressed her lips together, those eyes analysing as she raised an eyebrow, but her tone was much softer. "Do you have something to be nervous about?"

"No," I blurted, shaking my head, my fingers wrapping around the edge of the chair, pressing into the hard moulded plastic. "The process makes me nervous."

I wasn't sure why she chose to believe me, but her face relaxed, her head tilting toward me.

"Not a fan of blood?"

I managed another weak smile, this time meeting her gaze as I took her excuse. "Is anyone?"

"Try to take your mind off it."

I swallowed down the lump in my throat, pressing my foot into the marble floor to stop myself from jiggling it. Searching for any possible distraction, I chose the first thing that came to mind. "I never got to say congrats on your win at the French Open last year."

She'd fought Dylan for the title, losing the first set but coming back strong for the second and third. I hadn't watched the match, only caught up on the recaps. The men's competition was fine, but the women's always left me feeling queasy and uneven, the itch to be there myself overwhelming.

"Oh," she said, sitting up straight. "Thanks."

"You don't sound too excited about it."

She shrugged. "You must get it. The pressure. And then immediately being out on injury. It doubles the intensity. Most of the time, I want to hide away."

I looked around at the empty hallway of the villa, seeing the paradise of the luscious garden outside. "I guess you came to the right place."

She laughed. "You'd think, but somehow, being surrounded by other tennis players is worse. It's like living around a pack of wild tigers."

I sat forward, glad somebody had said it. "It's weird being so friendly over breakfast."

"When in a few weeks, we'll be competitors across a court?" She finished my thought with a knowing smile, her head nodding.

"Exactly." I had never trained like this, alongside other players so intensely. Usually, it was Matteo and coaches. We would get a hitting partner in every so often to change it up, give me a new challenge, but for the most part, this villa was a foreign experience.

"How are you finding it? Being back on the court?"

"Hard," I admitted, feeling the ache in my body down to my bones. "But I'm pretty certain that's Jon's style of coaching."

"Did you train at all while you were off?"

"I kept up my fitness. It's hard to let bad habits die."

She smiled. "True. Even on my days off, I wake up every day for my 5 a.m. run."

"Exactly. And I don't think I have the ability to stay still. I always need some sort of movement, or I start to feel a little unhinged." I had tried to stay in bed late for the first few months after quitting, but I'd missed the exercise. It was less intensive, of course, but I'd found ways to do it for joy.

"And I'm sure Dylan being around doesn't help," Inés added with a raised eyebrow.

"There could be nicer roommates to have," I joked with a nervous grin. Who could be a better person to be around 24/7 than the woman who thought I stole a Wimbledon title from her?

"She's mostly bark. You must know that by now."

"It's a pretty terrifying bark."

We both laughed, my nerves almost forgotten. Almost. Until the door to my left cracked open, and a nurse stepped out. She looked up from a clipboard at the two of us, before asking, "Rossi?"

My heart leaped into my throat at the mention of my former name. "That's not my name," I barked suddenly, the words sounding so much harsher than I had meant them too, but I couldn't help it. The name felt like ripping open a fresh wound, still healing and sore.

"I'm sorry," I said quickly, stuffing all the feelings of anger and rage back down into my chest, and into the box where they belonged. "My name is Sinclair now."

The nurse nodded her head, writing something down on her notes, before instructing me to follow her in. Slowly, I stood up, flatting my clammy palms onto my tennis skirt.

"Do you want company?" Inés offered. "Somebody to hold your hand?"

I quickly reeled myself back from my surprise at her offer, asking, "Are you sure?" When she nodded enthusiastically in response, I turned back to the nurse. "Can she do that?"

The nurse looked between us, her lips pursed with indecision, before nodding. "Okay. But don't touch anything."

Inés jumped up from her chair and followed me into the room.

The room was set up simply for first aid, a bed laid out with a fresh paper top, the bloodsucking kit set out, still in its packaging. The nurse gestured to a chair, asking me to sit, before taking her place next to me.

"So, has anyone caught you up on all the tour gossip since you've been away?" Inés asked, distracting me as the nurse took my right arm.

"No, tell me everything!" I smiled in reply. All the while, her hand slid into my left, squeezing and holding it tightly. Inés began to dish—or as much as she could dish, since she had been out for a few months following her surgery on her wrists.

I forgot for a moment about the last two years, remembering instead our time spent in locker rooms and bars. Sometimes, you never know how thankful you are for someone's friendship until it's gone.

The nurse worked quickly, and all the while, Inés's hand stayed in mine as she kept me company and sufficiently distracted. She finished without me even noticing, and all because I had found an old friend by my side.

Second Set

CHAPTER ELEVEN

Scottie
Shatter – Maggie Rogers

C ome on, give me ten more minutes!" Jon shouted from the sidelines. My body protested vehemently. I didn't have one more minute left in me, let alone ten. On the opposite side, Nico's lean figure stood out against the bright backdrop of the tennis court, his muscles taut with exertion and his chest soaked with sweat. The sun was relentlessly beating down, intensifying the challenge.

It was the first day of our intensive training. The clock had barely hit ten in the morning, and I was already planning my escape route off this damned island. We woke up to a run, gulping down a quick breakfast before spending the rest of the morning practising drills and footwork. After an all-too-short recovery, we were unceremoniously dumped into the gym, with a personal trainer adapting the workout according to whatever cross-training supreme ruler Jon dictated was the focus for the day.

In the afternoon, I faced the double whammy of yoga and Pilates, while Nico enjoyed some pool time for his knee rehab. If, by some miracle, we managed to survive, our reward was the "luxury" of stretching, cooling down, and recovering in the jacuzzi-turned-ice bath Jon seemed convinced was a treat instead of torture.

I was close to chartering a private helicopter to come pick me up. If he kept up being nice, I might let Nico come along.

"Pick up the pace, Scottie!" Another yelled command had me plotting Jon's murder as we ran suicides between the lines of the court, rackets in hand for extra intensity. Jon's authoritative presence loomed over the court, his tall frame casting a shadow as he pushed us to our limits. The court's white lines taunted me as I struggled.

Jon's phone erupted in a ring. He yanked it from his pocket, delivering a terse "hello" before turning away, leaving Nico and me to push forward. But instead, I halted, my hands on my knees as my lungs caught fire, gasping for air.

Seizing the stolen moment to rest, I hoped Nico would be doing the same when a ball attacked me from out of nowhere. My body twisted to avoid it and with a scowl, I turned to the other side of the court, spotting Nico. Despite the sheen of sweat on his forehead, he was sporting a smirk, one eyebrow playfully arched.

"No slacking now, Sinclair," he shouted, pulling another ball from his shorts pocket. The hem grazed halfway down his tanned, muscled thigh. Every time he'd moved around the court, the shorts inched up a little, revealing glimpses of skin and ink, which left me wondering how much farther they could creep up.

"Jon's gone. Can't you leave me to die already?" I whined. It was still early in spring, but with the court outside and unshielded from the sun, I was melting away. Removing my navy cap, I kept my blonde hair in check before wiping some sweat-soaked escapee strands from my face. I had recognised the hat from the pool when he'd stolen it back, but if he didn't want me to keep stealing it, he needed to stop leaving it lying around. And judging from the way he'd eyed it when I'd arrived at practice, his jaw clenching with what I hoped was annoyance, there was a possibility he might still expect it back.

"Come on. Let's see what you're made of," he challenged, mischief dancing in his voice as he looked from me to my racket that sat just to my side. "Then we'll get a delicious protein shake."

The thought made me queasy. While I knew getting back into shape after such a long break would be challenging, I'd underestimated how brutal these training sessions could be.

Another ball smacked into my side, this one delivered with more force than the last. I scowled, locking eyes with Nico, who was all too pleased with himself. He bounced another ball against the court surface before launching it my way with a stretch of his arm. My attention was hijacked by the sight of his shirt lifting as he moved, revealing a precious sliver of his lower abdomen. I lingered on the tantalising trail of muscle, only to be cut off by the waistband of his shorts.

Muscle memory kicked in, my hand adjusting into the correct position on the racket, my body moving toward the ball. An exhausted grunt escaped me as I swung, the sound reverberating around the court. The ball sailed over the net, bouncing once in front of Nico before he returned it. With a sly grin, he let out his own strained groan, mimicking me. Narrowing my eyes, my suspicion raised, and as I hit the ball, I did it again, the yell both helping to relieve tension and mocking his own. A smirk spread across his face as he swung, and this time there was no mistaking it as another loud, truly pornographic groan left him.

A single laugh escaped me as I broke, unable to contain myself, before stumbling forward to return the ball. I mirrored the noise, each of us getting louder and increasingly ridiculous with our groan as we each returned the ball over the net. We were both smiling despite an ache that felt like it permeated all the way to my bones, running around the court rallying with each other, being loud and silly, our laughter echoing against the court's white walls and the distant sound of waves crashing nearby.

As Nico reached for the next ball, he misstepped, his right leg buckling under his weight and he slid backward to the ground.

A groan of pain filled the air, and I knew from the scar the right was his bad leg. Without a second thought, I tossed my racket aside and, fuelled by a surge of adrenaline, sprinted across the court to where he lay.

"Are you okay?" The words escaped me on a heaved breath as I found him still on his back, his chest rising and falling deeply with exhausted breath.

"I'm fine," he snipped, tone tinged with irritation. I reached out a hand, but he shook his head, ignoring the offer. "I said I'm fine. I don't need help."

"You sure about that? Considering you're the one rolling around in pain," I retorted, frustration bubbling up. His hand clutched his knee, and I moved to assist, remembering techniques from my own past injuries.

"Scottie—leave it alone," he said, swatting my hand away. "It's not like you can do anything about it!" His brows furrowed in anger, lips pressing together as he rolled off the ground to sit up. His face was red and flustered, the mask of anger slipping for a moment.

"I'm trying to help," I reassured, but Nico withdrew further as he attempted to stand, hissing in pain with each breathless attempt. He tried to shake me off as I pulled him by the shoulder, attempting to ignore how the firm muscle felt under my fingertips. His chest heaved with every painful breath, and the sheen of sweat on his forehead accentuated his rugged features.

"I don't need it." His gaze connected with mine as he stood, anger radiating from his body. He shook my hand from his arm and brushed past me, slowly making his way to the side of the court. He limped away, favouring his left leg. My frustration boiled up again, spilling out as I stormed the short distance between us.

"Hey. We need to be a team, so if there's something up with your knee, you've got to be honest with me."

"What? You mean apart from it being fucked?" He laughed as he reached the bench. He stood for a moment, attention stuck on one of the stray cats that had been watching us play from the bench. Quietly he shooed it, flapping his hands while still keeping some distance from the cute animal. The feline stared intently, head tilted as if trying to understand what this buffoon was doing, before giving up its position and striding away. Nico almost fell to the bench as he pulled out a towel and threw it over his head, as if to hide. Closing the distance, I pulled the towel off him, forcing him to look up at me.

He did not look any less mad.

"Yes," I continued. "Like if there's anything I can help you with. If you need somebody to stretch with. You can't snip at me because I'm checking to see if you're hurt." I held the towel in between two fingers, keeping it away from him. I didn't need to touch Nico's sweat towel any more than necessary.

He looked away, grinning as if I'd humoured him, one arm holding on to his uninjured knee, propping him up. "I'm not sure why you're even here. You were pretty adamant about not wanting to come back to tennis. I only trust you'll stay clean because of Jon. And even then, what does he know?"

His words did exactly what he had meant to do—hurt. The unhealed wound within me stung with his accusation. I was on the brink of snapping back, tempted to call him an old man and remind him of how far past his prime he was. But instead, I swallowed down my retort.

"He knows me, you ass. I won't do it." I crossed my arms, standing strong against him.

"You did it before," he added, but his attention was distracted, pain etched across his face as his fingers worked along the top of his right leg, massaging along and causing him further ache.

"Are you going to throw that in my face every time we fight?"

"Are you going to keep being an annoying pain in my ass?" He tried to make the words snarky, but they escaped him in a pained gasp. I couldn't take it anymore, dropping down to my knees in front of him, the court's surface warm under my bare skin after being baked by the morning sun.

"If it means otherwise we lose, then yes."

"Well, ditto." He laughed again. Before he realised, I'd closed the space between us. "What are you doing?"

"Can I try something with your knee?" I asked, but he only eyed me suspiciously. Nico's piercing gaze bore into mine, his darkened eyes reflecting a mix of scepticism and vulnerability. "I had a similar injury a few years ago. Of course, I had youth on my side." He scoffed, but I ignored him, pressing on. "But I remember the massage technique. Maybe I could help?"

Maintaining our eye contact, his reluctance to let me touch him was evident in his flickering gaze. He tried to sit up straight, putting too much weight on the bad leg and letting out another small groan of pain.

I bit my lip, pressing once more. "Please, Nico. Let me try." I realised I was begging, but it was so clear he didn't have any trust in me. Without it, there was no chance we'd survive the competition.

His gaze met mine, and apprehensively, he nodded. Smiling at the acceptance, I began to very gently press my fingers to his knee, my eyes trailing the length of the scar across it. I tried to apply soothing pressure to his knee joint, my fingertips gliding across the healed skin. The tennis court's uneven surface was unforgiving beneath my skin, but I ignored it, trying to focus on the massage. He flinched at the contact, and I looked up at him, frightened I'd further hurt him.

"Sorry," he croaked before clearing his throat. His eyes were glassy, and I realised this might be the rawest version of Nico I'd seen. "Keep going, I'll try not to move."

"Tell me if you need me to stop," I instructed, waiting for him to nod before I continued.

I tried again with slow, deliberate strokes, gradually working my way around the knee as I pressed in with a sweeping movement. His leg moved, stretching out and relaxing, giving me better access to continue. With that, I grew bolder, increasing the pressure as I worked around his knee.

A quick glance up at him and I found him slack-jawed, eyes shut and relaxed. He looked peaceful, and with a smug smile, it was all the confirmation I needed to know I'd given him a bit of relief.

Continuing my work, my fingers massaged and kneaded when, without any warning, he let out what at first sounded like a groan. The noise was throaty and deep, a low, guttural growl that resonated from deep within his chest. Nico's well-defined jaw clenched and unclenched with each noise, his hands flexing absentmindedly as he relaxed into my touch. My fingers paused as I lost all track of what I was doing, my mind scrambled from the moan.

He jerked upright, his knee recoiling from my touch. Looking up, I found his face was burning a deep scarlet, his wide-eyed panic contrasting with his previous calm. He cleared his throat, his words wavering in pitch.

"T-thank you," he stammered. "It's better now. I'll see you at lunch." The words tumbled out abruptly as he leapt up, acting like nothing had ever been wrong. He tossed his equipment bag over his shoulder, and without another word, stormed to the exit, leaving me speechless.

My brows were furrowed together in confusion, my throat dry as I tried to process the noise he had made.

He paused mid-step, dropped his bag on the floor, and turned back, marching over to where I was still on my knees on the ground. He refused to make eye contact with me as he closed the gap between us, and without so much as another word, his strong arm reached out toward my head.

I jerked backward, not sure what his intention was, but he grabbed the navy cap from the top of my head.

"This is mine," he grumbled. Nico took the hat and placed it unceremoniously on top of his own head. Then he was gone, walking around the stray cat that had decided to take up a sunbathing position in his path. I was left on the floor, hair a complete mess from the hat thievery, his moan still replaying in my mind.

His eyes shut, his pink lips parted, and that seductive noise. There should not be this visual of my mixed partner making that noise in my brain. But there was, and I was pretty sure I wasn't going to be able to forget it. Finally pushing myself up from the floor and wiping my legs clean, I tried to collect myself, attempting to figure out what on earth had happened.

CHAPTER TWELVE

Nico
Norgaad – The Vaccines

I f watching Scottie Sinclair drop to her knees in front of me, her blonde hair tucked under my favourite cap, wasn't enough to push me to my limit . . .

If her blue eyes, steadily holding mine in a silent challenge, didn't fracture the tiny bit of resolve I still had . . .

If the touch of her fingers massaging my injured knee, erasing that persistent pain in a way pharmaceutical drugs hadn't come close, wasn't my complete undoing . . .

Then it would be living on with the embarrassment of forgetting where I was, who I was with, and letting that goddamn moan escape me.

Followed promptly with what I did in the shower later.

CHAPTER THIRTEEN

Scottie
NDA – Billie Eilish

F ailed?" I repeated back. Jon's stony expression seared into me as he held the letter from the agency that had performed the drug tests. "How is that possible?"

He'd leaned back, his desk chair creaking on its hinges. "I mean this in the most respectful way I can say it, Scottie—"

"I've taken nothing," I assured him. "Not even during my time off. Did I enjoy my fair share of champagne and cocktails? Yes. But drugs, no. Not even once. I'm enough of a lightweight as it is."

When he'd asked me to meet him in his office after practice was finished, the last thing I'd expected was to be accused of cheating. Again. But now the result of the test from a few weeks ago had come back as a fail, and there was an accusation in Jon's tone that didn't sit right with me.

His eyes softened slightly, his head tilting to the side. "If there's a chance of anything, you know you can tell me."

I pushed my hair out of my face, tucking it behind my ears before pressing my hands to his wooden desk. "I've put everything on the line here, Jon." I tried to calm my nerves, almost scared to ask my next question. "Do you think I'd risk that? After everything?"

"I don't," he said quickly. "But you understand, I had to ask."

Relief relaxed me back into my chair opposite his desk, nodding my head as I did. "I know."

"With everything that went down with your dad, how you reacted, I knew this couldn't be right from the moment I read it." I tried to hold on to his words, let them soothe the growing anxiety building, but it did little to alleviate it.

How did this happen? Was something happening to me without my knowledge again? I tried to recall the opportunities somebody had to mess with my food. I mostly drank bottled water, and always checked the seal was intact. It was a habit I'd picked up after Wimbledon, a distrust of where my food and drink came from. For a long time, I prepared my own, choosing only to drink bottled options when I was out at restaurants or bars. Therapy had eventually helped me manage the fear, but I was still easily triggered from time to time. Here, I'd felt safe with Elena preparing our food. After all, she had the Jon seal of approval, right?

"When did you get the letter?" I asked.

"Yesterday morning."

My eyebrows pressed together. "And you waited until now?"

He shrugged off my reply. "I needed to think. It's not only our reputations on the line. Nico's is wrapped up in this now too."

Panic raced through my body at the mention of his name. If Nico found out about this failed test, there would be no partnership. He would never trust me. He'd have the paper evidence of exactly why he shouldn't.

"I don't know how this happened, Jon. I promise, I haven't touched anything."

"I believe you."

I let a deep breath out, the tightness of anxiety loosening for a moment. Those three words soothed me more than anything.

"Thank you."

"But I need to understand how this happened. I'll dispute the test with the agency and try to get it straightened out before it all goes public."

"Public?" I repeated.

He waved a hand, dismissing my obvious worry. "Don't worry, I won't let it get to that stage. We know this isn't right."

I nodded, trying my best to register his words. "My suspension isn't officially over yet. Could they add more time because of this?"

He shrugged. "I'm not sure. We're going to sort this out, I promise." He was trying his best to be sincere, his expression relaxed and friendly. I knew Jon and could trust he would do his best to stop this. After all, it had been him who approached me, who came up with this plan for mixed doubles. His career would be affected by this too.

"Thanks, Jon."

"But until then, this is best kept between us. Don't tell anyone and let me sort it out."

I paused for a moment, uncertainty ringing in my words. "You don't think we should tell Nico?"

"He tends to . . ." Jon trailed off, his hands motioning in mid-air as he searched for the right words.

"Overreact?" I offered.

He squinted his face before rewording. "Nico reacts quicker than he can think sometimes. You haven't told him about what happened . . . with Matteo?" I shook my head in answer. I couldn't be sure he would have believed me if I told him, and now that there was something else, the truth was even riskier. "Then he might not understand. We know how this looks to an outsider, but we know the truth. Let's figure this out, and we'll tell him once it's resolved. It'd be less messy that way."

I thought over his words, recognising Jon knew Nico better than I did. "Okay, I can do that. But I don't want to lie to him."

"I know, but you aren't lying about anything. Just . . . waiting."

I nodded. "Okay."

"Good. I'm glad we're on the same page." Jon smiled, sitting up straight in his chair as the conversation came to a close.

"And you'll let me know as soon as you hear anything?"

"Of course," he replied. "But until then—"

"Keep it inside these four walls."

"Exactly," Jon confirmed.

Taking a deep breath, I got up from the chair, thanking him again for his help. All the while, my head kept spinning, trying to figure out if there could be any truth to the result. I had to believe there was some sort of mistake, a contamination or mix-up. I'd been consistent about giving samples during my time off to ensure nothing else was happening to me without my consent.

As I opened the door of the office and slipped into the hallway, distant footsteps caught my attention.

On the other side of the long corridor, walking away from the office, was Dylan Bailey. She turned, a quick glance over her shoulder revealing the same icy expression she'd been giving me for weeks, but this time there was something resembling a knowing smile on her lips.

CHAPTER FOURTEEN

Scottie

ballad of a homeschooled girl – Olivia Rodrigo

I had planned to try to avoid Nico for the remainder of the week, but apparently, I didn't even need to try. It seemed, from the way he deserted me after practice on the court and turned around if he saw me walking towards him in the corridor, Nico wanted to avoid me as much as I needed to stay away from him. By Friday, I was ready to request a separate training time. Outside of our tennis practice that we *had* to have together (according to Jon), he barely looked at me, let alone spoke to me. And the navy cap didn't leave his head for a moment. I was beginning to suspect he slept with the damn thing on.

When our day finally split up, with yoga down on the beach for me and physio inside the villa for him, I was glad for it. That was, until Dylan and the others showed up for yoga, which had now apparently switched from an individual class to a group setting.

A sharp foot hit mine as I balanced in a three-legged downward dog position, the instructor facing outward across the beach, missing everything. My foot stayed firm on the mat, the lumps of the sand underneath giving me extra balance.

I glanced to my left, where the back of Dylan's brunette head obscured my view. She'd been doing this throughout the entire class, blocking my space and making me wonder if I'd soon be covered in bruises.

"Now exhale as you gently lower your extended leg back down to the mat," the instructor suggested. As I released my breath, I tried to imagine my deep-seated frustration with the woman next to me dissipating like a rolling wave receding into the sea.

It didn't work.

We transitioned into a new position, legs holding strong, rooted to the ground, while my arms stretched out wide for balance. I had taken a deep breath, focusing on the taste of the sea salt air when an arm connected with my face, the skin burning with the sharp impact. I wobbled, falling out of the pose to stop myself from tumbling into the sand.

"Hey," I snipped, immediately turning to Dylan. "Do you mind?"

"Oh, did I catch you?" she asked with feigned innocence, her sharp features betraying none of the mischief in her actions.

"You hit me," I stated bluntly, sick of her already. All class she had been pushing her luck, and I'd reached my limit.

She shrugged, her slender body returning to the position as if I wasn't worth spending any more time arguing with. "Maybe you were too close to me."

Irritation pricked at my skin too incessantly to ignore. "Stay out of my way."

She barely flinched at my demand. "Or what?"

"Maybe we should all get into child's pose for a moment and take a few breaths to calm down," Kyra, the instructor, suggested, stepping in. I had been all but ready to put Dylan in corpse pose and call it a day.

Clenching my teeth, I tried to rein in the overwhelming anger swirling around me like an out-of-control freight train. Dylan stared me down, her unwavering gaze bringing me right back to our last match up at Wimbledon.

"Kneel on your mats, big toes touching, and knees spread apart," the instructor said, her light tone successfully pulling my attention from Dylan. Somehow, I convinced myself getting into a physical fight on the beach was not the way to solve the situation. "Gently lower your hips back toward your heels and extend your arms forward. Allow your forehead to sink down, releasing any tension. Take a few deep breaths, surrendering to the serenity of this pose."

I tried to do as she instructed, sinking deeply into the position, but my mind was anything but clear.

Two summers ago. Hot heat pounding down on the Wimbledon centre court grass.

One last set to go.

Matteo watching my every move.

I shuddered at the memory, still unable to stop it from having a physical effect on me. I'd cried for weeks after they stripped me of the title, haunted by headlines and tabloids and interviews with Dylan declaring me a cheat over and over. But I couldn't blame her; my disqualification didn't make her any more a winner, and with no other titles under her belt other than runner-up, that had to hurt all the more. In the end, we both lost out because of someone else's actions.

"Hey, can I join?" a familiar voice asked, and I twisted out of the position to see Nico standing at the front of the class.

"Of course," the instructor said, smiling up at him. "You can take the free mat next to Scottie."

He nodded in reply, walking to where I was stretched out, my head propped up, eyes following his every step.

When he lowered to the mat, getting into position, I hissed, "Don't you have physio?"

He turned to me, eyes meeting mine. "Day off."

"So, you're here?"

He looked at me weirdly, as if it was none of my business why he had come to interrupt my only escape from him. "It's what Jon said to do instead."

I sighed in frustration. First Dylan, now him. Turning back to the mat, I tried to surrender to the pose, but, if anything, the tension in my body only increased. Yoga was supposed to be effective at decreasing stress, not become the source of it. I had found solace in the fact that apart from having to stare at the back of Nico's head, I wouldn't have to interact with anyone else.

"Since we have the numbers, how about we do a couple of partner poses today?" And with a single question, the instructor sealed the deal on yoga being the source of my heightened blood pressure.

I wanted to die. I knew I couldn't go with Dylan. The woman would sooner drown me in the ocean and call it fish position. The instructor, sensing my moral danger, thankfully paired Dylan with another person in the class, which left Nico and me staring awkwardly at each other. I watched as his throat bobbed for a moment, mesmerised by the movement.

"I guess we're partners." His words were hesitant, as if he had also been rethinking the class. Drowning in the ocean suddenly didn't sound like the worst case scenario. Last time we did anything like this, he basically ran away and stole my hat. Well, his hat, but it was on my head. Technicalities.

Grumbling with disdain, we moved into position, sitting at opposite sides of the mat, our spines lengthened, feet meeting in the middle. Our hands slid into each other's, and I tried not to lose my concentration to the roughness of his well-earned calluses against the softness of my wrist. He pulled me forward, the muscles in his forearms flexing and tightening, and my throat dried up at the movement. We took turns using each other to stretch for the required pose, and the silence that fell between us screamed at me.

"I can't get over the tweener you pulled today," I said, trying to fill the silence with reflections of our earlier session. He'd caught me in our final game with the move, hitting the ball between his legs and causing me to lose the set. Sarah, the PR photographer for ELITE, had joined us during our morning practice like she had been since she arrived, but disappeared after the first twenty minutes, saying she had enough "action shots." I suspected she wanted some time beside the pool.

He grunted a simple response, his gaze focusing on the space between us. Frustration started getting the better of me, and on his next stretch forward, I pulled tightly, forcing him to deepen his stretch. Nico looked up at me, his brows furrowed together as he tried to figure out if I did it intentionally or not.

"You're ignoring me," I stated plainly.

"That's no—"

"Let's do some stretches," the instructor suggested, cutting off whatever bullshit excuse was about to come out of Nico's mouth. "One of you, please lie on your back." I looked around uneasily, but a quick glance at Nico told me clearly that it wouldn't be him.

"Are you going to lie down?" he asked, his tone agitated, and I was unsure why he was so uncomfortable with this instruction. Pressing my lips together and swallowing my anxiety, I lay down on the mat, my arms stretched down my body, pressing into the ground.

The next instruction came as I shimmied into position. "Now, extend your legs straight out. This is where your partner will come in and help you lengthen your legs over your chest as you inhale and exhale." We both froze, watching the others as they did as instructed, realising what this entailed. When I turned to Nico, he was on his knees, his jaw clenched and eyebrows pushed together.

"What do I do now?" he asked, clearly not paying much attention.

"Grasp her ankles with your hands," the instructor began, "and with one leg at a time, stretch it up and over her body until she's doubled over." Judging by how wide his eyes grew, his throat bobbing again with another nervous swallow, he finally realised what position we were supposed to get into.

He looked down at me, wild panic stretched across his features. I stared at him blankly, unsure what he wanted me to do now that he had made me lie down.

Eventually, I caved. "Look, the sooner we do it, the sooner we get this over with."

Nico took a deep breath, like he was trying to collect himself and build the will to touch me. Was he really so repulsed by me? I flinched when he finally gripped my ankles.

"Sorry," he mumbled, his eyes flickering up from my legs to my face. "Is this alright?"

"Yes, it wasn't you . . . I'm ticklish."

A grin stretched across his lips for a moment as he grabbed my legs again, lifting them up. It was awkward, but gradually, he pulled them over my body, my lower back rising up off the mat, leaving only my arms and shoulders to make contact with the ground.

The aching stretch in my lower back was easily forgotten by his focused eyes meeting mine, wisps of his dark curled hair falling into his face, and the compromising position he had pulled me into. I'd been in less compromising positions with one-night stands, let alone my mixed partner.

He cleared his throat before speaking again. "Are you sure this is okay?"

I nodded, not quite able to form a string of tangible words. The feel of his hands against my ankles. The upward view of his face and strong arms stretching me. I shouldn't have been distracted by the ripple of muscle. But I was.

Whose bad idea was it for him to join this class again?

"Why do you keep avoiding me?" The question slipped out of me of its own accord. After all, I knew my reason for avoiding him, but what did he have against me? I was a delight to be around.

His face creased with denial. "What are you talking about? I'm literally holding your feet over your head."

I kept my voice hushed. "This is the longest conversation we've had since Monday."

I'd foolishly thought we were getting somewhere when I'd tried to help his knee, like he was finally trusting me, even slightly. I suppose it hadn't helped that I was keeping things from him in return. Was it worse if he knew I'd failed the test or that I'd kept the results from him?

He bit his lip, looking uncomfortable in the face of my accusation, but he didn't deny it.

I took a deep breath, before admitting on a whisper, "It's like you can't bear to be around me."

"Believe me, Scottie," he whispered back. "That's not the problem here."

I was frozen, staring wide-eyed in confusion at Nico, all the while his gaze burning down right back at me with something else entirely. The already small space between us felt claustrophobic and tight, like I hadn't realised how close our bodies were until it was too late.

With a camera flash, the world came tumbling around us. We'd been so lost in the moment we hadn't noticed Sarah's arrival.

She stood there, camera in hand, looking down at the screen, a grin wide on her face. Nico's hands released me, and in a split second he was so far away, it almost felt like it never happened.

"Did you just take a photo?" I asked, my tone wavering with doubt.

Sarah grinned. "This is perfect for the campaign. When I heard Nico was joining the class, I knew we'd get some tasty shots."

"Tasty?" I repeated as I pushed myself up from the mat, still arranging the moment as if it was a jigsaw. She took a photo, with Nico and I . . . in that position. I could see it in my mind's eye, how close we had been, the momentary connection we had shared in the vulnerable moment. How it would look splashed all over the front pages of a tabloid, paired with a stupid clickbait headline like "Scandalized Scottie gets bent over on a public beach." I cringed at the thought, my cheeks burning red. Not only for myself, but for Nico. This agreement with ELITE wasn't supposed to be moments like this, twisted and scandalous.

"This will get the traction we need online," she added, as if it was a done deal.

"No." I shook my head in denial. "There's no way you can post that photo."

She furrowed her thick brows together in confusion. "Why not? It's perfect. You guys are together, and we can see the brand names perfectly. It's exactly what we're after."

"This isn't the kind of photo we agreed to." I curled my clammy hands into fists, keeping my voice low as I attempted to keep the conversation private. Behind me, I knew the rest of the class had stopped to watch the drama unfold. Their eyes burned holes into my back.

"It's just yoga." Sarah shrugged innocently, glancing down again at the photo.

I sucked in a deep breath, running dangerously out of patience as I stood up, my legs feeling anything but strong. "Sarah, please delete the photo. I'm not comfortable with it."

She tilted her head, raised an eyebrow, and with an exasperated sigh, she said, "Really? You have a problem with this?"

I knew what she was thinking. *This? Never mind the hundreds of photos out there of you in compromising positions. Never mind the fact that you're a girl who always gets into trouble, lies, and does all the party drugs she can get her hands on.* Everything and anything a tabloid or a so-called friend has ever said I've done, I knew Sarah believed it.

I felt two inches tall as she looked me up and down, filled with smugness. She held the camera in her hand, reveling in the power she had stolen from me. I was beginning to suspect she'd have me get on my hands and knees to beg.

"She said delete it," Nico said, stepping beside me. There was no room in his tone for argument, the authority of it sending shivers down my spine. I turned to him, eyes dancing along the set line of Nico's jaw, his gaze locked in an icy fury directed at Sarah.

"Our contract doesn't state what we can and can't take photos of," she replied.

"I don't care. Delete the photo before I do it for you." He stood tall compared to how I felt, unwavering in his authority. I looked from him to Sarah, watching as her lips were pursed together in displeasure.

She lifted the camera, pressing a few buttons. "Fine. It's done."

Instant relief washed over me, but for Nico, it wasn't enough.

"Let me see," he pressed, stepping in front of me. "I don't believe you deleted it." She attempted to stare him down, debating whether she should stand her ground. With a sigh, she passed him the camera.

Staring over his shoulder, I watched as he expertly pressed the buttons on the camera, navigating to the gallery. I had been stupid enough to believe her, but the picture was still there. And when I saw it, I realised how much worse the scene looked.

Our faces were so close together, our gazes connected. In reality, what was a simple stretch looked like an intimate moment captured between lovers. Or that was how it would look if it ever made its way into anyone else's hands.

I released a shaky breath as Nico pressed the delete button, the photo disappearing from the memory card. The previous photo flashed up, one from our earlier practice on the court.

His stony demeanour didn't crack as he handed back the camera to a pouting Sarah.

"You should be more careful if you don't want photos like that," Sarah said. "Next time, I might not be so obvious."

My heart was in a panicked frenzy, beating so loudly I could hear it. This place was supposed to be private and safe, but with ELITE's presence, I was as vulnerable here as I was out there. Maybe more so.

"Well, the next time, I might not give back the camera at all," Nico warned, earning himself another glare from her. Out of retorts, she stormed away and off the beach. Nico's shoulders didn't relax until she disappeared from view.

He excused himself from the class, his jaw still set tight as he walked away. I looked around at the others, all eyes still on me. Without a word, I slipped on my sandals and ran after him.

"I'm pretty sure Jon's going to have your ass for that," I said as I caught up to his furious speed.

He didn't look at me, eyes set on the horizon. "I don't care. There was no way she was keeping the photo."

I wondered for a moment if he had done it for me or for his own self-image. I doubted he wanted to be connected to me in that context. In *any* context, if he was truthful, but here we were anyway.

"Thanks for having my back," I said. Whatever his reason, it didn't matter. He was entirely to thank for the picture no longer being in Sarah's hands. He'd protected me.

Nico stopped and flashed me a look that caught me entirely off guard. His eyes were stormy, jaw set tight as he spoke firmly. "Don't thank me."

"I want to."

He pinched the bridge of his nose and groaned, the noise tinged with disappointment as his gaze fell to the warm sand below our feet. "You shouldn't thank somebody for treating you like a human being."

"You'd be surprised how little it happens." I truly thought my words would break the tension, relax him and remind him this was nothing new to me. Then I remembered how he'd looked at me that day in Jon's office when we agreed to all of this. How his face turned to concern after Jon showed us the article about us landing in Rhodes. Did he actually care?

"What do you mean?" he asked, his tone still sinister, that dark look in his eyes anything but a comfort. Did this man live somewhere without an internet connection? Or did my existence before now mean so little to him, he didn't even brush up on tabloid gossip?

"What do *you* mean?"

I was beginning to think maybe I thought too much of myself, that I was still unimportant and my impact on the world over the last two years didn't extend off the gossip pages of the Daily Tea, when he softened, his shoulder relaxing somewhat.

"People . . ." He trailed off, losing track of his thoughts for a moment. When he looked at me, his gaze was a little wild, a little unhinged. I was begging to know what he looked like truly feral. "People should treat you better, Scottie."

My throat was dry as I nodded. "I know."

"No matter what you've done."

"You haven't exactly been pleasant to be around," I pointed out, remembering our first meeting. The handshake he refused, everything we had said on the plane. Every bit of ground we gained felt uneasy. Every time we got closer, one of us went too far and we ended up further apart.

His hand went to the back of his neck and rubbed it uncomfortably. "I'm sorry for everything."

I didn't need him to explain. I was just as guilty for twisting the knife between us. I was wrapped up in secrets, sensitive when he dug too deep. He had no reason to trust me other than Jon's word, and less when I lashed out like I had.

"I'm sorry too," I said, before a small smile creeped onto my lips. "Especially all those times I reminded you of how ancient you are."

"Thirty-three is not old."

My jaw opened wide in fake shock. "You're *how* old?"

"Oh, shut up," he retorted, the darkness almost completely erased.

"What was it like back in the old days? Did you use a horse and carriage to get around everywhere?"

Nico rolled his eyes at me. "I'm only eight years older than you."

"That must feel like a lifetime at your age."

We turned together and headed back up to the villa, leaving the incident behind us. I was cautious but optimistic that maybe this could work. We could work.

"I thought you were going to play nicely, *katsarída*," he murmured, curiosity sparking inside of me.

"Are you ever going to tell me what that means?" I already knew his answer.

"Ever going to tell me where the coffee is hidden?"

"Maybe if you actually win a game on court, I'll take pity."

"I think you are seriously misremembering our training sessions."

I smiled brightly, an edge of satisfaction there. "Then I guess more coffee for me."

CHAPTER FIFTEEN

Nico
Meltdown – Niall Horan

mean, what were you thinking?" Jon's face was almost the colour of a tomato as he grilled me.

"Sarah was being inappropriate." I paced back and forth across his office. Just like Scottie had said he would, Jon was reaming my ass for what had happened on the beach. I didn't care. Sarah had deserved it.

"Then let me handle it. It's my job," he stressed, but I couldn't help but scoff. Anger fuelled every step I took.

"It's your job to protect us from situations like this in the first place," I argued. Scottie's face when she saw the photo replayed in my memory. "She was unprofessional, the way she treated Scottie—"

"I also heard you threatened to break her camera. Is that true?" Jon asked, standing from behind his desk, one eyebrow raised in question.

I didn't back down, not regretting it for a moment. "Only if she did it again."

Jon buried his face in his hands before I had finished the sentence, his fingers massaging his temples as if trying to ease the stress I'd caused him. "Nico." His voice was muffled. "You put the entire contract at risk."

"I don't care," I replied. Not if that's how Sarah was going treat Scottie.

"You should care!" he exclaimed, throwing his hands in the air. "ELITE is covering everything. Without them, you and Scottie will have to bear the financial burden."

"There are other sponsors."

He shook his head. "Not like this one."

I rolled my eyes, familiar with this attitude from coaches over the years. I'd always maintained strong partnerships with my sponsors, never allowing them to overstep boundaries we'd set. Somehow, I got the feeling that wasn't how it had worked with Scottie. And now, I was struggling to remember why I'd agreed to this in the first place.

"We gave them too much power."

Jon groaned in frustration. "Trust me when I say it's worth it. Yes, they demand a lot, but they're also providing us a lot in return."

What was a lot? What was the point of working for decades on end if I was still at the mercy of sponsors? If I was still having to sell my soul for a brand partnership?

"She can't talk to Scottie like that."

Jon eyed me as I continued to pace, his attention clearly on my knee as the tension in the room grew thicker. It's like he could tell it was beginning to ache after today's activities, and the lack of relief physio brought.

"Take a seat," he suggested, his voice calmer now.

I shook my head. "I need to move."

"You're stressing me out. Sit down so we can talk instead of arguing because we are getting nowhere," he pressed, his head indicating to the chair opposite him. "And I don't want you to wear that leg out."

I considered being mad at him for bringing up my knee, but as a familiar twinge of pain began to niggle under my skin, I realised he was being a concerned friend. I sat down, immediately itching to get up and walk around some more. It had been hours since the beach and I still had the pent-up rage in my veins. Instead, I shifted, struggling to find comfort in the hard leather chair.

"What exactly did Sarah say?" he asked, eyes softening momentarily.

"It was . . ." I trailed off, searching for the right words. It was the look she'd given, the subtle hostility in her words that had made Scottie shrink in on herself. I hated seeing that. I knew the look; Scottie had given it to me before, when I'd still been calling Matteo her dad. I hated it then, and I hated it more now that I'd seen somebody else do it to her.

"It was the *way* she said it," I conceded, knowing he couldn't grasp it without being there.

He let out a deep breath, as if counting down his exhale. "I'm not sure I can do anything about her tone."

I huffed. "How do we know she won't pull this stunt again?"

"We don't. But if she does, let me deal with it. We still get final say on any photos they publish."

My tense body relaxed as I processed what that meant. Anything we didn't like, anything like the yoga class, she was safe from.

"And you're sure they'll listen?"

He cleared his throat as he shuffled some papers on his desk. "They could always ignore our request; they hold the photos. But without my written confirmation, we could sue them. It doesn't stop anything, but it should make them think twice."

I tried to remember why I'd agreed to this deal. Scottie had said she was used to this. Used to being used like this. And I'd allowed another person to come and take advantage of her again.

"Nico, let me do my job. This is a standard contact, with a brand that is excited about the partnership. They want us as much as we want them," he explained, his hands pressing down into the desk. "But if something like this happens again, you need to keep a cool head and let me handle it."

Still unsure, I crossed my arms. Jon had never let me down, neither as my coach nor my friend. Even when he was poached, he'd set me up with a choice of other coaches, making sure everything was in hand before he abandoned me for the dark side. I might not trust Sarah after today, but I had to trust his judgement.

With reluctance, I nodded once.

"Good. Glad you're back on board," Jon said, a little more pep in his tone than I would have liked, before his attention turned to his PC monitor. I'd fought the urge to slump down in my chair when he'd spoken again. "I can't complain too much. It's nice to see you and Scottie on the same side of something. I just wish it was something less problematic for me."

I shrugged off his comment, pretending it meant nothing. "Guess all that team building is paying off."

In truth, I wasn't sure why I'd caused such a big deal. Off court, I usually had a more level head. While I wouldn't have let Sarah talk to Scottie like that, I could admit to myself that threatening to take her camera was maybe a step too far. I didn't dare allow myself to dig deeper, to wonder why out of everyone, I'd cross that line for *her*.

"Now let's talk about how you can make it up to Sarah."

"Make it up to her?" I asked, confused and a little agitated. "I admit I overreacted, so I'd understand if you want me to apologise to her. But she should be apologising to Scottie too."

He waved his hands as if to calm me down, but all it did was feed the reawakened rage monster living inside of me. "And she will, of course. But we also need to keep ELITE happy, and since they aren't exactly happy about how this photo situation has been handled . . ."

"They want something in return?"

"Exactly," he said with a nod.

Resigned, and out of fight, the pain in my knee growing and sapping my remaining energy, I asked, "What do they want?"

"Oh, don't look so sour. You might actually like this one."

I looked at him with a blank expression, waiting for him to put me out of my misery.

"You guys are going off campus."

CHAPTER SIXTEEN

Scottie
Brazil – Declan McKenna

I wasn't sure if the trip to Lindos was supposed to be a punishment for what went down during the yoga class, but it sure hadn't felt like it. We'd been locked up forever, working so hard with no break in the routine, that any change felt like a much-needed escape.

As we all clambered out of the rented minivan, the streets of the tiny village of Lindos too small for the car to venture any farther, I took a deep breath in, savouring the salt air from the ocean and the sweet scent of corner creperies for tourists.

"This way," Jon shouted, pulling our attention from the white-washed streets and instead, leading us toward the acropolis that sat atop a steep mountain. I was tracking the long and twisting path up the hill when I was jostled to the side, Dylan storming past me through the tiny streets.

Of course, Jon had invited everyone in the villa along, otherwise the escape out of the villa might have been too close to enjoyable for what was supposed to be a punishment.

"Didn't see you there," she muttered with a scowl. Henrik and Inés followed behind her, Inés giving me a softer expression that I chose to read as "sorry for my asshole friend."

"Scottie, can I get you a little closer to Nico, please?" Sarah asked, no further sign of her attitude from the beach. I looked over at him, smiling slightly as I took in his relaxed demeanour, his hands stuffed into a pair of navy shorts, the ELITE brand stitched on the top left of his pocket. We were both head-to-toe clad in ELITE clothing, my entire wardrobe now overflowing with the brand. I was pretty sure Jon had the rest of my clothes shipped back to my mum's, in case I got any ideas.

I stepped closer, walking alongside him as Sarah took some candid photos. Even I had to admit, he looked good, wearing a white linen shirt unbuttoned with a plain white T-shirt underneath, the colour matching with my own outfit. I had gone a little sportier, matching the top with a short white pleated skirt, shoving a blue shirt on top in case it got chilly. It didn't help that most of my wardrobe was tennis outfits, but they were cute, so I didn't complain much. Just over his shoulder, nestled onto a small set of stone stairs, sat three stray cats, all fixated on Nico.

"What do you think the chances of us being allowed a crepe are?" I joked, trying to give Sarah something to work with rather than two silent people walking. After all, we were supposed to look like we were together. Or at the very least like we liked each other.

"I can't remember the last time I had one," he admitted, glancing at me for a moment. "Maybe never."

My jaw unhinged in mock shock. "Never?"

His shoulders rose on a shrug. "I don't think that much fat and sugar is recommended by a sports dietitian."

I tsked, trying to shake his words off. Truthfully, I'd been finding the restrictive training diet . . . well, restrictive. There was plenty to eat, but dried fruit and handfuls of nuts only satisfied me so long. I'd been craving a burger with melted cheese and an entire order of salty, crispy chips for at least a week. It was the hardest part of returning to training.

"I had one every day for a month when I stayed in France. I tried every topping they offered in my local creperie," I admitted. The cafe was on the corner near my hotel, and it had turned out to be the best food for confronting a well-earned hangover.

"What was your favourite?" His eyes betrayed a hunger I recognised too well, certain it wouldn't be satisfied with another protein shake.

"I was a big fan of peaches and crème fraîche, then I'd get them to add a drizzle of honey." My mouth watered at the memory, the sweetness of August ripe peaches with the tartness of the crème, all wrapped in the delicate pancake.

"Can you guys get a little closer?" Sarah pressed, reminding me of her existence. Nico cleared his throat on a cough as he eased, our arms brushing as we walked. How much more could she ask for? My tongue down his throat?

My gaze caught behind us, and I found the three cats from before, all trailing behind us. When we stopped to let a car pass, one tortoiseshell came right up to Nico and began to rub against his trainers, weaving in and around his legs.

Nico lifted his leg, a scowl forming on his face as he tried to escape the assault of the feline.

I laughed. "What is it about you and cats?"

"I'm allergic," he mumbled while bending down and waving his hand to shoo the cat. Instead, the cat lifted its delicate pink nose in the air, booping his palm and taking a good sniff. Nico pulled away, shaking his hand as if he had been burnt.

"If I didn't know any better, I'd say you're afraid."

He didn't take his eyes from the cats for a moment, narrowing them as if he was contemplating a hiss to seal the deal. "Only afraid of my throat closing up."

We had made it to the beginning of the steps up to the acropolis, and while standing at the base of the hike, I allowed myself a moment to take in the true size of the mountain.

My mouth was dry as I leaned over to Nico, my eyes stuck on the tiny figures at the top I was sure were other people. "Are you sure you can manage this today?"

"Yes," he snipped, his tone turning defensive. I looked at him, finding his brows pressed together, his face set in a serious look. I glanced behind him at Sarah, who was distracted by her camera.

"I'm sorry. My own legs are ruined from today's practice." My apology did little to soothe his frustrated look. "Maybe if we give Sarah some good shots on the way up, really play it up, they won't mind if we slip away early."

"Why would we need to do that?" he asked innocently. I didn't bother to argue with him any further, not pointing out that he managed to walk comfortably at the end of a day of practice. Over the weeks, I had seen improvement in his performance. Jon had been right; he was slower than he had been, but he was older, so it was a given for most. Even if he wasn't ready to admit that.

"Just in case."

Sarah continued taking our photos as we scaled the mountain steps, the climb taking its toll on my already battered and bruised body. Quietly, I damned Jon for making us do those extra exercises today. I knew this trip was too good to be true.

I pulled myself up a tall step, thighs and calves burning as I climbed another, the rugged stone almost carved into the hill. Fighting weariness, I took a moment to rest, stopping to admire the view, the sea, a deep Mediterranean Aegean turquoise, contrasting the tangerine sky as the sun journeyed toward the horizon.

Nico appeared by my side, pulling my attention from the scene, his tanned skin aglow with the golden light. I swung my hip into his side to pull his attention. "You taking a break, old man?"

He tilted his head to me, an eyebrow raised playfully. "Dare I remind you that you stopped first?"

I feigned innocence with a shrug. "I thought you'd give up by now."

With what I'm sure was a smirk on his lips, he pushed past me to the next step. "Come on, before we lose the rest of the group."

I turned to follow him, the path becoming increasingly rough as we went higher. Nico had to help me up the steps, offering me a hand to keep me moving up. I didn't admit it to him, but I was grateful for it, unsure how he was able to manage it with his knee. I was beginning to wish I had worn appropriate footwear instead of a pair of ELITE sandals when Jon yelled from ahead.

"Almost halfway, guys! Come on, keep up the pace."

I pulled back in shock, the realisation that we weren't even halfway up hitting hard. My will and motivation were already waning. If it hadn't been a training day, a full morning on the tennis court followed by strength training in the gym, then it would've been easy. But my legs had already been tortured enough, and with Jon's words, I'd found my limit.

Nico was a step ahead of me, turning back to help me up again when my face betrayed me, showing him my reluctance to take a single step farther. He narrowed his eyes at me for a moment, then his expression changed, his head tilting as if he was having an internal debate.

He yelled out, "Jon, I have to go back."

"What do you mean?"

"Sorry, it's my knee. I wasn't expecting a hike."

Jon grumbled to himself before looking over at Sarah. "Have you got enough for today?"

She nodded. "But I'd still like to make it to the top. I can focus on the others."

"I could go back with him," I offered, my heart skipping. "Make sure he gets back to the van. Find some ice to take down the swelling."

Jon appeared uneasy, looking between the both of us suspiciously. The moment was long and tense as the gears turned in

Jon's brain. I was sure he was about to tell us to put on our big person pants and suck it up.

"Fine," he relented. He dug through his shorts, throwing the minivan keys to me. I caught them, trying not to look too relieved we'd been excused. "It will be another two hours, so I don't want to hear any complaints that you had to wait for us."

I didn't need to be told twice as I turned around and stormed down the hill. Nico, still feigning injury, was hot on my heels.

Jon yelled as he became but a tiny figure in the distance, "Go straight back to the minivan!"

CHAPTER SEVENTEEN

Scottie
Wildest Dreams – Taylor Swift

We did not go back to the minivan.

Instead, we took a path down the hill towards Lindos town, the cosy alleyways lined with tiny shops selling everything from fancy soap and jewellery to cheap souvenirs. Open bars blasted music as we navigated the busy streets, swerving around groups of tourists and dodging waiters trying to lure us in with promises of cheap food and large portions.

It was like stepping into another world. I could've lost myself in the atmosphere, in the buzz the crowds offered, but when I spied the green glowing cross, I turned to Nico behind me.

"Is your knee hurting?" I asked, looking at the pharmacy.

His face crumpled into a grimace. "A little, but I just need to rest."

I nodded understandingly, looking around and spotting a bar sitting off the street, a football match playing over the screen. I sent him a charming impossible-to-say-no-to smile, gesturing towards the bar.

"Jon said to go back to the van," Nico reminded me.

"You heard him. They won't be back for another two hours! Do you want to sit in the hot sticky van, or do you want to have a drink for the first time in weeks?"

"Are you always this rebellious? First coffee, now alcohol?"

"I said drink. You can have a Pepsi if you want," I pointed out. "Or you could go wild and order a diet."

Nico paused, narrowing his eyes on me. "Fine, but only one."

We found a table, sitting along the busy street, which provided us a perfect view for people watching. When the waiter arrived, placing a bowl of pistachios between us, I ordered a beer. Nico eyed me before ordering the same.

Taking that first sip almost washed away the stress and tension of the previous weeks, of the worry and gruelling labour of getting my body back into the shape necessary. When I looked over at Nico, his expression was relaxed as he drank the cold amber liquid.

"Better than a Pepsi?" I teased.

His eyes met mine, lips pressed together. "It's been a while since I had either."

"You don't ever cut loose?"

"I used to," he admitted. "Everything recently has been aimed toward recovery and keeping my body in the best condition I can."

"And what? One beer will destroy your entire recovery?"

He smiled. "That, and my dietitian was a very scary person who ruled what entered my body with an iron fist."

"Sounds . . ." I trailed off, grimacing at the memories. My life had been like that once. "Terrible."

"Are you much of a beer drinker?" he asked.

"It's fine. I'm more of a cocktail person. Give me a tequila old-fashioned and you'll make my night," I joked, remembering my favourite drink as a part of me began to miss my London life. But while those years had been fun and wild, and the training had been demanding, tennis was in my bones.

"Do you watch football?" My head nodded to the screen behind him. I reached for the nuts and deshelled one.

"I don't follow soccer, but I know enough to follow the rules," he corrected, his mouth turning up into a cheeky grin.

Forcing a terrible accent, I picked up the discarded shells and threw them playfully at him. "So American."

He tossed his own shells over at me, one getting stuck in my hair and the other hitting me on the nose.

"Such a Brit," he teased back, his eyes dancing playfully over my face. My fingers tried to dig the shell from my long, thick hair, but I struggled to pull it out.

"Let me," he said, leaning over the small table. His fingers met mine, concentration focused on untangling my hair, his eyebrows locked. I couldn't help but take in the line of his jaw, covered in a rough, unshaved stubble, his eyes unblinking as I took in their colour. He was so close I could smell his familiar aftershave, the scent mixing with the sweet air.

"There you go." He pulled back, breaking the spell he had cast over me, the shell held in his fingers. I smiled, my mind still reeling from the close contact. Then, in an instant, the shell hit me again on the cheek as he pinged it over.

I sent him a flat look, suppressing a laugh. "We are children."

He chuckled, relaxing back into his plastic chair, turning to see the screen again. I got distracted by the pull of his shirt sleeve around his biceps, eyes following his tattoo across the muscle. I took another drink, hoping the liquid would be enough to cool me down from a sudden wave of heat, before my attention moved to the opposite side of the street.

"It looks like your friends are back." Lined up along the pavement sat a trio of cats, their attention squarely on Nico. "Did you roll in some catnip before we went out?"

He swallowed another gulp of beer, his throat bobbing. "It's the same back at the villa. They won't leave me alone."

"Maybe they know their power over you."

"Have you somehow trained a legion of cats to take me out so you can steal my hat again?"

"Oh, that's unnecessary." I smiled knowingly. "I'll get it back next time you leave it lying around."

"It's my lucky hat. I'd appreciate it if you didn't."

"Maybe I could use a lucky hat of my own."

He leaned forward, elbows resting on the table, his grey eyes teasing. "We could get you another hat."

I met his gaze, arms folded over as I sat up. "But I'm quite attached to yours."

We stayed like that, staring straight at each other, waiting for the other to look away or blink. *Anything.* But instead, his teasing look turned deeper, and his eyes a little darker. I couldn't look away. At that moment, I found the curve of his face and the sharpness of his jaw the most fascinating sights in the world.

Did he have to be so damn handsome?

His eyes were similarly assessing me, but I couldn't read what he saw in my face. It was as if he was marking each freckle splashed across the bridge of my nose, connecting them with invisible lines.

Then the table shuddered as a waiter squeezed past us with a tray full of food, and we found ourselves disconnected again. Nico cleared his throat as we both took a drink, washing the moment away.

He moved on. "When did you visit France?"

"Last year. I watched your US quarterfinal there."

"Against Oliver Anderson?"

I nodded. "You were still good then."

He laughed, the noise loud and bright, catching my insult.

"I mean," I added, "for your age."

His attention switched from the TV back to me, the cheap plastic of the chair underneath him creaking. "I remember your French Open semi, what was it? Three years ago?"

It was my turn to laugh before I took another sip of beer to drown the sting of that match. "Yeah, I lost."

"You almost had her," he added. I took another sip, still attempting to drown the memory. I was about to beat her in straight sets when I fell, injuring my leg. She saw the weakness, exploited it, and won. That was the injury that snowballed into—

"Who were you playing again?"

I blinked, trying to pull myself back. "Dylan."

"Seems you two don't get on very well."

"Oh, you couldn't be more wrong. We have sleepovers every night, braiding each other's hair while we gossip about boys."

"I would pay to see that."

"She'd probably chop my hair off in my sleep."

"At least I'd be guaranteed to get my money's worth."

The moment lulled as we turned back to the TV, watching the cute men in tiny shorts kick a ball around a field for fun. Half of the bar cheered when the striker scored while the others grumbled about the goalie before taking a long sip of their drinks.

I started to eye the food menu, and turned to the only section I was interested in: burgers, flame-grilled and served with crispy onions, a fresh slice of tomato, and a brioche bun.

"Hungry?" Nico asked before finishing his beer.

I lowered the menu, smiling evilly at him. "When in Rome," I said, returning my attention to the limited burger section. It was a choice between one cheesy patty or two. The waiter returned, and ignoring a rather disapproving glare from Nico, I ordered us two more beers and a burger for myself.

"Do you want anything to eat?" I asked him.

"No, I'm fine," he said, smiling. The waiter was about to leave when I caught him, deciding to test Nico and see how far I could push him.

"And two shots of Fireball, please." The waiter nodded before disappearing.

"You're trying to get us into trouble."

"What's wrong with a little trouble, Nico?" I waved away his concerns. "It's just some shots."

"And a burger and two beers. You could've had Elena make you a burger back at home."

I squished my face. "It would've been made of beans or mushrooms. No, thank you. I've had enough diet burgers for one lifetime."

"I feel like I've been on a training diet my entire life." His face straightened, wiped of the previous joy. "My previous coach had me on a plant-based diet. No meat, nothing that came out of an animal, nothing that could've been near anything that once had a face. I can understand it if you're against animal cruelty, but my own mother didn't know what to feed me when I visited. Hell, I wasn't even sure what I could and couldn't eat." He leaned forward, a serious look on his face. He said the words in a whisper, as if he was revealing the nuclear codes. "Did you know Oreos are vegan?"

I laughed, not sure what I was expecting to hear.

"And don't get me started on what that type of diet does to your stomach," he added.

I clutched my middle, all the while hating how much I could relate. When I collected myself, I shared my own memory. "One time, my trainers decided I had put on too much weight over break and put me on a weeklong liquid diet cleanse. I think I passed out twice during practice."

He blinked at me, his mouth parted as if he was processing what I've told him. I shifted uncomfortably in my chair.

"That's not normal," he said. "Don't think that's normal."

I shook my head, finishing my beer in one mouthful. "I don't anymore. Extensive therapy helped with that. A lot of the shit that happened wasn't normal."

I almost told him what Matteo had done, the secret buried just beneath my skin. The one that cost me everything but let me escape. Led me to Mum. Took me halfway up a Greek mountain and to this tiny, packed sports bar.

"You know, after everything went down with Wimbledon—" The word was almost strangled in my throat, but I continued. "The first normal meal I had was a burger. It was in an airport. You know how they always have a Burger King in an airport, but it's always the worst Burger King you could ever eat? Well, I ordered a double Royale with cheese, like in that movie. And they asked me if I wanted fries . . ." I trailed off, seeing the image in my brain. I could still smell that Burger King, could still see the cashier's face perfectly. "And there was nobody to stop me. So, I did. I had the burger *and* the fries. And then for a drink, I had regular Pepsi. Not diet, not that zero crap they market to men. The one with all the sugar. And an ice cream. Then I sat in a corner, and I ate every single bite. I felt sick after the burger because, like I said, airport Burger Kings are the worst. But I ate it all."

He looked at me for a moment, trying to read me. There was a moment where I became concerned he might have missed the point I was trying to make telling that story. That despite what they had done to me, to my body, to that young girl who was trying to impress her fucking father, I had still escaped and gained control of myself, once and for all.

With or without this competition, all this training, I would still retain that control of my body. Nobody would ever take it away from me. No one could control me ever again.

Then he reached out, grabbing the attention of a hurrying waiter. "Hey, sorry—can I order a second burger for the table? Hold the tomatoes."

"Welcome to the dark side." I smiled. "But removing the healthy part of the burger? How ever will we explain ourselves to Jon?"

"He can never know." His hand stretched out to me. I took it, his fingers wrapping around mine, the calluses of his palm brushing against my skin.

"It's our secret."

WE LOST TRACK of time, ordering another round of beers (this time, minus a scowl from Nico) and eating our burgers in peace, taking time to enjoy our first comfort meal in a while. But when the final whistle blew on the football game, we realised we might have forgotten one important thing.

The rest of the group, who thought we'd be back at the van.

We paid the bill, rushing to make it back to the parking lot where we were supposed to be when the sky split open with heavy rain. The streets emptied, shops pulling out awnings to run the rain away from the entrance, while bars closed shutters over their windows to keep the water out. Very quickly, the small alleyway street of Lindos turned into a river, and with a quick glance at Nico, I'd known we didn't have time to sit this one out. If the group wasn't already back at the van, they would be soon.

Whether it was driven by need or the three beers I'd drank, I hadn't thought twice as I grabbed Nico's hand, our fingers interlacing, and dragged him out into the warm rain. It was like we jumped fully clothed into a shower, our clothes soaked through to our skin as we ran through the streets, attempting to dodge the worst of the rain by jumping from cover to cover.

We stepped out unprotected into the rain, the tourist area coming to an end as we surpassed the last awning. Heavy rain pelted down on us and any concept of the word "dry" was washed away. Halfway up the street, we found a doorway to give us some shelter, but not larger than for one person. We stood face-to-face, our bodies pressed together, squeezing into the tiny space.

He was as soaked as I was, strands of his hair stuck down on his forehead, shirt clinging to his frame, accentuating every muscle of his arms and chest; a hard chest that was pressed against mine.

Without the lights from the shops and restaurants, nighttime blanketed the streets. But as I looked up at him, his eyes darkened and wandered over every inch of my face. Just like before. I tried to ignore the feel of the length of his body against me as it rose and sank with each breath, the humidity in the air making it warmer and harder to inhale.

My chest tightened as my gaze caught a raindrop rolling down his cheek, and acting on an instinct I didn't know I had, I raised my hand to his rugged face and wiped it away, enjoying the feel of his unshaven stubble against my fingers. If the action was unwelcome, he didn't let me know, unmoving under my touch.

His stormy ocean eyes caught mine, the firm line of his jaw slackened into an expression that I couldn't quite decipher. It was like the water had washed away his armour, stripping away a veneer of control he held on to, and instead, he was vulnerable and exposed.

The pounding rain faded into a distant murmur as the tension between us, always simmering beneath the surface, now hung heavy in the air, like an electric charge waiting to ignite. Rain continued to pour, but it was as if the world had narrowed down to the two of us, locked in an unspoken conversation. His eyes held a hint of vulnerability, one that matched my own.

The pounding of my heart in my ears replaced the noise of the rain as I hesitated, my hand still resting against his cheek, our faces mere inches apart, his eyes searching mine.

And then he moved backward, and my hand fell to my side as

he slid from under the porch and out onto the street, the rain continuing to pelt down. It took me a moment to process everything, watching him as he looked back at me. With a silent nod of his head, he gestured for me to follow him out. His vulnerable expression was gone, his guard back up.

Wordlessly I followed, stepping back into the downpour, which only served to wash away that one precious moment in that doorway, where for a second, with my hand on his cheek, and his eyes burning into mine, there was a possibility that Nico Kotas could be more than my teammate.

Tweets

EXCLUSIVE PHOTOS: Scandalous @ScottieSinclair and
Tennis Legend Nico Kotas spotted sharing drinks in Greece.
Witnesses report seeing the two on a romantic sightseeing
trip before roaming the streets of Lindos. SEE PHOTOS HERE
—The Daily Tea

See the summer collection here, modelled by Scottie Sinclair
and Nico Kotas —ELITE

Are Scottie Sinclair and Daddy Kotas together? My life is over.

CHAPTER EIGHTEEN

Nico

The Walls Are Way Too Thin – Holly Humberstone

Shorts and a sports bra. That's all she was wearing. Black shorts that cut off mid-thigh, rising up her waist before revealing a canvas of soft skin that no amount of Greek sun seemed to be able to tan. A matching sports bra that sent my brain into such a spasm, I couldn't even begin to form the words to describe it.

A ball bounced into my side of the court, but I was too mesmerised to even move, watching the stretch in her arms as she returned the ball to me. We'd been in practice all morning, an extra hour added on, which I'm sure was Jon's personal punishment for not returning to the van.

"You should've hit that!" Jon shouted at me from the sidelines, and my brain scrambled all over again from the double entendre.

Her face close to mine, droplets of rain running down her freckled cheeks, blonde hair stuck to her face from the rain, the length of her entire body pressed against mine as we hid in the small alcove from the sudden downpour.

Another ball smacked me in the face.

"What are you doing, Kotas? Daydreaming?" Scottie grinned from opposite the court, my hat on her head. Again. I fought the urge to storm over and steal it. Distance was what I needed from her. Distance made up of miles, countries, and continents, and maybe then I'd forget the sweet scent of her shampoo on the rim of my hat.

Vanilla and orange. I wondered if my hat would smell of her again when I took it back.

Trying to keep my concentration, I bounced the ball and served, using as much of my strength as I could muster. Scottie's forehand return sliced through the air, the ball skimming the net before landing inside the baseline. She moved with grace and precision, her footwork impeccable, and so the rally began. We chased each other around the court, and even when I thought I finally had her, she surprised me, making a race across the court look too damn easy for these old legs to catch up. Scottie won the point, her smile a triumphant ray of sunshine, and she mouthed the running score to me, so Jon didn't notice.

For a while now, we'd been keeping a tally across our morning practice, and up until now, I'd been winning. Not by a lot, but enough to taunt her with. She'd pretend she was fine with it, tossing her hair into a messy bun at the end of practice, refusing to make eye contact. I could feel the heat of internal rage burning her up. Neither of us liked losing. You had to hate losing more than you love to win to stay in this game.

But with my brain buzzing on what I was certain was the pebbling of nipples under her sports bra, I was falling behind. And in need of yet another cold shower. Maybe this had been her plan all along. The shorts and the bra and the soft bare skin on display was a Trojan horse. If it was, it was working.

"Keep it up, Nico. She's handing you your ass." I was sure that was Jon's way of trying to motivate me, but when she won—again—I grew only more flustered. Was I seriously getting more turned on by her winning? What kind of sick masochist had I turned into?

Sarah had hung around earlier, taking up precious time trying to get shots of us while we did our warm-up routines, getting Scottie to do some moves with a jumper on and off, sometimes wrapped around her waist. I was already sick of this so-called partnership with them. Didn't they know we were supposed to be in boot camp?

When Jon finally called practice, she was an entire game up and I was completely ruined.

I headed over to my gym bag, taking a long, cooling sip from my water bottle, and rested a little from running back and forth in the baking morning sun.

"How are you holding up, old man?" Her grin was a wild thing as she marched over, grabbing for her own water bottle. "You look tired."

"Some of those balls were out," I argued. "I know it's been a while for you, but that video referee will bite you in the ass."

She shrugged me off. "Fine. Want a rematch?" The challenge hung in the air for a moment, my overheating, overstimulated body screaming in horror at the idea. But I couldn't let her know.

"No more today. You've still got the rest of your practise," Jon cut in, squashing Scottie's offer. My body relaxed with relief. We still had a gym session left, and then laps in the pool to continue the rehab on my knee. Truthfully, I was doing a lot better, Jon's plan paying off. Despite my performance, I was faster than I had been in months.

I looked up at Scottie, finding her sending Jon a look of disappointment for spoiling her fun. I knew she was partially to thank. Our games kept me on my toes, both of us taunting each other with our hunger to beat the other. I had wanted to do this alone, but now, I wasn't sure I could imagine it any other way.

Pushing myself up from the bench, I stretched to my full height, her eyes engulfing mine. With a swift motion, I snatched my hat back, placing it backwards on my head.

I was right. The scent did transfer.

My lips stretched into a satisfied smirk as she narrowed her eyes at me, strands of her blonde hair in disarray. Her hands went to the top of her head, delicate fingers flattening and pushing it back into place. Even with her messy hair, a flush of pink across the freckled bridge of her nose from the exercise, she was beautiful. If anything, the more undone she became, the more beautiful she was.

"Stop stealing my hat," I said, leaning down to pick up my gym bag. She took a swipe at my head, trying to take it back, but I caught her, moving out of her reach.

Her eyes switched from the hat, rolling back as if to say "whatever do you mean?" She sealed it with an innocent shrug of her shoulders. "Maybe stop leaving it lying about."

I grumbled, "I only took it off for breakfast. Elena hates when I wear it at the table." If I did, she would attack me with the wooden spoon until I relented. My knuckles learned that lesson the hard way.

"And I picked it up," she chirped, shouldering her own bag and heading for the path back through the gardens to the villa. I chased after her, only allowing my eyes to dip south for a couple of torturous seconds. Damn those shorts. Damn that ass.

"Use one of the hats ELITE sent. I'm sure they would love to have their name plastered all over your head," I suggested.

She let out a laugh that sounded like it was made of pure gold. "Should I offer to have their name tramp stamped on my lower back while I'm at it?"

It was a chore not to think about black ink tattooed into her skin. If she had one hidden under what little clothing she was wearing today, what would it be?

"I could get one matching," I joked. "They'd like that."

"I've always wanted one."

"A tattoo?" I asked, and she nodded. "Why haven't you gotten one?"

She was silent for a moment, glancing at the path ahead. She didn't need to say it for me to be able to read the answer. Her father. I wasn't sure what had given him this power over her, stretching over her like a dark cloud, even if she insisted he wasn't in her life anymore. What had happened there was a question I was dying to ask again.

I'd always hated him. He'd been cocky and arrogant back when I was coming up the ranks those fifteen years ago. Unbeaten for too long, he'd convinced the world he was a god.

That was, until I—unseeded and accepted in on a wildcard— made it to that final. And in one gruelling match, I dismantled an empire.

It was clear to everyone that Scottie had been his second chance at success. That he had her pick up his mantle while he pulled her strings. The question remained: how tangled up had she become before everything fell apart?

"I almost got one in Ibiza last summer," she admitted, smiling at me. "It was three in the morning, and I was drunk. We'd had bottle service at the club, and nothing had ever been a bigger mistake. I thought it was a great idea to get a tattoo half out of it; I told him what I wanted in some lame cursive they had and passed out in the chair. I came to with the man this close." She holds up two fingers a centimetre apart. "Then I threw up on him and they kicked me out. Thankfully. It did not look hygienic there, even before all the sickness."

I smiled at her memory. She had so many stories of her last two years, and none of them sounded anything less than carnage, chaos, and a hell of a great time. Just like she was turning out to be.

Curiosity got the best of me as I asked, "What was it?"

"What?"

"The tattoo?" We were almost back at the villa, the glass doors leading to the kitchen in sight. "What terrible mistake were you going to get on your body forever?"

She made a noise that almost sounded like a laugh. Her gaze looked straight ahead while her arms crossed in front of her. I was certain she was nervous when she answered, "It said 'clean.'"

"Clean?" I repeated, and she gave me the smallest nod. My brows pressed together. "Like not . . ." I trailed off, and before I could say another word, she clarified.

"Like 'Scottie Sinclair is fucking clean.' Or at least, I remember trying to get the tattooist to write that, but he refused, said something about it already being dumb enough getting a tattoo drunk, never mind a curse word along with it."

I didn't know what to make of it. What any of it meant, but one look at her and I knew it was important—the emotion in her eyes, the set of her jaw. I knew not to question, not to push. If she wanted me to know, she would tell me.

"I like it. It's badass," I said, trying to comfort her. She sent me a nervous smile, and I opened the door to the kitchen. The AC-cooled air made it feel as if I'd stepped into an icebox. I held the door open for her, watching as she slipped by me, a single shiver as she faced the cold.

"It was dumb," she said as I closed the door.

My shoulder rose on a shrug. "Better than getting an ELITE tramp stamp."

She laughed, the noise warm as it prickled under my skin. "At least they'd pay me to do it."

An idea bloomed, and before I knew it, the words tumbled out of me. "I know a good artist in London. We could go together."

"To get an ELITE tattoo?"

"No. I mean, in general. If you still wanted one."

Her eyes narrowed playfully at me. "Why? Do you enjoy watching people wither in pain?"

"I thought I'd distract you through the pain, but now that you mention it, it could be an unexplored kink." Scottie's eyes grew wide for a moment, her pink lips parting before she pulled herself together.

"Funny," she said as we reached the break in the hallway where we would go our separate ways. "I might just have to take you up on that."

I raised my brows in surprise. "That so?"

"I meant the tattoo, not the kink," she replied, patting me cheekily on the shoulder. "I'll leave you to figure that one out on your own."

My cheeks burned red with embarrassment as I nodded, gaze avoiding her. I was getting too close to her, too open. If the moment in the doorway had taught me anything, it was that. We said a quick goodbye before heading to our respective rooms to wash up. I continued to beat myself up the entire length of the hallway. This was supposed to be a professional relationship, with professional thoughts and not an entire training session distracted by the curves of her body or how she looked bending down to pick up a ball.

Scottie Sinclair might as well have had the words "bad idea" tattooed in block capitals on her forehead. The absolutely opposite type of person that I would normally let myself get close to. Too impulsive, too wild, too young.

And yet, here I was, offering to take her to my favourite tattooist and hold her hand. Keep her distracted while she got her first ink because when she opened up to me, allowing me to peer into the real Scottie, things weren't adding up.

She wasn't impulsive or reckless. She was hurt and growing through that. She had some wild moments, but to me, it sounded as if she had gone out and had some fucking fun for once. Whatever happened two years ago with the doping, I wasn't sure. But it didn't sound like the Scottie I'd gotten to know.

In fact, just the opposite.

Shocking Blood Test Results Serve Doubts on Comeback

The grapevine is buzzing with hush-hush talk of some mysterious substance uncovered in Scottie Sinclair's recent blood test.

Rumour has it she's eyeing a comeback soon, but will this revelation slam the door on her plans with a ban extension?

Apart from some promotional shots by the athletic clothing company ELITE, Sinclair's been playing hide-and-seek for the past month. The last time anyone laid eyes on her, she was soaking up the sun on the island of Rhodes, getting cosy with none other than Nico Kotas—yes, *that* eight-time Grand Slam champ! The two have remained tight-lipped on the latest dating rumours, but with the newest campaign from ELITE, these two stars look rather steamy together.

Stick around as we dig deeper into the chaos of Sinclair's meds mayhem. Game, set, and drama—the court chaos is far from over.

CHAPTER NINETEEN

Nico
Family Friend – The Vaccines

"Are you calling or folding?" Henrik's voice pulled my attention back to the table and away from the one person who always seemed to capture it. We'd been playing cards all evening out on the patio, but when I'd caught a glimpse of Scottie through the doors to the kitchen, I'd lost track of the game entirely.

Looking around the table, I took in the chorus of puzzled faces and lips pressed in firm, concerned lines as Inés and Henrik stared back down at their cards. Dylan, however, who sat opposite me, was calm and collected, a smirk spread on her lips.

"You gonna call, Kotas?" she challenged, raising her eyebrows confidently. I tried to ignore her, learning over the course of our stay here that she was impossible to read. I'd never played her on the court before, but after seeing her in a card game, I'd quickly figured out how terrifying an opponent she would've made.

I looked over at the kitchen again, spotting Scottie's messy blonde bun sticking out above the door of the fridge, and without another thought, I folded. Dylan made an unintelligible noise of glee, scooping the hoard of chips to her side.

"I'm going to sit this next round out," I announced, pushing myself out of the chair.

Inés eyed me suspiciously, her glance flickering behind me to the kitchen. "Are you going to get yourself a snack?"

I picked up my empty glass from the table. "I'm just getting a drink."

"Mhm," Dylan hummed. "Sure you are."

"You got something to say, Bailey?"

"Nothing." She refocused on the pile of chips in front of her. There was a long silence as I looked around the group, waiting for somebody to crack and tell me the truth.

Henrik finally broke, saying somewhat playfully, "You two just seem to spend a lot of time together."

"Yeah, because we're mixed partners. We train together all day."

He smiled, lifting an eyebrow. "So are me and Inés."

I looked between them as if I was still missing something. "And you guys are hanging out right now."

"Yeah, but I don't chase her around."

"And don't get me started on the way you guys look at each other," Inés chirped in. "It's like watching a rom-com unfold."

"It's sickening," Dylan said, just loud enough for me to hear.

My gaze caught on Dylan, her tone sharper. She didn't look back up at me, but it was clear what she thought of Scottie. I could understand her view. While it was good that Scottie came clean and confessed to the doping, Dylan was robbed of the precious Wimbledon win. If somebody had stolen that from me, I'd never forgive them either.

Inés pulled my attention back to her, playfully adding, "So, you both ditched us in Lindos for no reason at all?"

"Then turned up soaking wet?" Henrik smirked.

"It was raining!" I defended, throwing my hands in the air. I realised that I had almost shouted, and after a quick glance to the kitchen, found Scottie there, unaware of the discussion that was going on.

"You were supposed to be in the van." Inés smiled. "And you were gone for hours doing God knows what."

"We were just talking." My mind stuttered under their accusations.

I knew we were growing closer. After all, we'd been working together for a while now. We had a relationship where before there was misunderstanding and a little arrogance, but now there was communication and friendship.

And maybe, just maybe, I thought about the moment in the doorway. The way her pink lips had parted. How her eyes looked into mine. How the front of her soaked body pressed against me. Maybe I even thought about it in the shower when I most definitely should not be thinking about my mixed partner.

"There's nothing going on." I wasn't sure if I had said the words for their sake or for mine, but I said them firmly, trying to put an absolute end to this conversation. The last thing I needed was for Scottie to hear any of this, to think that . . . to know that . . .

"Yet," Dylan said, looking across the table at me, her gaze icy and cutting. Inés and Henrik looked at each other with raised eyebrows, their lips pressed into small smiles.

I was stuck for a moment, unsure if I should continue my plan to see Scottie. I had only wanted to check on her after today, to make sure Sarah hadn't done anything that we needed to speak to Jon about. Henrik had begun to shuffle the cards, and Inés looked over at me, a knowing smile on her lips.

I waited for another sarcastic response, but she just rolled her eyes at me and looked away.

"Just go," she mouthed, nodding her head in the direction of the kitchen. I hesitated for a single moment longer before relenting. Behind me, hooting and hollering rose from Henrik and Inés. I turned on my heels, sticking my middle finger up at them, sick of their childish antics.

Pulling the door open, I found Scottie sitting at the breakfast counter, snacking out of a box of granola. Her neck was left exposed by her swept-up hair, while she wore ELITE joggers and a tank top with thin straps that I made a mental note to ignore.

"I sincerely hope that's not a communal box," I grumbled, taking in the sight of her arm disappearing into the box, her cheeks full like a hamster as she still chewed on the last handful of granola.

"It's not," she said after swallowing, a smile curving onto her lips. "I charmed Elena into buying a box for me."

I scoffed. "Like the coffee?"

"That's one secret I'll never tell," she said with a wink. Every morning, she taunted me with that mug she somehow managed to acquire and successfully hide from Jon. And every morning, she refused to tell me how, or where, she got it. I was getting pretty sick of green tea, antioxidants be damned.

"How were things with Sarah today?" I asked, leaning back against a kitchen counter opposite to where she sat.

She shrugged. "Same old thing." Her words did nothing to stop my concern. "You would've hated it. They've moved me on to Tik-Tok," she added, digging out another handful and eating.

I scoffed, my fingers gripping the edge of the cool marble countertop. "I'm surprised they didn't want me involved."

"I think Sarah's a little apprehensive, given what happened." She almost side-eyed me, the glare soft but ever so accusatory.

"But she didn't push it again today?" My heart dipped, waiting for her answer, the same rage ready to rear its head again. I'd hated it when they'd sent me off to the gym instead of being able to keep an eye on the situation.

Scottie shook her head. "Nope, she was on her best behaviour.

Jon was helping out, so I doubt she would do anything like that again."

"Good," I said, trying to hide the relief behind a mask of indifference. Even knowing Jon was there helped keep me calm. My grip on the counter loosened, my shoulder blades relaxing into my back. She was okay.

"You guys sound like you're having fun out there." Scottie nodded her head towards the garden where the three others were still playing cards.

"Dylan is wiping the floor with us."

"Sounds like her."

"Want to join us?" I offered. "Maybe you can read her bluff better than the rest of us."

"I can think of about one hundred other ways I'd rather spend my evening than giving Dylan any of my money."

"You never know, you might end up taking it from her instead."

"Tempting." Scottie pressed her lips together, scrunching her nose with fake indecision. "Maybe I should watch her take yours instead."

"Be my guest. That's how the night seems to be going anyway." I laughed, watching her face light up with similar glee.

"I'm not sure who I'd prefer to lose to."

"If you play, you could end up beating both of us." I hold out the offer, trying to tempt her into joining us. So many nights she has spent alone, kindly turning down my offers to join us.

"I don't even know how to play poker," she admitted, biting her lip, and my gaze couldn't help but watch, paralysed by the soft movement.

I cleared my throat, a lump forming, and then the words were out before I could even think them through. "I'll teach you."

Her head cocked to the left. "You're that desperate for me to play?"

I shook my head in denial, stuttering out a response before I could string words together. "You always hang out on your own. I don't want you to feel left out."

"Thanks, but I'm okay." Her attention turned back to the box of granola.

"Is it Dylan?" My words hung in the air between us, an unspoken question playing over in my mind. *Is it me?*

"It's . . . it's hard. I know what they all think of me." Her voice was low, barely louder than a whisper. When she looked up at me, I could see the tremble in her pink lips, the watery effect washing the blue of her irises out. I wanted to step forward, close this small gap between us, and wrap her up in my arms. Keep her safe from everything she was too keenly aware of. Her voice nearly broke as she grew louder, but no longer confident. "And I don't blame them. But it makes it hard to want to hang out with them. It took a while for me to . . . move on from everything. Being around them only reminds me of what happened."

My control snapped as I pushed myself away from the counter, leaning forward on the breakfast bar opposite where she was sitting. She straightened, her body going stiff as if taken aback by the movement.

"Scottie, you came clean. You owned up to what you did," I started. We were face-to-face, her eyes looking into mine before glancing down to where her hands were pulling at each other nervously, her nerve lost. Apprehensively, I reached out, my fingers tipping up her chin so she would meet my gaze. A lock of blonde hair fell into her face, and I pushed the soft golden strand behind her ear, keeping her freckled face clear.

"I don't know what happened," I continued, "but I know you now. And I know I can trust you. As both a teammate and as a friend." The word "friend" felt wrong, like it wasn't big enough to encompass everything I felt for her, but it was the only descriptor

I could think of. "Not many people would've ever had the courage to step up and take responsibility for what they did, but you did. I'm proud of you for that. And I swear, I don't think I've ever seen anyone work as hard as you do." The lump in my throat reappeared, and no matter what, I couldn't swallow it down as the truth poured out, like I'd been cut with a blade, the injury deep and sharp, and now I couldn't stop from bleeding out. She had to know. She had to see.

"Watching you these weeks," I continued, "I can see why Jon had so much faith in you after everything. His career was in ruins after you came forward, and I couldn't understand how, after that, he could ever trust you. But he believed you'd changed, and . . . and so do I. You're committed, you work harder than anyone else here."

The air was thick with tension as I kept my eyes on her, wanting to make sure that she knew I meant every word I had said. After a moment to collect myself, my lips broke out into a slight smile, trying to ease us out of the tension. "I'm not sure how an old man like me is going to keep up."

She scoffed, some of that playful brightness returning to her eyes. "You aren't that old."

My smile widened. "So, you admit it?"

She tilted her head, looking at me through her thick eyelashes. "Don't get too cocky there, Kotas."

My name on her tongue—nobody had ever made it sound so good.

"Wouldn't dare, Sinclair," I replied, her own smile growing at the rhyme of my words. I lost myself for a moment staring at her, forgetting the point I was trying to make, but a quick glance over my shoulder reminded me.

"Give them a chance to get to know you. Stop hiding yourself away. You spent the last two years running. Don't you think it's time to stop?" I asked, watching as her gaze dipped away from mine, a soft sigh escaping her lips.

"Since when did you become so convincing?" she murmured, shaking her head. Pride welled from inside of me. *That's my brave girl.*

I hummed to myself, unable to tear myself away from her for even a second. "Probably right around the time Jon convinced me to start playing with you."

A laugh escaped her on a breath and when she looked up at me again, her usual mask of confidence was restored. She looked ready for battle, a knowing smirk playing on her lips.

"You coming?" I asked, looking to her for an answer.

With a deep breath in, she nodded, before leading me out into the garden, ready for the battle. And as I watched her leave, confidence in her stride, I realised everything Inés and Henrik—even Dylan—had insinuated about us might not be so far from the truth after all.

CHAPTER TWENTY

Scottie
Final Girl – CHVRCHES

There was one fundamental issue with Nico's plan to talk me through the game: there were only four seats around the garden table.

At first, he offered to stand, help me from over my shoulder. A perfectly reasonable solution that I fought. Nobody takes a seat away from another person without arguing about it. I offered to sit on the ground, or even go find another chair, maybe drag one outside from the dining room. Then, with a smug smile I couldn't quite understand, Inés piped up.

"Why don't you sit on Nico's lap?" she oh-so-innocently suggested.

And why wouldn't I sit on Nico? Why wouldn't that be the weirdest thing in the world to make a comfy seat out of my teammate's lap? Maybe it was the way he looked at me in the kitchen as he told me he trusted me, the way his fingers brushed my hair back behind my ear. Maybe it was the fact I liked it far too much.

Now there I was, sat on Nico's lap, like this was a normal thing to do around other people. Like this was a normal thing to do for *us*.

He held the cards out in front of us, explaining how the game should be played, while his head rested above my shoulder, his chest pressed into my side.

"If you look in the middle," he murmured into my ear, trying to keep our hand a secret from everyone else in the game. His breath was hot against my neck, and I had to suppress a shiver from running down my back. "You can see we have a straight." His finger flicked the corner of two cards he held.

I nodded my head as he continued to explain the rules in a whisper. I had to stop myself from fidgeting, wriggling around and digging into his lap with my thigh bones. This was awkward as hell, and I had somehow been convinced to agree to it.

"I'll play this hand, explain the logic, and you can play the next one," he said, his voice sounding slightly hoarse.

"Sure." My own words were filled with apprehension, trying to keep the contact to a minimum so I wouldn't focus on how good his body felt against mine again. The taut muscles of his torso, the firmness of his legs. Even if I didn't dare look at his face too closely, it was impossible not to notice how good he looked. Long eyelashes framed grey eyes—a ring of sea green around his iris was visible now that I was so close to him—and a jaw so sharp it cut its own way into my memory and had me longing to trace it with my finger, to feel the rough edge of his stubble against my skin.

"Alright, let's keep this interesting. We'll bet twenty." Nico confidently threw a couple chips into the middle of the table.

Dylan scoffed, sitting up straight in her chair as she eyed Nico behind me. "Only twenty? Not feeling too confident, Kotas?" I stiffened further as her eyes glanced past me, narrowing in an all too familiar way. She didn't need to tell me I wasn't welcome; I could read it all over her face.

Nico's response was a soft grumble I felt reverberating against my back. "Put your money where your mouth is, Bailey."

Her attention slid back to Nico as she smirked. "Big words." The large pile of chips in front of her told me that Nico was correct when he said she'd been cleaning them out all night. She lifted a couple of dark blue coins and tossed them into the middle. "Make it fifty."

Nico's body straightened against mine, shifting with surprise, and I had to bite my lip to stop myself from thinking about how good it felt to have Nico Kotas underneath me. The muscle of his thighs stiffened and the fight against the distraction was back to square one.

Inés shifted in her chair, letting out a puff of nervous breath. "I guess I call the fifty."

"Same." Henrik shrugged, his cards face down on the table, as if he had already given up. They both looked like they'd seen easier times, apprehensive but matching Dylan's bet anyway.

The game continued, the next card on the table turning to reveal a three of hearts. I knew, from what little Nico had explained that I had actually managed to pay attention to, this wasn't very good for our hand. And if Dylan's growing smirk wasn't a bluff, then it was very good for hers.

Nico moved again. This time, his arm wrapped behind my body, fingers pressing against my lower back as if to support me. I wanted to melt into the touch, the feel of his hand on my back, even over my clothing, making me weak. I fought the urge to curl into him. To feel his broad hands not only on me, but trailing along any exposed skin, feeling over every curve and tracing every part of my body.

Instead, I stilled, not daring to move a muscle. Frightened that if I did, he'd remove his hand, and I'd be left with nothing but the ghost of the memory of his touch.

Focusing on anything that wasn't Nico, I watched as Dylan raised her bet, throwing a few more chips into the centre. That was more than enough for Inés and Henrik, as they threw their cards down on the table, folding under the pressure. That left only Nico and Dylan.

Dylan's dark eyes were challenging, a look I'd been on the end of more than a dozen times across the court while we both waited to exploit the other's moment of weakness. But for once, it wasn't me that she was staring at.

"Well," Nico said, sounding rather confident, "let's see what you've got."

Dylan lowered her cards, her grin unmoving as she spread them out for all to see. "Three of a kind. Queens."

Nico laid his cards out, revealing the straight he held. The confidence drained quickly from her face, and her lip curled in frustration. She stood up, pushing the chips across the table toward Nico. He thanked her, stretching over me to sort out his winnings. Dylan sank back into her chair, grabbing her phone from the table, her pursed lips giving way as she scrolled through her notifications.

"Think you know the rules well enough to play?" Nico asked me.

"According to this," Dylan said, interrupting my reply, "she might need a little more practice in understanding the concept of rules."

All attention turned back to her, her phone screen directed towards us displaying the homepage of the Daily Tea. The headline was clear for everyone to see: *Scottie's Shocking Blood Test Results Serve Doubts on Comeback.*

My heart sank into my stomach. How did they find out about the test? Jon said he'd keep it under wraps, he'd protect me. But . . . this? Nico's hand wrapped around my waist as he pushed us up out of the seat, everyone around the table leaning forward to read the screen.

"Once a cheat, always a cheat," Dylan said.

I couldn't breathe as I blurted, "It's not what it looks like."

She raised an eyebrow, a sick satisfaction curled onto her lips. "It looks like a failed test, Scottie. Are you seriously denying this?"

"I've done nothing." My hand curled into a fist, fingernails pressing into the palm of my hand, pushing until I found my resolve in the pain.

I turned around to find Nico, his face tightened, sharp jaw clenched.

"Did you know about this?" he asked, his stony eyes searched mine for an answer, his large shoulders squared. I considered lying, pretending this was the first I'd heard of it. But what good would another lie do? I took a deep breath in, searching for any conviction, but finding none.

"Yes," I answered honestly. "I knew the test was a fail."

Dylan's response was immediate. "I told you!"

"But Jon is disputing it; the test is wrong." I shook my head, trying to hold his gaze, even as the weight of his disappointment began to feel unbearable. "I haven't taken anything that—"

"How are we supposed to believe you?" Dylan asked. Irritation pricked at my skin as I turned to her, finding her leaning forward, fists pressed against the table where her cards laid forgotten.

Dylan had been wronged; I knew that. And as far as she and the entire world were concerned, I was the one who had wronged her. It had been my choice to take the blame. I didn't make this mess, but I had tried my best to clean it up. That title had been stolen from her, but my entire life had been taken from me.

Instead of giving in to her, I turned to another. "Inés, you were there for the test." She had taken a step back from the table, as if trying to stay out of the conversation. "Did I seem like somebody worried about failing a test?"

She bit her lip, thinking to herself for a moment. "You were nervous, but . . . I didn't think it was because you were afraid of the result."

Dylan threw her hands up, groaning. "Why are we even debating this?"

This time, I couldn't help but snap. "I could ask the same question. This is medical data. It's my test, and it's been leaked."

I realised for the first time that, yet again, something else had been stolen from me. First my body, now my private information. Did I have any right to a choice in this, or should I have continued to be exploited at every turn?

"I can't believe you kept this from me," Nico said, taking a step away, his body shifting from side to side with hurt and indecision.

"We knew the test wasn't right." I scrambled to help him understand the deep regret I had for not following my instinct of just being honest with him.

"We?"

I started, "Jon and I, we didn't want you to—"

His body jolted with a sudden strike of anger, his patience running thin. "To what? Think my mixed partner was cheating again?"

"Nico." I had to make him understand, get him to trust me enough to see this test wasn't correct. Something wasn't right here at all. The failed test, the leaked result . . . What was going on?

"You kept this from me. What am I supposed to believe?" he practically growled, his hands curled in, the lines of his biceps defined by flexed frustration. I hated this. Seeing him so angry at me, so distrusting. It hurt.

"Me," I cried, unable to hold myself back now. "You're supposed to believe me. All these weeks and you think I would do this?" His chest rose up and down, his focus fixed on me, as if he was reading me, trying to align what he knew with what he had been told. I sucked in a deep breath, closing my eyes as I tried to pull myself together again. "I've never touched drugs, I've never taken anything—"

"But that's a lie," Dylan hissed, her eyes narrowed. I clocked my mistake, the slip of the tongue that revealed more truth than I'd intended.

I shook my head, not trusting myself to clarify the wording. "You know what I mean."

"You can't even keep your story straight," she continued. "I don't know why Jon let you come here. Why do people pretend like you deserve a place here? You aren't anything like us. You're a fraud and a liar, and we only have more proof of it."

I felt every word she said, the wound from where I'd been ripped open by the betrayal like a raw scar, stinging with every accusation. There was nothing I could say to her that would help her believe me. She had no reason to. Defeated, I instead turned to Nico, my last ace in hand.

"We've been here. Every day for weeks. I've been nothing but truthful with you. I've never lied. Everything with Matteo, every single story. I didn't tell you about the result because there was no way it was true. If you still believe I would do this to you, fine. Then let this be over because I'd rather play alone at this point than with somebody who couldn't believe me when I'm honest." My voice was a desperate plea, but he was silent, lips pressed into a thin line.

I'd had enough of being hurt and disparaged. I'd done this before, seen headlines calling me a liar, a cheat, a slut. I'd lived through this, and I had no intention of doing it again. I'd let them in the past, but not anymore. They couldn't hurt me more than I'd already been, and I wasn't going to stand there and let anyone try again.

I stood straight, shoulders back as I dug into that strength I held on to, the one I'd never allow anyone to take away from me again. I spoke once more. "I'm not a liar, Kotas. I promise you that."

And then I walked away.

CHAPTER TWENTY-ONE

Nico

Could've Would've Should've – Taylor Swift

S cottie walked away, her blonde hair disappearing as she headed down the path that led to the tennis court, my mind reeling.

"Coward," Dylan spat. I narrowed my eyes on her, heart beating so loud it drowned out almost every other sound.

"Don't call her that," I replied firmly. I wanted to follow Scottie, figure this out, but first I needed to deal with Dylan. "Where do you get off saying those things?"

She rolled her eyes, throwing her head back on a huff. "I think I'm more than entitled. It's all true."

I paused for a moment, weighing up what Dylan had said. For weeks now, I'd been trying to match up the Scottie I'd assumed she was: the daughter of my rival; the party girl who didn't take any of this seriously; the cheat. But also trying to connect her with the person I had spent countless hours on the court with. The person I knew she was.

"You don't think there's a chance she's being honest?" I asked, brows pressed together. I didn't know her before, but Dylan had.

"You can't trust her, Nico." She pressed forward, waving her hands dismissively before staring me down. "This is your career.

Your fucking legacy. And agreeing to play with that cheat is going to cost you everything."

I hesitated, Scottie's words echoing in my head. Jon had believed her, enough to invite her here and pair us together. Enough that he kept this from me.

"You don't know that," Inés said, stepping closer to the table. "I had never expected her to be a cheat before. We used to be friends. It never felt like her. It took us all by surprise."

Dylan huffed a laugh. "Not me."

Inés let out a heavy breath, looking at Dylan before meeting my gaze. "For what it's worth, I believe her."

"Ridiculous." Dylan shook her head. "You know what you're risking with her."

I clenched my fists as I felt the weight of the decision I was making. Dylan was right. The wrong call here and I could be throwing away my last chance. But there was something, an itch at the back of my head, that told me Scottie was worth the risk. "I don't think any of us truly knows what happened with Scottie," I admitted.

"We know she cheated before. This test shows that she's more than willing to take shortcuts again."

I knew the facts, understood there was hard evidence to back it all up. But these weeks, every glance and secret shared, they'd told me something new about her, and what I thought I knew altered with every moment spent with her.

"*If* it's right." I said the thought out loud. She'd sworn it wasn't, begged me to believe her. I closed my eyes, and I could see the desperate look on her face, the worried press of her eyebrows, the sadness in her eyes. "I know her."

"You've only known her for a few weeks," Dylan retorted. The truth of her words somehow stung more than they should have.

"And it was long enough to know she wouldn't do that. Not again." I shook my head as I made a decision. I hoped I wouldn't live to regret it. I'd seen how hard she worked. She was quick and smart and strong, and I couldn't help but doubt everything I'd once held true about her.

Dylan bit at her cheek, anger and frustration lacing her words. "Once is already enough, but twice? She's not trustworthy. You're an idiot for thinking she is."

"Dylan," Inés interrupted, trying to calm her friend down by reaching out to touch her shoulder, but Dylan only shook her off.

"No, Nico is. Him playing with her only helps validate her stupid comeback. That's probably why Jon paired them up in the first place. Give her the best tennis partner, ignoring any player more worthy." She turned her attention from Inés back to me. "He knew you were her father's rival. Imagine all the attention it's going to get on court. It's a circus act, and we're her clowns."

"Enough." I broke. "You don't have to move on, but if you keep talking about her this way, then we *are* going to have a problem."

"Move on? You're delusional, Kotas," Dylan scoffed. "Scottie Rossi, or Sinclair, or whatever she wants to be called, is a fucking cheat and we all know it. Does she really think changing her last name will make us forget what she did?"

I turned to Inés. "You better keep Dylan away from Scottie." And then I stormed down the same path where Scottie had disappeared. I nearly made it all the way to the beach looking for her before I turned back, but when I saw lights in the distance, I knew exactly where she was.

The clench around my heart relaxed as I found her, bathed in the stark illumination of the towering floodlights on the practice court. I watched from behind the fence for a moment as she bounced the ball against the opposite wall of the court, sprinting back and forth as she responded with precise, powerful strokes of her racket.

Her face was focused, teeth gritted together as she swung again and again. Each movement was perfect, her racket gliding through the air to meet every ball, knocking each one with a force I was almost scared to interrupt. Every stroke sizzled with lingering fury, each hit seeming like a personal vendetta.

Pop.

That was for Dylan.

Pop.

Probably Matteo.

Pop.

I stood there hoping I wasn't next.

Finally, she missed, her footwork slipping. I still couldn't take my eyes from her as she swore, the pain ringing as she leaned forward, raising the racket over her head before mercilessly driving it down, smashing it into the unforgiving court surface.

Again and again, she raised her arm, relentlessly pummelling the racket until it lay in shattered ruins at her feet before her knees hit the grass, collapsing alongside the remaining pieces. I kept silent, standing at the gate, watching her as she sat, slumped, staring at the ground.

She looked up, her tone accusatory. "What are you doing here?"

"Thought I'd hit a few balls around." I walked into the light as she attempted a forced smile. It only lasted for a couple of seconds before disappearing. I lowered myself to the ground next to her, resigned to sit in silence until she felt like talking. It had been a lot, watching Dylan tear into her like that, and I didn't want to leave her alone unless she specifically asked for it. I had also been hoping to get to the bottom of these blood test results that Scottie swore weren't real.

It was a few moments more before she spoke again, her gaze halfway across the court, the tone of her voice resigned. "I can't do this anymore."

"Play tennis?" I cracked a weak smile, before nodding to the bent racket that lay in pieces in front of her. "Not with that racket, no."

"I don't belong in this world anymore, and I'm done pretending that I do. I'm going home."

"Home?" My brows furrowed together. Weeks spent together, and I still wasn't sure where that truly was for either of us. With all the travelling I do for the sport, I'm never in one place for too long.

"London. Paris. Wherever," she said, her shoulders sagging as if she was weighed down by her next words. "I'm done here."

My chest grew tight. "Like hell you are. You can't quit on me now."

She looked at me, her lips pressed into a firm line as her spine straightened. "Quit on you? This *is* for you. The entire world sees me as a cheat."

"I don't." Shaking my head, I swallowed down all my remaining reservations. "I don't think you're a cheat."

The expression on her face twisted into confusion. "What about the test?"

"We'll have them retest the sample. If you say something isn't right, I believe you." The words sounded a little strange, strangled, even as they left my throat. But nonetheless, I knew them to be true.

Scottie Sinclair, despite everything, had my trust.

"You know this could ruin you? What will everyone think? Nico Kotas snuggled up with Matteo Rossi's cheat of a daughter."

"Don't speak about yourself like that." The words tumbled out of me on a stern command. I hated hearing anyone talk about her that way, hated it more coming from her own mouth. Whatever she had done in the past, it didn't matter. It didn't define who she was, nor did it give anyone the right to judge her for it. I'd done that too, assumed the worst before I'd even known her. I still felt bad about our first meeting, the memory of her hand stuck out for me to shake, and me ignoring it like she didn't even deserve the respect of a simple handshake.

"It's what they'll think," Scottie repeated, pushing herself off the ground, before turning to walk away. I scrambled to my feet, knee aching as I rushed to stand, and grabbed her elbow gently, causing her to still. Part of me felt a wave of relief at the physical connection. It was often hard to know where Scottie's head was at, but at that moment, she didn't seem so far away. That was, until she glanced down at the spot where we were connected, and although it pained me, I released my grip, cutting the tether between us.

"What Dylan said, it's what everyone will say. I'll be a stain on your career, and . . . I don't want that." Her voice was tinged with a vulnerability I wasn't used to hearing. It was all over her face, she was . . . scared. I hated seeing her like that; it drove me wild with my own panic. I tried desperately to read her, but it was as if she was pages of a book written in a secret-coded language and nobody had bothered to show me the cipher. "Tell Jon thanks, but I'm done. I'm exhausted pretending that this is working."

"So, what?" I snapped back with agitation, my trainers scuffing against the brightly lit court as I paced back and forth. "Things get hard, and if you can't cheat your way out of it, you quit? Is that what the last two years have been about?" She stiffened, and I realised my words hit their mark. "I guess so."

I ignored the twisting in my gut that told me this was wrong, pushed away the want and will to get on my knees and beg her to stay, if not for herself, then selfishly for me. These weeks, I could see the change in myself, feel it in my body. Having Scottie around lit my world on fire. Whether that was good or bad, I was past caring, I just wanted her carrying the matches.

"You know, I was beginning to think I had you pegged wrong." I couldn't stop myself from twisting it all further, angry that she'd give up like this. She'd throw it all away? Quit and call it a personal service? "I thought you were better than this. But here you are, leaving because things got a little tough."

"A little tough?" she scoffed. "Do you even realise the shit I go through on a daily basis? From the tabloids, to Dylan, and now you? I've not even done anything wrong!"

"The world already thinks you're a cheat and now you want them to think you're a quitter too?"

"Nico. Just stop!" she shouted, but like an asshole, I ignored her.

"Then why are you quitting? Why are you throwing everything away again? Why are you le—"

"It wasn't my fault." She cracked open, cutting me off, but what spilled out was unexpected. "I didn't even know it was happening."

I froze in place. "What's that supposed to mean?"

"I didn't do it." Her lips trembled as she spoke. Even in the silence of the night, it felt like the crashing of the nearby sea waves against the sand was louder than her voice. But she kept staring right at me, those blue eyes piercing, holding my attention as I tried to place the puzzle pieces together.

"Are you saying they got the test wrong back then too?" I asked, trying to make sense of her words. It seemed unlikely they had gotten it wrong twice. Surely she wouldn't have just accepted the error. After all, she had personally admitted to cheating. I could almost taste the unease and tension hanging between us, a salty tang that lingered on the tongue.

She shook her head, loose blond hair swaying with the movement as the moonlight illuminated the worry lines creasing her forehead. My muscles were so taut with frustration, and I was at the end of my patience of waiting for her to tell me the truth.

But instead, I smoothed out the feeling, taking a moment to consider how hard this was for her. Her chest heaved desperately for a full breath of air, her fingers running through her hair, pushing the golden locks out of her face, behind her ears, only for the wind to undo all her work. What a beautiful mess.

I took a step forward and closed the gap between us. With her gaze meeting mine, my left hand stretched out, fingertips finding the delicate line of her jaw. Drawing upward, her face leaned into my touch, my fingers sliding below her ear as my thumb stroked at the soft velvet skin of her cheek.

There was a single thought that cemented itself in my brain. A new desperate weakness to understand her.

"Tell me, please." My voice was a trembling plea, an unspoken bargain that no matter what she said, I would believe her. "Tell me what happened."

"My dad—I mean, Matteo . . ." Scottie started, slipping up as her words rushed out. She looked away again, her blue eyes shimmering with tears as she stumbled, trying to find the words. Trying to find the strength.

After Scottie came forward, it was easy to believe he'd turned on her. His legacy, now tarnished. It had been his driving force all those years. Had he really thrown her out? Had they had some kind of argument? Her spine straightened, arms falling to her sides momentarily, before her hands met again, her fingers intertwined, like no matter how much she tried, anxiety couldn't let her stay still. She took a deep breath, her pink lips pressing together before she pulled the bottom in between her teeth and finally, the secret she had been keeping from the entire world spilled out.

"He drugged me."

My thumb stopped mid-stroke, my body frozen as I reeled from the shock of the confession. My eyes searched her face for any sign of humour, waited for her lips to curve into a playful smile and tell me she was joking. But she didn't. And my heart shattered.

"For months, I had no idea. My own father." Her words were shaky, like she was recalling a nightmare.

A wave of guttural horror sank deep, goose bumps pebbling along my arms. "Will you tell me what happened? Please?"

Her gaze held on to mine, as if she needed me to know, to see, that she was still telling the truth. "He spiked my protein shakes. I was injured in the French Open, before Wimbledon. It was doubtful I'd recover in time. But they kept me training, and recovery should've been harder, but it wasn't. I didn't find out he did it until I got home the night after Wimbledon."

Her arms wrapped around her body as she shivered from the cool breeze, the scent of the salted sea riding it. I could see the weight that had been freed from her as her shoulders pulled back, her expression more relaxed, but still tinged with the worry that I might not believe her.

I replayed her words over and over, trying to understand what she had endured. She'd set herself on fire, her career on fire, her whole damn life on fire, all to get away from him. Questions tore through me, but they were nothing compared to the fiery rage that had reignited in the pit of my stomach. A flame that burned white hot, as an almost primal instinct clawed at me.

"How did you find out?" I asked, needing to know. Needing to know everything. She gnawed on her lower lip and I pressed further. "Scottie, help me understand."

She released a heavy breath. "I had just got home from a Wimbledon after-party, and overheard Jon and Matteo talking about it in the kitchen. More like fighting about it. And I—"

"Jon was there?" I saw red. Of course Jon was there. He was her coach then, he had to have known. And even if he didn't, he had a responsibility to look after her, to keep her safe. Instead, she was taken advantage of. And now, with these fake results being leaked to the press, his empty promises to protect her, it was happening all over again. With veins simmering, I was ready to rip apart the people who had failed her.

And Jon's name was at the top of my list.

CHAPTER TWENTY-TWO

Nico
Easier Than Lying – Halsey

"Nico, wait," Scottie called after me, as I stormed through the villa. I ignored her pleas, focused on locating Jon to find out for myself what part he had played. We turned a corner and I almost ran straight into Elena.

"Do you know where Jon is?" I asked her with gritted teeth as Scottie's hands landed on me, one holding on to my shoulder, pulling back, while the other slid into mine, our palms connecting. Her touch calmed my muscles instinctually, but the anger was still boiling within me. They hurt her. *He* hurt her.

He drugged me. For months, I had no idea. My own father.

Elena eyed me suspiciously, assessing my anger. "I think he's upstairs, in his office," she answered, looking uneasily between us.

"Thanks," I said, making my way towards the stairs, my hand slipping free from Scottie's.

"What are you doing?" she shouted after me, but I only increased my pace, trying to get ahead of her. I could barely stand to look at her without breaking down.

All these years, she'd been holding on to this secret? Ruining herself to keep it? While a part of me begged to know more, the dumb, reactive side just wanted to hurt whoever had hurt her.

My heart raced as I pushed my way through the office door, Jon already rising from his chair, eyes wide in surprise at the sight of me. His mouth opened, but before he could get any words out, I delivered a clenched fist to his nose. He fell back against the bookcase; its contents shook and fell around us. Gripping his shoulder with one hand and pressing my forearm into his throat with the other, I glared into his shocked face.

"How could you let it happen?"

"What?" Jon stammered, his face a mix of confusion and fear. His eyes darted from me to Scottie, standing in the doorway, her hands clenched at her sides, eyes red-rimmed from crying.

"How could you let Scottie be drugged?" I almost choked out her dad's name. "How could you help Matteo do that to her?"

"I didn't! I swear!" he shouted. I glanced at Scottie, and she gave me a small nod that told me he was telling the truth.

"When?" I continued to push him for answers, my voice hard and unyielding. "When did you find out?"

"I—" he stumbled, so I pressed again.

"When?"

"The same night Scottie did."

"Bullshit," I swore at him. It was impossible for someone as observant as Jon not to have noticed the unnatural speed of Scottie's recovery. It was his damn job to notice things like that. "I've known you long enough to know nobody can get shit past you. When?"

The room filled with tension as we held each other's gaze.

Jon's hands were shaking as he tried to explain himself. "It's the truth. When I got to the house, he was crushing the pills up . . . I didn't know what else to do." His eyes darted around the room, looking for any sign of forgiveness. "I-I'd noticed she was recovering quickly, but her training regime was advanced. I thought that it might be diet, even age or genetics . . . It was easy to explain away."

I held Jon there for another moment, reading him. The anger in me boiled over at his betrayal, making me want to lash out again. But I took a step back and released him from my grasp. My simmering rage had cooled enough for me to think clearly.

"You were supposed to protect her."

Jon's hand rose to his face, to where I'd punched him, as his gaze dipped to the floor, his voice sullen as he spoke. "I know."

"You let him do this to her."

Scottie interrupted, taking a couple of steps into the room. "It's not his fault, Nico."

My heart split in two as I took in her appearance. Her skin was so pale that it looked almost translucent, dark circles appearing under her red-rimmed eyes. The fatigue etched onto her face showed how much she'd been through.

Jon replied for me. "It might as well be."

I took a few steps back, away from them. With shaking hands, I rubbed at my face. But when I closed my eyes, all I could see was her standing in the centre of the court, vulnerable with guttural hurt. It made me want to scream.

"I'm so sorry for failing you, Scottie," Jon said earnestly. "It's haunted me every single day. Nico's right. It was my job to protect you, and I . . . I let Matteo explain it away. That night, when you came home, I swear that's when I found out. I guess he was getting lazy with his preparation since he thought we'd all be out. I wasn't going to let it continue."

"Were you going to tell me?" Scottie asked hesitantly, arms wrapped tightly around herself.

Jon exhaled deeply, his hand still rubbing his face in self-disgust. "I was trying to convince him to tell you. I couldn't have kept a secret like that from you, kid."

Scottie nodded, her eyes assessing, glancing from Jon to me. "Are you done now? Is it safe for me to leave the two of you and get him some ice for that face?"

I swallowed, nodding. My voice was hoarse, almost burning up my throat as I spoke. "I'm done."

She looked at Jon, a silent question exchanged.

"It's fine. Nico and I should probably talk," he answered, and with that she slipped from the room, the sound of her retreating footsteps echoing against the tiled hall. Slowly, the tension in the room began to dissipate like fog burned off by sunlight.

"I guess she told you?" he asked. I nodded in response, slumping into a chair opposite the desk, my knuckles stinging and my gut twisting with guilt. He ran his hand through his hair, wincing at the pain that seemed to radiate from his cheek.

"I needed to know," I admitted, the throb of my knuckles stinging as I flexed my hand. It was far from an excuse, even further from an apology.

He tilted his head, a hiss of pain escaping him with the motion. "I . . . understand. I can't say I didn't want to do the same to him when I found out."

"Why didn't you?"

He paused for a moment, lost in memory. "I was trying to reason with him when she came in. I knew we had to tell her, even if it was the hardest thing I had ever done. Even if it meant losing my job. But I didn't mean for her to walk in and find out like she did. I didn't know what she was going to do next. I tried calling her afterwards, but she wouldn't answer, and then two days later I got a call from the ITIA."

My stomach twisted further at the thought of her learning about it all so suddenly. She found out like that? Walking in on her father midway through, arguing with her coach? The two people she had trusted the most, wrapped in a scandal she'd been pulled into? I'd had a coach bring it up once, when the problems with my knee started to get worse and even training started to feel impossible; they suggested some "outside resources." The decision had been in my hands that day, and I chose to walk away, firing him on the spot for the insinuation. I hadn't wanted to be involved with it at all.

Even the idea of partnering with Scottie had been too much. If it hadn't been for Jon, I wouldn't have done it.

"She took the blame for it all?" I asked.

He let out a heavy breath. "She told them she had done it all on her own, kept both of us out of it."

My brows pressed together, distaste twisting me up at the very idea. "Why?"

He shrugged. "Only she can explain that. I would've wanted the world to know."

I hummed in agreement, silence falling between us for a moment. I coughed, clearing my throat before I spoke again. "I'm sorry . . . for your face."

Jon looked at me plainly, an eyebrow raised. "No, you're not."

I winced. "I'm sorry for not being sorrier?"

"For two years I've been waiting for somebody to punch me in the face over this, for not doing better. Maybe I wanted a reason to stop feeling so bad over it."

I hated that I had doubted whether he was in on it. He had always been one of the best coaches, which was why Matteo had hired him out from under me in the first place. But that had never stopped us from meeting up every so often. He'd joke about my recent performance, and I'd tease him about being bankrolled by Matteo, like he was being paid by the dark side, my enemy.

"Is this why you were so persistent about us working together?" I asked.

Jon nodded his head back and forth with indecision. "Partially . . .

I believed you would make a great pairing and, obviously, I was right. You need her as much as she needs you."

I couldn't argue with him there. Training with her had changed my game, given me a drive I didn't have before, and . . . well, it had me caring about our success in a way I wasn't sure I understood yet. With her, sometimes I felt so out of control of my own body, like she was the guiding force to everything I was driving toward.

"But yes, attaching her to you, it makes it easier for her to return. There's a reason for everything she's done, I believe that, but she's too good to keep out of the game," he admitted. I couldn't help but think of Dylan's words.

This is your career. Your fucking legacy.

She believed Scottie would ruin it, but in truth, I was beginning to think she would define whatever came next for me. Whether it was for better or worse, I was slowly tying myself to her.

"I agree there." I slumped further into my chair before another thought came to me. I raised an eyebrow at Jon. "And then there's the failed test."

Jon sat up straight at my words, swallowing before he answered.

"You know about that too?" he asked, and I nodded in response. "It was my idea to keep it from you. She didn't want to. I had to convince her."

I grumbled, not quite happy that he had kept that from me too, but I moved on. "And you think the test result is wrong?"

"I've been looking into it. I've asked for the full breakdown in the results, and something definitely seems off. I mean, even her blood type is wrong. I don't know how they didn't notice that."

My eyebrows pushed together, suspicion taking hold. "Her blood type?"

"I didn't need to see the breakdown to believe her. There's no way she'd put this at risk like that. But the more I dig, the less it makes sense."

I wasn't quite sure what he was implying, but with everything her father had done to take down my own career at the beginning, could I doubt he wouldn't do the same to his own daughter? Perhaps I just didn't want to believe any parent would do such a thing.

I tried to imagine what she had been through these years living with this lie she had told, using it to keep him away. She was strong, on and off the court, and far more than I had known and already admired her for.

And as if he could read my mind, Jon asked, "Is there . . . is there something going on between you? Something I should know about?"

A denial made its way up my throat, but died before I could verbalise it. There was nothing going on . . . right? Nothing had happened . . . but did I want it to happen? When she sat on my lap, I had to put a hand on her to stop her moving about before I lost all my goddamn control. She was the sole focus of all my attention during the daytime, and then the memory of her had me tossing and turning all night, keeping me in the shower five minutes longer than it should've. I couldn't think straight when somebody crossed her boundaries, lost all power over myself when they didn't give her the respect she was due.

I hadn't signed up for any of this, hadn't wanted to be attached to anyone in a long time. But her? Golden blonde hair, a smile and a joke that always managed to light me up no matter what grim mood I was in, the hidden strength I envied. It was like my favourite baklava from my family's Greek bakery back in Florida. One taste, and I couldn't get enough.

"There's—" I began, blinking a few times as new realisation crashed into me. The image shifted, coming into view, like I'd found glasses and now the world was no longer blurry.

"Ah, good. You didn't kill him while I was away," Scottie interrupted, entering the office again. I turned to her, watching as she walked to the desk, passing Jon some ice covered with a cloth. Jon's gaze was still on me, a small grin on his lips.

Well, I guess he had his answer.

She appeared in front of me, her blue eyes icy as her lips pressed into a firm line. "Here," she said, passing me my own cold compress. "For your hand, so you're not useless on the court tomorrow."

Surprise flickered inside of me as I took it from her, pressing it to my knuckles, which had turned swollen and red from the punch. Considering my entire profession relied on my hands being in perfect condition, I may not have thought the punch through.

"Thanks." She slipped into the chair beside me, crossing her arms, and a cool silence fell over the room.

Jon cleared his throat, breaking the uncomfortable atmosphere. "I'll leave you two to talk." The chair creaked as he got up and shuffled past us, placing a heavy hand on my shoulder as he passed me.

We weren't alone for more than a second before Scottie snapped, "Are you finished beating up our coach now?"

"I was just . . . I'm sorry. I jumped the gun a bit on that one," I apologised, knowing that wasn't going to quite cut it for her.

"Maybe next time wait for me to finish my story before you speed off and start punching people?"

"I thought he helped Matteo . . ."

She flinched at the mention of his name, then shook her head, a heavy exhale leaving her as she tried to restrain herself from beating me up in revenge. "Do you honestly think I'd be working with Jon if I thought he would pull that shit?"

"No, of course not."

"So, as I said, how about you listen to me next time instead of going all macho man on the person who holds both our careers in his hands?"

I took a moment, guilt weighing on my shoulders. "I'm sorry. I really am."

She could hardly stand to look at me, her gaze directed out the window, her jaw set firmly. I couldn't take it. "You scared me, Nico. I didn't know what you were going to do."

"I didn't expect . . . I never thought for a second that somebody would hurt you like that, Scottie. I . . . I had to do something. Even if it was dumb."

"I was scared you didn't believe me." Her words just about broke me.

"Of course I believe you." My gut churned further. The hurt held in her words, her tone like a dagger that kept twisting. Her eyes caught mine, the deep blue pools captivating, holding me hostage.

Her mouth opened, as if to speak, before she hesitated, losing her nerve. I couldn't stop myself from reaching out to her, my hands finding hers, and finally I held her attention long enough to see the fear still there.

"I believe you," I repeated, my tone firm, words clear. "I trust you, Scottie. What he did to you . . ." I trailed off, my own eyes closing. How he took everything from her. I couldn't bear thinking about it.

"It hurt," she said. "It took everything to survive." Her fingertips pressed into mine, hands squeezing with reassurance. "But I survived."

Something in my chest squeezed tightly at her words. I'd known she was brave—that was hard to miss—but the depth of her endurance still shook me to my core.

My next question hesitated on my tongue, lingering for a moment as I tried to find the right words, the correct way to say it. "Why didn't you tell anyone?" I didn't understand. "You could destroy his entire world."

She took a deep breath in, as if she was almost sick of the question. As if she's spent the last two years justifying her reasoning to herself over and over. "Do you think they would believe me? Believe that the legend, tennis God Matteo Rossi, would lower himself to doping his daughter without her knowledge? I'd be labelled another woman crying wolf, ignored and tarred as a cheat anyway." Shame ate away at me as I realised she was right. Some might believe her, but with the influence that Matteo still had over tennis, it would take a lot more than only her words to convince people.

She swallowed before continuing. "I took the only revenge I could. He was so obsessed with legacy, and I was it. I didn't see it until I left, how poisonous his love was. I wasn't a person, I was a tool to further his name, another trophy on his goddamn mantel. My life didn't exist outside the tennis court, my body fodder for the machine. It took me a long time to see that, to rebalance my mind on what is a healthy give and take."

Scottie shook her head before continuing, "But I'd had enough. I couldn't let him destroy me. If I was a possession he thought he owned, then I needed to make sure he couldn't use me, that he wouldn't want me anymore. I blew everything up. I told the ITIA. I told the world. I called the press and leaked the story myself. Then, I did whatever I wanted for years. I actually saw the cities I travelled to like a tourist, I partied and had fun, and I slept with whoever I wanted. I threw his name away and used my own. I cleansed my life of him. Hell, I wanted the words tattooed on my skin." She shook her head, looking up for a moment, a small, proud smile on her lips. "He was a poison and a stain, but I finally feel clean of the mark he left."

I fought the urge to lean over, close the gap and wrap my arms around her, hold her there, but I knew that wasn't what she needed. She didn't need comforting or somebody to lean on. She was strong enough on her own. A survivor.

"So why come back?" I asked, curious. "If you were so intent on not continuing his legacy?"

"Jon convinced me that with you, I could keep twisting the

knife. That making a comeback with the man that finished his ca-reer would be too big an insult to his legacy to claim. And I missed the sport. He might have almost destroyed me in the process, but tennis was my life. And I was good. I wanted to prove to everyone that while Scottie Rossi was dead and buried, Scottie Sinclair was back for revenge."

I was almost at a loss for words for how proud I was of her. She'd faced hell and come back stronger. I couldn't blame her for earlier, when she told me she was quitting. It must've been too much for her. You can only take the blame for a crime you didn't commit for so long before it breaks you.

"Scottie," I said, staring deep into her eyes. Begging her soul to feel what words I couldn't bring myself to say out loud. *I need you here.* "Please, don't leave."

She stared at me with a sad smile. The room falling silent.

One breath.

Two breaths.

Three breaths.

Then she finally put me out of my misery. "I'll stay."

All the air returned to my lungs. "And . . . you still want to work together?"

She rolled her eyes, the tension relaxing a bit as the smallest smile appeared on her lips. "Who else is going to beat up my enemies for me?"

Relief flooded my system, my body relaxing at her joke, at the crook of her lips. That smile, I needed to see it more, wanted to trace it with my fingers and lips and memorise everything about it.

"Good," I said, leaning forward, closer to her. "Because me and you, we've got a trophy to win."

CHAPTER TWENTY-THREE

Scottie

Dream Girl Evil – Florence + the Machine

T he early morning air was a cool breeze as I sat on the rocky shore, waves quietly drifting against the beach as the sun peeked out from under the horizon. I hadn't slept all night. Instead, I scrolled through social media, going through every tweet that mentioned my name since the article came out. It didn't look pretty. It was still an unconfirmed rumour, but that was enough to send the internet alight again with further rumours, even past articles being rehashed and shared.

Year-old photos of me leaving clubs and bars. Selfies from parties with people I'd regretted knowing. Yachts that had sunk to the bottom of the Med.

We made Jon aware of the leak, and within seconds he'd called the lawyers. When he'd told me what he'd discovered, the discrepancies with the test results, what had happened became clear to me.

The tight band around my stomach tightened as I looked down at the screen, seeing *his* named contact. All this time, I'd never deleted his phone number. I never understood why, but somehow I knew I'd need it one day.

With a deep inhale, I pressed the number and lifted the phone to my ear. Dread beat on me like a drum with every unanswered ring. My fingers pressed to the sandy floor for support. Any planned script went out the window at the sound of my father's voice.

"Hello?" he answered, still sounding groggy. It was still early back in the UK, but a 5 a.m. wake-up time was his usual. "Hello? Anyone there?"

I moved to speak, but no words came out. My voice was missing in action. Gone. My hand felt slippery around the phone, and I was almost sure I was going to drop it or hang up.

"Scottie . . . is that you?" The sound of my name on his lips stung enough to snap me back into my body.

I closed my eyes and replied, "It's been a while."

"Two years." The sleepy tone disappeared from his voice, as if I had grabbed his full attention. I was desperate to ask him how he was, the memory of the father I'd grown up with just within grasp. But he wasn't that person.

I cut straight to the point, summing back up all the courage that had previously abandoned me. "The test. Did you leak it?"

The silence on the other end of the phone almost felt like an answer.

"You call after all this time, and this is what you ask?"

I pushed away the implied guilt. He didn't deserve any of my time. I wouldn't have even called him if I didn't desperately need to know the truth. Like an uncomfortable sunburn that had kept me awake all night, and hearing the truth from him would be the aloe vera.

Keeping my tone firm, my fingers curled into the sand as if I was trying to root myself to the ground and pull yet more strength from it. "This is the only thing I want to talk about."

"And here I thought you'd want to chat," he murmured. "Catch up with your old man."

"Can you just answer the damn question?" I snapped, losing

my patience. It felt good to shout. We'd never fought before. He ordered, I followed. No arguments. And why would I? I had trusted him. He was my father, after all. He'd never do anything to hurt me. Until he did.

"Take a moment and think about what you're doing." He paused. "Training with Nico Kotas? Did you think I could let that happen?"

I almost wanted to smile, knowing that I had managed to do exactly what I'd wanted. Get under his skin. "I don't think you have much choice in the matter."

"You'd be surprised at the strings I can pull."

I swallowed down my discomfort. The very idea that he still felt he could control me made my skin itch. "So it was you."

He fell silent for a moment, his hesitation hanging heavily, as if he couldn't decide. "Stop training with him. Come back to London and we can talk. This can all go away."

"No." I didn't need to think about my answer. "I'd stop playing before I went back to you."

Go back to him. To that cage.

"Then stop playing."

I inhaled sharply, shaking my head before looking out at the sea, watching the waves wash away at the shore.

For two years, I had done that. I paid the price for his mistake and quit. And that . . . that had been just fine. I had done things I'd never done, lived in a way I'd always dreamed of. I'd escaped.

But now, with my feet back on the court, I remembered the strength in my arms, the speed of my serve. I had found the power he had taken away. And I wasn't going to give that up.

"No."

"You'll regret it, Scottie, playing without me," he warned.

"You're wrong." I didn't believe him, not after everything that had gone down between us. I'd happily walk away again if it meant keeping my life away from his. "Tell me how you found out about the test. Then I want you to leave me alone."

Another grumble rang through the phone, one that sounded like it was on the edge of a laugh. Like a parent who has reached the end of their tether with their bratty child. "Not everyone in that villa is your friend. Remember that."

And then he hung up the call. Leaving me alone again on the beach with nothing but suspicions.

Sinclair Test Mayhem Leak Proven False

Contrary to earlier reports, it has been revealed that the leaked information regarding Scottie Sinclair's blood test was inaccurate.

The undisclosed substance that supposedly sent shockwaves through the tennis community has turned out to be a swing and a miss.

With this correction, any suspicions of a potential ban extension due to the medication revelation can be put to rest.

The gossip mill grinds on with Sinclair's rumoured relationship with Nico Kotas, all eyes still pinned on Rhodes. The couple has been spotted sharing cosy moments off the court, and gracing the spotlight as the faces of the latest ELITE campaign.

Third Set

CHAPTER TWENTY-FOUR

Scottie
True Blue – boygenius

Salt air and an endless blue ocean, the waves rolling in over the beach, did it get any better than this? It had been over a week since everything went down. Jon's bruised face had gone through every shade of black, blue, and purple, and Dylan had left the training camp the morning after our argument without even so much as a goodbye.

"I don't know how you can stand that," Nico said, his eyes assessing as I dug my feet into the sand, warm from the afternoon sun, my toes completely buried.

I looked down at his own trainer/sock combination, a grin stretched wide along my face. "Good luck getting all the sand out. You'll still be finding it months from now."

He shrugged, relaxing into the large ELITE-branded towel we'd put down. "I'll throw them out. Better than putting up with sand," he complained, his voice bitter, but when he looked up at me, leaning back on his elbows, his smile was anything but irritated.

"And if you could hold that position," Sarah said, interrupting the moment with her camera held up to her eyeline. I watched as his smile faltered. That expected irritation appeared, but he did as she said, holding his position. "Perfect. This sunset is giving the best lighting."

It had been her idea for this beach shoot, trying to collect as much content for ELITE's upcoming campaign as possible. The entry list for Wimbledon had been announced a few days ago, and with my and Nico's names mentioned in our own separate singles categories, and together in the mixed double category, both of our social media mentions had shot up.

The internet was abuzz with rumours of us together at the breakdowns of our careers. Apparently, ELITE had been beyond pleased with the influx of attention and had started to kick off their PR campaign featuring us a little earlier, and Jon was more than happy to allow them to shoot extra content while we were available.

With a careful smile, I mouthed, "She'll finish soon."

A flat look from him argued back. All the while, my eyes danced over his familiar stubble that covered sharp cheekbones.

"Just hold on. I need to adjust the settings." She took a couple steps back as the camera absorbed her full attention. We relaxed, our bodies freed from the position we'd been frozen in, and slumped into the warm sand.

"I hate this so much," Nico needlessly admitted, his tone grumpy.

"I know. I don't love this either."

"Did you always have to do this?"

I nodded. "I'm surprised you didn't."

"I was good at saying no." He stretched lazily backwards, his arms pressed up. His T-shirt pulled up at his stomach, revealing tanned skin stretched over hard muscle. My mouth watered at the sight, my body reacting as if I hadn't already studied the sculpting of his topless body from across the court a hundred times. Now, however, I was beside him, and distracted from a much closer view.

A squawk from an overhead seagull reminded me to stop checking out my doubles partner.

I smiled at him and joked, "What happened?"

He squinted against the sunlight as he looked up at me, before raising a hand to cover his face from the direct light despite the cap sitting backward on his head. "Jon's gotten good at being convincing." Somehow, I sensed there was more to his words than allowing Sarah to take some photographs.

"At least Sarah's good," I said, trying to move the subject along to something less likely to cause a physical reaction. "I've had plenty of embarrassing experiences on shoots."

"Like what?" he asked with a cheeky smile. I let out a breath, trying to pick from the many, many possibilities, before deciding on one that felt harmless.

"Wardrobe malfunctions, for one. Sometimes, those tennis skirts are hemmed a little too short, even for me. I'd spent the entire shoot trying to keep it from riding up while I leapt around a court after a ball. At least ELITE's clothing is actually comfortable."

He laughed, the sound as calming as the rolling waves in the background. "I should ask them to send a new hat." His gaze moved from my face to the navy cap sitting atop my head, a ponytail threaded through the back. "My baseball cap has been going missing for weeks." He flicked the cap with his forefingers, moving it up, the hat going loose around my crown.

"Hey!" I cried, my free arm flying up to press down on the hat before the wind took it. "I don't have a clue what you're on about."

He was about to say something else when one of the cats from the villa came up beside him, nuzzling its small brown head against his arm as it purred for more attention. Nico rolled his eyes at the animal, but relented anyway, his free arm coming round to pet the cat.

"What happened to hating cats?" I said as the cat rolled onto its back, exposing its belly to him.

Nico, the weak man a feline reduced him to, complied to the animal's will and began to rub its belly instead. "I do. I'm allergic."

"You don't look allergic," I argued, taking in the scene. A man like that was far too attractive to add a pet into the mix. He'd be lethal on a dating app. I almost cringed at the idea.

"Just wait until my throat begins to close up and my eyes start bulging out of my skull."

I hummed, unsure. "I don't think that's going to make Sarah very happy." When I started to worry if I should grab an EpiPen, he came clean.

"It's okay. I started taking an antihistamine when I saw the cats around the villa."

"Is that for your benefit or the cats'?"

"I'm trying to survive them."

"Sure. As if I'm supposed to believe that it's not because those cute little faces have melted your heart."

"My heart is still safe in its deep-frozen state." His eyes remained fixed on the cat, which let out a wide yawn, exposing large teeth that had never looked so adorable. My eyes flickered to his face, his lips pressed into a loving smile.

Frozen state, my ass.

"Did you have any pets growing up?"

He thought to himself for a moment, pushing his hair out of his face; it had grown a little long without a haircut. Shaking his head, he answered, "No. My brother always wanted a hamster though, but the way Mom acted, you'd have thought he was asking for a rat."

"They are rodents," I reasoned, imagining somebody as large as Nico holding the small thing, with its beady little eyes and hands and scurrying feet. A cat made more sense.

"My parents moved to the US with very little, and after food and rent, it left no time or money for a pet of any kind."

"What part of Greece did they move from?" I asked, enjoying the moment of openness with him. It was a far cry from where we'd started. He'd been a closed book, and I was too wrapped up in my own stuff to even ask. But talking with him, being around him, was easy. Even with Sarah taking our photos in the background.

"The mainland, Athens." He smiled. "They moved when my brother was young. I wasn't even born until a few years later, and they didn't go back for decades, not until I made enough to take us back on holiday. We still have family in the city, so it was good to see my parents reconnecting after so many years away. I always thought about representing Greece to honour them, but I was born in the US. I didn't want to overcomplicate it. They run a Greek bakery down in Tarpon Springs."

"Where's that?"

"Just northwest of Tampa." Nico grinned madly, as if he was lost thinking about it. Then, he shook his fist in the air in a mini celebration. "Sponge capital of the world!"

I looked at him as if he had gone slightly insane, but instead I tucked the memory away, enjoying this side of him too much to tease him.

Nico spoke again. "It's been hell not asking Elena to stock up on more baked goods. Loukoumades used to be my favourite; it's like a dough ball, but soaked in honey."

"You should! I'd love to try some."

"Jon wouldn't be happy. He still doesn't know about the burger."

I tried not to smile wider at the memory of us scrambling back to the van in the pouring rain, getting back just as the rest of the group joined us, but not enough time so that Jon couldn't smell the beer on our breath. "And he never can. It was bad enough when he found out about the beers."

He glanced up at me, and for a moment, I wondered if he was thinking about it too. The doorway alcove. The rain having soaked us through to the skin, our bodies pressed together. He cleared his throat, looking back down at the cat. "We didn't have much growing up, but it didn't matter. I had tennis. I didn't need anything else."

"You started young, right?" I could see the pictures in my head. A tiny Nico, the racket half the size of him.

"I was six when I went to my first training camp. I'm not sure I remember doing anything else."

"How did you get into it?"

"What is this? Twenty questions?"

I leaned over, elbowing him, the smile that had curved onto my lips out of my control. "Just trying to get to know my mixed partner. Make sure he's up to scratch."

"You mean you didn't google me beforehand?" His tone was dripped in sarcasm, but it raised a good question.

I answered his question with one of my own. "Did you google me?"

I hadn't. Had I considered it? Of course. But I knew from what the internet had to say about me, that the truth about a person could be stretched.

He shook his head. "I didn't feel I had to. Everything I had to know about you, I already either knew, or I'd learn it from you."

"But see, if you had googled me, you could've found out about my annulled marriage with a billionaire and secret love child with his father."

He paused, his eyes assessing as his lips pressed into a thin line. "I'm not sure if you're joking or not."

I waved him off, relaxing backwards as I let my head roll back, closing my eyes to let the sunlight warm my skin. "You could read about it. Doesn't mean it's true."

A momentary, easy silence fell between us, and when I cracked an eye to look at Nico, I found his gaze slowly grazing up my body, the length of my neck, the lump in his throat bobbing as he swallowed. His attention snapped to mine when he noticed me watching him. I thought back to that night. A stray raindrop rolling down his cheek, and how his stubble felt under the pad of my finger as I wiped it away. The tension that pulled me close to him in the already cramped alcove, the storm of grey in his eyes. How would it feel to reach out and touch him again? How easy would it be to shatter everything?

"I was given my first racket when I was four," he started, answering my original question. "Apparently, I'd been a violent child and Dad thought this would give me an outlet. Turned out, I was an angrier child than they'd anticipated and could hit a ball at top speeds by the time I was ten. I became obsessed, wouldn't miss watching a slam, and dreamed of winning Wimbledon. I turned pro at sixteen and won my first open by eighteen."

I blinked once, my throat dry. This part, I'd never had to google. "And that was . . ."

"That was the US Open," he said, with a gentle nod, his eyes still assessing mine. "Against Matteo."

It was fifteen years ago, but that game had changed my life; both of our lives.

I bit my lip as I rolled the admission around my brain like a ball. "I remember that match."

His eyebrows popped up as his eyes widened. "You were there?"

I nodded. "In his box."

"That's weird." His nose crinkled and my stomach was full of butterflies, the usual sting of the memory erased.

"It is what it is." I shrugged, my toes digging further into the sand as I admitted, "I watched that match back a lot."

"Really?" His jaw was slack, a goofy grin curved at the edges of his lips. I nodded, choosing not to mention that the primary reason it was on was because Matteo was obsessed with finding that one incorrect step that led him to lose everything, the missed opportunity that toppled the entire tower of cards.

That was the reason it had been played over and over, but I'd watched it over and over for him. The way he played. The way he moved across the court and caught all of Matteo's tricks, unravelling all of his confidence, and reducing him down like no other player had before.

It was David vs Goliath, and David had walked away triumphant.

"It stuck with me. He was always unbeatable, at least as far as I had known him to be. Until you walked onto that court, cocky—"

"I was not cocky," he interrupted with a bemused smile. "I was eighteen, going up against the biggest name in tennis. I threw up in a trash can before I went out."

"Seriously?"

He cocked an eyebrow. "Wouldn't you?"

I let out a breath, debating for a moment, remembering how he'd strutted out to Centre Court that day. He'd stared Matteo down any opportunity he got, playing mind games even when they weren't playing. Matteo had complained about it to the umpire, but he'd listened to none of it.

"Could've fooled me."

A laugh escaped him, his body relaxing. "You know what they say. Fake it till you make it."

"I guess so," I hummed. "There was something about how you dismantled his defence that I'd never seen before. You destroyed him in that match."

He shook me off, his attention turning back to the cat. "He was old."

"Don't play dumb. You knew what that match meant. He was almost unbeaten that year, and you . . . you tore into him. He wasn't expecting that." I watched as his shoulders tensed, his fingers scratching at the cat's fur as it rolled onto its back.

I wondered, for a moment, what it had been like for him. I didn't allow myself to think very long on my only win, the memories best left to be forgotten, but I had holed up in hotel rooms for a very long time before I ventured out again. The press was very different, but with Matteo, I'd grown up with that. I was used to it. But for Nico, he'd stepped onto that court, a relative nobody, and walked away a Legend Killer.

"How fast did everything change after?"

A heavy breath escaped him. "I couldn't walk down the street for the first few weeks. That was scary, everyone suddenly knowing my name. Tabloids trying to dig up every bit of dirt they could after I took down their favourite player. And competitions got harder, but there were a lot more opportunities." He paused, the moment stretching out, until with a heavy head hung lower, his voice lower, he admitted, "It changed my life."

I nodded knowingly before speaking again. "Changed mine too."

"How so?"

"His attention wasn't split anymore." I shrugged, before folding in on myself a little, trying my best to match Nico, to share the parts of myself I kept hidden. "I was his backup. I'd been in training since I had developed basic hand-eye coordination. Then it was time for little Scottie Rossi to step up. I had just turned fourteen when we went pro."

His voice was hoarse when he asked, "Would you change it?"

"What?"

He motioned with his hands. "Playing tennis? If you could, would you go back and Tonya Harding my ass?"

I smiled at his joke, shaking my head. I didn't need time to ponder his question. It wasn't something I didn't already ask myself in the early hours of the morning on those nights where sleep seemed impossible. "Even if you hadn't beaten him, somebody would've. And besides, I was already playing. I just had more time."

"So . . . you wouldn't change it? If you could?" I knew what he was saying. Every moment for the last few years. Wimbledon, every mistake that was made, the two years I had.

In a voice that was quieter than I had anticipated, I answered, "Would you judge me if I said no? If none of it had happened, I don't know where I would be. And, I mean . . ." I looked around at the beach, the waves washing onto the sand, the sun low in the sky surrounded by hues of orange and pink. I thought about the last few weeks, and as much as there was struggle, I'd not felt more like myself in years.

And then I looked at him, those eyes burning into mine, his sculpted cheekbones, his lips. If any of it changed, would I have met him? Gotten to know him? Would I trade this for an easier ride? Did that even exist?

I looked right at him as I spoke. "I don't regret tennis, just the shitty dad. And besides, it brought me here, right?"

He kept looking at me, those grey eyes unreadable. A smile crept onto his lips, full of comfort and a little relief. "Yeah, I guess it did."

I forgot to breathe, my lungs useless, when he looked at me like that. Like there was nobody else in the world. For a moment, it was made only for the two of us and the curve of his lips. And I knew that wasn't right, that I shouldn't think things like that. This was a professional partnership, we both had everything on the line: our careers, our reputations—or at least, what was left of mine—and . . . and an "us" put all of that at risk, no matter how much I wanted it.

But when he opened up to me and told me things that made me feel like I belonged in his world, I couldn't help but want it all. Every moment he could give me, every smile breaking through that cloud of grumpy grey moodiness. I didn't know what life would be like without him anymore.

"Hey, guys." Sarah's voice pulled me from my thoughts, dragging my attention reluctantly over to her. She was standing a short distance away, and I realised then that she'd been taking photos all this time. It wasn't a problem, like the yoga on the beach, instead a testament to how effortlessly I got caught up in Nico Kotas. "Can we get rid of the cat? It's pulling the focus," she asked.

I looked up at Nico, who's attention was on Sarah with furrowed brows, clearly offended on the cat's behalf at Sarah's comment. But without any argument, he stopped, lifting his hand from the cat and resting it on the top of his thigh. The cat turned, staring up at him with what I could swear was a similar furrowed brow to Nico's own, before letting out the loudest, most strangled meow I had ever heard.

I struggled to contain my laughter and found it even harder when I took in his raised eyebrow as he directed his attention back to Sarah, who was now standing with one hand on her hip, waiting to restart her work.

He looked at Sarah and shrugged. "I guess she's determined to be the star of the show."

My smile broke out, knowing that despite his reluctance, or anything he said, those cats had crept into his heart and dug out their own piece. And maybe it was near the piece I'd started to claim as mine.

CHAPTER TWENTY-FIVE

Scottie

How Not To Drown – CHVRCHES

Nico served first, the shot powerful and clean as his racket sliced through the air with precision. Inés returned it with a swift forehand, and the rally began. My heart raced as we glided around the court, taking up and defending our space. Nico was at the back on the baseline, while I was closer to the net, ready to intercept any shots that came my way.

We all defended for a few volleys, managing to return the ball before Henrik had an opportunity to unleash his lethal backhand. Reacting on instinct, I ran, meeting the ball with millimetres to spare, and sent it back over the net with a perfectly executed volley. Inés ran, finding the ball easily before returning.

Nico's calculating eyes locked onto the ball's trajectory, and with a swift leap, he smashed it with an overhead slam that left Henrik rooted to the spot. The ball rocketed past him and landed in the corner of the court, well out of Inés's reach.

The game was ours, and so was the match.

We'd been playing all afternoon, and while they had won their fair share of games, we had beat them in straight sets. It was clear to anyone on or off the court what a great team we were making.

I grinned over at Nico, only to watch him as he lifted his hat, biceps of his bare arm tightening as he moved to wipe the brow of his forehead after hours in the Greek sun. Apparently, halfway through today's practice, it had gotten too hot for a top.

I bit my lip as my gaze trailed down his powerful arm, the dark ink of the tattoos that wrapped around his limb only heightening the experience. Silently, and on behalf of humanity, I cried a hallelujah to the tennis Gods for what the sport had done to that man's forearms.

"Good save there, Sinclair." He nodded, and it took a moment for his words to sink in, my brain switching gears from topless Nico to whatever he had said.

"Not so bad yourself, Kotas." I smiled nervously, forcing myself to maintain eye contact. "Maybe next time you won't get caught short on Henrik's backhand."

His eyebrows pushed up. "I wouldn't get caught short if my partner was in the right place."

"I was in the right place." I pressed forward to argue, but Inés got there first.

"If I hear you guys picking apart your game piece by piece, I will be forced to shove this racket up your asses." She spun the racket in her hands, looking rather threatening.

Nico hummed. "Like, collectively, or one at a time?"

"Not the point, Nico." She gave him a blank stare. "You guys are impossible to beat. Stop arguing so much and it will be fine."

The nervous ball that had been building in the pit of my stomach for weeks returned. We were due to leave our little bubble soon and fly back to London. The week after, Wimbledon would begin. It was my first competition in two years, and I wasn't sure I was ready.

What if I let everyone down? What if I took one wrong step and these weeks, all of our hard work, had been for nothing? Before, it had been me and the expectations that I had to fight for. But now,

I had a teammate who relied on me to not misstep. How could I handle it if it all went wrong, and it was my fault?

I turned to Nico, deflated. "I wasn't in the wrong place, but I should've gotten the shot after. I missed it."

"You did, but I got to it, so it's all good." His tone was soothing, the easy look on his face telling me to calm down. "You saved my ass countless times. It's what teammates do."

Teammates. Six weeks together and that was all we were. But teammates didn't think the things I had been thinking about him.

I let out a deep breath, but it did very little to loosen the knot. Turning, I made my way to the side of the court to take a moment for myself, trying to pull myself back from the edge of the dark thoughts that had begun to shadow at the edges.

Grabbing my water bottle and taking a long sip, I watched as Inés and Henrik still stood in the middle of the court, picking apart their own game.

"Whatcha doing?" Nico nudged into my side, the momentarily warm press of his sweaty body overwhelming.

I twisted, looking up at him as I recapped my bottle. "What do you mean?"

He sat down on the bench as he dug his towel out of his bag, swinging it over his neck. "You know you didn't do anything wrong, right?"

I turned back to the court, watching Jon as he joined the conversation with Inés. I recognised the expression on his face, the movement as he used his hands to count all the things he was listing off. It was a typical Jon talk down, a post-training download of every misstep and mistake we made.

"I shouldn't be making mistakes like that," I admitted. I had to do better. I could do better. If I'd played like that before, with . . . with him, I'd be back out there, doing drills over and over until holding the racket was more from sheer will instead of capability, blisters ripping on my palm. Because that's what it took to be a winner. I sat down, slumping beside Nico, my back leaning against the metal net of the tall fence.

"That's why there's two of us out there. We have each other's backs," Nico said, his head tilted.

The last point continued to repeat in my head, over and over. Catching the moment I made the wrong decision, misread my opponent. It couldn't happen again. Henrik was good, but a better player would've exploited the weakness in a heartbeat.

"All the same, I shouldn't be doing something stupid. It could cost us the game."

"What about the mistakes I made?" he argued. "Do you want to see me beating myself up over them?"

"No, of course not."

"And do you know why you won't catch me doing that?" My focus pulled to him, those grey eyes on me. "Because it's not worthwhile. A million things can go wrong between the start of the match and the final bounce of the ball, and about ninety-nine percent of them are out of your control. The mistakes you made, out of your control. Just don't get . . ." Something in his voice changed, the firm line of his jawline stiffening. "Don't get distracted."

The word hung in the air between us, like a secret code. *Distracted.*

Did he feel it too? I'd seen how he looked at me, it was getting hard to pretend I hadn't. It was even harder to pretend I didn't do my own fair share of looking. See: my eyes fixed on his instead of trailing down the hard line of biceps that had been teasing me. But he'd given it a name, and I couldn't argue with it, not with everything that was already on the line.

Distraction. We were walking on a knife-edge, trying to keep ourselves upright before the hardest three weeks of our lives. Anything new, any move unconsidered, could put that balance at risk.

"Yeah." The word croaked out of me as I nodded my head, looking away from Nico, and instead down at the gritted ground of the court, rubbing the sole of my trainer into the grass. I shook my head. "Of course. You're right. We've got to focus."

I knew what this would take. For us to get anywhere, to win, I had to stop with the flirting and the staring and the constant thinking about how hard the muscle of his thick thigh must be, how they would feel under my hands.

All of that had to wait. Or better yet, disappear entirely. That would be easier. Cleaner.

"This next bit, it's all about confidence," he began again, the tone changing as the tight air loosened around us. "Trust me, if something went wrong, Jon would be over here kicking your ass about it. But he wasn't. He was busy chewing Inés out for her mistakes because they were avoidable."

I looked across to where they had been standing, finding that they had dispersed, Jon finished with his complaining for the day. Then, catching me off guard, Nico's hand slipped against mine. The contact almost had me flinching until I realised it was supposed to be harmless, but my heart pounded all the same.

That tightrope came into view. A balancing act between staying the course, keeping our focus, and falling into whatever had been building between us. But he spoke again, and I would've taken a pair of scissors to the rope if it meant I could keep feeling how he'd made me feel.

"There is not a single shred of doubt in my body over being your partner, Scottie. I trust you implicitly." A caress of his shoulder against mine threatened to be overwhelming. I was quickly learning that anything that seemed simple about Nico was in fact the opposite. Instead, he was layered and nuanced, and I was beginning to grow addicted to every scrap of closeness I could gain from him.

"Whether we win or lose, we do it together," he finished, and I could see it in my mind's eye. The result of our work, standing Centre Court on a summer's day in London. Standing with *him*. That was beginning to feel like it would be enough of a reward.

All I could do was nod because words were beyond my capability as I watched the bob of his throat before tracing the curve of his comforting smile. When we arrived six weeks ago, I wasn't even sure he could smile. He was just grumpy. All the time. Now, all he seemed to do was smile.

"Together," I echoed, trying to return his smile. With one last squeeze, his hand slipped from mine, and he stood up and helped me to my feet. Looking around, we found the court empty, everyone else having disappeared.

"We better head inside before they send out a search party for us," he said, but there was still a reluctance in my bones, telling me I wasn't quite done.

"You go ahead. I'll save Jon a job and clean up here."

"I can help."

"No, it's fine. You should probably hit the shower." I winked, trying not to protest too hard. He narrowed his eyes in mock disdain before lifting an arm and taking a strong whiff. And judging by the twist of disgust that appeared across his features, he didn't disagree.

"Okay, maybe you're right," he conceded, before reaching for the hat atop his head. I tried not to feel the well of emotion opening up inside of me, the soft twist of my gut, the begging of every nerve end to touch him as he stepped close and placed the hat on my head, adjusting it so it sat snugly.

He took a step back, analysing his work. "It looks better on you anyway," he admitted. The squeeze of my heart was a cruel and beautiful thing. A reminder that he was forbidden. At least, that's what I had to keep telling myself.

"See you inside." Nico slung his bag over his shoulder and left me alone. It took me a moment to collect myself. My fingertips ran over the stitching on the edge of the cap, trying not to read into his actions, but failing. I shook my head and set up the ball machine, then grabbed my racket, and redid what I had messed up during practice until I got it perfectly.

Each ball I hit, I put something of myself into it, this ballooning feeling that had grown too big for my chest. I needed to vent it before it overtook me, before it knocked me from my balance.

Before I did something stupid.

CHAPTER TWENTY-SIX

Nico
Hoax – Taylor Swift

had been feeling good about my knee, experiencing less and less pain after practices and making sure I kept up with my physio's recommended exercises.

Only to get taken out by a cat.

As I headed back to the villa, four of them had rushed towards me, coming out of their various hiding places amongst the flower beds. But when one large grey monster got under my foot, causing me to misstep, lose my balance, I fell squarely on my newly recovered knee.

I'd limped the rest of the way back, swearing under my breath every time I had to put weight on that leg. Sliding through the kitchen doors, I aimed right for the freezer, digging out one of the trusty ice packs that Elena had left for me there, and attempted to rest up for the remainder of the evening, my anxiety swelling as the pain refused to dissipate.

We were days away from London. If my knee could still hurt this badly from an incident with a pack of rabid cats, was I even strong enough to get through Wimbledon? I had weeks of competition ahead of me, hours of matches to play.

This was my shot. My chance. But was I really ready for it?

It wasn't until I limped downstairs for dinner that I noticed Scottie was missing. I asked around, trying to find out if anyone had seen her. When the answer was no and a quick trip to her bedroom upstairs also showed that she wasn't hiding from me there, I reluctantly started the journey over to the beach. It wasn't far from the villa, but it was far enough that I shouldn't have risked it on my injured knee. I made my way through the gardens, avoiding any more of the damned cats, when I spotted the floodlights of the tennis courts still on. I pondered for a moment, thinking of the last place I had seen her. She couldn't still be there, could she?

Yet, there she was. Standing at the baseline, the crack of the ball meeting her racket echoing through the cooled evening air as the ball machine fired at her. Her blonde hair was in a ponytail, falling out from under the cap I'd given her earlier. Seeing her wearing the baseball cap, my name stitched into the back, gave me a low hum of comfort, a continuous murmur in the background of my heart. I remembered the last time I found her here alone. The night she had come clean about everything.

"What are you still doing here?" I asked over the noise of the machine. Scottie jumped, snapping out of her zone. A ball pounded into the side of her, and she yelped.

"Jesus, you scared me," she complained, stepping out of the line of fire.

"It's been hours, Scottie. Have you rested at all?" I questioned as she pulled the remote out of the pocket of her pleated skirt, and the machine powered down.

"I wanted to get it right."

"That's what this is about?" My brows raised in surprise. Had she come back to work some more on that? "That move is simple, easy to correct next time in training. You must've been done hours ago."

"But then . . . then I started running drills, and I started to get slow, so I started again and . . . and I wanted to practise," she explained with a slight grimace, her shoulders slumped and out of their usual strong pose.

I shook my head, still unsure of what to make of this. Why hadn't she come inside? We needed to rest as much as we needed to practise, especially this close to the competition. The last thing we needed was her burning out. I'd seen it before, even experienced it myself, and it made an already gruelling few weeks feel impossible.

"Come inside. You need to eat dinner."

"I'll get something soon. I need to practise this backhand swing."

"Your backhand is fine," I stressed.

"It could be better."

"Then we can focus on it tomorrow."

"Five more minutes," she pressed again, her fingers adjusting oddly around the handle of her racket. The movement caught my attention, her grip all wrong for something so fundamental. Then I noticed the skin looked a little red. Closing the gap between us, I was fully able to read the exhaustion that was written all over her face. Her usually dull gaze with her blue eyes almost washed out.

"Show me your palm, Scottie." I reached out for her left arm, my hand open to her.

Her brows pressed together. "Show me your knee. I saw you limping. Is it sore again?"

For a moment, I considered lying, shrugging it off and telling her it was nothing. But if I wanted her to open up, maybe I should do it too. "One of those damn cats got in my way. I'll get an ice pack soon."

Scottie looked up at me, her face flushed pink, trying unsuccessfully to contain the stress across her face. Slowly, she relented, swapping her racket to her right and lifting her hand to me. I gripped her wrist and softly rotated it, her fingers clenched into a painful fist, but I could already see that her palm was a bright, painful shade of red.

"Can I see . . . please?" My hand slipped from her wrist and instead went to her palm, softly rubbing at the outside in a comforting motion. Slowly, her fingers unfolded, and I finally saw the state of her injury.

The palm was red raw, the skin broken and swollen slightly, with small blisters forming on the heel of her thumb and along her fingers. I could make out the strain in the creases of her palm, the line deep and more pronounced from the constraint flexing and stretching of her fingers.

My heart didn't break—it shattered. Regret overwhelmed me. I should've never left her. I should've made sure she came inside and rested. As much as I hated that she'd done this to herself, I hated the fact that I had let her even more.

But the question still scratched at me: Why? Why was she still out here? Why had she let herself get hurt like this and then carried on, anyway?

I smothered down my anger, letting it burn away instead. I couldn't look at her injury without wincing myself, the thought of how much pain she must be in too much.

"Can I take you inside? Get this cleaned up?" I still held on to her hand, almost unable to let it go. "We'll need to make sure it doesn't get infected."

"It's not that bad." She pulled her arm out of my grasp, her fingers curling back into a fist, wincing as she did. Her pain was clear for a moment before her mask fell back into place.

I ran my fingers through my hair, pulling as irritation pricked at my skin. "This . . . this isn't normal, Scottie. I told you, you played well today."

She shifted her weight from foot to foot, her attention lifting to me as she glanced around the court. When she answered me, her voice was so small and breakable.

"I just . . . I don't want to risk you losing everything because of my mistakes."

I let her confession hang in the air for a moment, before dismissing it, my anger shining through. "And what about you? Now we have to wait for this to heal before you can play again."

She looked reluctantly at the ball machine, like she wanted to keep practising, like she still couldn't leave yet. But there was no way I was letting her stay here like this. I knew I couldn't trust her not to keep playing.

"It'll take five minutes," I said, the lie easy to say. "Then if it's okay, you can come back."

I had zero intentions of letting her return. But I'd take whatever means necessary to get her to stop. Her body was a tool, as much as the racket in her hand. Misuse it, and it could cost her everything. She relented, her body almost caving in to my offer as she nodded.

"I should clean this up." She looked around at the court with that last shred of reluctance.

"Leave it," I said. "We'll clean it up later." Another lie that Jon would make me pay for tomorrow when he saw the mess. I switched off the floodlights of the court as we left, the stray cats our companions as we headed back down the dark garden path to the villa.

"Hold still." I gripped Scottie's hand gently, keeping it in place as I tried to stop her from squirming around. She groaned, sending a frown at me, a first-aid kit thrown open all over the counter beside us.

"I'm trying," she complained, relenting slightly and resting her arm along the marble counter. I'd been trying to disinfect her wound with some antibacterial wipes, the strong smell of stinging alcohol hanging in the air.

"You're doing a terrible job of it."

Her eyes narrowed on me as she replied, "It would be easier if you weren't intentionally trying to hurt me."

"If we don't do this, we have to chop your hand off. You won't be much use to me with only one." My joke distracted her long enough that when I wiped again, she didn't even flinch.

Instead, her gaze fixed on me as she challenged, "One arm is plenty enough to play tennis."

"That's true." I smiled. "But I'd still beat you."

She tsked before examining her palm. Somehow, even though disinfected, it looked worse. Blotchy, raw red, bruises appearing on the sensitive skin. I ached at the thought of the pain she'd tried to cover up.

"Are we going to talk about it?" I asked, only to be met with a raised eyebrow. "Why did you let it get this bad?"

She let out a deep, annoyed breath. "It's not that—"

"Yes, it is," I said. "And if you disagree, then I'm probably due another conversation with Jon about what kind of practice injuries you're used to."

She fell silent, and I used the moment to squeeze a small blob of the antiseptic cream onto my finger, laying my hand out again for her. Thankfully, without further argument, she let me gently dab the cream into the worst affected parts until it was all smoothed out and absorbed.

"I already told you," she said under her breath. "I . . . I don't want to be the reason we fail. I know how important Wimbledon is for you."

I kept my eyes on her palm, committing it to memory as if I needed to remember the cost of what that worry had done to her. Shaking my head, I tried to reassure her. "You won't be."

"What if I am? What if I make another stupid mistake?" Her voice rang with anxiety, and I swore she turned to look outside again, across the vast garden and over to the court, as if she was already wondering when she would be able to get back out there and start all over again.

"If you really think one stupid misstep can derail our entire game, we obviously weren't playing very well to begin with."

"I'm scared, Nico," she admitted. "This . . . I don't think anything has ever meant so much to me."

"Me either." The words were hushed, but nonetheless true. This last title was my only goal. And with my knee and age, a second shot wasn't guaranteed. If I failed now, my career could be done. However, as I grew faster and stronger, this admiration for her didn't simmer out. "But we make a good team."

"Somehow, that makes it worse."

I dropped her hand, searching through the kit for the bandages, the cream on her palm making things look a little better. Tomorrow, I'd get Jon or Elena to take a look, make sure I had cleaned it correctly.

Pausing, I held the bandage out to wrap her with, but instead I met her gaze. "Scottie, even if we did lose, I would want to keep playing with you." *I would want to keep you.*

She swallowed nervously. "I wasn't sure you'd want to keep playing together."

I moved her arm closer before running the material over and under her injury, keeping it tight, but not enough to cut off circulation. "You know I do like you, right?"

She let out a single laugh, rolling her eyes playfully. "I couldn't tell."

We stayed like that for a moment, her bandaged palm in mine, her blue eyes meeting my grey, lost in the small contact. She lifted her arm, inspecting the wrap as she stretched her finger out. She still winced with pain, but the reassurance that the wound was at least well-kept for the evening soothed my worry somewhat, as if somebody had tried to smooth a crumpled piece of paper. Better, but not as it was before.

"I mean to start off with, you were annoying." I smiled, thinking back to those early days where I was just as bad as she had been. Two arrogant players, unwilling to work with someone else. My own ego had been too inflated to admit I needed her.

"Dare I remind you about the plane?" she asked.

I let out a snort of laughter, titling my head slightly. "Dare I remind *you* about the plane?" She shrugged her shoulders innocently, her expression clear. I let it go, knowing she was toying with me. There had been moments where we both weren't our best selves. "We've been on this journey together. Before you, I wasn't sure I'd really make it this far. My knee, the pain made it too hard to keep going. I kept pushing myself harder. Wondering why I wasn't getting any better? But I think Jon knew I needed somebody to distract me, to push me in a different direction."

"Or just somebody who would push the right buttons." She smiled playfully. I realised for a moment how right she was. She had pushed all the buttons, like a Vegas slot machine, and somehow I'd been the one who won the jackpot.

"Exactly. We started off fighting each other, but really, you lit the drive in me to keep going," I admitted, leaning forward on my stool, the gap between us closing. Those early days, they were rough. We were on opposite sides of every argument. Everything was made as difficult as possible just to annoy the other. But there was something in that, a drive I'd lost the months living through the physical rehab. It was back.

"I didn't think I had this much fight left in me before you." The words left me without thought, unsure if she would understand what I was truly trying to say. How much I'd admitted.

"I'm not sure what that says about our relationship."

The moment stilled, her words hanging in the air. Did she

really not know how I felt? Was it not obvious enough? Somehow, that overwhelmed the dam I had built that was holding back the flood of every too-big emotion I'd had for her. Every truth I'd tucked away.

"Let me make it clear in case it wasn't before. No matter what happens in the next few weeks, I've only made it this far because of you."

She leaned back, waving a hand as her nose crinkled in apprehension. "You would've been fine without me."

I pushed up from my stool, unable to sit still anymore. My legs, despite their previous pain, ached to stretch and work out the frustration that had built up. I inhaled sharply, looking right at her, and with another burst of courage, I started again.

"You helped me train harder. Taught me to take a break and eat a burger, and run through Lindos in the pouring rain, to hell with the rules. You saw when I was in pain and helped. Even when I pushed you away."

Her pink lips pressed into a thin line, her eyebrows creasing together, and I took the opportunity to keep going until she believed what I was saying. Until she understood what I meant.

"I don't care if something goes wrong next week. If we lose the first match, it will suck but I'll get over it." I almost closed my eyes to escape the piercing blue of hers, but I knew that even if I did, their colour would haunt me in my memory. "I only care that you're okay and safe. It hurt to see you driving yourself to this, especially if it's because you're afraid for me. That . . . that broke my goddamn heart, Scottie."

"Nico . . ." The gentleness her tone held as she said my name almost brought me to my knees, a warning to stop, but my words wouldn't stop spilling out. I'd reached the limit of what I could reasonably smother down and save for a more convenient day. It might've been fine before, but she'd hurt herself for me. I wouldn't be another person Scottie Sinclair ruined herself for, not when all I wanted was the opposite. When she meant so much.

"You're all I think about all day," I confessed, as her face fell blank, her pink lips parting. "You. I wonder how I could make you smile, how I could show you that you're worth more than you give yourself credit for, how I could keep you safe. How do I show you how special you are? How your strength is the thing I'm most proud of you for, the thing that leaves me in most awe of you?" I tried to swallow the lump in my throat, nerves getting the best of me. "Then, after everything else, right at the bottom of the list, I think about tennis. You have managed to plant yourself before everything else in my life, and I didn't even realise you were doing it."

Her gaze was fixed on mine, a completely unreadable expression spread across her features. As seconds passed like hours, I couldn't help but wonder if I had made a huge mistake, baring my soul like this. But I had to make her understand how much she meant to me.

How I couldn't watch her destroy herself.

"Nico . . . I . . ." she stuttered, her eyes searching my face. "I don't know what to say."

"Say you feel it too." I cracked wide open, every part of me exposed and vulnerable. "Tell me you think about me too."

"All the time," she admitted. "Nobody has ever . . ." She trailed off, and I couldn't help but reach out to comfort her. My palm slid along her neck, tracing the line of her jaw. Her eyes closed as she melted into my touch, accepting it. I tilted her head up, her eyes opening to reveal a hungry blue that too easily consumed me whole. Never had I ever felt like this.

"Tell me, Scottie," I begged, my voice breaking. "Tell me."

"I thought we agreed on no distractions," she murmured, a sly smile on her lips. She was toying with me, but I was already too close to my limit.

"I feel pretty distracted, don't you?" I'd been so dumb to say that earlier, but it had been a last-ditch attempt to stop a runaway train that travelled far away from me. A last act of desperation, but instead it had done the opposite, propelling me towards her.

"I've always thought focus was entirely overrated." She breathed. "Restraint too."

"Scottie." Her name was a sin. Touching her was too close to heaven, and I was all too sure of the hell it would bring my life to go without her any longer.

She pulled her pink lip between her teeth and my knees weakened further with the need to run my thumb over it, to finally know how it felt to press any part of her to them. Her hand rose to where mine was on her jaw.

"I want you too, Nico," she admitted, the words tattooing themselves into the fabric of my soul. The dull ache in the centre of my chest I'd been carrying for weeks dissipated, replaced with a heart that felt as if it had grown ten sizes too big for my chest.

"Can I kiss you?" I asked, needing to know this was for her what it was for me.

There was no hesitation in her answer. "Yes."

CHAPTER TWENTY-SEVEN

Scottie

Don't Delete The Kisses – Wolf Alice

The taste of Nico Kotas's lips, the gentle rub of his stubble against my cheek, and the way his fingers gripped the back of my head as we kissed was all information I hadn't woken up thinking I would learn.

But there we were, one hand on my face, pulling my lips close to him, the other at my lower back and gliding farther southward, mouths moving together and exploring. My uninjured fist at his shirt, the feeling of the tight muscle underneath pulling at something in my lower stomach.

He was a filthy pleasure I couldn't wait to unwrap.

He moaned into my mouth as he grabbed at my ass, the noise addictive as my skirt pulled up to reveal the thin shorts underneath. I melted into his body, pressing forward, needing to feel him against mine.

In one quick motion, Nico moved past me and used his arm to clear the counter, before he leaned down, his arms hooking at the backs of my thighs and pulling me up. I instantly wrapped my legs around his waist, the centre of his body pressing into mine. The kiss turned desperate, my fingers interlacing with his hair and tugging, lightly at first, but as I felt a curve grow on his lips, I used them to leverage his head into a different position, taking some control and deepening the kiss.

We grew hungry, pulling at each other, teeth grazing. I needed as much of him as I could get, desperate to satisfy the endless starvation that had only grown for him. The feel of him was impossible, a ripple of firm muscle and soft skin. My nails dug at his shirt, desperate to remove it so I could trace the black lines of his tattoos that disappeared underneath.

I needed every inch of him. Everything he said before . . . nobody had ever made me feel the way I did with him. Safe, secure, cared for, and nobody had ever driven me quite this wild.

I breathed him in, losing myself in the smell of his shampoo, wondering if he'd notice if I stole his body wash to cover myself in it. He was, for me, a basic human need. Oxygen, water, shelter, Nico Kotas. And judging by the hardness rubbing in between my legs, it was the same for him.

His hand pulled at the back of my top, finding his way underneath. The way his touch felt against my bare skin sent sparks up from the base of my spine to my neck. His fingers spread, digging into me and pulling me closer—as if there wasn't any space to begin with. His mouth left mine, kisses trailing across my jaw, finding the base of my neck and sucking at the sensitive skin. My fingers curled on his back, eyes rolling back at the sensation.

He made his way to my ear, pulling at the band of my ponytail and letting my hair fall past my shoulders, then breathed out, "Tell me to stop." It was a desperate plea, begging for a mercy that I wasn't going to give him. A mercy that neither of us even wanted. The smile on my lips was out of my control, my brain drunk on the knowledge that as much as I needed him, he needed me back all the same.

"What if I say keep going?" I replied, my hands sliding to his face, pulling up, so he left my neck to look at me.

"Then I will."

He looked undone, torn, and desperate. His lips red and swollen, grey eyes wild. I imagined mine looked much the same. My chest heaved for air, my heart thundering in my chest as I looked at him, committing every detail to memory. I never wanted to forget seeing the great Nico Kotas looking at me like this. Like I wasn't just a want, but a wild, unabandoned need.

"Then keep going." I squeezed my legs, pulling where he was hard against the centre of me, and moved my body against his. We both moaned at the touch, the relief driving us again as he thrust, clutching at me for grip.

If we'd been lighting a fire, then the rotation of my hips had thrown petrol on the whole damn thing.

We moved, craving and frenzied, as we found a rhythm, the perfect friction between us driving us further together. I needed more, needed the length I could feel growing against me, my dirty mind hungry to know how impressive he was, how good it would feel when I lowered myself onto him. His touch left my back and moved to the band of my skirt.

"Can I?" he breathed against me. I nodded enthusiastically, words out of reach with the anticipation of feeling him against me. He continued, his palms sliding down my front, under my skirt and underwear until he reached me.

"You're soaked." His voice was low and controlled. The feel of his finger trailing down, the tease of it, had me moaning into his ear as he continued, "Is this all for me?"

"Yes," I whimpered at his words as he played with me, his finger gently teasing against my clit, making perfect round circles that were driving me to the edge.

"Would you let me taste you?"

"Yes."

He grinned, his own wickedness teasing me now. "The things

I've been dreaming of doing to you. It's going to take us a while to work through them all."

I was ready to beg, and would've too, if it hadn't meant moving from our position and losing the contact that was driving me wild, pulling my body tighter and tighter, winding me like a coil, ready for release. My reply was nothing more than a hungry moan as he continued. I rubbed desperately against every point of contact, feral for the pleasure he promised me.

I could feel the release nearing when there was a noise outside the kitchen door. My body tensed as I let out a sharp inhale, glancing around the empty kitchen, suddenly remembering where we were. Anyone could have walked in and found him all over me. Sarah could have taken a photo, making any possibility of denying our relationship impossible. Labelling us as fuck buddies before we even got the chance to make our Wimbledon debut. One moment, and this could all be over. And then the chair screeched to the side. Nico yelped slightly, bringing my attention back to him, his face creased with pain.

"I hit my leg," he explained, letting out a deep breath as some distance grew between our bodies. Some very necessary distance. It felt like a bucket of ice water had been thrown over me as reality really kicked in.

"Are you okay?" I asked, eyes searching his. The air was hot and tight, but nevertheless, the coiled knot of need that had been tightened by his every touch loosened somewhat.

"It's fine," he tried to reassure me with a grin, but this time it was weak, like he could sense the imminent end had arrived too.

"We should stop," I whispered. *Stop before I let you take me raw, hard, and fast against the counter and it's too late.* I hated saying the words, but I knew it was for the best. We were out of control, risking something both of us had put everything on the line for. Him, more than me.

His hand pulled out, resting on my back as he moved back to look at me, expression full of concern. "Did I go too fast?"

I shook my head, still catching my breath. "The opposite."

He crooked an eyebrow, that devilish smile appearing. "Not fast enough?"

"We can't." I tried to release the tight knot inside of me with a breath. I was wound so tight, I was surprised I could tell him to stop, surprised I didn't jump his bones to finish the job.

"We can."

"We shouldn't." I shook my head, telling myself that this was for the best.

"I can feel how needy you are, and I can't think of one single good reason to stop." His eyes broke from mine, looking down at my ruffled skirt, his hand disappearing inside the white material. His fingertips moved against my aching core. "Say the word and I'll get down on my knees and tell you exactly how sweet you taste."

I almost cried out with the overwhelming want I felt for him. The throbbing absolution I needed from him. I leaned forward, my head resting on his shoulder, his comforting smell overwhelming.

"Wimbledon," I muttered into him. The excuse was easy. I'd been making it to myself for weeks now. "That's a reason."

My head lifted from his shoulder as he hummed his reply. "Hmm, try another?"

His forehead tipped forward to meet mine, the moment softening slightly. I wanted to cry with how desperate I was to continue, with the effort it took to fight this tsunami of need for him.

"Nico."

"I want you." It was a strangled final plea, not made to influence me, but only to remind me what I meant to him, that this had been more than a spill in the kitchen. As if he had to say it; I could still read it in his eyes.

I had to take a moment, swallowing down the impulse to kiss

him again. I was an addict, doubting I'd ever crave any other plea-sure more in my life as much as I wanted him.

"I know," I managed. "But we should stop."

He nodded, just once, before taking a step back, clearing his throat as he did. He wiped his hands along the front of his shorts before offering me help down. I couldn't even meet his eyes as I shuffled off the counter. In awkward silence, we cleaned up the mess we'd made, putting the kitchen back as it should be, leaving it almost as if we'd never been there in the first place. As if it had never happened. The way it should be, I told myself. Even if it broke me to keep him at arm's length.

"I think I'll head to bed," I said, unable to will myself to stay another moment in his presence, not without caving and making him mine over and over, not without giving in to the temptation to add my name to his tattoos, tucking it away somewhere hidden.

Property of Scottie Sinclair.

"You should eat," he reminded me. "Elena probably has leftovers from dinner in the fridge."

I shook my head again. "I'm not hungry."

Not that kind of hungry, at least.

He gave me a look, pressing the urge to shovel food down my gullet. Like I could think of food when I was wound up like this, my body aching for his touch. I needed a shower, a long one. I wondered if there was enough water in the world to cool me down after him.

"I promise I'm not hungry," I insisted, the look on his face not diminishing. I sighed. "If I want to eat later, I'll come and raid the fridge."

It took him a moment, his eyes still more black than grey, fo-cused on me, before he relented. "I'll head up too."

I almost teased him, considering what we had been up to less than a few minutes ago, but it died before I could say it, unable to will myself to make the situation more awkward.

Silently, we headed out of the kitchen and upstairs, the already long corridor feeling more like miles than metres. He walked alongside me, our arms brushing every so often, and each small touch had me closing my eyes, breathing in. The heat inside of me spurred hotter, the need for him only growing. We reached my room first, and the already awkward air grew heavy and almost unbearable.

"This is me." I immediately fought the urge to slap myself in the face. Six weeks living together, as if Nico didn't know where I slept? My cheeks burned hot as I watched a teasing smile curl onto his lips. I almost missed the more difficult days when he would've already grunted and run.

Instead, he looked at me, his eyes filled with something I couldn't quite place, leaned forward, and kissed me on the cheek. The simple touch was electric, his lips pressing against my skin. My fingers, despite the injury, curled into fists, my breath restricted, my lungs tight.

"Goodnight, Scottie," he said softly, taking one last look. Then he turned and continued down the hallway.

I didn't dare to move until he turned the corner, disappearing into the night. All the while, I cursed myself with every name under the sun for letting him go.

CHAPTER TWENTY-EIGHT

Scottie

Superbloodmoon (feat. d4vd) – Holly Humberstone

Nico smirked across the breakfast bar at me, the curve of his lips yet another reminder of exactly what had gone down on this very surface just the night before.

My lips against his. My legs wrapped around his waist, pulling and rubbing. His hands down my skirt.

I swallowed yet another uncomfortable mouthful of oatmeal, looking down at the bowl as I tried to avoid eye contact with Nico and another blush threatened to rise to my cheeks. He was already there when I came down for breakfast, a cocky look all over his face, as if he had been waiting for me since the sun had risen. As if he might not have slept at all.

"Did you get up to anything last night, Scottie?" Nico leaned forward on his elbows, his head between his hands, as if he was a schoolgirl looking for his dish on the latest drama. I gritted my teeth, trying to find some resolve.

It had been tempting for a moment to tell him what I really did after he left me last night. What I did when I was finally alone. How I couldn't stop myself from crying his name. How the thought of him had kept me twisting up in my sheets all night. How I ran the batteries of my vibrator flat trying to chase away the memory of him telling me how wet I was when he'd had his hand down my skirt.

Instead, my answer was the squeak of a mouse, heat rising to my cheeks despite every effort to contain the embarrassment. "Nothing."

I should really be a lot cooler than this. It wasn't even sex. I'd done worse with many more people, but there was something different about it this time.

Being with me, what I would bring to his life—drama, and that lack of privacy I'd given away over the last few years, the press following my every step, hunting me around cities . . . Nico was used to putting on a baseball hat, enjoying his peace. When we'd arrived at the airport here, that was the first time he'd been pap-ed in years. I'd checked last night, trying to find topless photos of him. Meanwhile, these last weeks were the longest I could remember not seeing any paparazzi. I was surprised they hadn't reported me missing.

He took a bite from the corner of his toast. Chewing had never looked so self-satisfied. "Aren't you going to ask what I got up to?"

"I'm not sure I need to ask."

"Ask what?" Jon appeared from over my shoulder, storming through the kitchen as he grabbed a bottle of water from the fridge.

"Nothing," I stammered, almost choking on air. "Doesn't matter."

"It's good you're both here anyway. I thought you might be taking advantage of the day off to sleep in."

We had practice later in the day, but mostly we were wrapping up the intense schedule of the camp. We'd be travelling tomorrow, and then the focus would be adjusting back to London conditions.

"Didn't get much sleep last night," Nico said, his tone unusually chipper for a man who apparently didn't get his full eight hours.

Jon took a sip from his bottle. "Why not?"

"I was a bit distracted."

"I guess that's to be expected." If Jon had any inkling of something going on between us, it didn't show. "Are you both packed?"

"Still a bit to go, but I'll finish after breakfast," I managed, trying to stop myself from looking over at Nico.

"Good." Jon moved on. "Listen . . . I've got some news."

His words pulled Nico's gaze from me, the burning spotlight finally turned. "What?"

"I need both of you to stay . . . calm. I don't want to get punched again."

Nico's brows furrowed, his arms crossing. "I won't punch you."

"Just . . . tell us," I said, despite a dry mouth.

Jon looked from Nico to me. One last hesitation in his voice before he delivered the blow. "Matteo is going to be at the competition."

"What?" Nico snapped, standing up from his chair. His palms pressed into the marble surface, fingers spreading out. It was all I could focus on, the space right in front of me.

Jon paused momentarily, giving himself time to make sure that Nico wasn't about to do something stupid. Again. "The rumour is that he's attending as a coach. And my sources are pretty reliable."

Nico swore, pacing across the kitchen, his hand rubbing at his face. I didn't hear the rest of their conversation, the words out of focus, a high-pitched noise drowning it all out. He was attending as a coach. My body had turned cold, my food turning into a brick in the pit of my stomach.

Finally, I managed a single question. "He's been training somebody else?"

Jon nodded. "I didn't expect it, either."

"I can't believe he would show his face. He knows she'll be there," Nico said, missing the point entirely.

I had known on some level that he'd try to crawl back. Tennis had been his world too after all. But what I had never predicted, stupid and self-centred as it was, was that he'd take somebody else on to coach.

"Do you know who?" I asked.

"No, I'll try to find out more," Jon promised, his words weighing heavy on me. If I had told the truth of what Matteo had done instead of taking all the blame, this would be different. Revenge had been the only thing I had been concerned with, my judgement clouded by foolishness to think he'd never take on another person to train. Someone he could hurt like he hurt me.

I looked down at my bandaged hand, the pain across my palms burning like wildfire. He had been a loving father. I knew that. I had memories of that. He had been with me from the beginning of my career. We'd eat together, drill together, play together, train together. He'd smile at me, tell me that I could be the best in the sport, that we would do that together.

But when I got injured, maybe he got impatient, or his ego had been bruised one too many times. Or maybe I'd been too young and foolish to see how willing he was to break his daughter to keep his own legacy in tennis going.

But I should've seen he wouldn't stop.

"This is my fault."

Nico's head snapped to look at me, his eyes narrowed. "What do you mean?"

"If I'd told people what he had done . . ."

Jon pulled out the chair next to me, softly placing a comforting hand on my shoulder as he shook his head. "There would always be somebody who would take him on."

Nico took a step closer to the counter. "None of this is your fault, Scottie."

I closed my eyes, trying to believe their words, trying to convince myself that even if I had spoken out, this all would've happened anyway. Nobody would've believed me. They wouldn't have listened. I had no proof, one witness at best. And despite years of being confident that would've been the case, I didn't feel so sure anymore. Nico believed me. If he did . . . could everyone else?

I pushed up out of the chair, my thoughts overwhelming. "I need some air."

They were silent for a moment, both sets of eyes assessing as I turned, walking around them to the double glass doors that led out into the garden.

"Is there anything I can do?" Jon asked.

I didn't even turn, craving the fresh salt air of the beach. "Just find out who, if you can. And how long he's been training them for."

I WATCHED THE waves roll over the sand, listening to the seagulls, feeling the grit of the warm sand on the palm of my uninjured hand. I wasn't sure how long I'd been sitting out there, basking in the sun. *He* would be there. I would have to face him. And the entire world would watch. Would I have to play in front of him as well?

"Scottie."

I turned, and found Nico struggling up a dune, a grimace on his face as he battled the hard walk through the soft sand, his baseball cap backward on his head. I turned back to the waves as he sat down next to me, saying nothing else.

"Did Jon send you out?"

"He actually made me wait. Said you needed to be alone."

"How ever did you escape?"

"Elena distracted him for a moment, and I snuck out," he said. "I had a feeling you'd be here instead of the court."

"I figured I'd destroyed enough rackets for one camp," I joked, but it wasn't even like I was angry. It felt like somebody had thrown a bucket of water on the raging fire that had been fuelling me for the last few years, all my fight extinguished.

I let out a heavy breath, knowing I was safe here, watching the waves roll in with him. "I could've stopped this, Nico. I should've stopped it."

"You had your reasons."

"What if he does the same thing to somebody else?"

His hand found mine, fingers rough as his palm slid against my own and squeezed ever so tightly. "He might not be. Jon's going to find out who, and then we can go from there."

I nodded, knowing he was right. "I . . . I knew I'd have to face him someday, but . . . I thought I'd at least have more than a few days' notice." I closed my eyes, now able to face the truth. "Nico, I'm . . . I'm scared."

"He won't be able to get to you," he promised.

"He'll always get his way. That's why I ran, why I did all of this."

"I won't let him." He shook his head, a stern look on his face. "He's done hurting you. You ran when you needed to, but now, you're strong enough to fight. I'll be with you the entire time." Something flickered in his eyes as he bit his lower lip, releasing it before he spoke. "You aren't alone in this."

I breathed in the salt air, choosing to believe what he said. Whether it was my fault or not, he was right. I wasn't alone.

"You'll be there?" My voice was a stupid fragile thing, my mind cast back to the night before.

I only care that you're okay and safe.

He smiled softly. "Even if it means I can't leave your side."

A single laugh escaped me before I tilted my head, looking at him. "I wouldn't go that far."

"If it kept you safe, Scottie, I would." There was no humour left in his voice, his lips pressed into a firm line. Then, his body relaxing somewhat, he lifted the hat from his head and placed it on mine.

"You keep leaving me with your lucky hat." I smiled, despite the size being a little too loose on my smaller head. Comfort, safety, and the smell of his shampoo almost overwhelmed me.

He tilted his head to me with a knowing smile. "I don't need it anymore. I've got you, *katsarída*."

I loudly huffed, breaking the tension. "Not that nickname again."

His smile was incomparable, teasing me with the name I hadn't heard for weeks, as he leaned back into the sand.

"Are you ever going to tell me what it means?"

He hummed, looking uncertain for a moment. "I'm not sure we'll be friends after."

"It can't be that bad, right?" I urged, eyes glancing over his face, taking in the tight restraint. "Right?" I repeated, in a much smaller, less confident voice.

"Look, I was being a dick when I said it. I didn't really mean it." I thought back to the plane journey here. I felt like a different person, somebody who was holding on to a secret so tightly they could hardly breathe. Being with him, working and growing closer, I'd never been able to be so open with somebody and feel comforted in the knowledge that I was truly safe with them.

"Yes, you definitely did." I laughed, calling him on his bluff. He grimaced, but I pressed on. "Just tell me."

He let out a deep breath. "It means . . . cockroach."

"Excuse me?" I stared at him, slack-jawed and confused.

"In Greek," he added, unnecessarily. I paused for a moment, looking ahead at the rolling ocean waves, before returning, my brain a stalled engine.

"Cockroach," I repeated.

He nodded.

"Like . . . the little bug with all the legs. The disgusting, garbage thing?"

I knew what a cockroach was. What I didn't know was why the

man who almost had his head between my legs last night was calling me one.

"I didn't mean it," he said, as if that was supposed to be a comfort. "At first."

"At first?" I shrieked in confusion, really not sure how to take it.
How was someone supposed to react to being called a gross trash
bug in a different language?

"Look, yes, it's a bug. It was a mindless insult, I promise. But
it . . . worked? They say if there was ever a nuclear winter, like world
ending shit, that the cockroaches would survive."

Another shriek. "So?"

"That's you."

A single eyebrow pushed up. "I'm a bug?"

"No, you're strong." His words caught me off guard, if still
recovering from the true meaning of the nickname. "You went
through hell and survived it. You're a force to be reckoned with.
On and off the court. I don't know how, but you survived the un-
imaginable and came back. I don't think many people could do
what you have."

"Okay, well . . ." I trailed off, still very unsure of this. "I think
there was a compliment in there. Somewhere. But I still don't appreciate it."

"I can understand that."

"Maybe I should come up with a meaner nickname for you," I
teased, trying to move on.

"Because calling me ancient wasn't mean enough?"

"It was 'old man' actually," I corrected. "And at least it wasn't a
literal bug."

"True," he admitted, still looking rather guilty. "How about I
come up with another nickname?"

I paused, lips pressing together. "How about just use my name?"

"But where's the fun in that?"

I couldn't help but laugh, hating how effortlessly I had *almost* forgiven him. "You'll have to make it a really good nickname."

He opened his mouth to reply, when a cat from the villa pushed in between us, rubbing its head and neck against Nico's arm.

Nico tsked. "What do you want? I don't have any food for you." But instead of shooing the cat away, he rubbed its head, giving in to its little feline demands.

It wasn't until he had the cat scooped up into his arms that I interrupted, "What happened to hating the cats?"

"Annoying," he admitted. "They've clawed their way to my heart." Then he smiled at me, a self-satisfied look spread wide across his face. "Almost like somebody else I know."

Doubles Partners with Benefits? Rumoured Lovebirds Scottie Sinclair and Nico Kotas Announce Partnership at Wimbledon

Fans were shocked today when tennis players Scottie Sinclair and Nico Kotas announced their joint return to the world of tennis, both in the singles and the mixed doubles category, with the competition beginning next week.

In recent weeks, the two were spotted arriving on the Greek island of Rhodes, and rumours of a relationship set the internet ablaze, especially after sportswear brand ELITE launched its summer campaign with the two athletes looking rather cosy together.

Now, with their return to the grass confirmed and a mixed doubles attempt, fans are left wondering what this means for the suspected couple.

The move is surprising for Kotas, who historically has kept a low profile compared to the scandalous Sinclair, who herself is returning after a ban from tennis due to doping.

Only time will tell if this partnership spells success, but we suspect fans won't be complaining about any extra action on or off the court.

CHAPTER TWENTY-NINE

Nico
Lullabies – CHVRCHES

N ico, how has your gameplay changed since your recovery?" A reporter in a sea of many inched forward, his phone held out in his hand to capture my words. The hush over the packed room continued, the only noise the incessant clicking of a camera intent on capturing every moment.

I adjusted uncomfortably in my seat, squirming again under the spotlights of the press conference. "I . . . worked on my movement and footwork, making them more precise and efficient. We've also done a lot of work on my serve, adapting my playing style to be more strategic."

Jon, sitting farther down the table from me, leaned forward to his mic. "Nico's recovery has been a collaborative effort. In addition to enhancing his serve, we've also worked on developing a more strategic game plan. The injury allowed us to reassess his playing style, and I have no doubt that these changes will make him a stronger competitor in the upcoming tournament."

I nodded my head to Jon. "What he said."

A small murmur of laughter filled the room, relieving the tight knot in my stomach. I had never liked these pre-competition press conferences. The fear of saying the wrong thing always took control, making me look like a grumpy and mumbling idiot. The journalist said a quick thank you before sitting back down as a hundred voices yelled out for attention, the battle for their morning headline recommencing.

We'd been in London for a week. Time that was supposed to be spent preparing and adjusting to the summer weather had turned into the biggest media circus I'd ever seen. From the moment we landed, photographers chased Scottie and me down. Apparently, ELITE had started their campaign to coincide with the beginning of the competition, and the internet was alight once again with the speculation that we were together.

This was one of the most chaotic press conferences I'd ever been a part of, journalists fighting each other in the pit to ask another question. A winner from the crowd was picked, and an older man stood up. My lips pressed together at the sight of the Daily Tea logo clear on the press pass that hung around his neck.

"Scottie," he grumbled, looking down at the notes in his hands. "Who are you wearing today?"

I, and the rest of the room, turned to look at Scottie to find her rolling her eyes at yet another stupid and sexist question. I'd been asked about my return, my training, what had made me want to return to the sport. She was asked about her clothing or if she was missing partying or if she regretted burning the yacht. Jon moved that one along before she could answer.

"This is from ELITE's spring collection." She smiled somewhat politely, although I could still read the ire in her eyes.

"Would you be interested in doing another collaboration collection with them in the future?"

Her smile wavered, and I wondered to myself how much longer we had until we could escape this madness. "I guess so."

When the room immediately broke back out in its usual noise, I leaned over to her, placing one hand on the microphone, the other on her shoulder. Her long blonde hair fell over her shoulder as she leaned in to listen. Being this close to her, her face inches away from mine, was the closest we'd been since that night in the kitchen.

A small teasing smile broke out on my lips as I whispered, "Why don't they ask you what brand of underwear you're wearing and get it over with?"

She pulled back with a loud laugh, her head flung back as she snorted, before remembering how many people had a camera on us. But for a moment, I didn't care. All I cared about was the momentary joy in her blue eyes, the curve of her pink lips, the sound of her laughter. Our instruction from Jon was to look friendly, almost together. Feed the media a little something, without telling them anything at all. I didn't like it, but it was what we agreed to do with ELITE.

"One last question," Jon said into the microphone. "These two still have another round of practice to go."

An attendant nodded, looking around the group before picking another man. Tall and thin, with beady eyes. A chill ran down my back under his assessment.

Silence fell as he spoke. "Nico, you've been very vocal throughout your career about your feelings on doping in the sport. Has that changed since this"—he pointed a pen between Scottie and me—"partnership has begun?"

A hot rage built at his words, and I was almost ready to explode at him when, out of the corner of my eye, I watched Scottie stiffen, her back straightening as her gaze dipped to the table. It quelled, the sight of her extinguishing the rage like an ocean wave crashing in, washing it away.

"No comment on that," Jon said for me, but I stretched out a hand to stop him.

"Hold on, I'd actually like to answer that one."

He eyed me suspiciously, issuing a silent warning.

I turned, my gaze finding the reporter who was still standing, staring him down for a moment before I responded. "I've always been passionate about a clean, fair competition in tennis. That hasn't changed," I began. "It's important to remember that behind every player, there's a team of coaches and support staff who play a crucial role in our careers. There is a constant immense pressure on athletes, and it's not always easy to strike the right balance between pushing for excellence and ensuring our wellbeing."

I thought of her hand, now healed well enough for her not to bandage it, but the memory of finding her on that court still fresh. I remembered the stories we had shared that night in Lindos, of fad diets and burgers that tasted like freedom. I thought of what her father had done to her; and even worse than that, I thought of what I didn't know, what she hadn't told me.

"I've seen firsthand how the line between tough training and potential harm can blur. My feelings on doping haven't changed, but I'm also committed to keeping this sport free of abuse and maintaining the wellbeing of the athletes that take part. Thank you."

The room erupted into questions, but I ignored them. All three of us stood up, exiting to the left. I didn't look at the crowds, the odd shouted-out question on whether we were dating or sleeping together finding my ear. I kept my head ducked down as we left, following an attendant into an empty waiting room.

"So how did we do?" I asked as the door clicked closed behind us, the noise of the hotel outside instantly turning quiet.

"Alright by my standards." Jon shrugged, looking around the grand room, before his eyes found a fresh pot of coffee sitting on a trolley beside the door. He looked over at me as he poured himself a takeaway cup. "You did well with that last question."

"Thanks." I looked at Scottie. She seemed smaller than usual, like all the questions had reduced her down in size. I ignored the pull, the need to wrap my arms around her and feel her heartbeat in her chest. "Can we pre-approve the questions next time so Scottie doesn't have to deal with so much sexist bullshit?"

Jon nodded. "We might have to."

"It's alright," Scottie said, sitting down on one of the vintage sofas. "I'm used to worse. And I don't want to get on their bad side, not with the competition."

My answer was immediate, the same reaction every other time she'd said those four words. "You shouldn't be. Those questions weren't worth your time."

I hated it, their disrespect for her, her being used to it. It made me sick every time she shrugged it off. That it was so commonplace for her, she didn't even fight it anymore.

"It's what they expect from me," she replied, her voice almost nonchalant, but I could see it in her eyes, the annoyance at each question. They had all chipped away at her, slowly eroding her confidence. The last thing we needed was her getting any pre-game jitters. That could throw everything off.

"Well, they should expect more," I grumbled, turning to pace some more. Silence fell over the room, the only noise Jon's slurping of his coffee.

"I'll go get the car, then we need to head to practice," he said, finishing up his cup. I nodded in reply as he slipped from the room.

He had just disappeared when Scottie's gaze snapped to me, her brows pressed together in confusion. "What did you mean back there?" she asked, before repeating my words. "'I've seen how the line between tough training and potential harm can blur.'"

"Exactly what I said."

Her pink lips pressed together is dissatisfaction. "You don't think it gives too much away?"

"No, I don't think it gives enough away."

"Nico." Hearing my name on her lips, I could only think of the night in the kitchen. Her legs wrapped around my waist, pulling me in. Her mouth at my ear, moaning my name. "This isn't your secret to tell."

I rubbed my hands over my face, falling onto the sofa opposite her. I leaned forward, my elbows propped up on my knees for support. "Don't you think I know that? Don't you think things like this remind me what he has gotten away with? What he did to you?"

"You can't hint like that again," she pressed. "It's too risky."

"It's too late for that. You're both here, everyone is already talking about it." Between the media and the comments I had caught offhand, everyone had their eyes glued to Scottie. Watching her every move with suspicion. Nobody had said anything directly to me about it until the press conference, but I knew the place was buzzing with the news of them both being here.

The great father-daughter duo, a drug scandal and a falling-out. Everyone wanted to know what had happened. How the daughter had betrayed her legendary father. Meanwhile, I knew the truth, and it was weighing heavier and heavier.

"I know. I hear it too. I'm the one in the changing room getting looks from all the other players. Every second question is about it, or something filler, like who did my bloody hair today. But at least the beauty questions aren't bringing him up again."

She ran her fingers through her hair, pulling the strands back from her face, uncovering the look of grief and stress etched across her features. I was fighting with her because she was so used to this, but I was taking her problem and making it my own. This was survival for her. I had to learn to respect that, and know when she really did need my help.

I took in a deep breath, reaching across the distance between us to take her hand. She looked up at me, questioning, as if she was trying to figure out what my next move was. Unable to hide the surprise on her face as I said, "I'm sorry."

"I know you mean well, Nico." Her hand squeezed in mine, her fingers so delicate despite the calluses. "But, please, remember this is what I want."

"I will, I promise."

"Car's here." Jon popped his head in the doorway before disappearing just as quickly.

We both pushed up to our feet as she dropped my hand; it felt so empty without her palm pressed to mine. She headed towards the door, but I reached out and grabbed her arm, getting her attention.

"I promise, any more questions like that, I won't answer." She nodded understandingly. "But if anyone says something to you, if anyone hurts you in any way, you tell me."

An eyebrow twitched up. "You can't beat them up, Nico. You'll get us kicked out."

"Not that, I promise." I shook my head. "But if somebody is rude to you, I need to know. We are expected to be friendly over the next few weeks, but I don't want to waste a single moment of my time playing nice with somebody who doesn't pay you the respect you deserve." My throat was entirely too dry by the time I finished, but I kept my eyes on her, pressing for an answer. "Promise?"

"I promise. Now, let's go before Jon adds an extra hour to practise."

I followed her out, staying close as we walked through the busy hotel reception. There were a few stray photographers waiting and they pushed forward, shouting questions at us. I ignored them completely, instead storming around Scottie, making sure to keep my shoulders broad and walk behind her, protecting her from their view as much as I could. As we stepped outside into the sunny London street, one of them ran up beside me, trying to push past to Scottie. Instead, I carefully shoved back, making sure not to knock him over, but ensuring a safe, respectful distance was kept.

When we reached the car, Jon already settled into the front seat, I leaned past her, my arm slightly grazing her, and opened the door. My world slowed as she looked up at me.

"Thank you," she mouthed to me before climbing inside, and something primal settled in my stomach, knowing that she was protected from those who would exploit even a simple image of her for their own gain.

In this car, next to me, she was safe. And safe my girl would stay. Even if she wasn't really mine . . . I was hers, ready when she was.

CHAPTER THIRTY

Nico
Eat Your Young – Hozier

"All I'm saying is, at least try to behave yourself," Jon gruffed, folding his paper back up as he straightened in the corner armchair. I eyed his reflection in the mirror as I attempted to tie my bow tie. Again. It was all for nothing when I caught a glimpse of my and Scottie's faces front and centre on the newspaper.

"I have no idea what you mean."

He raised a single eyebrow. "Press will be at the gala," he reminded me. "The last thing we need is more distractions before the tournament."

My fingers twisted the soft material, pulling it through the knot the way I was sure my father taught me, before it came out all wrong. I yanked at one side, almost tempted to give up and go with a tie. That had been the plan before Jon showed up five minutes ago, bow tie in hand, as he reminded us that the event was black tie.

"Again, no idea what you could be referring to."

And for once, it wasn't a lie.

It had been a busy few days since the press conference, too busy for any drama, with the day taken up with almost constant practice as we tried to attune to the local conditions. We'd each played a few matches in our own singles category and some as doubles partners. So far, they'd all gone well, both of us walking away victorious.

I turned my attention from the bow tie, taking a moment to focus on cuff links and watches and everything else this stupid event demanded. It was another thing ELITE had signed us up for, a charity event with a ticket price of $15k each that attracted everyone who was anyone before the stress and competition of Wimbledon began.

I'd always managed to avoid it, spending the evening in practice. But if ELITE said jump, we said how high, apparently.

"So, there isn't anything going on between you and Scottie?"

My back stiffened at the mention of her name, but somehow, I managed to keep my attention on my fingers, twisting to get the cuff links in position.

"Absolutely nothing," I confirmed. I certainly wasn't thinking about what happened in the kitchen. Or how well she had played a match yesterday, with a short white pleated skirt that held my attention almost the whole time. Or seeing her at breakfast this morning, her hair tied back, my hat on her head. She wore it like it had always belonged to her . . . just like I did.

"That's not what it looks like." He laid the newspaper flat on the table beside me, the headline staring back up at me.

Doubles Delight: Are Nico and Scottie Scoring On and Off the Court?

My blood ran cold as I scanned the photo. It was from a few days before, during a match that had been closed to the public—not that it mattered to anyone.

We had just won, Scottie hitting a dropshot over the net to secure the final set. I'd immediately run to her, dropping my racket as I wrapped my arms around her, pulling her feet off the ground and holding her close. I'd breathed her in, her unmistakable shampoo mixing with the sunshine happiness that had filled me up.

Winning had always made me happy, no matter how small the

stakes. The grind was so hard that anything was worth even a small celebration. But winning with her by my side felt like taking the gold at the Olympics over and over again.

And that was what they had captured, that moment of her in my arms. Two teammates congratulating each other. In reality, I'd been losing my grip and was releasing Scottie to the ground. The camera angle had caught one of my hands as it was hovering over her ass. God, I wish that were the case . . . If I had actually touched it, I'd still be trying to work the memory away, with either a merciless gym session or with my fist.

But, of course, that was the shot they had managed to capture.

"Isn't that what ELITE wants it to look like?" I moved on, tearing myself away from the photo.

Jon shrugged. "For the cameras, but I don't want this kind of distraction during the tournament."

"She's my teammate. Didn't you want us to get along?" Annoyance had begun to creep in at the edges. I'd always hated this plan, never wanted to play this up for the tabloids or ELITE for that matter. But I'd gone along with it, and now they were exploiting us for every move, every gesture. And if they really knew what was going on, how I felt about her, they'd use that too.

"So, there *is* something."

Jon's face was a twisted mix of delight and suspicion. The look threw me just enough off-balance that the white lie almost choked me, and the knowing curve of his lips grew. I stumbled to respond, but found myself cut off by a knock at the door.

"There's nothing." As my back was turned to him, a look of panic crossed my face, a slackened jaw exhausted from the tightness that had appeared the moment he laid the newspaper out. How much longer could I keep pretending?

He shouted again as I headed towards the door, "You know I work for you and Scottie, not ELITE. I'd keep your secret."

I ignored him, and instead, with a deep inhale, tried to pull myself together, only to be winded by the sight of Scottie on the other side of the door. Her blonde hair was swept up off her bare shoulders, collarbones exposed as the dress plunged down to her breasts, revealing just enough to drive me to the edge of insanity before the gold sparkling material began, hugging every curve of her body. My hand ached to reach out, memorise those curves.

She pursed her lips together, a hand on her hip. "They've waxed every single part of me. I'm pretty sure I now have the sleek, aero-dynamic skin of a baby seal."

My brain did not know how to process that new information, still struggling to catch up with the sight of her before me. She looked up at me strangely, her blue eyes darkened by eyeshadow, before I got the message and conjured up enough brain power to step aside. Any self-awareness I had reclaimed instantly evaporated as she stepped past me, a leg stepping out of the high slit, reveal-ing yet more perfect, soft, bare skin, before meeting the thin black straps of her tall heels.

This dress had to be designed by Satan himself, every inch against Scottie's soft skin, begging me to sin.

"Baby seals are fluffy, Scottie," Jon corrected as I closed the door, desperately trying to fight the urge to kick him out and find out how easy it would be to rid that dress from her body. See what she was wearing underneath.

"All I know is I'm counting the hours until I'm free of this dress."

If Jon would leave it could be seconds . . .

I remained at a safe distance, leaning in the doorway, my eyes taking in every inch of her. The dress sparkled gold against her skin, which had also been given a golden shimmer, lighting her as she moved around the room. The straps sat delicately off her shoul-ders, as if they had fallen off, but it was just another thing to add to the list of reasons that dress would kill me.

"What do you think?" She spun around the centre of the room to face me.

"You look . . ." I trailed off, unable to think of a single word that encapsulated how she looked. Was there even a word that would give her beauty the justice it required? She was starlight personified, gorgeous, and golden, and beautiful. Beyond beautiful.

"Like an Oscar trophy. I know." She huffed, turning back to look at Jon, who had made himself comfy on my bed. "That beauty team you hired was torturous."

"What do you ladies say? Beauty is pain?" Jon pushed himself up from the bed. "I need to go grab something from my room, then I'll get the car round the front so we can head over." We both nodded in his direction.

Jon looked at me, raising his head slightly, a finger indicating to his neck. "Nico, your bow tie."

I recalled my abandoned task, my hands pulling at the two ends of the material. Jon left the room as I headed over to the mirror, taking up my old position. But this time, it was Scottie who offered a tempting distraction from the task at hand. After a moment, my memory still uncooperative, I sighed loudly, pulling the bow tie entirely off my neck, and turned around, determined to find the regular tie I had been planning on wearing, only to find Scottie behind me.

"Here, let me." She laid a hand out between us, but I only shook my head.

"I can do it."

Her lips, which had been painted a dark seductive red, turned up into a smirk. "Do it wrong, more like. Come on, one of us should look decent for this thing."

I narrowed my eyes at her for a moment before relenting, and handing her the tie. She looped it around my neck, taking a step closer to me as she did. My body almost went into fight-or-flight mode at the closeness, the gravity of the attraction to her too over-whelming.

"You shouldn't do that, you know?" I said, trying to distract my-self, desperate to look anywhere but her face, with her attention fixed on her fingers at my throat, her lip pulled in between her teeth.

"What? Tie men's bow ties? Does it emasculate you?"

"You shouldn't pretend like you aren't going to be the most beautiful person in the room tonight," I continued as her hands released, her work finished. I kept my eyes on her. "I think you've been sent here to torture me because Jon just warned me not to make a scene, but I already can't keep my eyes off you. No one else will be able to either, and I just want to keep you all to myself."

She tilted her head, not stepping away, not moving a muscle. "Weren't you taught to share your toys, Nico?"

I locked my jaw, hating how she thought about herself. My hand rose to her, setting under her chin to keep her eyes on me, my touch soft but demanding. "You're no toy, Scottie. You're a goddess in that dress. I don't know how I am supposed to keep my hands to myself all evening."

There would be so many people at this event, and every single one would have a camera in their pocket, waiting to capture one moment of weakness from me, from us. And she was dressed like temptation incarnate.

"Tell me not to, Scottie, and I'll be good." My voice grew husky, the need to close the gap and touch her growing more intense.

"Nico, I—"

A knock on the door cut off her reply.

Neither of us moved. Neither of us looked away.

She just had to say no. Tell me she didn't want me to touch her and tonight . . . tonight would go more smoothly if I just knew that was what she wanted. Then I could keep my hands to myself.

"Well?" I challenged, my eyes scanning every inch of her face.

In one movement, she'd stepped forward, her hands going to the back of my neck, and her lips met mine. For one moment it was soft, the next I was lost in her, my hands skimming down her curves, hungrily pulling her body to mine. I'd found the slit in her dress, my hand sliding up her bare thigh so I could have her even closer.

One second we stood apart, the next, we were tangled up in each other like we had been starved of touch. She pulled at my hair as my hand explored every curve, desperate to commit her body to memory after the sudden, cruel separation last time.

Her lips pressed against mine, teeth grazing as we lost ourselves, lost our minds, until another knock pulled us apart, bringing us crashing back down to earth. She looked from the door and grinned up at me, blue eyes utterly wild.

"Nobody can see," she instructed, still trying to catch her breath.

I nodded, barely understanding her meaning, my brain buzzing with lust. All I could think about was the feel of her lips, my hand wrapped around her thigh, how much I never wanted to leave this bedroom.

Not as long as she was inside too.

She leaned past me for a moment, looking in the mirror as she patted her hair back into place and fixed her makeup, before her hand slid into mine and she practically dragged me across the room toward the door. She paused as we reached it, her eyes examining me.

Her hands went to my neck, fixing my bow tie, pulling my shirt straight before her fingers met my lips, and rubbed slightly at the edges.

"Lipstick." She smiled, with an all-knowing grin.

"We could tell Jon it's the new fashion," I managed, wishing I could replace the stain, make her press her perfect lips to every inch of my skin, and leave the imprint of her lipstick for everyone to see. Let her claim me.

She crooked an eyebrow up, eyes lighting at the devilish idea, before wordlessly she pulled the door open, and we stepped out, not at all expecting the storm we were walking straight into.

CHAPTER THIRTY-ONE

Scottie
Slut! – Taylor Swift

Nico ran his fingertips along the soft, sensitive skin of my bare thigh, the slit of my dress leaving me exposed as we sat together in the back of the car. His gaze was pinned to the back of Jon's head in front of him, giving absolutely nothing away.

Meanwhile, I was working extra time to keep myself composed as his hand pressed into my skin, fingers making small teasing circles as it slowly inched up the length of my thigh. I'd known this dress would come back to haunt me.

He looked incredible. Dressed in a designer black suit, the material perfectly tailored to every swell and dip of his body, accentuating the muscles of his arms, the broadness of his shoulders. Even just looking at him was a damn meal.

Nobody can see.

The words continued to echo around my head. His touch had me caving in to the need, pretending like I hadn't tried to deny him less than a week ago.

His hand reached the top of the slit, dangerously high up my thigh, and his fingers slowly traced the seam, leaving delicate touches that sent shivers along my leg. The proximity of him was not lost on me. One small slip, an accidental break from the car driver, and his hand could slip much farther up. I couldn't tell if I was praying for an emergency stop or not.

"You know the script. Make sure you walk around the room, interact with people. We don't need to make any more enemies," Jon began to grumble from the front seat. Thankfully, his attention was still on his phone as he talked to us, only twisting his head so we could hear him.

Nico's hand remained at the top of my thigh, the rough pads of his calloused hands against my skin just as intoxicating as our kiss in the hotel room had been. That had surely been a mistake, but one I hadn't quite brought myself to regret. Not yet, anyway.

Being that close to him as I tied his bow tie, watching his throat bob as he so obviously tried to control himself. The heat burned in his eyes as he looked at me, and only me. And not to mention I'd been on edge ever since the kitchen. It had been months since I'd had any action at all. And endless practice and work with this surly, muscled giant had left me with a craving so intense I was floored by a simple look from him. There was no question I was weak for him, desperate and hungry. And this itch, the one that had been growing in intensity since yoga on the beach and running through Lindos in the rain, only to erupt all over a kitchen counter . . . well, I was primed for a good scratching.

"Me, talking to people?" Nico said. If he was enjoying teasing me, there was no indication, with the usual stoniness to his voice.

Jon ruminated for a moment, all the while Nico continued to draw tiny tortuous, teasing loops. I almost counted them in my head alongside my breaths, one hand on the handle of the passenger door, as if it were my grip on the situation. "You stay silent. Let Scottie do the talking."

I could barely maintain my composure, let alone form a sentence.

My gaze locked with Nico's, a cocky grin spread wide on his lips. "Because there's no issue with that plan."

I swallowed, before trying my best to keep my voice level, not letting on to anyone in the car about the heat building between my legs, the need and anticipation rising. "I'm not sure I enjoy that implication."

"I'm sure you'll find a way to deal." Then his fingers achingly slid under the hem of the slit, pushing up the sparkling material. My cheeks burned red as I readjusted, trying to give him more access while also slyly placing my small handbag on top of my knees, to hide from any prying eyes.

His fingers slid under the material, and my eyes closed as I tried to bottle up this feeling, this desperate need for him. I attempted to find my control in the situation, but that was long gone. My lips parted, hand clenching the satin material of the handbag as I held it in place, waiting and waiting for his fingers to graze at my centre. The feel of his hand up my skirt, exploring high up my thigh, nearly drove me to the edge itself.

I needed his touch. I fought the urge to move my hips again, slide down the seat and move him along already. But it would be too obvious, too exposed, so I didn't dare move an inch, instead focusing on my breathing, keeping it level and stifling every noise that threatened to erupt the moment he touched me again.

His hand moved over my thigh, my legs automatically parting for him. A hiss of breath escaped him as he slowly inched up, the slit of my dress fully spread open, one leg out. Then suddenly, I felt his body freeze and stiffen beside me.

"Fuck," he swore, his voice barely audible. Barely but enough that when the radio fell silent at the same time, the entire car heard. Quicker than I realised a person could move, his hand was gone, and my legs pressed back together.

"What was that?" Jon asked, a wild panic taking over me as my face burned red hot.

"Just something I saw on my phone. It's nothing." Nico's reply was suspiciously fast, but Jon must've had bigger fish to fry, and his attention soon turned back to his own phone, his fingers typing away furiously.

I managed to look at Nico and found his gaze already on me. I noted the shock, his gaze wild as he searched my face for an answer to a question he had not yet asked. Nervously, he licked his lips, glancing to the front of the car where Jon was locked in a conversation with the driver about the traffic. He leaned over, closing the gap between us. I leaned in, brows furrowed together. He met me in the middle, his lips at my ear.

"Are you . . ." he started, before he pulled back a little, letting out a breath as he blinked, trying to collect himself. He pulled in again, his voice low, even with the closeness.

When he finally spoke, a cruel smile curled onto my lips, a reminder of what I'd left behind in my hotel room, my stylist having forgotten to bring one crucial essential when it came to a dress like this.

"Are you not wearing underwear?"

And then, with nothing more than a knowing smile, a crook of a raised eyebrow, we pulled up outside the venue, a crowd of photographers waiting beside a short red carpet. The door next to me was opened from the outside, just as Jon shouted further instructions to us about conducting interviews, but I was still looking at him, and he sure as hell was still looking at me.

I leaned close again, taking in the smell of his aftershave, allowing myself to bask in the scent for a moment before I took my own chance to whisper in his ear.

"I guess you can find out later." And then I slipped out of the car, my legs shaking slightly under my weight as I was greeted by the flash of a camera and the roar of a nearby crowd of fans. After a tiny adjustment, I walked confidently away, a wide, satisfied grin on my face, knowing that his eyes were still burning into me as I left him.

THERE WASN'T MUCH opportunity for anything more once we were inside, with Jon shepherding us around to various sponsors and reporters, all but holding our hands through the conversations.

But we did as we were told. I turned on the charm, smiling and laughing at their jokes, while Nico stood beside me, almost entirely silent unless spoken to. The small talk was nearly unbearable, ranging from the placid "yes, it's so exciting to play at a Grand Slam again" to the more strange "no, I haven't tried that strange foreign vitamin you're suggesting would enhance my performance." Either way, eventually Jon would find a friendly excuse to exit and move us on to the next group. Apparently, he had a list.

That was when, while we shuffled through the busy room, making our way past friendly and unfriendly faces alike, Nico would lean into my ear and whisper little grumpy observations.

"I didn't think he would ever stop talking."

"I'm sure that pack of old women was checking me out."

"When do you think he will remember that he uses that vitamin for erectile dysfunction?"

Every time he'd have me laughing, distracting me from the room full of people waiting to take their slice, recharging me for another social interaction. I could feel the ghost of his hand on the small of my back, both of us needing the touch but not daring to risk it in such a public place.

"Have you noticed I was right?" he whispered in my ear as we moved away yet again, the noise of my forced laughter still ringing in the air as we turned away.

"About what?" I asked, trailing behind our coach, brows furrowed.

He smiled, his eyes connecting with mine for a moment. "That you're the most beautiful person in this room."

My brain short-circuited at the reminder of his words from before, body aching to feel his against mine again. I didn't have any time to respond before I was colliding into someone else's back. Nico's arm pulled me back, holding me steady and allowing me to find my footing.

"I'm so sorry," I stammered, my cheeks flushing with embarrassment, my grip on the champagne glass miraculous. I looked up, my eyes finding the familiar face of Imogen Foster. On instinct, I gulped.

Foster was a legend. Holding the highest number of Grand Slam wins of any player, period. I'd grown up watching her matches, been inspired by her delicate movements on the French and Spanish clay court, the battleground where her talent excelled the most. I'd met her once before, in passing with my father, but seeing her now, ten years retired, she was still intimidating.

Her dark eyes were assessing, as if to recognise me too, before a flicker of kindness appeared as she chuckled, her Australian accent clear. "No worries at all. These gatherings can get a bit chaotic."

Jon beckoned us yet again to another group of unfamiliar faces. I yearned to fight him off, stay a little longer, but I was so shocked to see her, reduced to a fangirl, that I just apologised nervously again before turning away. Nico stayed behind me, his presence a reassuring anchor, as he also greeted Foster before following me.

We headed towards the cluster of older men engaged with Jon who, ever the master of introductions, began the process. "Gentlemen, may I present Scottie and Nico, two remarkable talents in the world of tennis. Scottie is making an astonishing comeback, and Nico, well, I'm sure you're more than familiar with him."

The crowd looked us up and down like we were dinner. Jon went around the group, somehow knowing every single person's name.

They fell into easy conversion, Jon repeating the same jokes he'd already told ten times.

"Scottie, is it true what they say about you?" one of the men, who had been introduced as Alister, said with a crooked smile.

I took a long, necessary sip from my champagne. "I'm not sure. They say a lot of things about me."

Nico grumbled again, his shoulder rubbing against mine. "Yeah, Alister, what is it they say?"

"Just, you know, your travels around Europe. I heard you had quite a lot of fun." My stomach twisted uncomfortably, reading into the look that spread across his thin face . . . I could see the tabloid headlines all over again, but that didn't matter. I had nothing to be ashamed of—not that, anyway. If this man thought he could bring it up without even a simple hello, he had another think coming.

I smiled politely but very plainly. "That was a great time, but I'm happy to be back competing now."

He leaned over, close enough that I could smell the whisky on his breath. I felt Nico's body stiffen beside me as Jon tried to pull him into another conversation, but he only grunted a response. I knew he was still listening. I was never alone.

"Oh, come on now, that doesn't mean you can't have a good time."

I pulled away from him. "What makes you think I'm having a horrible time?"

Alister talked again. "All I'm saying is, it must be quite a bore."

I shook my head, a smile from Nico's joke still spread wide. "Not at all. I've got a doubles partner to keep me entertained now."

He read my expression, obviously thinking I was laughing with him instead of at him, and his drunken confidence grew. "Let me buy you a drink, for old times, Scottie."

I struggled to hold on to that edge of politeness. "I'm good, thanks. I've still got a full glass of champagne."

"Exactly, full. You've hardly touched it."

I refused again, before holding the glass up to my lips, and took the smallest sip to satisfy him. His beady eyes watched every moment.

"Unlike some people," Nico muttered.

I somehow managed to force a smile to my lips, tilting my head to my coach at the other side of the group. "I'm savouring it. Jon will have my neck if I show up hungover tomorrow."

"I insist." Alister's voice rang around my skull like a headache, and I knew I had just about had enough of this ass. There was no way I would be going anywhere alone with him.

"I'm fine," I snapped, before remembering Jon's words. This was a public gala, full of people who could decide any number of things about my career. I had to behave. "Go get yourself something," I suggested politely. "I'll wait here." I would disappear so fast he'd wonder if I'd ever actually existed.

"Maybe I'd like the company." He leered, and I was too disgusted by the look he was giving me to notice his arm curling around me, pulling me into him. I yelped, trying to wiggle out of his grip, but his hold only tightened, fingers digging into my arm.

"I suggest you keep your hands to yourself." Nico's hand was instantly on my arm, thankfully pulling me out of Alister's grasp, before stepping in front of me. And his darkened focus narrowed on Alister. "She said no."

"Nico." My hand found his large shoulder, urging him back, but instead he stepped closer to Alister.

"I was only offering her a drink," Alister spluttered, throwing his hands up.

"I think you've already had enough for all of us." Nico's voice was low, the tone threatening, even if the words weren't. "Go find someone else to bore."

Alister's brows pressed together. "Do you know who you are talking to?"

"Doesn't matter who the hell you are. If you lay another fin—"

Jon interrupted before Nico could issue his threat. "Alister! I have to say, have you tried the thirty-year-old Highland Park?"

Alister turned away from Nico and faced Jon, apprehension still ringing in his voice. "Why, yes, I'm quite the fan."

Jon continued acting very friendly toward Alister, stepping in front of Nico and me, his body practically a wall separating us from him. I took the moment to pull Nico back, stand alongside him, my arm wrapping around his as if to ground him to me. "I think there's a bottle behind the bar with both our names on it," Jon said, then his voice slowed to signal to us. "You know, to thank you for the deal you helped set up with ELITE."

"Oh, well," Alister grumbled, seeming a little confused, but Jon was persistent and convincing as he stepped forward, hand over the man's shoulder, and escorted him over to the bar.

"The last thing that man needs is another drink," I muttered to myself, still feeling entirely gross from the way he had touched me, his breath on my neck. I tried not to get mad that this man got a free pass, that he could touch me and get an expensive drink as compensation. All Jon had seen was Nico getting angry at some-body who was important to the brand that had given us our meal ticket, but if he did know, would his reaction have been different?

Jon's attention snapped my way, the warning in his eyes very clear. "And meanwhile, my tennis players can have a conversation between themselves about what is appropriate behaviour."

Nico pressed forward. "I think Alister is due that reminder him-self."

I stepped in front of Nico, pressing my hands to his chest, look-ing up at him. "Nico. Stop."

"No, he was . . ." Nico was full of rage, so much so that mine dis-appeared in order to ease his. We had just narrowly escaped mak-ing a scene; we didn't need to try again.

"He was what? Rude? That's all," I hissed. Around me, I could feel eyes directed my way, people murmuring and trying to figure out what's happened. His gaze found mine, the intensity in the storm of grey almost too much.

"No, he was being a sexist asshole. How can you be so calm?" His question left me dumbstruck, a slice of the anger I still had bubbling away under my skin very much redirected at him. I swallowed it down, washing it away with the rest of the champagne left in the flute. So much for savouring it.

I tilted my head in the opposite direction of the bar. "Come with me."

I eased away slightly, but he didn't move an inch. Instead, he frowned. "Where?"

I sighed, discarding my empty flute onto a passing waiter's tray. I let my hand slip into his, squeezing once with persistence. "Just come with me."

He turned again, watching Jon and Alister heading in the other direction toward the bar. I could sense his urge to follow, to really let that rage out of his system, but when I squeezed his hand again, his attention returned. I led us on, cutting through the busy crowd. I forced smile after smile as we passed some friendly faces, people calling our names for attention. We both made more than a few false promises to return, catch up or get a drink, and by the time we reached the edge of the crowd, my cheeks hurt from forcing a grin.

I kept walking, pulling him down a corridor, and when I thought we were far enough for the distance to be deemed safe from the crowd and any prying eyes, I opened the very first door I came across, pushed Nico inside, and closed it behind us. Darkness and the strong stench of bleach surrounded us until I found the light switch.

Nico's eyes searched around the small dark room, scanning

shelves of cleaning products, brooms, and mops propped up against the walls. "Why are we here?"

"You needed a moment to calm down."

"I don't get it." He let out a huff of air as he shook his head, the space between his eyebrows crinkling with frustration. "Aren't you mad?"

"I'm furious. But maybe you're taking up all the oxygen, there's none left for me."

His eyes scanned my face, the anger in his features soothing as his frustration relented. "I'm sorry, Scottie. The way he spoke to you like you were . . ."

"A piece of meat?" I snipped at Nico, a little harder than I'd meant to. "I'm aware."

His voice lowered, his own fury finally making way for mine, understanding what I needed. "Then he touched you and I just . . . I lost it."

I crossed my arms, suffocating down another bite of frustration. I didn't want to be squabbling in a cupboard over an asshole comment that, honestly, I had practise in handling. "So?"

"I didn't like him. Really didn't like how he spoke to you. Hated it when he thought he could touch you." His eyes didn't leave mine, burning with intensity.

"I wasn't the biggest fan of it either. But I can handle these things myself," I said. I had to admit, it was nice for somebody to have my back for once, to see how easily one person could make another feel like dirt and actually step in and call them out on it. My anger smoothed out at his protectiveness, the comfort of it invaluable, but not when it put everything at risk. Nico nodded in the dim light, the ancient lightbulb above us dimming.

"And what he was saying about Europe . . ." He trailed off, the firm line of his jaw becoming more pronounced as he tried to bite down that frustration. At least he was trying.

"He was teasing." I knew I was downplaying it for him, but if we got into a serious topic of all the sleazy things men had said to me since I'd grown boobs, we'd be in the cupboard all night.

"You know what he was implying." For a moment, I hated the way he looked at me, his eyes soft, lips crooked in a sad smile. It was pity. Pity I didn't want or need for a second. Something snapped, fuelled by that asshole grabbing me, by the thought that anyone thought I owed them anything because of my past.

"That I fucked my way around Europe? The tabloids get a lot wrong, Nico, but not that. I was doing whatever and whoever I wanted. He brought it up to sleaze, which is gross, but I won't be made to feel ashamed."

"You shouldn't be. I didn't mean it like that." He raised his hands, fingers spread out wide as he tried to calm the situation. "I'm sorry." I scanned his face, waiting for the judgement, the look of disgust at my admission, but it didn't appear. Instead, there was clear regret and confusion as he carefully attempted to navigate his way through this conversation. "I was just . . ."

I raised an eyebrow, a smirk hanging on my lips as I finished his thought for him. "Jealous."

"No." His answer was immediate, his brows pushed together in denial. I could see it then, the realisation that I was right, the strong line of his jaw setting.

"Liar." My challenge hung in the air, the line of my smile growing as the fact cemented itself as truth. I couldn't take my eyes from his, waiting for that delicious moment where he'd finally relent. Whether it had been entirely jealousy-fuelled, I couldn't say. That man had been acting like an ass, and quite frankly, he deserved worse than being shouted at by Nico. But after the hotel room and the car, and everything else that clearly lay between us, I knew there was more to his actions than just protectiveness. I knew he wanted me. And God, did I want him too.

His voice was a low murmur. "You don't deserve to be treated like that, Scottie."

"I know."

He lifted his arm, his hand hovering over the pale skin of my biceps, waving like he wanted to touch me, wanting that connection, but couldn't quite bring himself to it. "You deserve better."

"I know that too."

"I want to treat you better."

My smile wavered with the admission, realising that we were very much alone. Alone, in a darkened room. "Well . . . I don't see anyone around now."

A second passed. Then another. As if Nico's brain was on a delay and it needed a moment to catch up with the implication of my words. And then, his control finally snapped. He stepped forward, catching me in his embrace, before his lips smashed into mine like he couldn't bear any distance for a moment longer.

CHAPTER THIRTY-TWO

Scottie

bet u wanna – Sabrina Carpenter

My back was pressed up against the door, his hand sliding down my jaw, tilting my head up as his lips pressed hungrily against mine, all in a matter of a single heartbeat. My hands rose to his face, feeling his stubble against my palms as I pulled him close. Our mouths moved against each other, desperate and starving for a taste.

He pressed into me until there was no more space, our bodies hard against each other, grinding and needy. The feel of him against me only left me addicted to him, every inch of him hard from muscle and want.

His head pulled away from mine and I groaned, instantly missing the touch of his lips. I was quickly rewarded with hot, lingering kisses trailing across my jaw, his hand tilting my head as he needed it. He trailed down my neck, across my bare collarbone, and left me breathlessly moaning and panting.

My fingers pulled at his jacket, clawed at his clothing like I was trying dig my way to his naked skin, wanting to feel the heat of him against my own fingertips, wanting to trace every ripple of tight muscle, craving to find out how he tasted against my tongue.

"Nico." His name left my lips on a whine, aching at my core for more of him. His lips on my throat weren't enough. I needed all of him.

"Fucking love hearing you say my name." He spoke against my skin, as if he couldn't dare stop himself for a moment. "Need to hear you moan it."

"Make me, then."

His head lifted, my body instinctively following to keep him close. His eyes met mine, the grey darkened with need. His hand rose to my lips, the pad of his finger running slowly over the swollen bottom lip.

"I should've known you'd be so demanding." He smirked, and a knot yanked tight inside me as I pressed my thighs together, fighting the urge to rub them together and give myself any edge of pleasure.

"Show me how much you want me. Show me how desperate you are." He grinned, satisfied. I could see the power trip going straight to his head as he realised how much he was in control here, that I was too weak to fight him any longer. I wanted him, needed him to take control. If it meant the smallest bit of satisfaction from him, I'd do exactly as he said.

No question asked.

His left hand ran up my bare thigh, but he didn't play with me like he had in the car. This time, he wasted no time pushing up the sparkling material of my dress, the high leg slit giving him perfect access.

"Was this on purpose?" His grin turned curious as his hand reached between my legs, his middle finger teasing me as he moved forward. "Did you leave your panties at the hotel just to tease me?"

My legs struggled under the weight of my body, the teasing pleasure too much. I shook my head truthfully. I couldn't have expected this, but I didn't once regret it.

"I bet you did," he said as his finger found my clit, running small teasing circles around it. My eyes closed, breathing in as he spoke again. "Now I'm tempted to make you pay for it. Bend you over and fuck you from behind until you can't stop yourself from screaming my name. I bet you'd enjoy me using you like that."

Another moan escaped me as his movements grew in momentum. I couldn't help myself as I began to grind against his hand, needing more and more pressure as the pleasure began to build.

He leaned forward, his lips leaving another trail of kisses against my bare neck, leading up to my ear, where he whispered in between kisses, "Let me make one thing clear. You're mine from now on, Scottie. I'll do anything for you. I'll treat you like a princess and a pretty little whore. Whatever you want. But I don't share."

His name on my lips was a breathy, strangled plea for more. I could feel his grin against my skin as his hand moved again, finding my entrance, two fingers lined up.

"I need you. Please," I begged for more. For him.

"You're so wet for me. I wonder how perfect your pussy is. Wet and tight and needy," he teased, refusing to move any further. I desperately ground against his fingers, pressing in, but every time I did, he pulled back a little, leaving me more frustrated, crying for more.

"Nico, please," I begged, pushed to my limit. My usually strong body felt reduced to a fragile little thing too close to snapping. He was the rock I was clinging to, absolution pulling me in the other direction.

"Look at you, legs spread for me, desperate to ride my fingers. Is this what you want? A dirty quickie in a cupboard?"

"I want . . ." I could hardly form the words. "I want you."

"Do you know what I want?" A devilish smile curled onto his lips. "I want to fuck the name of every other man you've ever had out of your brain. I want to be the only one you can remember taking this pretty cunt. The only one you want."

"You are . . ." I could feel how embarrassingly wet I was, his fingers working my pussy in every way except the way I needed. "I only want you."

"Prove it," he challenged, his fingers realigning at my entrance. I wasted no time pressing down, and this time, instead of moving away, his hand pressed inside of me. He forced me to work, making me fuck myself on him.

I opened my eyes and held his gaze, his eyes dark and challenging. "Prove you can take me, Scottie. Show me how good you'll be for me."

I ground on his fingers, low and deep, my pussy aching and stretching to take them. I couldn't stop the loud moans escaping my mouth, his name, every curse under the sun following it. His other hand found my mouth, closing over it to muffle the noise.

"Keep going," he demanded, as if it was something I could control. I felt him working his fingers inside of me, pressing and massaging against my G-spot as wave after wave of pleasure crashed against me. I moved faster and faster, growing greedier for the satisfaction that was building.

"You are so fucking beautiful like this," he crooned, the mood changing. My attention pulled to his face again, finding his eyes soft, the smile on his lips one of disbelief. His hand lifted from my mouth, wiping a strand of hair from my face. The moment was delicate, like the mask had slipped, and I was seeing the smallest hint of what was hiding behind. It only made me want him more.

I'd never felt like this for anyone. All the hookups and flings; they had nothing on Nico Kotas and this cupboard. Not from the way he was touching me, his obvious need, and how fucking special he made me feel. Like I was made for him, a precious thing he wanted not to keep or lock away, but to let shine.

Then he did the most despicable thing. He pulled away, leaving me a whimpering mess. His fingers removed, and I almost screamed at him, would've done so, if that dark look hadn't returned to his face, challenging me not to say another word.

His fingers rose to my mouth. "Clean," he commanded. "And taste."

My lips opened, mouth taking whatever he gave me without question. As he instructed, I greedily tasted myself on his fingers. He watched me, his breathing deep, lips parted on a breath. Then he rewarded me with the sight of him on his knees before me.

He kneeled in between my legs, his hands underneath my dress, easing the material up and out of the way. He unwrapped me. Slowly. Painfully. One look at his face and his devilish grin told me it was on purpose.

"Please," I begged, his hand snaking around my leg, pulling my right over his shoulder, opening my legs for him.

He looked up at me, his eyes hungry. "Are you going to beg me to taste you? Are you going to beg like a needy brat?"

"Yes. Please, I need . . ."

"What do you need?"

"I need your mouth."

"And . . ." His spare hand rose up to my pussy, trailing again between my legs, teasing. "Where do you want my mouth?"

I almost cried out as he leaned forward, kissing my thighs, trailing his lips, biting and grazing his teeth on the sensitive skin. My hand found his hair, fingers knotting.

"Show me where you need my mouth, Scottie. Use me." He no sooner said the words than I pulled his hair, moved his head to my centre, and pressed him to my pussy. He didn't need to be told twice, his tongue licking, mouth sucking, my hips grinding against his face as I tried to open my legs as wide as I possibly could for him.

My eyes rolled back, moans escaping me, his name delicious on my tongue, his hair between my fingers. Pleasure built higher as his finger joined his mouth, pushing hard back inside me, moving with my hips. I could feel him moan against me, the heat of his lips, the grip of his other hand on my hip, holding me close to him. I gripped the nearest surface, holding on like I was holding onto the edge of release that was building, the tightness squeezing between my legs as I worked against his fingers.

He didn't stop when I whispered to him that I was close; instead he intensified his efforts, just as hungry for my orgasm as I was. I was desperate and close and needy, living for every lick and suck and grind. And then it crashed into me, my legs weakening under my weight, but he held me up with his shoulders and the support of his free hand, lapping up every moment of my orgasm, feeling me grow tight against his fingers.

When he pulled away, his grey eyes were incredibly bright in the dim light, his lips pulled into a slack, satisfied smile as he said, "I'm going to need you to do that again."

CHAPTER THIRTY-THREE

Scottie

History Of Man – Maisie Peters

There was something cooling in the June air, a breeze coming from the Thames. After the small supply closet, followed by a quick escape through the busy ballroom, I was more than thankful for the cool wind on my rosy cheeks. Nico had disappeared to find the valet and get us out of there. We'd both agreed we'd had enough for one night. Enough small talk and sucking up to people with their father's and grandfather's name.

I hadn't had a chance to overthink what had happened in the cupboard, but now that I was alone outside the gala, I had plenty of time for it.

Nobody could know. That was the one rule of all of this going on between us. They could speculate, take photos and use them to sell their cheap trainers and gym clothes. That was going to happen whether we were really together or not. But they couldn't know the truth of it.

The second they did, I feared they'd strip me of a part of myself I wasn't willing to give away or sell any longer. I'd never been in love, always playing fast and loose with my reputation because there was nothing at stake, nothing to protect or to keep just for myself. But now there was Nico, and my heart that beat too quickly when he was around, and the growing anxiety that it was bound to get broken with so much at risk.

It wasn't only my reputation at stake anymore, something I treated with frivolity, used as a weapon. It was my heart.

"Scottie." I knew that accent. Knew immediately whose voice said my name. I'd heard it a thousand times. I'd heard it in my old kitchen, telling me not to overreact. I'd heard it on the phone on the beach in Rhodes. I'd heard it growing up, yelling at me to get my serve right. I turned too quickly and found my father. His dark brown eyes stared down, lips pressed into a thin, assessing line as he took me in. After two years of only seeing me in tabloid photos paired with scandalous headlines, stumbling out of clubs in the arms of strange men, me wearing skirts inches too short or dresses too revealing, it must've caught him off guard.

"Dad." The word slipped out from between my lips. Matteo. His name was Matteo.

"It's good to see you." His arms moved from his side, reaching forward as if to wrap around and pull me into an embrace, of all things. I took a step back, keeping my eyes on him. He inhaled a sharp breath and let his arms relax again, apparently getting the message.

I was frozen to the spot, throat dry as I searched for the right words, but all I could think was how much older he looked, how much thinner. His hair, once a pure black, was now heavily salted with grey, and the thin lines around his eyes had grown more defined. He looked so frail compared to how I last remembered him. In the middle of the kitchen, standing powerful in front of the island counter, his body trying to block the evidence from my view as he still fought to hide the truth of what he had done to me.

"How are you doing?" he asked, still looking disappointed that I'd moved away from him.

My hands curled into fists. "I'm fine. What are you doing here?"

"I was invited."

I forced my reply out through gritted teeth. "I mean Wimbledon. Why are you back?" I thought back to our phone call. His attitude, the bargaining. He wanted me away from Nico and to go back to training with him. "I told you to stay away."

He shrugged, like it was so simple. "And I told you to come to London."

I laughed at the irony, motioning my arms around the tall limestone buildings, the busy London street just ahead of us. Walk for five minutes in any direction and you'd find yourself at any London landmark. "I'm here now, aren't I?"

"Not what I meant." A bitter smile curled onto his lips as he pressed his hands to his temples in what I was sure was supposed to be disappointment. "I was willing to train you again, you know."

My jaw slackened as I pulled back again, and I looked at him, as if to wait for the punchline to the joke he had clearly just made. When it didn't deliver, my shock turned to incredulousness. "Are you out of your fucking mind?" I barked another laugh, leaning forward as a disbelieving smile grew. "You really think I'd come back after what you did?"

His eyes narrowed on me. "You're my daughter. I know what's best for you."

Oh, he was a real comedian now. I wondered if he had an entire stand-up set planned.

"You think ruining my career—drugging me—is what's best for me? Jesus, I can't wait for your guide to raising children."

His face remained stony, not seeing the situation the same. "Raising a child and a winning athlete are not the same thing."

"Is that all I was to you?" My question hung in the air a moment too long, as if he wasn't sure what to say. In the end, he left it unanswered. But it didn't matter. I could see it in the bob of his throat, the way he shifted from foot to foot. I was his daughter, but I was more a legacy, another thing to sit in his award cabinet and look sparkly. He couldn't even admit it, but I knew.

He coughed, clearing his throat. Taking a step forward, pointing a finger down, he started again. "If you want to win, Scottie, you've got to be willing to do anything."

"I was willing." I ground the three words out as if it was painful. Painful that he didn't see that I had given it everything I had.

He raised a single eyebrow. "Clearly, you weren't."

The implication was enough to turn my rage up from a simmer to boiling. "It doesn't count if you cheat. That is not winning, that's not what competition or tennis is about. I don't want to win if it means breaking the rules to get there. If that level of desperation is truly what it takes to win, then you're right, I don't have it. And I don't want it either."

He let out a loud sigh, as if he was already exhausted by me. Had considered the past all settled up. "Scottie, I was just trying to help."

"Help?" I hissed, almost disgusted at the word. "Help is giving somebody a hand when they need it, doing something useful. Not drugging them without consent for months."

"I couldn't watch it all slip past you again."

I turned at his words, trying to walk away before I was forced to listen to his excuses. But he followed me away from the venue, refusing to stop. "You were injured and slow, and it was risking everything we had been working towards. I've seen it before, the defeat creeping in. I wasn't going to let my daughter become a failure. Rossis don't quit."

A quitter. I thought of all the times I'd run, I'd given up. I'd run for two years, but the first time was that night, when he'd stolen everything from me, when every single thing I'd worked for turned out to be for nothing.

"I was never a quitter before you. You . . . you ruined everything."

"Ruined?" He barked a single laugh before his eyes narrowed, the mask of the frail father before me slipping, the hungry competitive beast rearing his head instead. "I gave you everything you have. You think you would have made it this far without me?"

A smile crooked on my lips. "I made it this far, despite you."

He took a single step forward, finger pointing down, his expression stony. "You only lifted that trophy because of me."

"And I lost it because of you." I shook my head, feigning disbelief with an almost laugh. "When are you going to give up? I'm not yours to play with anymore."

"As always, it's all about you, isn't it?" He shook his head, eyes stuck to me. "It can't be about anyone else."

"Then who?" I challenged, itching to really know why he was here, who had fallen into his grasp. "Who are you coaching? If you think I'm going to allow you to come back and ruin someone else's life, then you can think again. Whose life are y—"

I cut off as my eyes caught Dylan stepping out from the building, brown glossy hair down. Without any hesitation in her step, she headed straight over. My throat went dry as she stopped beside Matteo, a sly grin stretching across her blood-red lips.

"Hello, Scottie." Her voice was a light sing-song thing, but I felt anything but jovial. Instead, a pit of regret had ripped open, and I'd fallen through the cracks.

"I'm sure I don't need to introduce the two of you," Matteo said, but his voice sounded so distant, my attention and horror glued to the woman beside him. This was her revenge. She'd always blamed me for what happened, and I'd let her.

But by doing so, I'd sent her directly to the true enemy.

This was her revenge, but it was the wrong kind. It was payback for not telling the truth, for not being strong enough, for taking the easier path, pretending this only affected me when the ripples were still being felt. The consequence of my running.

"What are you doing with him, Dylan?"

Her eyebrows pressed together as she scoffed at my words. "I'm winning, of course."

I wanted to grab onto both her shoulders and shake her. Shake until she saw the truth and understood who it was she had partnered with. Everything he had done, everything he masterminded, what he had stolen from both of us.

"Did he tell you what he did?"

"He didn't do anything, Scottie. We all knew you'd go changing your story because you want to come back now and play like nothing happened."

My hands were shaking, fingers rubbing together as I searched for some control in all of this. I couldn't just scream out the words, but the secret was on the edge of my tongue. I knew if I said it aloud, it would be wasted. There was little chance she'd believe me before, and now that he'd sunk his teeth into somebody else, there was none.

"Dylan, you need to listen to her." Nico's firm voice was a welcome surprise, the noise wrapping me up, relaxing my tense muscles, even slightly. He appeared beside me, jaw set, his narrowed eyes set on Matteo.

"Nico, it's been a while." Matteo grinned at his former competitor.

"Not long enough, if you ask me." His voice was a soothing grumble as his attention slid to me, Nico's eyes searching, as if to ask if I was okay. I fought the urge to take his hand, root myself in his stability and protection, and instead, I simply nodded.

Dylan sighed. "And here's Prince Charming coming to her rescue." Her nose scrunched up as if the thought disgusted her.

"Dylan." Nico stepped closer to her. "You used to be better than this."

"You used to be better than working with a cheat, but I guess we all change."

"Now, shouldn't we be nice?" Matteo interrupted, his calm demeanour leaving me with hives. "Let's just play out on the court. I'm sure it will make for an excellent game."

I couldn't help but run my fingers through my hair in frustration. I refused to fall into this man's trap again. Refused to become a pawn in his game again. I refocused my attention on Dylan, taking a deep breath. "I swear right now, you don't deserve my help. But you can come find me when he fucks this all up for you."

"Sure, thanks for the offer," she dismissed, but all I could do was hope she would take me up on it, that she would get out earlier than I did.

"Enjoy your new coach." I turned around, meeting Nico's eyes and making sure he turned with me and didn't make more of a mess of this situation than it already was. I managed to control my pace, just fast enough to get away from them, but without looking like we were running for the hills.

"Enjoy fucking your doubles partner," Dylan shouted, louder than necessary. "Can't wait to see what kind of mess that gets you into."

We slipped into the back of a car so quickly I had to rely on Nico to confirm that it was the correct driver, desperate to get away, desperate to wrap myself up in him and pretend the rest of the world didn't exist.

Tie Break

CHAPTER THIRTY-FOUR

Scottie
Tennis Court – Lorde

Sinclair vs Murphy
1st Round – Court 4

The first day of the competition brought a palpable buzz of excitement to the court. A hot summer sun mixing with anticipation of the crowd. I felt the hum in the air, similar to the one that had been simmering in my blood. An anger beneath my skin I'd been itching to get out.

For the last week, we'd been participating in qualifiers and some warm-up games, and I was learning how fun it was to play by Nico's side. I'd never wanted to share the glory of a win with anyone else. It was mine, after all. I'd earned it.

But turning around, after we'd secured victory over our opponents, to find him with a wild, prideful grin spread wide across his perfect lips, his fist pumped in celebration, joy radiating from him . . . It made the win that much sweeter.

And playing with him was more fun too. We had this ability to read the other plays from only our bodies, written in those almost imperceivable movements and small coded expressions. Our own secret language that only the two of us spoke.

But today, I was on my own, and against Chloe Murphy. She was younger, only twenty or so, and had gained entry on a wild-card. It was her first Grand Slam. A baby at the beginning of their career—if a baby had been training since they were five and had three other titles under their belt.

She was smiling brightly, as if she expected this match to be fun. It certainly would be. But not for her.

I remembered my first Wimbledon. I was the same age as her and I'm sure I smiled just as wide. I had no idea of the fight that lay ahead of me. The competition, the training, the betrayals and the wins. All of it took its toll. But looking back, would I have changed any of it?

When the coin toss fell my way, and Murphy's perky smile deflated slightly, I felt as if she was already questioning her decision to be here. This was my town, my court, and she was only beginning to realise it.

We got into place, and I could already see the wobble in her couched stance. I pulled back my arm, tossed the ball in the air, and spun it into Murphy's service box. It flew past her—ace. She barely even moved. Let the games begin.

15 – Love

30 – Love

40 – 15

I took the point, feeling smug at how quickly I'd claimed it as my own. She looked uneasy, but after a quick glance to the crowds, she refocused, finally realising this was no playground.

I ran circles around her. She won a few points. There was an arm on this girl, that with a few more years, would strike fear on the court. But today, she was lazy, her footwork still needed refining, and she couldn't break my serve. She stuck to the baseline, and it was easy to pick her game apart.

I hit screamer after screamer, forcing her all over the court. It was almost too much fun to run her side to side on the grass. The first two sets were mine. The match was mine. I'd forgotten this feeling. My feet on the grass, the thrill of fucking winning. It was a rush, and I'd been cold turkey for too long.

When we shook hands at the end, she looked on the verge of tears, and I felt a little regretful for being relentless.

"Good match," I said, trying my best to keep my smile friendly and hide my delight at the win. She only nodded in reply, lips pressed together in a small line.

I collected my things and walked off the court, finding Mum waiting for me. She was dressed in a pair of blue jeans paired with a cream top and a Chanel blazer. A pair of sunglasses pushed her blonde hair out of her smiling face, her arms stretched open. My heart almost doubled in size at the sight of her.

"You might not want to hug me. I'm all sweaty," I warned, watching her grin grow.

"That's what dry cleaners are for," she said, pulling her slim body against mine, her long, slender arms wrapping around me. I instantly melted into her, my head landing on her shoulder.

"I'm so glad you could make it," I said to her, her perfume a comforting blanket on my still racing pulse.

She pulled back, eyebrows pressed together. "How could I miss this?" Her attention was pulled from behind me, and Murphy paced past us, heading to the changing rooms. Mum whispered, "I never realised you could be so mean to somebody in a game."

I laughed, tilting my head. "Have you watched much tennis?"

She hummed for a moment before shaking her head. "But I'll catch up. I have a feeling I'll be following this to the final." She sent a confident, playful wink my way. I'd been playing like Matteo was nipping at my heels. I was pulling drive from his words, a new strength. I wanted this more than ever before.

I shook her off, heading toward the cool-down area. "I think I went too hard on her."

"You won. I wouldn't worry too much about it."

My bag strap slipped from my shoulder, sparking a memory. "Oh, I have something for you. Jon mentioned you'd gotten tickets."

"Oh?" She drew back in surprise as I pulled the bag in front of me, unzipping one of the compartments. I wiped my hands on my skirt before I pulled out the black silky material from inside.

"My dress!" my mum cried, her fingers instantly taking the satin material from me. She looked longingly at it. "I knew we would be reunited soon!"

"I looked after it." I fought to hide my smile, but failed completely.

She only narrowed her eyes on me, clutching the material close to her body. "You stuffed vintage Versace in your tennis bag?"

"It was safe there, and you wanted it back." I shrugged. She rolled her eyes at me, muttering some complaint about "children" and "dresses are not play things" all the while she refolded the dress perfectly, placing it delicately in her tote.

"It's older than you are," she noted, still holding a look of disdain in her eyes.

I waved her off. "Throw it in with your dry cleaning. It will be fine."

"You know, there's a reason I got that particular dress." Her anger dissipated, the smile on her lips turning coy. "I waited a long time, made connections and friends in high places, but if there was one thing I wanted to remember my runway days by, it was this."

We reached the cool-down room, other players stretching out. Mum was temporarily distracted, eyeing the other athletes.

"What is it?" I pulled her attention back to me.

"On this particular runway, I showed up puking my guts up. All morning the stylist was getting so irritated with me because I could hardly hold it together. She said 'you shouldn't party so hard if you can't handle it.' And then made some very harmful and out-dated comments about it keeping me skinny." She rolled her eyes, her smile growing on her lips as she continued. "Which turned out to be very ironic because it was morning sickness, and I was about to put on a lot more weight."

I paused, putting together her words. "You mean . . ."

"You, my darling, were part of the Versace 1998 runway." She smiled, looking rather pleased with herself. "The entire London Fashion Week, actually. But this show was when I knew that you were with me."

I paused, taking in the information, and found myself thinking that it was strange that it had been the dress I'd chosen to take to remind myself of her. For a moment, I felt myself mad all over again that I'd missed out on an entire childhood with her. She was young, had an entire career ahead of her. If I found myself in the same position, I wouldn't be in it for long. But she'd still had me. I'd never asked her why. I tucked the question away for another time, knowing that no matter her choices, I was just happy she was here with me now.

"That's pretty cool." I smiled softly at her. "I need to shower, then can we meet? Maybe go watch a game?"

She nodded enthusiastically back at me. "I'll go find us some Pimm's to celebrate with," she said, before she leaned forward, kissing me softly on the cheek. "I'm so proud of you," she whispered gently against me, pulling me into another quick hug. "Now go shower. There's only so much sweat this Chanel can take."

I SHOWERED FAST, keeping the water roasting hot to soothe my aching muscles, but as I was leaving the locker room, a familiar male voice rang from the row of lockers opposite mine, keeping me completely hidden from view.

"What were you doing out there today? Your footwork was a complete mess."

I'd have known that voice if it spoke quietly in a crowded room. It was Matteo. For a moment, I thought the words were aimed at me, as if he had come back to tell me off. But then I heard her.

"My footwork was fine. I won after all." Dylan's response was snarky. I could practically hear her furrowed brows and crossed arms at his comment. She'd been playing a different match today, and obviously, had walked away successful. Apparently, she still had to learn that it wasn't enough for her new coach.

"Barely! Did you forget you have a backhand? I couldn't tell if you were avoiding it on purpose."

"I played like I normally play." Her response was flat, and I could hear her shuffling about as if she was emptying her locker, not even giving him her full attention. I felt a small pang of delight at that, at how angry that would make him.

"Your game plan was nonexistent. It's like you were hoping your opponent would get bored and leave." He started to walk back and forth, so I creeped farther up my row of lockers, making sure I was hidden from sight.

"I didn't like the game plan we had discussed beforehand. I made some adjustments, I didn't wa—"

"We only won because you got lucky."

A moment of silence fell, only to be broken by a heavy exhale. "I," Dylan's voice rang, tired and dry.

"What?" Matteo questioned.

"*I won.* Not 'we,'" she corrected, her voice not losing her edge for a moment. A locker door banged shut, and then she continued. "I ignored your game plan because it was wrong. And *I* won."

There was a long pause, tension tightening in the humid air of the locker room. "Next time, you'll play as I tell you to. Don't forget, you signed a contract with me. You can't use another coach, you can't switch teams. You play with me, or you don't play at all."

I listened, committing every word he said to memory. Could he really put that in a contract? It couldn't be binding? But Dylan didn't argue. She didn't say anything at all.

"Now change and meet me in the car," Matteo instructed as he left, the room turning silent. I took a moment, unsure of my next steps. I thought about waiting until she left. I was almost sure she wouldn't find me here and I could avoid the confrontation. Dylan had made it clear she didn't want my help, but she didn't know how much she might need it.

I curled my hand into a fist, fingernails digging into my palm as I reluctantly pushed myself out of the corner. Did I want to talk to her? No. But after everything that had happened, this still felt like my mess to clean up.

I swallowed down the lump in my throat as I crept along the row of metal lockers before, finally, I turned the corner to the row over, and found her sitting on the middle bench, still dressed in her usual Nike white skirt and top, her head held in her hands.

"Dylan." She twisted to find me, her body jolting up straight. In a heartbeat, her guard was back up, any sensitivity in the moment vanished.

Her eyes scanned me up and down. "What do you want?" she sneered.

"I heard what he said," I admitted cautiously. I held my hands up as if to try to soothe the situation, prove to her I was here as a friend, not a threat.

"So?" Her sharp tone was accusatory, rough around the edges, as if to miss my point completely.

"So? He can't speak like that to you." I shook my head before remembering his final words. "Is it true what he said? About the contract?"

She rolled her eyes at me, pushing herself up from the bench to reopen one of the lockers in front of her. "He's just a tough coach. It isn't anything I can't put up with."

"There's no putting up with him." I tilted my head to the side. "I would know."

She let out a cold laugh as she hastily began to stuff clothing into a large gym bag. "You were weak."

"Excuse me?"

She paused, her expression fed up. "You think that was anything worth getting upset about?"

"Come on, Dylan. You've been coached by Jon, you know that's not normal."

"Jon's soft. I didn't need soft. I needed to win."

I laughed at the irony. "Then Matteo's definitely your guy because he will stop at absolutely nothing to get you there." Memories threatened at the edge of my mind, the brutality of that man's appetite for winning, but I pushed them back down. "But don't think for a second any of it is about you."

"What? Is it about you then? Revenge on the pretty little daughter who betrayed him."

"No." I shook my head simply. "It's about himself. His legacy. There's only one person he wants to see succeed, and it's himself. Everyone else is collateral."

"Right." She drew out the word before she slammed the locker door closed again. "And who am I supposed to believe? The cheat, or the man who just told me how to win?"

"Dylan, wake up. He threatened your career." I stopped short of pointing out that he was the threat, the one she should've been concerned with.

She shook her head again, that smile a mean thing as she hoisted her bag strap onto her shoulder. "The only threat to me is you, Scottie."

She started to barge past me, but my hand went to her arm, clutching tightly. She immediately stopped, looking down with disgust where I held on to her. But my grip only strengthened, desperate to hold her attention.

Her eyes met mine, confusion all over her features. Holding her gaze, I said, "I meant it, before, when I said when you need help, I'll be there."

She pulled back at my words, yanking her arm out of mine, and after a moment, a pause, she blinked and walked away without so much as another smart retort or insult.

I turned on my heels, watching her leave, the door swinging back and forth on its hinges as she disappeared through it, leaving me all alone in the locker room, hoping that this time, she would listen before it was too late.

CHAPTER THIRTY-FIVE

Nico
You First – Paramore

A *nd it's an unexpected first win at Wimbledon for Scottie Sinclair.*
She won in two sets today against—" The voice from the TV of
the sports commentator disappeared into the noise of the packed
hotel bar, the rest of his words lost, but the screen already had my
attention.

I'd been nursing a glass of whisky for ten minutes waiting for
Scottie to arrive. A tequila old-fashioned I had ordered for her sat
untouched, swimming around a large ice cube. After her first victory earlier today, I promised her a drink on me. And after a raised
eyebrow from Jon, I promised just the one drink, but stopped short
of inviting him along.

The screen held my attention as I watched the replay. I'd missed
it with my own match playing at the same time. I'd won, but the
after-match dip in the ice bath had been both torturous and heavy
on my knee, the joint throbbing. It wasn't anything I couldn't handle. I smiled as they showed her final point, her joy palpable as she
celebrated. It was almost too easy for her, tracking down each ball
like her life depended on it, hitting every serve with exact precision.

It had been a week since the gala and the cupboard and her father, and things had been . . . different. Like the tension between us had both broken and grown. Now that I'd had a taste of her, I wanted more. More of the noises she had made, the needy movement of her perfect hips.

My head turned as another person walked into the bar, eyes assessing to see if it was her yet. She was late, of course, which normally I'd hate, but I didn't mind waiting for her. I took a sip of the amber liquid, enjoying the burning at the back of my throat.

I grinned to myself, feeling the heavy weight of the whisky glass in my hand. Jon had told us that he had never bought Alister a drink at the gala, instead escorting him out and shoving him in the back of a cab. I'd made sure to order the Highland Park, the distillery Jon had promised him, and very much enjoyed tasting something Alister had been robbed of.

"Nico." I turned to my left, hearing my name come from a strange man who had taken it upon himself to sit at the bar next to me. "Got a moment for some questions?"

My eyes narrowed on him, scanning his face before I figured out where I'd seen him before. The press conference from a few days ago, asking Scottie frivolous questions.

"No." I turned, staring straight ahead.

"Come on, my editor will kill me if I don't get something on the record." He stuck his hand out to signal the bartender.

"Tell your editor to go to hell." I took another sip of my whisky, hoping it would wash him away too. Instead, he ordered us both a drink. My hand gripped my glass. As if getting me drunk would help his cause. The second whisky arrived quickly, the reporter placing it in front of me.

"I'll charge it to the newspaper. Call it a business expense." He laughed, the smell of the cigarette on his breath forcing me to bend away from him slightly. How long had he been stalking this hotel for somebody to harass?

"Who do you even work for?" I sighed.

He sounded almost proud as he announced, "The Daily Tea."

"Then you can get fucked." I pushed the drink back over to him, refusing to take anything from him. If I hadn't known to avoid his cheap tabloid before working with Scottie, I sure as hell knew it after seeing the crap they wrote about her.

"Aw, that's not fair," he crooned, before placing his phone out on the bar and tapping the screen. I glanced down at it long enough to see the microphone icon, the phone clearly recording audio. I fought the urge to hurl it at the mirror opposite me at the bar. "Can you confirm or deny for me if you and Scottie are sleeping with each other?"

"No comment," I grumbled, my finger tapping the red button on his screen.

"What about dating? Can you give me that?"

"No comment."

"There's nothing? Absolutely nothing going on between you both?" He dug further, obviously deciding to irritate me into an answer. He'd sooner irritate me into a brawl.

I took another sip of my own whisky, the ice cubes clinking together as I put it back down on the bar. "No comment."

He tried again. "It must suck having to tarnish your spotless career record by partnering with somebody like her. I mean, doping? Who would've thought it, eh?"

"No comment," I said between gritted teeth. It took tensing every muscle in my neck to prevent myself from swinging towards him, fist raised.

"Of course, the ass you're getting on the side must be pretty nice."

I flinched. One irritating muscle spasm that told him to go on, let him see the anger building inside. I kept her pretty face in my head, her gorgeous smile, blue eyes. Getting into a bar fight now would do nothing but get me kicked out of the competition and possibly arrested for assault. And judging from his employer, that would only mean a good news day for them.

He let his words settle before he poked again. "I wonder . . . is she around? Maybe I'll take a shot. After all, she's got a lot to thank me for. My editor gave me my first byline when I came up with the nickname Slutty Scottie."

"That was you?" I sneered. I hadn't thought I could get more disgusted and yet . . .

He smiled, the expression more snake-like than human, before he raised his glass as if to say cheers. "What about her dad? He's back in town, right?" He let the question hang unanswered in the air. "Sources say they were seen outside the gala a few nights ago. Is there a family reunion in the cards?"

"You don't know what you are talking about."

"Wanna clear it up for me, then?"

I sucked in a breath, turned back to the bar, and took another sip of the smoky liquid, trying not to fall for his questions again. This is what he wanted, what this man preyed on for headlines and bylines and clicks.

"No?" He sounded almost overjoyed at my silence. "Okay, back to you and Scottie. How does it feel to be sleeping with your former rival's daughter? Must help that she's an easy lay. Or what? Has she been in every other man's bed but yours? I bet I could have her in mine in no time."

"You really want to go there?"

"I mean, is a slut like her even worth it?"

I was on my feet before I realised it, using my full height to loom over him. My hand gripped the now empty glass, accidentally turning it to the side, the half-melted ice cubes scattered on the bar.

My chest heaved as I spoke, as anger boiled up inside of me. "Don't."

I could only get the one word out, the edges of my vision turning blurry as I focused on this asshole who dared to call her that. Who said it so casually. Who fucking came up with it in the first place. Years of disrespect boiled down to this snake sitting in front of me, and I wasn't supposed to do a damn thing about it.

"Don't call her that."

He smirked back, taking a sip of his beer as if totally unaffected. But I could see it, that trickle of fear in his eyes. I knew I was playing into his trap, but I was done caring. There was a low hum playing in my ears, drowning everything out but his sneaky voice.

"Can I put that on the record?"

I gritted my teeth, staring him down. I wanted to throw the glass. At him, at the bar. I wanted to watch it smash and see if this anger dissipated. "Do what you want."

Apparently unsatisfied with this, he decided to push his luck once more. "Do you want to comment on the rumours that you and Scottie Sinclair are in a relationship?"

I grabbed the drink he ordered me, downed the amber liquid, and took a moment to enjoy it, looking at the empty crystal glass before placing it back on the counter, the so-called journalist watching my every move, hopefully out of fear.

I didn't bother looking back at him. If I did, I might not leave at all.

"No comment." My eyes found the bartender, who had been watching the entire exchange. "My drinks are on him."

And then I left, grabbing the drink I ordered for Scottie before storming out of the bar and straight into the elevator.

CHAPTER THIRTY-SIX

Scottie
Peace – Taylor Swift

oming!" I shouted, answering the knock at the door of my hotel room. I'd been midway rushing to dry my hair after a long, hot bath to help relax my tight muscles from the match earlier today.

The game was more gruelling on my body than I could ever remember, and since I was playing double the number of matches—taking part in both the singles and the doubles—my body was beginning to suffer. I felt like I should have dark bruises where my body felt strained.

There was a second demanding thump at the door, and I toyed with the idea of leaving it a moment longer, to annoy whoever was so impatient they couldn't wait another goddamn minute.

Instead, I relented, hair dried but unstyled, and opened the door, forgetting to look through the peephole to check who it was. I should be used to the stern and stormy angular face of Nico Kotas, his jaw locked so tight I could feel the strain in my own, but somehow it felt an age since I'd been on this side of his irritation. And even worse, at the very sight of him, even the grumpy version of him, my body still ached to melt into his, see if his body heat was enough to help ease those knots in my muscles.

"I swear, I was on my way down," I lied, knowing I was at least fifteen minutes late to meet him at the bar.

"Did you even check the peephole before opening the door?" His question caught me off guard, my head pulling back.

"No? You were a very insistent knocker."

"I could've been anyone, just waiting for you to open the door."

I tilted my head, raising an eyebrow. I could smell the alcohol on his breath, confusion twisting as I caught sight of the glass of clear liquid in his hand, remembering our promise to Jon to keep on our best behaviour. "Well, Mr. Dangerous Stalker Man, would you like to come in?"

He nodded without saying anything, and I moved to the side as he stepped into the plush room.

"Is that for later?" I joked, closing the door. As he reached the middle of the room, he turned around, confusion etched on his features. I looked down at his hand. "The drink?"

His body tensed as if to remember he was even holding it in the first place, before he stretched it out towards me. "I ordered it for you."

Surprise washed over me as I took it from him, my fingers wrapping around the cool glass. I knew I was late, but he was acting like it was thirty instead of fifteen minutes. I raised the glass to my nose, taking in the orange scent.

"Tequila old-fashioned," he answered without me needing to even ask. "That's your drink, right?"

I grinned at him, taking in the moment before nodding. I looked around the room, although I already knew the answer. "We should get you something to drink. How else will we say cheers to our victory?"

He shook his head, body almost rigid, his shoulders pushed back. "I don't think I need another drink."

I hummed, drumming my fingers on the glass before placing it down. "Hold on a moment."

I walked to the tea station in the corner of the room, finding a clean mug before dipping down to the mini fridge underneath. I turned to him for a moment, noticing that he'd sat down on the bench at the end of my bed.

Nico Kotas on the edge of my bed. What a dangerous thing.

"Sparkling or still?"

His nose scrunched up at the thought. "Still, please." I pulled the bottle out and poured the clear liquid into the mug.

"Thanks." He took the white mug from me, his longer fingers splaying around the porcelain, and I tried to push all the dirty thoughts down. Tried to forget how well Nico knew how to use those fingers in very sensitive places, how easily he had me desperate for him. I smiled, pretending there was nothing at all going on in my head, before taking my place next to him, my own drink back in hand.

"I should offer you a coffee," I teased, nudging into his shoulder a little. "But then I'd have to tell you where I get it from."

He huffed, the smallest smile creeping onto his lips. "You're never going to let that one go, are you?"

I bit at my cheek, my broad smile spreading. "Cheers to us," I said, changing the subject and bringing my drink up to him. The storm on his face broke, like a ray of sunshine peeking through the dark clouds as his mug met mine, the dull clink of porcelain singing against my glass.

"To us," he repeated, his dark eyes not leaving mine. I was mesmerised as the curve of his mouth grew, absentmindedly taking a sip, the sweet citrus agave notes dancing on my tongue. He lifted his mug and took a sip, his shoulders slackening as he relaxed.

All I could think about was the press of his lips against mine, the rub of his stubble, and why on earth we were here in my hotel room when we should've been downstairs.

"Why are you here?" I asked. "I know I was running late, but it was only fifteen minutes."

His head dipped to the ground, the sunshine disappearing behind storm clouds again.

"I just . . ." He trailed off, the line of his jaw going tight. His eyes pressed closed for a moment as he exhaled, as if still trying to calm himself. His grip on the mug tightened, his knuckles almost turning white. "I had to see you."

I was confused for a moment. He had been with me all day, only taking a couple of hours to recover from the match. But then it dawned on me that something in those few hours, in those fifteen minutes, had gone wrong.

He was silent for a moment, his gaze lost somewhere across the hotel room instead of on me. "There was a man, a journalist, at the bar." He shook his head as a knot appeared in my gut. "He wouldn't stop asking questions, kept saying . . . things."

My mind raced with a thousand headlines, a thousand scandalous photos. I'd never regretted doing any of it and had enjoyed it, as a matter of fact. But I'd never considered there'd be somebody like Nico, somebody maybe worth being extra careful for.

My brows pressed together, trying to read the unfinished answers from his face. "What did he say?"

He paused, the bob of his throat swallowing as he tried to find the words. "He said things about you that I didn't like. Not at all."

His entire body was rigid, as if he was holding himself back from something, from storming back downstairs and making a terrible decision. Maybe another terrible decision.

"Did you . . ." I trailed off, almost afraid to finish the sentence. I could see him holding Jon to the wall. If he lost his temper like that again . . . this would be over. He'd be kicked out of the competition. I didn't know how to do this without him anymore.

Didn't want to, either.

I watched as he shook his head, his eyes dipping to the ground. "I didn't do anything. I told him to stop, and I left."

Relief washed over me in an instant. "And that's all?"

"I let him get under my skin, Scottie. I gave him what he wanted."

I didn't feel anything but sorry. Before me, he didn't have any of this trouble. He didn't have journalists hounding him in hotel bars, using me, my history, as a way to irritate him into a quote for their headlines. He wouldn't know that peace again for as long as he was with me. Another reason to add to the endless list of reasons why "we" were a terrible idea.

My eyes danced over his face, reading the regret, the annoyance across his features.

"You walked away, right?" I asked, before finishing the liquid in my glass. His eyes found me, and he simply nodded his head.

I didn't break his gaze. "And you came here instead of doing anything?"

Came here. Found me. Needed me?

He nodded again.

And I couldn't help myself as I placed the glass on the carpet floor, twisting around to face him. My left hand stretched across to his face, fingers tracing his rough jaw as I pulled his face towards mine. My lips found his, and I kissed him softly, my lips moving against his. I pulled away from him, taking a few millimetres of space, just enough to lift my gaze to meet his. His eyes were lighter, the storm settled.

"That's for not doing anything stupid."

His answer was a hand tangled in my wavy hair, his fingers pulling me crashing back to him, his lips moving urgently against mine with need. My body melted into his as I swung a leg over his lap so I was sat on top of him, his head cradled in my palms. His hand found my ass, squeezing and pulling me roughly against him.

His lips against mine, my hand on his jaw, the other travelling down and pulling at the edge of his T-shirt, needing more contact. Needing skin. I rocked against him, feeling his thickness pressing between my legs. I couldn't stop myself as I ground down harder, feeling how perfect he felt against my centre. A moan escaped my lips, and I felt his mouth turn into a grin against mine.

His hand on my ass held me down as I ground again, keeping me hard against him. I moaned again, unable to stop myself. A blush burned on my cheeks, realising how loud I was being. He pressed again, drawing another noise from me. I buried my head into the space where the wave of his muscled shoulder met his neck, my teeth nibbling lightly against the skin, muffling myself to stop the noise.

His hand on my hair pulled gently so that my head moved back, and my eyes met his again. There was no room for question when he spoke. "I fucking love the noises you make. It drives me wild. Be loud. Don't you dare hide them away."

With his eyes on mine, he guided my hips down across his length, watching me as my eyes rolled back. I moaned again, loudly this time, losing myself against him.

"Good girl. Just like that." Warmth radiated up at me under the smug curve of his lips, the satisfied gleam in his eyes. "Do it again."

His hips rolled up to meet mine. I moaned again, no longer holding myself back from him. Eventually, he lost his T-shirt, and I lost mine, my hands hauling it off, desperate to feel him against my skin. Chest to chest. My fingers ran down his back, tracing his spine, nails digging into the skin as he continued to elicit all sorts of noises from me.

All at once I'd had enough, needing more and too tempted by the promise of the bulge I felt straining against his shorts. I pushed up to my feet, leaving him looking dishevelled, topless with his hair all out of place from my hands, his face full of the same unhinged desperation I felt.

I dropped to my knees, my hand instantly finding the buttons of his shorts, pulling the thing open, fingers tugging at the edges. "Take them off," I demanded with a hungry smile.

A small laugh escaped him before he did what I said, his hands pushing the material from his raised hips, sliding them down his legs. My hands found his, pulling them the rest of the way. He moved to his briefs, his thumbs tucking under the black Calvin Kleins. But I stopped him.

"Let me," I said on a breath, wanting the delicious privilege of unwrapping him. His smile was a lopsided thing, almost awestruck from seeing me on my knees in front of him.

My hands replaced his, toying with the black elastic, slipping under and feeling the delicate, soft skin where his sculpted stomach met his waist, rolling over the strong bone of his hips. I hooked my fingers and dragged the material down. Slowly. Carefully. Tanned skin gave way to inches of hard, thick flesh. Once free, it sprung back, hitting his belly button.

I swallowed involuntarily, eyes racking up his length. It was a struggle to concentrate on the rest of my task, but I pulled his briefs over his muscular thighs, over the fresh scar on his knee. Then I met his eyes with a grin, and enthusiastically tossed them across the room.

My fingers went to his knee, running to the top of the long red scar. He flinched as I grazed it, and I almost jumped back myself.

"Sorry!" The apology fell out of me as I looked back at him. "Does that still hurt?"

"No." He shook his head before the lump in his throat bobbed as he swallowed. Despite clearing his throat, his voice still had a hoarse edge when he spoke. "You caught me by surprise."

"Is it okay if I touch it?" His only answer was a silent nod, a comforting smile, and a heated gaze. I leaned forward, my lips coming to the top of the scar, and I kissed, leaving a trail down the length of the healed skin. This scar allowed him to be here. It was the reason we eventually met each other. It brought him to me.

His breathing turned deep, the rise and fall of his chest growing, his fingers softening in my hair as if to comfort me. I met his gaze again, checking that he was still okay with this. His expression was so full of awe, so soft. I didn't think I'd ever felt that special to somebody.

My attention returned as I licked and sucked and kissed my way from his knee, up the inside of his thigh, tracing the thick curve and dip of muscle, all the way to the monster standing at attention in between his legs.

His eyes tracked my every move. Watched as I wrapped my hand around his cock, as I ran my tongue up the length, tasted him like he had tasted me. I kept my eyes on him too, watched arousal wash over him, and saw the moment all control slipped from him as I ran my lips and tongue along his length.

"Do you like that?" I asked, as if I didn't already know, teasing and keeping him on the edge. His head fell back, and a breathless moan escaped him as I tried to work my mouth downward, sucking and bobbing, determined to take as much as I could.

His hand rested on my head, knotting in my hair as he used it as leverage, helping me to keep a rhythm and encouraging me to take him deeper. I ignored the tears rising to my eyes, turned mindless with the one sole task at hand, desperate for more of his cock in my mouth, wanting to match that pleasure he had given me.

His hips started to move, his grip in my hair turning tighter as he began to fuck my mouth. I moaned around him, clenching my own thighs together as I grew hungry and impatient for my own pleasure.

"Look at you," he said, his hips bucking, my hand at the base as he reached the back of my throat. "So pretty choking on me."

His spare hand delicately brushed the curls of my hair that had slipped into my face, moving them away and taking them in his other hand. His hand returned to my cheek, wiping away tears that had escaped me.

"Look at me." My eyes met his, and that astonished look was erased from his face. "Can I fuck that pretty mouth? Will you be still for me, my love?"

His touch was so soft as I pulled back, preparing myself and switching gears. Then I nodded.

"Relax your jaw." The words were a whisper, so gently spoken as I readied myself for him. "Tap my thigh if you want me to stop. Just once, and I'll stop."

Then, with his hand on my head, he pushed my head down on his length and I took it greedily as he pulled me back up and down, fucking his length with my mouth.

"You feel so good," he rasped, pulling me deeper and deeper. "I'm so lucky. You make me feel so fucking lucky. So good for me."

I pressed my legs together, feeling how fucking wet I was between my thighs, growing desperate and hungry as he continued to use me. I moaned around his length, enjoying it.

"You love this, don't you? Taking my cock in that good girl mouth? It's driving me insane. I can see it now, you cleaning me up after I fuck you. Tasting yourself. And believe me, love, you taste so fucking good."

His words kept me going, turning me on so much that my body felt overheated and tight, every muscle aching, begging for release. Tears streamed down my cheeks, not just with the roughness but from the want building, the impossible need for release that my body was begging for.

And then he stopped, pulling my mouth from him. My jaw ached, but I wasn't complaining. His hand released my hair, and gently he brushed away my tears, rubbed around my swollen lips, and wiped me clean.

"You are fucking perfect for me." With his eyes on mine, pride washed over me as he held my face in both hands. Rough and gentle. Nico Kotas was a potent mix of the two.

"Now crawl. Get on the bed. Face down."

I smiled mischievously, my heartbeat pounding. "You want me to crawl?"

His hands were still on my face, rubbing gently, when he replied, "And I want to watch."

I took a moment, still processing his words, before I dropped my leggings to the ground, and fell back to my knees. I looked up at him, taking in the delicious sight, the taste of him still on my lips. And then, on all fours, my hands met the carpeted floor and I crawled, pushing myself past him on the bench.

I made my way up to the bed, my aching, needy body keeping my pace slow, but it only served to tease him as I crawled nearly naked into position.

Face down. Ass up.

Nico followed, grabbing a condom from his wallet and coming up behind me as he rolled it on. His hands instantly found my hips.

"Fuck," he swore under his breath as his groan rubbed against my soaked centre, my body clenching at the contact. "You've been so good for me. Do you want your reward now?"

I could hardly answer as his arm curled around my thigh, finding my throbbing clit and patting it teasingly with his fingers, every touch sending shockwaves through my heated body.

"Or do you want me to tease you more? Make you beg?"

His fingers tapped my clit harder, groans of pleasure my reply to his question.

"I thought that might be your answer."

And then his spare hand pulled at the hem of my lacy pants, even the friction of the material against my centre leaving me a moaning mess. He was slow, teasing as he pulled them over my ass and down my legs. All the while his fingers were still working against my pussy, wetness soaking down my thighs in anticipation.

As his hand tapped against my clit again, he spanked my ass, the pain and pleasure mixing. He did it again, the palm of his hand stinging against my sensitive cheek, but I was too lost in the feeling, in the indulgence of his touch.

"Nico," I managed, through gasps for air for relief from the need building impossibly tight. "Please."

"Please what?" He tapped again against my clit. "What do you need? More teasing?" He thrust his hips forward, so his length rubbed between my legs from behind, the tease of his length driving all possible responses from my brain. "Use your words."

"Fuck me," I begged, willing to do anything, say anything, for a release. "Please, fuck me."

"Do you want me inside of you?"

"Yes."

And almost as if it was a reward, he thrusted between my legs again. "Want me to stretch you out?" I moaned his name, lost in the anticipation of his suggestion. But he still wasn't satisfied with that answer.

"Well?" He moved again, lined up perfectly behind me, the head of his cock pushing at my entrance. "Show me how much you want it. Fuck yourself on me, beautiful."

I didn't dare waste another moment, pressing my hips into him. His length slid into me, my eyes rolling as I pushed past the resistance to his girth. I lost myself in the pleasure and pain as I moved against him, taking as much of him as I could. I wanted all of him. Every inch. I would take it all.

He groaned in ecstasy, his hand reaching forward to my hair, and using the tension to help me go deeper, bottoming out in my needy cunt.

We fucked hard, desperate, and loud. His fingers gripped at my body, moving from my hips to my hair to my shoulders, any leverage to keep himself buried deep inside of me. He leaned forward, his hand finding my breast. The feel of his cock inside me was overwhelming with need, with how good we felt together.

I gave in to the feeling, to the welcome closeness of his body. As if I'd never feel the same without him anymore. Now that I'd found this missing part, living without it was immeasurably harder. An orgasm finally ripped me open, my fingers curling into the bedsheets, my pussy greedy, taking everything he had to give me.

I swore, his name falling from my lips like a curse, the only tangible thought in my brain as he continued to ride me through the waves. He was so big it filled me up, but even without that, sex had never felt this good before. Not with anyone.

"You're so beautiful coming on my cock. You feel too damn good," he struggled out between broken groans of pleasure. I scarcely managed a response, mindlessly lost to the feeling of him inside me as he continued the unrelenting pace, nerve endings electrified.

"Keep going," I finally managed, still thrusting my hips to meet him, the intensity of the post-orgasm already faded, making room for another. His hand on my hips helped me keep up, a grip on my ass, squeezing, driving me wild.

"I don't think I can last much longer," he confessed with a single laugh. "It's too fucking good with you. Like you're made for me."

"I want you to come. Show me how good I make you feel," I ushered, mindlessly urging him on as I came again. "I want to take it all, Nico."

Another wave crashed hard into me as he drove on with fury, and I felt him push deep inside of me as he came. I groaned, overwhelmed all over again by the intensity, by how I felt for him. He rested on my back, the warmth of his body welcome, the heaviness of him against me a reminder that this was real. We were here. We were together. He was mine.

We stayed still for a moment, his chest leaning over my back as we both heaved for air. He turned his head, kissing the centre of my back.

"Has it ever felt like that for you before?" he asked, his voice no louder than a whisper.

"No," I confessed, still dazed from the connection between us. "You?"

He kissed me again. "Never."

CHAPTER THIRTY-SEVEN

Nico

Call Me Lover – Sam Fender

C an you flex your knee for me? Any sharp pain?"

I did as my physio asked, extending out to stretch my leg into his arms. Pain radiated up and down as I gritted my teeth. My hands fisted the edge of the chair I was sitting in. "It's a bit stiff, but nothing I can't manage."

Jon had all but wrangled me into an emergency appointment after my second-round singles match. I'd won it, comfortably, but it was long, gruelling on anyone. When I'd hobbled off the grass, Jon had made it clear that this appointment wasn't something I could avoid.

Ethan, my physio, cocked a disbelieving eyebrow as he looked from my knee to me, but he stopped short of pointing out the fact I limped into his assessment room.

His attention turned back to my knee, working it up and down. "The surgical site seems stable, but there's inflammation, probably due to the intensity of the matches you've been playing. Can you walk for me? Any noticeable limp or change in your gait?" Ethan asked, moving and letting me push myself from the chair. At first, any weight on the leg was unbearable, but it soon broke into an easy movement.

"It's not too bad when I walk," I said, eventually walking from one side of the room to the other. Jon stood against the wall, arms crossed, and an assessing look across his face. His gaze narrowed at my words, silently pressing into me like screws before I admitted to Ethan, "But the real pain hits when I pivot on the court."

Ethan crouched down to his knees, so he was in line with my legs. "Alright. Show me a quick pivot to the right, like you would during a match. Let's see what's going on there."

I let out a heavy breath, almost dreading doing the moments after gritting though it on the court, but I relented, showing Ethan the action, using my sore leg in the front, and pivoting through as if I was returning a shot.

Ethan hummed as he watched me. "'Okay, now try a few lateral movements, side to side."

I did as he said, moving my weight from side to side. "It's stable, but there's a bit of discomfort."

He nodded again, before explaining, "The stress is likely aggravating the knee. We might need to adjust your movement patterns on the court. Try incorporating a wider stance during lateral movements; it should reduce the strain on the knee."

I mimicked his movement, pushing my feet apart to widen the stance. Pain shot up my leg, albeit duller than before. "Feels a bit awkward, but I'll give it a shot."

Anything to make this easier.

"Great. And for now, let's limit the excessive sliding on the court. That can be harsh on your knee. And if the pain persists or intensifies, come back."

"We can try shorter steps too," Jon added roughly.

Ethan nodded in agreement. "It's late into the competition now, but I can send you some videos of footwork drills to help you get into the practice. Have you been doing your prescribed exercises?"

"Yeah, every day."

"Good, but let's increase the icing and elevation post-game. And I recommend cutting back on the doubles. You need some rest. Playing both is putting undue stress on it."

"Absolutely not." I shook my head, the finality of my words catching everyone off balance. Jon's eyes narrowed again, clearing his throat to speak again. "I can't back down. I'm playing both singles and doubles. I'll just tough it out."

"I get the commitment, Nico," Ethan started, sounding apologetic. "But pushing through might make it worse. It's a long tournament, and you risk jeopardising the rest of your season."

I wanted to tell them to fuck the rest of the season. I didn't care about what came after this. It was hard to think ahead when I was so caught up with winning this competition; my focus was purely on this win. This win, and her.

"I'm not cutting doubles." I crossed my arms, looking across at Jon, whose grim expression mirrored Ethan's.

"Nico . . ." Jon began, but I was too impatient to listen to whatever speech he had locked and loaded.

"No." I shook my head, looking at him. "You got me into this. Now let me finish it."

He tilted his head, his lips pressed together, and after a pause, he said two simple words, "She'd understand."

I could see her face in my mind, blonde hair tied up, that smile that she used to hide whatever she was actually feeling. She would understand. She'd always known I was injured, and part of her would've known the chances of me having to drop out. We had both been around long enough to have seen more than a few failed comebacks.

But this meant more than just a competition. Doubles was her revenge, her knife twist. And to me, it was what had tied us together. If it hadn't been for our training together, I simply wouldn't be here.

"I can do it, both of them. The doubles are best of three, anyway," I pointed out. "Half the work and guaranteed shorter gameplay. I'm not dropping out. I could be knocked out of the singles competition and still be ready to play the doubles."

Jon rubbed the back of his neck, sighing before he responded. "Just . . . remember this is a comeback. You need to be easy on yourself as much as you can."

I fought the urge to grind my teeth with frustration. Of course I knew this was a comeback. I could see how weak I was compared to the other competitors. Slower, and older, I was far too aware I was past my prime, but still longing for one more day in the sun. This struggle, the pain of the rehab, it had to be for something . . . right?

And if it couldn't be for another win, another shot at the singles men's title, then maybe it could be for her.

"I'll do everything I can post-match," I promised, determined to convince them that I could do this. "I'll limit the sliding, do the exercises like you said. But I'm not cutting the doubles."

Ethan looked at Jon and shrugged, as if to say "he's your problem." And a problem I was determined to be for as long as they had this idea in their heads about quitting. Jon readjusted his posture, ruffling slightly before looking at me.

"It means that much to you?"

I realised then that despite his suspicions about Scottie and me, he truly had no idea. Whether he thought it was a fling or a silly little attraction, Jon had not realised how deep these feelings went for me. Because if he thought this was still only about tennis, about competing, he had missed the point entirely.

"She does." I watched as his eyes widened, his mouth dropping into a circle as realisation dawned on him, watched as he saw that this was a problem entirely of his own creation, and that arguing against me was entirely futile.

He nodded. "Alright, but if the pain gets worse . . ."

"We assess options," I finished for him, knowing I couldn't let it get to that point. Not for her.

"You realise you are putting the run at the men's singles at risk," Ethan added. "And with your injury, you could start to undo the progress you've made."

His warning was stark in the silent room, Jon's eyes on me, searching for an answer.

With a locked jaw, I nodded, acknowledging what he was saying. This could be it, if I pushed it too far and didn't heed the warning. This was my second shot. Many had tried before, some had succeeded. More had failed.

Then I looked at Jon. "You can't tell her about this."

His eyebrows pressed together with frustration as his body straightened, finally stepping away from the wall. "Nico, she deserves to know."

I waved a hand to dismiss him. "I'll tell her if the time comes, but I don't want her to know until then. She's stubborn, she won't understand."

I knew she wouldn't ask me to carry on, wouldn't let me put it all on the line for her. But I wanted to give her this. If anyone deserved this revenge, it was Scottie fucking Sinclair.

"But you're doing this for her?"

I crossed my arms and kept my shoulders firm. "That's exactly why she can't find out."

Jon rubbed his hand over his face. "I think you're making a mistake. She won't like that you kept this from her."

"I'll deal with that—if the time comes." There was still a good chance everything would work out fine. "Until then, she doesn't need to know."

"Okay. Fine," Jon agreed. "But I won't keep anything else from her. She's my responsibility too."

"I understand." I ran a hand through my hair, relieved. A part of me was glad that he had her back too, that he was struggling with the idea of keeping this from her, even if it might not even be an issue.

On a relieved breath, I sighed. "Thank you."

Jon nodded curtly, his body still tight, as if still wrestling with the idea. It must have been hard having a conflict of interest like this. "Just don't hurt her. This is the kind of thing that could do that. Be careful."

I smiled faintly at him, trying to soothe his nerves. "I promise I have no intention of ever hurting her."

SCOTTIE'S HAND SQUEEZED my own as she winced in pain, the buzz of the tattoo needle filling the summer evening air. I'd surprised her with an off-campus trip (Jon approved, of course) after she won her game in the fourth round. It had gone the full three sets, but she'd managed to close it out in the end.

I had reached out to my favourite tattooist, Harry, last minute, right after Ethan wrapped up his lecturing on doing the correct stretches. When I'd promised the design I had in mind was small, he agreed to fit us in this evening. I had gone first, letting her explore the shop a little, while I sat in the chair and let Harry do his work, making sure to keep the result hidden from her. Then it was her turn.

She let out a small yelp of pain again as she lay on her back with her arm above her head so he could work on the inside of her biceps, the opposite arm to mine, but the same position. I held on to her hand, allowing an outlet for her pain, all the while running my other hand through her soft hair.

"Oh, come on, it doesn't hurt that much," I teased, earning myself a scowl in response.

Her pink lips pursed together. "Did your first one hurt?"

I thought to myself for a moment. It had been larger than this design, but in the same place. Five black Olympic rings. "It . . . stung."

"You liar." She hissed again, although this time with a smile, a playful look held in her blue eyes.

"Just squeeze my hand. It's almost over."

She did as I said, her hand tightening around mine as she winced. I hated seeing her in this pain, but I knew it would be over soon. "Can't believe I let you convince me to do this."

"You said you wanted a tattoo," I pointed out, remembering our conversation back in Rhodes. I'd not fully understood what she had been saying when she told me about her drunken idea for a tattoo, but now with the truth shared, I could understand how deeply she'd been hurting to want the words inked permanently on her body.

Scottie Sinclair is clean.

She laughed, the sound twinged with pain as the needle continued its work. "And you said something about exploring your S&M kink."

"Eh, two birds."

Scottie rolled her eyes, paired with a shake of her head. I could still hardly believe her reaction when the car had pulled up outside the shop. A wild, bright smile. My girl was really a rebel at heart.

"What was Ethan saying about your knee? You were there for a while." Concern twinged at the edges of a frown. She'd obviously seen that I'd struggled through the end of the game. "I tried to wait to see you after, but I had to go warm up."

I hesitated, unsure what to say instead of the truth. Jon's words played on the edge of my brain, his advice not to keep this from Scottie. I knew she should know, but I also knew she would force me to stop playing the doubles. I wasn't ready to quit, not on myself or playing with her.

"Oh, nothing new," I said, barely holding her gaze. "Just getting at me about doing my stretches. I need to stop sliding."

She nodded, thinking to herself for a moment. "We can work on that. Could you manage a practise after this?"

I shook my head, still feeling the ache in my legs from the earlier match. She must be some sort of superhuman to want to keep playing tonight after going for three sets. "We should rest up tonight. We still need time to recover."

"Nico Kotas taking a night off?" Her grin was wicked and unhinged, a dash of pride held in her eyes. "I have been a terrible influence on you."

My heart thundered its rhythm inside my chest, her grin infectious. "The worst."

"Alright, we're done," Harry announced, sliding on his stool and bringing back a mirror. Scottie hopped up, clearly excited to see the final product. Anxiety hammered at me all over again. She'd let me surprise her with the design, a decision I was now sorely regretting. What if she didn't like it? What if I'd permanently scarred her for life with a stupid little tattoo and she hated it forever and ever and—

"I love it," she said, eyes glued to the mirror as her fingers tentatively traced the pink outline of the little ruby red strawberry, a perfect callback to Wimbledon.

"Really? You like it?"

"Of course." The way she smiled was everything I'd hoped for. That very smile kept me going during doubles. Every point we scored, every game we closed out, she'd send it my way and it would just about bring me to my knees. I wanted more of it, and there was no way I would give it up.

"I got one to match," I added, twisting my biceps to show her my own fresh tattoo wrapped up in plastic to protect it. It sat inside the design already there, twisted up like she's already managed to twist herself into my life. "It felt like a good idea to get one that was Wimbledon coded."

"It's perfect."

"Really?" Worry cracked at the edges of my question.

She stared at me blankly, her voice dry. "Yes, the thing I let you permanently tattoo onto my body is perfect." Even when she was sarcastic, she still managed to be my favourite person. "It's really cute."

She jumped off the chair, saying a thank you to Harry as he went through the after-care routine, handing over a healing lotion to help speed up the process. When he was done, she closed the gap between us, her lips meeting mine.

"You know what this means, right?"

I hummed for a moment. "You've decided to go get a full sleeve of tennis tattoos?"

"Nope," she replied, her eyes on mine. "We've gotta win this thing. We can't get tattoos to commemorate the event, and then not win."

I smiled. "Let's give them hell, Sinclair."

"After you, Kotas."

CHAPTER THIRTY-EIGHT

Nico

I Like You – Harry Strange

A thunderous applause broke out as Scottie and I sealed doubles victory at the round of sixteen, Scottie's return bouncing twice, our opponents unable to reach the ball in time. We had played beautifully, reading each other's moves to dominate and take the match in straight sets.

She turned, beaming at me with pure joy, her hand forming a fist as she yelled out with victory. I stood no chance against the wide grin that broke out on my own lips at the sight of her.

My entire body ached with the need to run to her, close the distance, and pull her tightly into my body. I wanted to kiss her, taste victory on her lips. Instead, I planted my legs and promised myself *later.*

Our relationship was not for anyone else but us. They could believe what they wanted, read into every photograph and smile. They could use that to sell their clothing and brand, but they wouldn't turn what I really had with her into a spectacle.

We met our opponents at the net, shaking their hands before walking back to the bench to collect our belongings.

"You did good out there, Sinclair," I complimented, nudging my shoulder into hers, desperate for any physical contact, even if it was a friendly gesture.

"I know." She turned to me, meeting my gaze before shrugging. "You were alright."

I narrowed my eyes at her, pursing my lips. "Just alright?"

The playfully evil glint in her eyes told me she was just messing with me, flirting even. But that didn't mean my ego could take the dig.

"I mean, there were a few that went past you I would've been able to return." She pushed her racket inside her bag, before slinging it over her shoulders, a water bottle held in her free hand.

"Oh, yeah?" My eyebrows pushed up, shouldering my own bag and standing alongside her.

She shrugged again as she took a sip of her water. "I mean, if you can't handle a critique, I could keep it to myself and let Jon tell you instead." Then she turned, beginning to walk off court as if this conversation was over. *But it was far from over.*

I caught up easily, increasing the pace of my long strides to match her speed. "Do we want to talk about your second serve?"

She stopped dead in her tracks, a hand on the strap of her bag, keeping it on her shoulder, and she peered up at me with suspicion and confusion. "What *about* my second serve?"

I smothered a grin at how easy it was to get under her skin.

"Hey, if you can't handle critique . . ." I turned, leaving her frozen on the spot, and pretended not to notice the sexy scowl on her face. Scottie Sinclair was definitely still hot when she was mad. The only thing that made her hotter was a tennis racket in her hand.

There wasn't much distance between us before she yelled, "I can take it."

I immediately whipped around to her, eyes wide as she realised her innuendo. There was almost nothing I could do to fight the smile breaking out before I looked around, trying to see if the crowd had noticed us. But when barely anyone in the players' room had stopped to look, I turned back, finding her by my side, a slightly nervous look on her face.

I pressed my lips together. "Well, apparently you can't handle your second serve."

Frustration rushed back onto her face, her mouth opening with whatever retort she had prepared when somebody cut her off.

"Hey—good to see you out there again," Oliver Anderson, one of my competitors in the singles, said with a friendly smile. "It's been a while."

The last time we'd been on court together was the US Open quarterfinal almost a year ago. It was the last Grand Slam I'd managed to get through with my knee. I won the match against Oliver, but not without the game going late into a tie break.

I grinned confidently at him. "Just getting warmed up."

Scottie interrupted, her arms crossed. "Oliver, tell him there was nothing wrong with my second serve."

He looked uneasily between us, one eyebrow arched. "I don't want to get in between a lovers' spat."

I shook my head, refusing to acknowledge his comment. It was becoming more frequent as the press attention grew. After our positive performance on court today, I knew it would only get worse.

"It's about the lack of spin," I answered, keeping my attention on Oliver.

Scottie just about exploded. "A lack of *spin*?"

"Don't worry about it." I smiled. "I'm sure Jon's already constructing a last-minute training session about it."

She mumbled something mostly incoherent, but I picked up the odd word. That in itself was enough for me to know I definitely didn't want to hear what she had to say. Her gaze met mine, a fiery anger still burning. "I'm going for a shower. Don't think this is over."

She narrowed her gaze one last time at me, before her face softened, turning to Oliver as she said a goodbye to him. My attention caught on the sway of her white pleated skirt as she walked away, the bare skin of her thigh calling to me.

I wonder if she'd let me tattoo my name there.

"Did you see who your opponent is for the quarterfinals?" Oliver asked, bringing my attention back to him. I blatantly ignored the raised eyebrow and cocky smile combo he was sporting.

"No, I haven't had a chance to check. Who is it?"

His smile grew. "Me."

A laugh escaped me, the competitive side kicking in. Every time Oliver and I met on the court, we both knew we were in for one hell of a match. At thirty, he was younger than me, but fast and tactical, a defensive baseliner who would always try to force errors from my play. *Try* being the key word.

"Should I expect payback after our last match?" I asked. It had been brutal from the start, running until almost 3 a.m. It had taken all my strength to get through it, leaving me exhausted and unprepared for the quarterfinal a day after.

He nodded, before joking, "I'm excited to see what that new knee can do."

A tinge of pain struck through my leg at his words, the memory of the days after the US Open playing over, the joint swollen and painful. Even after today, I was desperately needing an ice pack and rest, the reminder from Jon and Ethan not to overdo it still at the front of my mind. I had to look after myself for Scottie. I couldn't let her down.

"How's Ava doing?" I asked, changing the subject to Oliver's wife.

Something flashed in his face, a shadow falling over his confidence. He swallowed, looking off at the crowd around us before answering. "She's alright, I think."

"You think? She's your wife."

He shook his head. "Not anymore. She left."

My shock overwhelmed me for a moment as I tried to fit this piece of information with the couple I knew well. We were, of course, competitors, but Oliver was a friend off court, too. When I'd been recovering, he'd visited a few times, made sure I knew I needed to get better so he could get his revenge after our last battle.

"What happened?"

He shrugged casually, but now that I knew, I could see sadness was clear on his face. Dark circles under his eyes, his face a little slimmer than it had been. "Turned out we wanted different things. It's just life sometimes."

His words played on my mind. *What did Scottie want?* After this? The touring could keep us apart for weeks, maybe months. And what would it mean for the future?

"Fuck. I'm sorry," I finally managed, a hand reaching out to his shoulder, fingers pressing firmly into his T-shirt.

Oliver's head swayed a little, jaw clenched as his gaze moved unfocused. "It's fine. I mean, it's not, but it is what it is."

"Is that why she's not competing here this year?" I asked, trying to make sense of the situation. They had been together a long time, both of them managing the juggle between their careers and relationship—at least, that's how it had seemed. After burning out in his early twenties, he took a relaxed attitude to competing in the sport, only playing when it suited him. But when he did compete, I knew I was in for some real fun.

He let out a heavy breath. "Honestly, I don't know. It's hard to keep in contact with her, different time zones with the tour."

"I'm sorry to hear that. Honestly, it sucks."

He raised an eyebrow, the hint of a smirk appearing. "Fancy throwing the match tomorrow out of pity?"

I laughed. "I'm not *that* sorry."

"Worth a shot." He shrugged.

"I'd wish you good luck . . ." I trailed off, head tilting in answer.

This time it was his turn to laugh as he raised his hand, letting his palm rest on the centre of his chest. "Just go easy on me. I'm a man with a broken heart."

"And I've only got one good knee," I retorted. We both started to go our own ways, knowing we would see each other again soon, only that interaction wouldn't be nearly as friendly.

His smile was wide but didn't quite reach his eyes. "Sounds like it's a fair match." And then, with a soft nod of his head, we parted, tucking our friendship away, somewhere down deep.

You play a lot of friends in this sport, but that didn't matter when they were standing on the opposite side of the court. Not when that person was between you and the rush of victory, a step closer to the title we all go to bed dreaming about.

CHAPTER THIRTY-NINE

Nico

The Lady of Mercy – The Last Dinner Party

I watched Scottie chaotically tapping her fingers on her thighs as she pushed her leg out to warm up for her next match, her body primed with anticipation. The player's area was filled with other competitors and their teams, all getting prepared for their next game. Jon had been pulled away by an emergency call, so I'd stepped in to help her prepare. Watching her stretch was still an effort not to get inappropriate in a public place (again), the memory of her long slender legs wrapped around my waist this morning still fresh in my mind.

"Calm down, you're making me nervous," I said with a smile as she moved into a new position.

"It's the quarterfinals, Nico," she gritted out, pushing her body forward over her legs, sounding stressed and distracted. "I think I'm allowed to be nervous." She barely looked at me. Instead, her focus remained on a singular spot as she pulled her muscles. Her white crop top stretched up, revealing inches of soft skin underneath, testing my resolve.

"We could go somewhere private, and I could find a way to distract you," I suggested, stepping close to whisper, my eyes catching on the edge of her skirt. Now that I knew how her thighs felt, soft perfect skin hiding powerful muscle, it was even harder to keep my hands to myself.

"Then we run the risk of becoming *too* distracted." I looked back up at her face, noticing that I'd managed to capture her precious attention. Her lips were pressed into a knowing smile, an eyebrow raised.

"I'll make sure to do all the work. We don't want you tired out right before you go on," I continued. She had stopped moving, her body pulling even closer to mine, which did nothing to settle the ache inside of me. It was getting harder to pretend there wasn't anything between us anymore, impossible even.

"Don't tempt me with a good time, Kotas." Her smile was addictive, and for a moment, I imagined leaning across and kissing her, really kissing her. Screw it all and show everyone how much she was really mine. Pin her to the wall and give her the distraction she needed—the one I was desperate for.

Her gaze fluttered behind me, catching on someone else, and the smile faltered, her nerves reappearing as her hand raised in a hesitant wave. I turned, my gaze catching on the dark hair of her opponent. Inés was smiling, looking all too friendly, considering what was at stake. The semifinal was only three sets away.

"I'll be back in a moment." Scottie smiled before heading over toward her competitor. Both of them pulled into a friendly hug before they began to chat casually. Scottie's hand landed on her hip, as a sly, competitive smile curled onto her lips. I knew it well, all too familiar with the way she liked to tease before a competition. Inés looked more than comfortable, however, an eyebrow raised as Scottie laughed at something she'd said.

"They seem friendly." Another voice broke my concentration. I turned, finding Kit, Scottie's mom, beside me. Her blonde hair was pulled out of her face, and it struck me how strikingly similar they looked. Identical dainty nose and round face. Same deep blue eyes.

I laughed. "Just wait till they get out on the court."

"It's incredible how quickly they get ruthless." She tossed her head back, almost recoiling at the memory. I'd met her mom in the family box during one of Scottie's games. She'd sat, her leg jigging nervously as she watched her daughter sprint across the grass, clapped and yelled a little too loudly for Wimbledon standards when she'd won.

I'd never sat with somebody's parents while they watched before, but I imagined my own weren't any different. They'd normally come to show support, but the last thing I needed was the rest of the Kotas family descending on Scottie. We'd struck an agreement that if I made it to the final, they could come then, no matter how reluctantly my mom agreed. I didn't need any more pressure.

"I'm just glad I get to play *with* her instead of against her."

Kit looked over at me before she said with a knowing wink, "In more ways than one, I hear."

I blinked, my mind panicking slightly at the insinuation. "I—" The silence stretched on and on, only jumbled sounds leaving my mouth. "Em . . ."

Her face cracked open with glee, her hand patting my shoulder in what was supposed to be a calming motion. "Relax. I just wanted a shot at being the embarrassing parent for once."

I coughed, trying to clear away the choke from my throat, but the words still came out strangled. "Did it live up to your expectations?"

"It certainly did."

Thankfully, Scottie interrupted the conversation before I could make myself seem like any more of a fool. "What are you guys talking about?"

"Just the match," her mom replied, still looking very happy with herself. "Anyway, I should head up. I don't want to be late."

Scottie nodded before pulling her mom into a hug. "I'll see you out there."

Kit turned to me for a moment. "Nico, are you joining me in the box?"

I realised that knowing my luck, I'd probably be sitting next to her. "I'll be right behind you." I smiled politely, hoping that would be enough time for me to be able to look her mom in the eye again.

She looked back at Scottie, waving as she turned away and crying a final, "Good luck!"

As soon as she was out of earshot, Scottie practically spun around to face me, a wild curiosity across her features. "What was she saying?"

"It was nothing."

"Did she embarrass you?"

This time, I didn't hold back. "I nearly choked on my tongue."

She smiled, looking a little pleased with her mom. "Sounds like her."

Looking at them together, you'd never have guessed that Kit had only been in Scottie's life for less than a year, the closeness they had clear. They spoke the same language. I was glad she had somebody outside of tennis to keep her grounded somehow, somebody who had nothing to gain from her win.

"How's Inés?" I asked.

Scottie grinned back at me, the expression twisted with something devious. "Nervous."

My eyes narrowed. "Now that you mention it, you don't seem so skittish anymore." Her earlier jitter was gone, her hands relaxed by her sides, her face calm and collected. It was as if she'd returned a new person.

She looked carefully around her, stepping closer to me and keeping her voice low. "I . . . I think I can win this, Nico. Like, a real chance."

"Yeah?" I beamed back at her, renewed by her newly found confidence.

"Inés is great. She always catches me off balance with her slice. But she's still recovering. Her matches have only gone two sets. I know how she plays, and I think if I can get her to play long points, maybe even get her into a rally and push her back behind the baseline, it might work. Keep it so she can't execute that slice. I could tire her out and win."

I thought over her words. It was good. She was right about Inés. Get her to that final set and she had a solid chance of winning. Pride welled up inside of me.

"Sounds like you've got your game plan."

For the first time today, she truly looked hopeful. "If I keep my head, don't play too hard and lose my own steam, I think I can do it."

I couldn't help but reach out, my fingers meeting her chin to pull her gaze to mine. It felt like I would never get sick of the way her face changed when she looked at me, the softness there.

"Scottie Sinclair in the semifinals." I smiled, loving the way the words sounded. "And then the finals."

She let out a single laugh. "Who would've thought I'd have any chance?"

But I didn't let go of her gaze, keeping my eyes on hers as I pressed, "I would've."

She pulled her bottom lip between her teeth, biting to smother what surely would've been a wide, confident smile from breaking out. An announcement called out, telling everyone that the players were expected out on court shortly. Scottie shifted in place, this time with impatience to get started. Her hands ran down her ELITE crop top, smoothing out any wrinkles.

"I can do this," she said to herself on an inhale, taking a deep calming breath. I watched as her chest rose, feeling her confidence, her fight. She had this.

My girl had this.

"I always believed that you could." My hand reached out to her, interlacing our fingers and squeezing. It was more than we'd ever done openly, but I couldn't help the overwhelming need to touch her, my own anticipation at watching her play beginning to rise. A goodbye and good luck was on the edge of my tongue.

"Scottie, can I pull you in for a quick photo?" Sarah, our photographer from the training camp, appeared from a crowd, camera in hand. She had been around us during our time here, usually taking photos during matches or after, always making sure we were still wearing the ELITE brand.

Scottie frowned slightly, her hand dropping from mine as her eyebrows pressed together. "Not right now. I'm just about to go out."

Sarah turned to look at the clock, calculating that we still had some time before she had to go out. "Three seconds, that's all," she pushed.

Scottie's face twisted with indecision, understandably not happy that Sarah had decided now of all the moments to request a photo. But I knew she hated arguing because of our contract with ELITE.

"Fine," she relented, and Sarah turned to lead her away. I picked up her racket bag, keeping by her side as Sarah pushed through the other players and coaches getting ready for their matches. There was no way I was leaving her alone with Sarah.

Scottie's gaze constantly flickered back over her shoulder as Sarah led us across the room, as if to keep an eye on the time and not be late to her game. The crowd finally broke, and my stomach dropped as I realised who was waiting for us.

If she knew what she was doing, Sarah's voice gave nothing away as she instructed casually, "Okay, if I can get you over here beside your dad, we can get this done."

Scottie's attention turned back, and she stopped dead in her tracks beside me. My hand formed a fist on instinct, anger riling up inside of me at the sight of her father, dressed casually in a button-up and shorts, standing beside the Wimbledon logo, looking photo op ready.

"Why is he here?" My voice was deep and low as I looked at Sarah, confusion clear in her face. She didn't even bother to answer my question as she shook her head.

"Just a quick photo. That's all we need."

"Good to see you, Scottie." He looked as slimy as ever, a snakish grin on his face as he peered across at her. I wanted to take her away. Get her away from him.

"What do you want?" Scottie's voice was full of frustration, her eyes fixed on Matteo. She turned to Sarah. "What is this? Why is he here?"

"ELITE asked for a photo of the two of you," Sarah said half-heartedly, her attention on her camera settings. Clearly, she either had no idea what she was doing, or she didn't care. Was this revenge for the beach?

Matteo's shoulders relaxed, his demeanour softening from smug to somewhat fatherly. "Come on. Take the photo. For old times' sake," he pressed, raising a hand and waving to her only. To anyone looking onto the scene, they'd see a legend reuniting with his daughter. They wouldn't know how dangerous this all was.

My hand found hers, pulling at her. "Scottie, you don't have to do this," I urged, desperate to make this stop somehow. I knew whatever this was, it wasn't good. The fact he was at Wimbledon was enough to set me on edge, but here, in this room, taking this photo? And where was Jon to stop it all?

I could see her fear and confusion in her expression as she silently looked back at the clock, the pressure folding in on her, the time ticking down until she was due on the court.

"Nico, let's get you in there too," Sarah insisted, her tone beginning to sound snipped. She moved, taking up a place in front of Matteo, camera raised and primed, as she ushered us over.

I shook my head, insistent on not cooperating. Fuck ELITE. Fuck whatever this was. "No, we aren't doing this."

"Really? Now you're making a big scene," Matteo said so plainly, he almost sounded like a reasonable person. I had to bite down my rage, keeping the monster contained. A scene would give him what he wanted. He pushed an eyebrow up, his palms out wide. "People do talk, you know?"

There was a lull, like the world had gone on pause. Scottie took a moment, looking around us. I could see it too, the eyes of people looking our way, their attention pulled by our arguing. We were drawing too much attention, and it was beginning to make her feel nervous. He was using everything to his advantage to twist her into this. I turned to her, readying myself to get her out of here, but instead, I watched her shoulders pull back, her spine straightening.

"Let's get it over with," she muttered, each word sounding painful. She took a few short steps over, standing on the opposite side of the logo. I followed, nudging her over further to the right so I was between her and Matteo, as if my body was a wall to protect her. I just wanted her as far from him as possible.

"Smile," Matteo reminded, my stomach twisting just as Sarah took a few shots. As soon as I registered the flash of the camera, the click of the photo being taken, my hand was around Scottie's, pulling her away.

His voice rang through the crowd as he shouted after us, "Good luck."

My anger was beating at me like a drum, a loud droning noise that threatened to erupt. But I knew I had to keep a lid on it, keep myself in check. Not here. Not now. She still had a match to win. I didn't stop until we were back at the door, and there was barely another moment before her name was being called, the game almost ready to start.

"Are you okay?" She didn't even look at me, her eyes pinned instead to the door. She nodded silently, but I could see it was gone—the confidence, the fight. She had been cut down just when she'd found it. Maybe that was the plan all along. Get in her head, under her skin. Take this from her again. Dread drained the blood from my face at the thought.

"Scottie." Her name was a plea, but it worked, and her eyes met mine. I did my best to keep my anxiety under wraps, keep myself composed when all I felt like doing was storming back over and making that man pay for what he had done.

"I'm fine," she snipped, pushing her hair back out, dragging her hands down her face. I could see her resolve flickering like embers of a dying fire. I took a deep breath in, trying to temper my panic. She could not go out there like this.

"You can do this," I pressed, placing my hands on her shoulders to root her back in the moment. "Remember your game plan." Her hands met mine on her shoulders, palms pressing against the top of mine as if she needed the connection.

"I know," she said, and I finally caught the spark, anger igniting and replacing the defeat in her eyes. "I've got this." Her name was called again, pressing the urgency of which she was expected on court, but her eyes stayed on mine.

"Scottie Sinclair in the finals. You belong there. Fight for it," I pressed as her hands clenched around mine. She let go of a deep, shaky breath, the exhale calming her, bringing her back. I could see it now. She was here. She was back. She was mine.

Her eyes closed for a moment, before she took a step away, my hands releasing her shoulders as they confidently pushed back, chest out, and grabbed her bag from where it had been sitting waiting. "I'm ready. I can do this."

And I believed her. I really did.

Sinclair vs Costa
Quarterfinals – Court 1

THERE WERE RARE moments of beauty in life. Most of them pass you by before you even realise what you've seen. But watching Scottie Sinclair glide across Wimbledon's centre court during the quarterfinals against Inés Costa was one where you immediately understood you were witnessing something special.

Inés took the first set, but Scottie the second, exploiting Inés's weakness just as she had planned. Now in the third and final set, Inés was slowing, struggling to keep the strength in her returns. The match was still a fight, the umpire challenging to work with.

Throughout the match, he'd made it hard on Scottie, calling various infractions. Some were fair, like her serves called out, but others had left Scottie frustrated. He had handed out a few time violations for her taking too long during breaks, sometimes a foot fault when it seemed like her footing was nowhere near the baseline. Once even a net touch when it was hard to even see if it had happened.

She'd used her challenges where she felt confident the call was unfair, the hawk-eye camera helping to determine if the ball was actually out. But despite that, it was clear her annoyance was rising at him.

My anxiety watching her was sky-high, unable to keep myself from fidgeting, rubbing my clammy palms up and down the nylon material of my shorts.

When I'd first gotten to the box to find Jon already there, all the anger I had pent up exploded, demanding to know why he wasn't with us. Jon, with a much cooler head than mine, waited until I had told him what had happened. A dark look had furrowed onto his face when I mentioned the photo, and he quickly disappeared again. When he returned, he'd informed me that Sarah had been dismissed and sent back to ELITE. Apparently, she'd claimed not to know the drama between Scottie and her dad, but I didn't buy the excuse.

It was Scottie's serve on game point, already up two points to Inés. I was mesmerised as her long body stretched up, and by the strength in her arms when her racket collided with the ball and she expertly sent it spinning over the net. My eyes were still trained on every tiny motion of her body as she moved from the service line. Inés sprung from her position, racket swung out wide to return, the ball just passing her as she missed when the umpire broke the hush over the crowd.

"Fault!"

Despite the distance, I could see Scottie's jaw locked in frustration, and behind her, even Inés looked to the umpire, her brows pressed together in confusion. Scottie challenged the call, her patience waning as she paced back and forth while the system processed the video from the camera. Inés, in the background, looked conflicted, gesturing slightly to the umpire as if she couldn't decide if she could make up her mind about speaking up.

The crowd around us began to clap as the video came into view, louder and louder as we followed the computer-generated trajectory of the shot. My hands curled into fists, agitation biting at me as the result came through.

OUT

My heart dipped at the result, some of the crowd jeering in delight. I tried to ignore them, immediately returning to Scottie, watching as she took a moment to pull herself together. Then, when she was ready, she pushed her shoulders back, shaking her head as if to shrug the mood away—a move I'd watched her do a hundred times when my shit talking during practice was getting on her nerves. She'd shake me off and ruin me with a big serve.

And that's exactly what she did next, the ball tracking system reporting her serve at an insane 114 mph as the ball slammed onto the opposite side of the court. Inés struggled to return it before finding her stride, and both began their back and forth.

Game point—Scottie. And they carried on to the next play.

Scottie waited for Inés to serve, clearly a little impatient for her to get on with it, but letting her opponent take her time. It was known Inés was extremely superstitious; she had to have the right count in her head before she would begin.

Finally, she served, Scottie being quick to return the ball. But ultimately, Inés was able to catch her off guard, rushing the net and volleying the ball out of Scottie's reach.

15 – 0

Scottie returned her next serve with ease.

15 – all

Inés's following serve was called out, and on her second serve, she hit an ace, the ball landing in the corner of the service box.

30 – 15

The game continued, Scottie chasing down every ball, every hit of her game perfection. The way she was able to read Inés's next play, react in a split second and glide across the court without missing a beat. Scottie was perfection on court, her body a tool, her mind a weapon. I wasn't surprised when we were onto the next game, her serve, with the previous game tucked safely into her pocket. She was closing in on the set now.

I watched Scottie as she counted in her head, preparing to serve. She tossed the spare balls to the side until she finally chose the one she wanted, then the umpire called again.

"Time violation, Sinclair."

At first, her expression was confused, looking around the court when her eyes found the serve clock countdown ticking down to zero. Her arms fell to her side, her head shaking. I knew she was trying to keep a leash on her anger, pushing it down. And as she set herself up for her second serve, returning to that focus on her movement, a hush fell across the court as we all watched, breath held, waiting for the sound of her racket whipping through the air.

"Foot fault, Sinclair. Point awarded to Costa," the umpire announced, and that was the moment her patience snapped. She dropped her ball, practically throwing it to the side, her racket pointing over at the umpire.

"Are you trying to distract me?" she shouted over at the umpire, taking a few steps closer to him. At first, he ignored her, waiting for her to serve, but she shouted again. "Well?"

Finally, he turned, waving his hand. It was impossible to hear what he said back, the crowd around me impatient, boos and whistles breaking the usual respectful hush of the court.

From the start, it was easy to see how the umpire had been slowly distracting her from her match, making all sorts of calls against Scottie, but none against her opponent. And now, one set down and the score heavily leaning in Inés's favour, Scottie had finally had enough.

"Keep it brief?" Her voice echoed around the court, growing louder as she got increasingly frustrated, she took a few steps closer to the chair. "I lost that point because of your calls. You are intentionally being distracting."

One look to my left and I found Jon's grim expression transfixed on Scottie, his voice low as he murmured softly, "You gotta calm down, kid. Don't let him get under your skin."

I couldn't hear what the umpire responded, but Scottie's shoulders slumped as she listened to his response. Turning away from him, she threw her hands out in exasperation, left hand still grasping her racket. The umpire spoke again, but his response was once again lost in the noise of the crowd.

She faced him again, feet planted as she pointed her free hand down. "No, we're doing it now. My last serve was in, and you called it out! Not to mention the fact that she's been going over time, but you've not said a damn thing about it."

Jon shook his head, his hands out as he tried to catch Scottie's attention while lowering his hands as if to indicate for her to calm down, but she either didn't see him or ignored his advice.

"Challenge? I've already wasted challenges and time on your other mistakes!" Both Jon and I stood up from our seats, watching helplessly as Scottie continued to loudly express her anger and frustration. Jon muttered under his breath, hands dragging over his face as he tried to keep his own actions under control.

A deep pit opened up in my stomach. Then, he caught my eye. Straight ahead, at the other side of the court sitting dead centre in the crowd. Matteo.

I immediately thought of Scottie, wondering if she knew he was also in the crowd, but when she shouted again at the umpire, I was almost comforted by the fact that she was too distracted to notice him.

"How am I supposed to play when I'm up against my opponent and this asshole? This is ridiculous." Her voice cut through to me, and I was desperate to go down, intervene somehow, even if it meant calming her, but I knew better.

"Third offence, verbal abuse. Game point awarded to Costa," the umpire issued, his voice booming through the microphone. Immediately, Scottie relaunched into an argument with him, wildly fighting the accusations.

It all went downhill as I watched her get increasingly frustrated, all emotions boiling over with the pressure and intensity of the game. Eventually, she gave up fighting the umpire, issuing a final challenge that he would never be on court for another of her matches again, and went back to the baseline.

But it was too late; her concentration was fried and her game in tatters. She played with too much fury, hitting the ball too hard, missing returns she would've easily made.

If the umpire had been doing this on purpose, then it would be mission accomplished because it took up all my strength to watch her miss that final point, sealing Inés's win, locking Scottie out of the women's single competition at Wimbledon for another year.

CHAPTER FORTY

Scottie
Castles Crumbling – Taylor Swift

Anger like this was a real, tangible thing. A beast, living and breathing. Normally, I had a leash on it, controlling it to my own advantage. The strength that sort of rage contained was a useful tool, delivering precise serves and driving me to success when all else had failed.

But that match against Inés, with that umpire, I hadn't just lost control—I'd let it consume me entirely.

I sat on the wooden locker room bench, a personal one this time since I'd made it to the quarterfinals, surrounded by the entire contents of my training bag. Emptied out, kicked around, and smashed into walls. Two tennis rackets sat in pieces alongside crushed bottles and snacks that had been demolished with angry stomps.

And yet, my blood was still molten lava, anger burning up my veins. My body didn't feel like my own, still finding my way back through my rage.

The game had been a car crash from the start. I was all for respecting the umpire, but he had some sort of vendetta against me, calling my shots out but ignoring my opponent's, picking on me for time discrepancies. It would've been fine if he was strict, but it was only for me.

He was intent on wasting my time, keeping me out of my focus, and ruining my game.

In the end, there was only so much I could take before I snapped, and boy did I. I played everything wrong, footwork turning clumsy, and any sort of strategic thinking was completely thrown out of the window. By the final set of the game, I was practically begging for Inés to knock me out in some freak tennis accident and end my suffering once and for all.

A knock on the door broke me out of my spiralled thinking, and I could barely manage a reply, my voice hoarse from yelling.

"Yeah?" The noise was croaked, but it was loud enough for the person on the other side to hear. I expected Jon, expected his disappointed grimace and shoulder pat, paired with a somewhat comforting, "There's always next time, kid." I'd probably end up snapping all over again.

Instead, Nico appeared, and relief washed over me. Dressed in a white T-shirt and shorts, he was ready for his own afternoon match. I could barely manage to look at him, the softness in his grey eyes overwhelming.

I expected him to pause, to look around and be ashamed of the mess I had made, of what my rage looked like. Instead, I listened to the door click closed behind him, heard his careful footsteps walk across to me, and stayed frozen as he sat down on the bench beside me, his body grazing against the side of mine.

I couldn't help but melt into him when his strong arm wrapped around my body, the warmth of his body and fresh scent of his shampoo surrounding me and all of a sudden, the dam broke. Instead of my earlier anger and frustration breaking through, I was crying, shattered and falling apart in his arms. He held me, one hand rubbing low on my back, the other stroking soothingly over my hair, letting me ugly sob into him.

"It's okay." His head leaned onto mine, leaving a single kiss on the top of my hair. "You tried your best. You were beautiful out there."

I sobbed into his clean T-shirt, more than sure that I was leaving embarrassing wet patches on the white material. "I was a mess."

His hand on my lower back stroked, the movement wide as he kept a strong pressure there, the moment calming my heartbeat. "You know that wasn't your fault."

"I threw it away. I let him get to me."

"It happens to the best of us," he comforted, before going a step further. His hand moved to my opposite thigh, wedging over and pulling my body onto his. Our chests pressed together, my head on his shoulder, legs around his waist. I pulled myself as close as I could, feeling his chest rising and falling against mine, deep calming breaths that reminded me of the waves softly crashing into the rocky Rhodes shore.

I could still hear them, the noises of the beach that day we sat out there, sharing stories like we were the only two in the world. How was it he always found me? Always knew what to say and do?

"I've done it myself," he admitted. "The French Open during the semis a couple years back. There was this umpire, and I knew it from the beginning, how he looked at me. Like I was trouble, and they were going to treat me as such. He made every possible call against me, and by the end, I . . . I lost it completely."

The memory resurfaced. Diva behaviour on court always made news. I could practically feel the headlines being drawn up as we spoke.

"Was that the time you broke your racket on court?" I asked.

"It was my lucky racket too," he joked. "The umpire did me for equipment damage, so I threw it at his head. Goddamn idiot move. Got me disqualified."

I remembered the video and felt his rage through the screen. It was easy to think he was being hateful and unprofessional, and maybe he was. But when you poured so much intensity into the practice, when you turned your body into a tool, walking the precipice of physical abuse, it was hard to stay rational in the face of unfairness.

When you felt like the opportunity was being stolen from you, it was twice as hard as when you screwed it up yourself. Usually, because it felt like weakness.

"At least I waited until I was alone to lose my shit," I hummed, every moment with him leaving me a little lighter.

He laughed softly. The feeling of it against my chest had me closing my eyes, revelling in his joy. "You sure did a number here. I'm quite impressed."

"I swear, if people knew how good it felt to destroy a racket, the entire anger management industry would collapse in on itself."

"Maybe we should consider taking a few classes." His tone turned light and playful. "It might save a few innocent rackets from total destruction."

"Nah." Slowly, my own lips began to curl with his words. "They had it comin'."

I pulled back from his shoulder and sat up to properly look at him. His face was clear of any judgement, any pity either hidden or nonexistent. Instead, his eyes were filled with concern as they scanned over my face. I was sure my red-rimmed eyes and puffy face were quite the look.

He asked, "Are you okay?" The immediate grimace on my face was a clear answer. "I mean, you know you're going to be okay?"

I shifted my head back and forth, still trying to decide that for myself. "We do still have a doubles competition to win."

At least we had that. Normally, this would be it for me. I'd be done and out until the next competition. But because we were here together, I had a second opportunity. I could win with him by my side, and now I realised I couldn't think of a sweeter ending to this story.

A smile grew wide on his lips. "Atta girl."

"And you a singles," I reminded. I could've sworn the smile faltered for a moment, something in his eyes flickering, but his hands moved to the side of my face, cupping and pulling me into him for a kiss as if to distract me. Which, it did, my body giving in to the moment, enjoying the momentary freedom from the heavy feeling that had still to loosen its grip.

"What time is your match?" I asked, resting my forehead against him.

He groaned, scrunching his face up. "Soon. An hour."

"Jon will be hunting you down for warm-ups," I warned, eliciting another noise of complaint from him. I smiled, kissing him once again as a comfort, before shifting my weight.

"No," he said, his hands keeping me on him. "One more minute."

I raised an eyebrow at his words, forcing my lips to stay pressed together in a disapproving line. I was ready to put up a small fake fight, but I was too weak against him and instantly I relented to his request, my lips meeting his again.

We stayed like that for a moment, wrapped up in each other, losing ourselves a little. It was so easy to be with him. He hadn't come here to make me feel worse; he'd come because he supported me, to be here for me. I'd been running from what used to be my life for years. Who'd have known that he'd be the person to help bring me back? I wanted to stay tangled up in his arms, in his bed, for as long as he'd have me.

"You gotta go," I reminded him, finding the physical strength to pull myself away from him. He narrowed his eyes at me, pursing his lip to one side as if he was considering bowing out of the competition entirely to stay here five minutes longer.

"Fine," he agreed, his tone grumpy. "But tonight, keep it free."

My eyebrows pressed up. "Why?"

"I think after today, we deserve some time off."

I paused at the idea, considering my options. Another late night analysing every misstep I took on court, every time I should've kept my calm at the umpire, every bad call he made?

Or a hanging out with Nico Kotas?

"I'm in," I said, watching his smile grow. I slid from his lap and raised a single finger. "On one condition."

His head fell back in fake annoyance. "What's that?"

"You gotta win."

His smile turned into a sly smirk. "Maybe you ought to stick around, be my good luck charm, and make sure I do."

"Me?" I let out a sharp laugh. "After today, you really think I'm lucky?"

He kissed me once, just a quick peck, but it was enough to leave me breathless. "Wear my hat and prove me right."

CHAPTER FORTY-ONE

Nico
Play God – Sam Fender

Kotas vs Anderson
Quarterfinals – Centre Court

I thought I'd been nervous before a match, but it didn't compare to knowing Scottie was tucked away in my player's box, watching me. Every break, my eyes couldn't help but go to her, see the tuck of blonde hair under a navy cap—my cap.

Instinct kicked in as the ball flew across the court. Oliver's serves were nothing to be trifled with, and I acted quickly to return them. The tense, hushed crowd left only the noise of our quick footsteps and the snap of the ball meeting a racket.

We both charged across the court, determined to take this point. I'd won the first two sets, and now we were in an all-out assault for the third.

The first point ended when he hit the ball over to my side of the court, and years of training left me with the assurance that the ball would be out. It bounced, and the yell of the crowd and an announcement from the umpire confirmed the point was mine.

I smiled, giving a small celebration before I couldn't help but look and find her again, her lips curled up into a knowing smile. My already erratic heart rate had pounded into overdrive at the sight of her.

Everything about her was perfect. Her drive, her strength, the way her lips pressed against mine. It was getting harder and harder to hold myself back from her, to pretend like I didn't want this to be something real, something that lasted after our partnership at Wimbledon. Impossible, in fact, when all I could do was think of her.

She mouthed the word "focus," and flicked a finger towards the court. I smirked back, shrugging my shoulders, wishing I could keep my eyes on her longer, but I knew she was right. I had to keep my head in this game if I was going to beat Oliver.

I'd played the cocky Brit many times in my career, and at Wimbledon, Oliver had the upper hand, playing to a hometown crowd.

15 – 0

The second point opened with Oliver's serve. My forehand return was quick and powerful, hoping to catch him off guard with the speed, but he was ready. We rallied for a while, each time the ball gaining momentum. Oliver finally hit the ball to the far right corner of the court, and I chased it down. My legs almost ran in an all-out sprint to make it into a position. With a firm wrist, I volleyed the ball over the net.

I almost claimed the point, Oliver having to readjust his play to compensate for my movement, but he hit it back over, sending it flying to the back corner.

I'd barely found my footing before I swung, momentum still pulling me forward as my arm swung back, racket facing to return as the ball spun over the net. I continued to slide forward. My body shifted under me, my knee unable to adjust to the unexpected weight from the quick moment, and then I came crashing into the ground.

Scarred skin met grass, and I nearly blacked out the moment my knee collided with the ground, the pain blinding, reverberating up and down my leg. I managed to roll onto my back, my hands cradling my knee, my fingers feeling up the scar to make sure the skin hadn't split open.

I was sure I was out. That the months of recovery had been for nothing, that my career was over. With the pain searing, it certainly felt like it was. But through the pain, I spotted Scottie, saw her through the crowd, standing up, a look of horror across her beautiful face.

And I remembered who I was fighting for. Without her, I wouldn't be here, wouldn't have any fight left. That was what she gave me—the strength to keep going, to remember why this was important to me. To us.

This comeback was supposed to prove to myself that I could do it, that I wasn't old and exhausted. That not only could I still play the sport I loved, but I could win.

Up until I met her, nothing felt as good as winning. Now, it only counted if she was by my side.

I took a deep breath in and focused, moving past the pain, pushing it down until I didn't feel it anymore—or at least, didn't feel it in that moment—and I pushed myself up from the ground.

I gritted my teeth as I took a step forward, the crowd clapping as I got up. Turning to my left, I found Oliver at the net, a worried look across his face, his dark hair stuck to his forehead.

"You alright?" he asked, head tilting, as the umpire appeared beside me, handing me back my racket.

For a moment, we weren't competitors. I knew him well enough when we weren't playing against each other, his fun, cocky attitude always bringing us back to our latest battle on court. He was a great guy, but there were no friendships strong enough to distract me from what I needed to do.

"I'm fine, thanks." I nodded, taking the racket and thanking the umpire, spinning it in my hand to find my grip. "Now get back over there so I can beat you."

He smiled widely, reassured. "It's like that, eh?" The crowd laughed at his response, the noise dipping just enough for them to hear our conversation. Oliver beamed all the way back to the service box, his abundance of annoying confidence shining out of him like sunshine.

I only re-focused on the win, on finishing this match once and for all. Oliver had managed to hit the ball back over the net while I'd been falling, so that had been for nothing. Tennis is nothing but brutal, after all.

The score was 30 – 0, and again, Oliver served. It was clear there was something wrong with my knee. My pace was slower, more painful, even my body felt different, reluctant to put down any more weight than necessary.

The tide turned on me. Oliver easily took the game, then soon after, the third set. I could feel the anticipation of the crowd in the charged silence of the court, every bit of ground claimed by Oliver gaining a louder and louder cheer from them. I shook my head at the reminder that by cheering for him, they were cheering for my own downfall.

In the fourth set, I only grew more pained, just trying to get through to the next break, tiredness setting in, panic wracking at my brain. I couldn't take another fall like that. The thought of the pain turned my stomach, but despite that, I wouldn't quit on this. They'd sooner carry me out on a stretcher than take this from me.

I knew if I didn't try something soon, I was going to lose. Victory was one set away for me, two for him. If I let him take this, we'd be playing another, and with my injury and exhaustion . . . would I make it through?

Defeat was not an option. Winning was all I had. I was struggling to serve, the ball shaking in my hands as I held it, my hand adjusting its grip on the racket. I was finally ready to serve when something hit my cheek. My head tilted to the sky, only to be hit on the cheek by another raindrop.

I only felt relief when another hit me, and another, until a heavy summer shower erupted over the court. The umpire made an immediate announcement, suspending gameplay until the next day as it was already late.

My knees weakened under my weight, almost falling back to the ground, but I carefully made my way to the edge of the court, getting out of the way of the grounds crew who were frantically rolling out a tarp to protect the grass. I grabbed my bag, stuffing everything inside as the crowd grumbled unhappily, quickly leaving to go find shelter.

I took one long look around the emptying court. I'd played here plenty of times in my career, but none had felt like this. The rain coming down heavy, highlighted in the bright lights that lit up the fast space.

There was a finality to it. Like this could be the last time I ever stepped out onto the grass.

CHAPTER FORTY-TWO

Nico

i don't want to watch the world end with
someone else – Clinton Kane

I knew from the grim look on Jon's and Ethan's faces as they stood in my locker room what was about to come next. Ethan was already there when I limped off the court, ready to help me cool down post-match, but his face had dropped into concern when he saw my grimaced, hissing through teeth, gritted reaction to his basic massage and stretches.

"I'm sorry, but you can't go on. We need to give you sufficient time to heal this knee, and playing in both competitions is untenable." Ethan's words were not a shock, but nonetheless, I was determined to fight them.

"Look, I fell—" I started to reason, sitting on the wooden bench opposite the lockers, hoping that I could convince them again that I was up to this. Give me an ice bath, some painkillers, and an evening of rest and I'd fight through tomorrow.

"Nico." Jon pulled my attention, his head leaning toward Ethan as he stood in the opposite corner of the room. "It's time to listen."

I stared at him for a long moment, the instinct to argue raging inside of me. A snarling beast who refused to accept defeat. The trained athlete who despised any sign of weakness and fought back in the face of failure.

Somehow, I swallowed it down, and looked to the physio, who continued, "The joint has significant trauma. I'm not sure I'd even recommend carrying on in either competition."

"We can announce you and Scottie are pulling out of the doubles at the press conference next. Then you rest up tonight and with what little game is left, you finish and win tomorrow." Jon laid out the plan as if it was that easy to accept.

I shook my head, hanging it as I gripped the edge of the bench so tightly, I was sure the wood would splinter. "Can't we wait and see how it goes tomorrow?"

"We need to make a decision; we can't keep avoiding it." Jon sighed, his tense body crumbling inward. "I know it's important to you, Nico, but this is what is best. It's better for you, for your career, to take part in the men's singles competition. The doubles were always supplementary."

"I can't." My memory replayed that night back in Rhodes when she told me what her father had done to her. How her face was etched with worry that I might not believe her, that she had kept all that pain wrapped up inside and had taken her revenge any other way she could. And this competition, training with me, partnering up for doubles, that had all been part of the revenge that still allowed her to come back and do what she loved. I gritted my teeth with a fresh determination. "I can't let her down like that."

There was a knock, and the door swung open, Scottie sticking her head in. She scanned the room quickly, seeing Jon and Ethan, taking in the mood of the room. Then her gaze turned to me, and I knew it was written all over my face—the guilt twisting up my gut.

"Can we have a moment, guys?" She stepped inside, holding the door open for Ethan and Jon. Without so much as another word, they shuffled out and closed the door behind them.

One long silence filled up every corner of the room as her eyes analysed the entire length of my body. She stood almost glued to the wall opposite me, biting her lip.

Then, with a tender look, she asked in her usual light tone, "So, how badly fucked is your knee?"

I rolled my eyes as I tried to shrug her concerns off. "It's fine, really, it's—"

"It's lucky you're walking without a walker, old man," she interrupted, that tender smile turning sneaky. I raised an eyebrow at her favourite nickname for me.

"Really? That's making a comeback here?"

She raised her shoulders. "Hey, I'm about to get all self-sacrificial here. I can say what I want."

I pushed down the shame, hating that she knew so easily what they were trying to get me to do. Meanwhile, I was still unwilling to accept that this was how it had to be. "What about what I want?"

She sighed, shaking her head. "What you want is probably stupid."

My brows furrowed in confusion. "Did Jon tell you?"

"He didn't have to," she said. "I knew what I was signing up for with you and your damn knee. Are they telling you to pull out of both competitions?"

"Just the doubles."

"They think you still have a chance with the singles?" she asked, and I nodded apprehensively. "A chance" might be stretching the definition of what they thought I had. "That's great." She smiled, her words sounding so easy. It cut me to my core, seeing how genuinely pleased she was for me, when all I could think about was what this meant for her.

"I want to give it more time."

She tilted her head forward, her voice going low and serious. "It's not going to get better, Nico. You need to prioritise. A shot at the singles title was your goal; you have a chance here."

"We don't know that it's one over the other," I argued, beginning to feel more and more unhinged, as if I was holding on to this argument by my fingertips. "Rest and ice packs really help take down the swelling."

"You know yourself, that's not enough," she said, before adding, "Let's walk this through logically. You can finish the game off tomorrow, and then it's the semis and the finals, with a good number of days to rest and heal in between. You've beaten Oliver before, you nearly did today, and you can do it tomorrow." Scottie took a beat, some time to recollect her thoughts before she pressed on. "But if you throw the doubles competition in there, you won't have any rest days. It's twice the work, and the competition is tough. Yes, I'm there too, but the singles competition is where you shine. You said yourself, it's the one title you don't have. I know how much that means to you."

"But . . . you," was all I managed to say before she waved a hand in the air, ignoring my concerns.

"Respectfully, fuck me." She smirked. "Do you think I'd give up the singles title for you?"

I considered her question for a moment, the answer deserving more time than a simple "no." I searched through every moment with her, seeing her competitive side on the court, knowing how deep that ran in all of us. We gave up so much for the chance at a win, for five minutes of glory before we do it all again. It was not about the fame or the money.

It was the moment you know you've reached the pinnacle, the thrill and relief when you beat everyone to the top. That feeling was addictive.

Part of me wondered if that was why her dad was still so invested in her. That if his time on top was over, at least he could still have the closest thing by succeeding through her. Like an addict, willing to do anything for their next hit. But Scottie, she wasn't anything like her father. Instead, I found the answer in her blue eyes. Ignoring her cocky smile, the slight playful mood she was using to mask, and there, the truth lay.

If this was as important to me as I knew it was for her, then she would not hesitate. She would fight for me, even if it meant giving up something, even if I didn't want or ask her to.

She was strong, and kind, and selfless in that way, and I loved her for it.

Loved her. Period.

I couldn't help but pull her back into my arms, squeezing her tight as I pressed my lips to her temple, basking in the feel of her body against mine, the sweet scent of her shampoo surrounding me. Her arms wrapped around my waist, her head nuzzled under my chin.

"I'll still be here for you," she promised. "Your lucky charm."

My fingers found her chin, tilting her face up to meet mine. "Good, because I'm really not letting you go anywhere without me anymore."

I watched her expression change as my words sank in, the worry lines smoothing out, her bright smile returning as my heart skipped a beat. And then my lips met hers, unable to hold back from her for another moment.

CHAPTER FORTY-THREE

Scottie
Green Light – LORDE

The press room was packed. Rumours had gotten out that there was some sort of announcement to come from Nico, and it seemed like half of London wanted in on the news.

I'd been in the box when he fell on the grass, and when I heard that gut-wrenching sound of pain, something . . . changed. As if my world narrowed in on that moment, watching him fall to the grass and seeing him at risk of losing his Wimbledon success made me feel like my chest was being squeezed too tightly for my heart.

And when he got up, playing through his obvious pain, my entire world reorganised itself and I realised how Nico had been able to weasel his way into my life, meaning more to me than a mixed partner is supposed to.

Seeing him in his locker room after, with that look of defeat and desperation spread across not only his, but his team's face, it wasn't hard to see how close he was to having it all snatched away.

It was easy, easier than it really should've been, to tell him to let the mixed go. I could almost feel the Scottie from two years ago, the girl who wouldn't throw away a chance at her own title, revolting against the idea. But he meant too much to me now to hold him back.

"Hi, everyone, if you could give me a minute, I've got an announcement to make." Nico's voice echoed around the packed press room as he sat at the front. I was standing to the side, safely out of sight while he and Jon took on the press junket.

His words did little to quell the racket of questions being shouted his way. I could hardly make out a single word except the occasional mention of my own name that I knew couldn't mean anything good.

"Excuse me," he said firmly again, his voice almost booming through the speakers. With that, the press fell quiet, calming as they settled into their seats.

"Thank you," Jon said, taking over. "If you can please give us a few minutes for an announcement, then we will allow some time for questions."

Then it was Nico's turn. I watched as he shifted uncomfortably in his chair, the lump in his throat bobbing with nerves. I smiled softly, as if trying to soothe him from the sidelines, calm him so he could do this.

I hadn't wanted him to feel bad for having to drop out. There would be other titles, other Wimbledons. I'd come back stronger next year because of everything he taught me. They wouldn't know what hit them.

"Over my fifteen-year career, it has been my dream of achieving the men's singles title here at Wimbledon. I think we can all agree, this is a special event. I don't think we can quite explain the effect it has on us players as a whole, but I think it's fair to say we all dream of winning this title." The crowd was hanging on his every word, waiting for his announcement.

"For the last year, I've had one goal, and that was to take part and win this title . . ." Nico's head turned and his eyes found me standing at the sideline, a warmth igniting in the usual cloudy grey colour, an emotion I was still trying to put my finger on when I realised that something had changed for him too.

"And that's still very much the same. Except it won't be the singles title I'm competing for."

My legs went weak under my weight, and I had to grab onto a chair for support, my hands gripping the metal back so I wouldn't fall to the ground.

And then he said the words. "I am pulling out of the singles title completely, in order to focus my efforts on the mixed doubles title."

And the room immediately erupted into chaos, reporters standing up out of their chairs once again, yelling questions, but it was all a distant noise to me as I processed what Nico had done.

He had pulled out of the singles. The last title he had dreamed of winning. For me?

When I finally had enough control over my body to focus, I found Jon and Nico deep in conversation, Jon's hand outstretched covering the microphone so their conversation wasn't picked up. Jon retreated into his chair, his face pale and features still wide with shock. He swallowed before speaking into the microphone. "I guess we will take some questions now."

The room did little to calm, so it took more than a moment for them to be able to pick somebody out of the crowd. When they did, Nico's face twisted with recognition. I moved forward to see it was the man from the Daily Tea.

My eyes rolled at the sight of the journalist, an impulse far beyond my control.

"Is this change of heart anything to do with your doubles teammate, Scottie Sinclair, and the rumoured romance between the two of you?" His question was predictable from a tabloid. Who on earth let this man go first?

Nico leaned back in his chair, his smirk ever telling. "No comment."

The man shook his head in disappointment, and I couldn't help but grin at Nico's delight in denying him an answer.

Another reporter was picked, and someone else in the crowd stood up. "What's your plan for taking on the rest of the competition? Is there a strategy?"

Nico took a moment before slowly sitting up, leaning into the microphone, his words almost a challenge as he said them. "The strategy is to win."

Something grew inside of me, pride that he was back to his normal grumpy self after so much stress with his knee. He was being cocky, annoying, and . . . I couldn't love him more.

Love. My heartbeat pounded in my ears, my head woozy. Months with him on a court, spent teasing and toying and playing. I'd learned so much from him, and somewhere along the way, I'd found my old self again. He'd brought me back. And I loved him for it.

Jon picked a final reporter, obviously seeing that they wouldn't be getting much out of Nico after his bombshell announcement. "Arguably, nobody expected you to do this well on a comeback. Some might say you're a favourite, given your past efforts in other competitions."

Nico looked confusedly between Jon and the crowd, before asking into the microphone, "Is there a point to this?"

"What's behind your motivation to give up the more prestigious title for a mixed doubles?"

The crowd fell silent, waiting to see if he would give them an answer. They could speculate all they wanted, but only he could give his reason.

Instead, he leaned close to the microphone, and with a smile aimed directly at me, he repeated, "No comment."

WE WERE SWEPT out of the room, the noise of the reporters louder than it had been as they desperately shouted their questions at him.

All I registered was the rough brush of his palm against mine, our fingers intertwined, as he stormed from the stage. Jon led the way down the hall back to Nico's locker room, not even waiting until we were alone before he exploded.

"What happened to what we discussed, Nico?" he yelled, a couple of paces ahead of us in the hallway.

"I did what I thought was right."

Jon turned around, the frustration clear on his face. "All this time it's been the singles title. You've made it clear several times that's all you've ever wanted."

There was a moment of tension before Nico simply shrugged. "Things changed."

Jon looked between us, his teeth gritted as he searched for answers. He let out a loud sigh, pushing open the door to Nico's locker room. We took a moment to breathe, my eyes going to Nico only to find his already on me. His hand squeezed mine, the reassurance silent but clear. I smiled softly in reply, still processing everything.

Had that really happened? Was it a heat-of-the-moment decision, or had he always planned this? Just as I formed a tangible string of words to say, Jon's voice boomed from inside the room, pulling us both in.

"Have you at least thought this through?" We found Jon pacing across the room, and as I closed the door to give us some privacy, his next question went right through me. "Is it just for Scottie?"

I almost froze, the same concern filling my brain. I knew how important this was to Nico, felt his anxiety around his injury and the ticking clock he couldn't help but be haunted by. I wanted this for him, this last title, but . . . had he given it up for me?

"Of course it's not only for her," Nico burst out, just as I shrank into a forgotten corner of the room. "But it's because of her I even made it here. And my chances are better in the doubles, we make a great team."

"I agree, you obviously do make a good team, but—"

"Then what's the deal? I'm still in the competition."

"You had a chance of winning that singles title. One last chance . . ." Jon trailed off, aware of how important this was to Nico. He'd been on this journey with him a lot longer than I had been and shared this goal. "I don't want you to regret throwing that work away," Jon finished, managing to stay still.

Nico stood solemn, his shoulders pulled back as he processed what Jon said. For a moment, I worried that he hadn't realised the full extent of what he'd done, what he'd given up. Like he'd been in a dream state and had woken up to absolute horror. But when he spoke, it was calm and resolved.

"I would've regretted staying in the singles," he explained. "It might've finally happened, but I was also sure it was going to break me. It . . . it didn't feel right when everyone was telling me to quit doubles. The singles—I've been in that fight before. I know what it takes to even get to that final, and I'm not sure I've got it."

His admission broke my heart. This last goal he had for his career, the dream, and realising that it wasn't going to happen for him. But also, the pride in knowing his capacity, in putting his body first when for so long, he'd abused it, pushed it far past its limit as we all did at this level of sport.

It was not normal what we put our bodies through, the intense training in order to reach the pinnacle of human athleticism. And then to realise we still came up short.

"But there's a reason you pitched doubles in the first place. Whether you realised it at the time or not, you were giving me a lifeline." He looked away from Jon, his gaze meeting mine again and his smile warmed me from the inside out.

Jon went quiet, his eyes assessing the two of us, before he shook his head, mumbling to himself, "I knew I'd regret putting the two of you together."

I fought a grin across my lips. "It was your idea."

"At least this means you both still have a chance to compete." Something about him relaxed, as if he began to accept what was right in front of his eyes. "You know, you both might be taking this PR campaign for ELITE a little too close to heart. We did specify that it didn't have to be real."

My grin only grew. "Again, your idea."

The hidden smile on Nico's lips confirmed the joke was funny, but Jon was apparently in anything but a laughing mood.

"I am happy for you guys, I swear. But whatever this is, it's giving me a migraine trying to untangle. Head back to the hotel." His attention turned to Nico. "Make sure you ice that knee, and I'll catch up with you later to go over the plan."

We both nodded, not wasting another moment before we disappeared out of the room.

CHAPTER FORTY-FOUR

Nico
Heart Skipped a Beat – The xx

With my relatively narrow escape from Jon's wrath complete, we didn't waste any time heading to the car. I was desperate for a moment that was just the two of us, where I could wrap my arms around her and breathe her in.

I'd always hated doing press after a match. Achy muscles and the anticipation to start preparing myself for the next game left me inpatient and irritated by their incessant questions—not that I was ever not grumpy while dealing with the press. It always left me on edge. But today, I'd planned exactly what I wanted to say. Despite what Jon and Ethan were advising, I knew staying in the singles was the wrong decision for many reasons.

And as her fingers intertwined with mine, I had no regrets about any of it.

We turned the corner together, reaching the front door, only for Scottie to pull me back at the last second with a quick yank of her arm. Flashes of cameras going off on the other side of the glass wall told me who waited for our exit.

"Maybe you should go first. I'll give them a few minutes and meet you in the car," she said, her hand pulled from mine, her face turning a slight shade of red as she became flustered, peering back round the corner that kept us safe from view. "Shit—there's so many of them."

I looked at her, confused. "Why would we do that?"

Her gaze snapped up to mine, her head pulling back. "Do we want to give them more photos of us together? This is already turning into a circus."

The sharp edge of my confusion softened, and I shook my head. "I don't care about that. There's no fucking way in hell I'm letting you go out there without me."

I'd seen well enough how they treated her. She was nothing more than a headline, a payday to them, and I was unwilling to leave her alone to deal with them.

"I don't care about people seeing us together, Scottie," I continued, reading the reluctance on her face. "I want people to know I'm yours. I want them to know that if they mess with you, they are going to have to answer to me."

She looked at me for a moment, her gaze trying to read anything other than the certainty spread across my features, like she was trying to unpick a lie. My hand rose to her cheek, brushing the soft skin there, as I couldn't help but pull her in for a kiss.

"I love you." The words were as easy as they should be. Confidence was an easy thing around her. She took a step forward, pushing me so my back found the wall, before her lips met mine in a rush. I smiled, my lips moving against hers, the taste of her all I ever wanted to know.

When she pulled back, her blue eyes were almost sparkling. "I love you too."

My hand pulled her face to mine again so I could kiss her, happiness warming in the centre of my chest.

She was mine, all mine. I'd never felt this way about anyone, never met anyone worth the hassle of opening up to.

But Scottie Sinclair had pried me open like a knife at an oyster. At first, she got under my skin—an irritation and an unwanted reminder of my weakness. But as the weeks went by, she became the reason I grew stronger, my recovery every bit a credit to her own resolve in training as it was mine. And then there were all the moments she allowed me to see past her facade, the forced confidence, and slowly she let me in, trusting me enough to be vulnerable.

She let me feel worthy around her. Whether I was old and broken and used up, I knew she'd never look at me any different for that.

And it was one of the many reasons I loved her as much as one person could love another.

Why she was a reason I'd changed my goals. Because what was it all for if she wasn't by my side while I did it?

We stayed there, foreheads pressed together as I held her to my body. I needed her alone, craved to feel her soft skin against mine, to ink her words into my skin and make them permanent.

My hand found hers again, and this time, I gripped almost too tightly, certain that if I didn't fuse our palms together, she might lose her nerve when we stepped outside and let me go. But I wouldn't let go, not unless she asked, and certainly not out of fear.

The pack of paps was ravenous by the time we stepped out again, the lightning storm of camera flashes blinding.

"Stay close, keep your head down," I murmured to her as we stepped outside into the summer air. We were swarmed immediately, the security outside just able to keep them clear of us. Making a beeline straight for the town car, I only looked up to make sure she wasn't being hassled. I pulled open the car door, stepping behind and allowing her to slip in first, before closing the door and going around to the other side.

As soon as my door slammed shut, the car took off, the hum of the engine bursting into life.

"Back to the hotel?" the driver asked, and Scottie confirmed, her voice still light despite the crowd.

"Is it normally like that for you?" I asked, watching as she relaxed into the leather seats, the executive car long enough for her to stretch her long legs out comfortably. The white skirt of her summer dress rose up against the pale skin of her thigh.

Her blue gaze caught mine, wisps of blonde hair escaping her ponytail and trailing across her face. She shrugged. "It comes and goes. I suppose I got used to it."

My jaw locked with irritation, a grinding anger growing in my gut. I hated that for her, that she was followed like that by strange, pestering men. Even when you thought you were alone, like I thought we were in the airport in Rhodes our first day, you never truly were. Privacy was a privilege that had been taken from her.

And then, I realised, by extension, it could be denied to me too. For simply being with her.

My eyes met hers again, and I found my uncertainty mirrored back in her shade of deep blue, dark iris lines of worry. I knew she had realised the same thing. The need to erase that worry from her face consumed me.

The car came to a slow stop, our attention pulled to the driver.

"Sorry, guys, looks like this is going to take a while to clear," he said, backlit by a line of brake lights in front. The roads were blocked, traffic bumper to bumper in the streets ahead.

"No worries, just do what you can," I said, before finding the control for the partition and raising it. Scottie raised an eyebrow at me, trying to read my next move.

I unclipped her seatbelt before stretching over to her farthest leg, easing her over to me. Her body relented, letting me guide her from her seated position so she was straddling me instead. Face-to-face, I could still see the concern in her eyes. My left hand slid across her jaw, while my right found the exposed skin of her thigh, her skirt pushed up revealing inches of soft milky skin, tempting me to drive my hand higher than it should've in the back of a car.

"There is nothing that could drive me away from you, Scottie." Her gaze dipped as I spoke, forcing me to lower my head to keep her attention. "If being with you means giving up pieces of my life, it's worth it."

"This is your privacy." Her voice was quiet. "I know that's important to you."

I shook my head, my resolve as firm as my jaw. "It's not nearly as important to me as you are."

The hand on her leg shifted, the delicate feel of her skin against my calloused hand intoxicating.

"You don't know what you'd be giving up."

"I think the last few weeks have been a crash course in exactly what I'd be giving up," I replied softly. "But more importantly, it's who I'm gaining that's far more tempting to me."

Her lips slowly curved into a smile, the band of anxiety around my heart loosening at the sight. "Tempting, eh?"

I groaned against her, lips meeting hers for a simple kiss, all the while my hand slid further up her thigh, finding her ass. "You have no idea."

"I think I have some ideas." She pushed her hips forward, grinding against my cock that was already hard for her. Always hard for her. Wearing shorts around her was a living nightmare. My fingers dug into her perfect ass, taking a handful as I helped guide her back and forth.

A breathy gasp escaped her pink lips, and I knew I was done for. This wasn't how I had imagined ever taking her. In the backseat of a town car, the windows darkened so nobody, including the driver, could see inside.

It took me only a moment before I was undoing my shorts, pulling them apart to free my cock, and rolling on a condom from my wallet. Letting her take control as she ground over it, sending waves of need through my body. I was desperate to feel her wet, tight pussy pulse around my length, feel how perfect a fit she was for me, stretching out to take my size.

I closed my eyes as she moved those perfect hips again, a wet patch through her lace underwear telling me how ready she was for me.

The only noise was the breathy, quiet moans of torment, the shared need between us overwhelming. She tilted to the side, her hand going to her centre and shifting the lace to the side. She pushed up on her knees, lining us up before she pressed down onto my cock.

Our heads buried into each other's opposite shoulders, trying to stifle our groans of pleasure. I felt her teeth on my throat, biting the sensitive skin as her pussy slid down my shaft. So wet and perfect, she felt like heaven, pleasure gliding down every inch as she lowered down, impressively taking the entire length until she bottomed out.

Her hands clung around my neck, her fingers pressing in through the cotton of my T-shirt as she hissed slightly at the pressure. I could hardly string a sentence together, the pressure of the tight grip she had around my cock driving all sense from my brain.

"Don't move," she begged, staying still for a moment. "I need a moment."

"Take your time. I love feeling you stretch to take me." I smiled, kissing the top of her head gently, overwhelmed myself by the feel of her so tight around my length. My body pulled at me, begging as the basic instinct threatened, knowing the pleasure that it gave. But even remaining still inside of her was enough to take me to the edge. Her hips moved, slowly at first, but the indulgence was all the same. The slow grind of her cunt felt like nothing else on this earth.

"Look at me," I commanded as my hand gripped at the top of her ponytail. She had begun to speed up, riding me hard and low. Her eyes caught mine, her mouth open wide while she lost herself to the feeling.

"Do you enjoy getting yourself off on my cock, beautiful?"

Her answer was a quiet moan that I stifled with a kiss. If the rocking of the car wasn't enough to give us away, there was no need to give any further clues, not wanting anything to interrupt us before she had a chance to finish.

"Such a noisy girl. Can you feel how hard it makes me?" I didn't dare tell her to be quiet. Every sound that escaped those perfect pink lips was a luxury I refused to live without. Breathy moans and uncontrolled groans, each drove me further until I was hammering my hips up to meet her movement. Each squeeze and pulse of her pussy along my length nearly drove me to insanity, and if I didn't come soon, I'd be driven insane. I closed my eyes, trying to hold on to the edge of control, not wanting this to be over.

"Fuck me like you mean it, Kotas." Her voice was a seductive whisper, my eyes opening at the control of her tone. The blue of her irises fixed on mine, those pink lips curved into a teasing smile. She had decided to play with me, but I could play back.

With my hand gripping her ponytail, I pulled her head back to reveal her perfect long neck. My hand found its position there, her pulse on my fingertips as I held her.

"You want to make me come over and over?" I asked, eyes darkened and hand pressing. Her skin was soft and perfect, every inch of her a drug.

She whimpered needily, the control slipping from her as I increased my pace from underneath, fucking her as hard as she was moving against me.

Scottie's eyes stayed on mine. "Make me yours."

I lost control, my hips driving forward as she came too, the feel of her perfect cunt pulling tight around my cock beyond anything I'd ever felt before. The love I had for this woman, and the edge of need she drove me to, was unmatched.

I made her mine, but I'd been hers for a long time.

CHAPTER FORTY-FIVE

Scottie
The Great War – Taylor Swift

We were hardly out of the steaming shower, trying to wash off a night spent twisted up in sheets, when there was a knock at the hotel room door. One glance at Nico's equally confused face told me he hadn't somehow secretly ordered breakfast before he hopped in with me. Too bad.

"What if it's Jon?" I whispered, as if they could hear. I sped up, drying myself off with the fluffy towel. Nico's face flattened as he tucked the edge of his in, securing it just low enough to make me want to unwrap him all over again.

He motioned between us. "I think it's somewhat obvious to Jon what's going on here."

I rolled my eyes, switching from the towel to the hotel dressing gown, speedily tying it around my body, my hair wrapped up in a towel.

"It's probably housekeeping," he answered, before he read the apprehension in my eyes. "Do you want me to answer?"

"No." My answer was said before I really gave myself time to think about it, but almost as soon as I declined, social anxiety kicked in. But we were in my room, and if it was anyone other than

Jon, it would look odd to find Nico Kotas, chest bare and lower half only covered by a towel, in my room, no less. The press would have another field day.

I shook my head. "You stay here. I'll go get the door." I took in a deep breath as all the possible options of who was actually there began to scroll through my head. Couldn't I pretend to not be here?

"Keeping me a secret, Sinclair?" Nico's wide smile, grey eyes so soft and light on me, still seemed a little strange. Despite the last few weeks, I wasn't used to seeing him so unguarded. I hung on the end of every second with him, committing them to memory like it could slip away at any moment.

But the longer he stayed, the more reassured I felt that this wasn't temporary. Like we both felt the same way, that his whispered 'I love you' spoken in between a trail of kisses as he traced the freckles on my back was truly real. And the possibility of that was enough to wrap me up warm, and squeeze my heart one notch too tight.

Another knock on the door interrupted my train of thought, keeping me paused in the doorway, before I turned to him, stretching up only to kiss him quickly on the lips.

"Just keeping you to myself." I smiled. "I'm too selfish to share you."

I gently closed the bathroom door behind me, hating every moment I was away from him, hating that he had to stay in the bathroom because of who could be on the other side of the door, obviously growing increasingly impatient as they knocked yet again.

I grabbed the doorknob before remembering the peep hole. Pressing my eye to the glass, I peered through, brows furrowing together at the sight of brown hair. When I finally opened the door, taking a moment to try to collect myself, I'd still not processed the single thought running through my head.

What the fuck is Dylan Bailey doing outside my room?

Her eyes narrowed on me instantly, as if it was instinct, her hand firmly on her hip as her lips pressed together into a firm line before she practically yelled, "You could've warned me."

My brows creased together. "About what?"

She rolled her eyes at me, head tilting on a huff. "Matteo? Your father?"

"I'm pretty sure I tried," I huffed back, fingers gripping the door as panic began to race through my body.

"Yeah, yeah." She shrugged off my words with a careless wave of her hand. "Vague, meaningless warnings from somebody I categorically don't trust will not fight off the devil."

"What happened?" I asked. She looked okay, relatively fine, that snarky mask of hers well in place. What had been so bad that it brought her to my doorstep?

It must've been my reaction, because she calmed down, the sarcasm turning serious as her brows raised. "Maybe you could at least invite me in first. Or do you plan on interrogating me on your doorstep?"

I hadn't yet fully registered her words as I moved out of the way, and she strolled into my room as if it was no big deal. As if her being here didn't signal that the worst had happened, that my actions had meant I'd failed to protect another person.

She looked around the room, her gaze catching on the unmade bed, both sides clearly slept in. "Where's Loverboy?"

I kept my eyes trained on her, trying not to give anything away. "Not here."

I still didn't know if I could trust her. After everything, she'd left Rhodes in the night with little more than a note telling Jon she was gone, and presumably ran straight to Matteo. There was still so much distance between us.

Her smirk only widened as her eyes went to the closed bathroom door. "Stuffed him in the bathroom? Real classy move there, Sinclair."

My patience snapped, my own protective instinct riled up by her comment. "You know, Dylan, I don't know what you want from me."

I regretted for a moment all those times I'd tried to warn her about Matteo, told her my door was open if she needed it. She obviously hadn't listened to a single thing I'd tried to say, and whatever had gone down, I was sure to get the blame for it again.

Dylan fell silent, instead slinking her way around my room as if she was still hesitating about even being here. Reaching the small dining table beside the large window, she pulled a chair out, before unceremoniously sitting down and crossing her legs. She took a moment to get comfy, as if wielding my own impatience against me.

"I want in," she said bluntly, her eyes fixed on me. I paused, still reading the room, trying to put the pieces together.

"On what?" I asked carefully, narrowing on her again. I still kept my distance, standing across the room near the entrance. At least if she turned on me, I'd be closest to the exit.

"Your revenge plot," she said, as if it was the most obvious thing in the world. "I want to take down Matteo."

I laughed. "Take him down? You brought him back. And what do you know about revenge? You don't even know what happened." I waved her off, ready to turn to the door, not even the slightest bit interested. She had nothing to offer me but more confusing, vague statements. Because if she knew what had happened, what had really happened, would she have shown up at my door?

"I know he paid that umpire off."

I hardly managed a single strangled word, turning again to look at her. "What?" I tried desperately to scan her face for some sort of sign of a lie, waited for the joke to crack open and the moment to loosen the band tightening itself around my gut.

Instead, she continued, her expression remaining straight. "The one from your singles match? The one who made a real stink about everything you did, to the point where even I thought it was excessive? I saw them together. They shook hands, and I didn't put it together until after your match."

I shook my head. "That doesn't prove anything."

"I sat next to Matteo during that match. He kept making these signals to the umpire. We all know what coaching during a game looks like, and it was like he was telling him what to do," she explained. I found myself sinking into the chair next to her, my legs unable to support my weight as I thought through her words, playing the memory back over.

I thought he'd been waving, trying to taunt me. But of course, he was smarter than that.

"When I asked him what he was doing, he said he was friends with the umpire. Something didn't sit right with me. He smiled and . . ." She paused, pulling back into her seat, uncertainty—another new emotion for Dylan—spreading across her face. She shook her head. "It could be that they are just friends. But it felt like too much of a coincidence when I saw them together after."

I sat silent, unsure of this new discovery. Could he really have done it again? Stolen yet another opportunity from me? But why?

Before, it was for his own gain, to see his name, the Rossi name, succeed again. I was just another trophy back then, something else for his mantel. And now I was on my own, with my own name, trying to reclaim what he'd stolen from me, but he'd denied me that opportunity once again. It began to dawn on me that he wouldn't let me go so easily. I could change my name, wreck my reputation, and team up with his former rival, but it would never be enough.

I'd win on his terms or not at all.

"I know now that he's been playing me," she started again, her eyes breaking from mine as she closed them. Her lips pressed into a thin line as if she was trying to pull herself together for a moment. "At the villa . . . the failed test."

I sat forward on the edge of my seat, realising what was coming next. Matteo had warned me when I called him to ask him about the leak. "Not everyone in that villa is your friend," he'd said when I'd asked him how. I'd had my suspicions. Dylan had left the very next day, only to reappear by his side.

"I told him, Scottie. I overheard you and Jon, and I assumed you were planning on cheating again. I called him up, told him what I had heard, and told him I wanted him to coach me. He agreed and told me to stay a few more weeks. When the story broke, I knew it was time to leave. I was so sure I knew what was happening. I'm sorry for that." I let her admission hang in the air, waiting for that rush of anger to hit me, the blame settling on the person responsible. How the test had come back a fail, I'd never know, but now I understood how it had all spun out. Instead, I only felt relief that I knew the truth now.

"Thank you," I managed, catching her attention. I nodded toward her. "I appreciate you telling me."

Her eyes stuck on mine, searching for an answer she hadn't yet asked. I braced myself, knowing what was coming, and what it would take to finally tell her. I'd kept this part from her as much as she had kept her admission from me. Her voice was soft but demanding. "I know there's more to this story, what happened between you and Matteo. I think I deserve to know."

I swallowed down the uncomfortable lump in my throat, my clammy fingers wringing with the opposite hand. I couldn't deny that after all this time, all this drama, she should learn the truth. If anyone else deserved this information, it was the other person who'd gotten swept up in Matteo's game.

I'd told two people, my mum and Nico, and each time, it felt like walking right up to the edge of a sharp ledge. Every step closer was a risk that the earth below you could give way, that they might not believe what you said. It was dangerous ground to tread. I had to trust Dylan, keep the faith that she would accept my side of the story, and have the confidence in myself that if she didn't, that if I walked all the way out on that ledge and fell, that I would eventually get back up again. No matter what, broken bones mended with time, and I would get back up again.

I took in a deep breath, filling my lungs up, and took a leap of faith.

"Everything about the cheating at Wimbledon. It was all true." My fingers curled in, nails biting at the skin of my palms, pressing in and leaving small half-moon imprints. I reminded myself that this wasn't a lie. I wasn't twisting the situation. This was the truth, and Dylan was ready to listen and believe me. "But I didn't know about the drugs. It was all Matteo."

The words hung in the tight air between us, my heartbeat soaring as I tried to remain calm. I was stripped bare, the hurt resurfacing. It was the truth, and somehow, it was more painful than the lie I'd crafted, wrapped myself up in like it would protect me. But taking the blame hadn't changed anything. He still found strings to pull.

"And you didn't think to tell anyone? For two years," she said, the words straight and to the point. No bullshit, the way I'd learned Dylan always was.

"I didn't think anyone would believe me."

"You didn't even try?" she snapped, eyes narrowed on me.

"I don't think that's fair. You have no idea what I've been through," I argued back, sick of apologising. The lump in my throat refused to disappear. No matter how hard I'd tried to swallow, the hurt from years ago resurfacing, refusing to be put back in the box I'd kept it stuffed in. "Who was going to believe me? Against him, with no evidence? I had no chance."

The air was full of tension, so tight I could hardly breathe. Then she let out a heavy sigh as her eyes pressed closed, a hand rising up to rest on her brow.

"I'm sorry." I almost fell off my chair at the words. An apology coming from Dylan Bailey? If I looked out the window, would I find flying pigs?

When she spoke again, her tone was calmer but still with that edge of Dylan slice. "I'm not trying to be nasty, Scottie. I just want to understand why you'd keep this to yourself."

I nodded, understanding her intention. I could see she was trying. That had to be something.

"So," she said tentatively. "You took the blame and ran?"

My only answer was a wince. There were those words again. I had been running away the day Jon appeared on our doorstep, and Mum convinced me to hear him out. When Dylan had yelled at me in the garden, and again, when Nico found me on the practice court after and I told him the truth, thinking it would drive him away.

All I'd done was try to outrun Matteo, and I'd ended up in the exact place where he could use his influence over me to extract whatever result he wanted. A win or a loss, as long as it was what *he* wanted. I could still feel his control all over me, those strings I was tangled in. And it made me sick. I'd been running for two years, but I was exhausted. So out of breath that I'd stayed in one place just long enough to see that I'd never really escaped him. If I really wanted to be free of him, I needed a new game plan.

"Scottie." My attention snapped to Dylan, realising that I hadn't given her an answer in a long time. "I know . . . we've never been close, right?"

At first, I wasn't sure if it was a trick question. I slowly shook my head, waiting for some sort of cruel trick.

"But when you won, that day at Wimbledon. I was bitter, and I held on to that. Do you know how many finals I've reached? Four. And I still don't have a title that I've truly won. I've lost every single one. But that Wimbledon title—it haunted me. Because while it was mine, it really wasn't? You know? We both know how it feels to lose, but to lose and then find out your competitor cheated? It felt like I'd been robbed of the thing I'd spent my entire life working toward. It never sat right with me, and I think I let you know that."

I bit my lip, answering very carefully, still treading on new ground. "You have a very angry communication style."

She nodded. "I'm in therapy, I promise."

I almost laughed then, realising as I held it back that I barely recognised her. She was no longer an enemy, at least temporarily. Her hand stretched out and met mine, her warm touch against my ice-cold palm.

"I want you to know that I'm sorry for treating you that way. I was hurt, but I believe you."

I felt the world shift under my seat, like a new lens had taken everything blurry and made it clear enough to see again. I couldn't keep the tears back, my eyes filling up. I took my other hand and wiped them away, but I kept my left on hers, the warmth of her hand grounding me in my body.

"You can't let him get away with this. Not again," she said, her voice firm. She'd always had more fight than I did, on and off the court. If anyone was going to fight their hardest until the very end, it was Dylan. All this time, I had been pushing her away, but maybe she was exactly the person I'd needed all along on my team.

On a deep exhale, I broke again, my hand gripping hers. "He's not going to stop . . . is he?"

She shook her head, her eyes not leaving mine. "But you can end it. There will be some evidence with the umpire, we can get them to investigate it. With both of our stories, and considering I have absolutely no reason to take your side other than I believe you, we will force them to act. At the very least, stop him from hurting anyone else."

She read the hesitation on my face. "Or we can set Loverboy free from the bathroom and make him force them." Somehow, she forced a gasping laugh through the tears running down my cheeks, just as a voice rose from the bathroom.

"Does that mean I can come out now?"

Dylan was quick with her simple retort. "No. I'm quite happy to keep pretending that I'm not sitting in some sex den." She forced yet another laugh from me. "I don't want to think about what you two animals have been doing on"—she pulled herself up from the chair, looking around suspiciously—"every surface in this room."

The door to the bathroom cracked open, revealing Nico wrapped up in his own robe this time, his hair still curly and wet from the shower. His expression was serious, but I could see the pride in his eyes. It felt like hours had passed since we were in there together. So much had changed.

"So, can we do this?" Dylan asked, pulling my attention back to her.

My answer was two years in the making. I'd stopped running long enough to let Nico in, to let myself come back to the sport I loved. I'd convinced myself that this life had been taken from me, that there was no return, nothing but the remnants of an old existence that I'd scarcely survived.

Now, I knew I could still have it. I just had to be willing to fight to keep it. All I needed to do was be brave enough to tell the truth.

"Let's end him."

Tennis Legend Faces Allegations of Abuse

Today, Scottie Sinclair and Dylan Bailey made allegations of abuse against Sinclair's father, tennis legend Matteo Rossi. Bailey, addressing the media after securing her place in the women's final, took the opportunity to shed light on her experiences working with her now-former coach, Rossi. Adding an unexpected twist to the narrative, Bailey invited her former rival, Sinclair, to join her onstage and share her own troubling allegations. Despite a historical rivalry, and Sinclair's two-year ban from tennis due to doping, she now claims ignorance and asserts that her father and then-coach Rossi plotted against her.

While both players lack concrete evidence to substantiate their claims, which include allegations of bribery of tennis officials, supporters have rallied behind them. Notably, a dozen current tennis professionals have stepped forward, inspired by this revelation, to share their own stories of mistreatment and abuse within the sport.

The International Tennis Integrity Agency (ITIA) has announced an investigation into the allegations made by Bailey and Sinclair. As Wimbledon unfolds, with both players reaching the finals in singles and doubles competitions, the story is set to continue.

Representatives for Matteo Rossi could not be contacted at the time of publishing.

CHAPTER FORTY-SIX

Scottie
Karma – Taylor Swift

All my life had been leading to this single moment. A hot summer's day in mid-July, Wimbledon's Centre Court, the Mixed Doubles Final, and Nico Kotas's soothing hand rubbing the tension from my upper back. We could hear the electric buzz of the crowd all the way from the locker room, and soon it would be time to head outside and meet our opponents.

"You okay?" Nico asked.

I let out a short laugh, looking across the room, searching for the nearest exit. "I think I'm going to throw up."

"Same." My gaze met his, and I found a small smile. "Maybe we can share a bin."

"How romantic," I teased. "I doubt we need any more team bonding."

"I'm sure we have time for one more quick practice session. I hear the cleaning closets here are pretty roomy."

"I'll meet you there if we win."

He stepped closer, his pull so magnetic I couldn't help but step in too, facing him head-on as he spoke. "And if we lose?"

"I'll meet you at the bar first."

"A public place? I don't think so. Make it your room, a bottle of tequila, and absolutely no clothes."

I hummed with anticipation, memories of the last few days playing over in my mind. His room had been all but abandoned as we spent almost every waking moment together, either in practice preparing for doubles, on the court fighting our way to today's final, or wrapped up in my bedsheets together.

A quick glance at the clock told me that we did not have time to sneak off to a supply closet.

"You know, whatever happens out there," he started, the lump in his throat moving as he swallowed, "I wouldn't have done it any other way, or with anyone else."

"Same." I smiled before leaning over and kissing his lips. "Even if you are a little on the old side."

His strong hands wrapped around my waist, pulling my body close to his with a groan. I heaved with laughter as he kissed all exposed skin, my skirt riding up as he squeezed and teased me.

"Just you wait till this 'old man' shows you up on the court."

He kissed my neck, his lips trailing up and down, the skin turning hot with the contact. Being in his arms, I never wanted to be anywhere else.

There was a knock at the door and we both turned, breaking apart, expecting to find Jon, but instead, a looming tall figure replaced him. My heart stuttered at the sight of my father.

"Am I interrupting something?" There was no smile to be found across his features. No smirking grin or snaky expression. Instead, he was just about the coldest I'd ever seen him look. Face stony, shoulders drawn back.

Nico's hand tightened against mine, his body shifting to go in front. But with one quick squeeze of his hand, he paused. Nico looked at me as I spoke directly ahead at my father. "What are you doing here?"

"I wanted to wish you luck." He said the words as if it was obvious. As if Dylan and I hadn't just told the world what he had done. I could've sworn he was puffing out his chest, trying to fill the doorway to intimidate me. But I was done being made smaller—I knew my strength now.

I shook my head, turning away from him. He wasn't worth it anymore. "Just leave me alone."

I looked at Nico, the strong line of his jaw locked with anger, his fury directed towards the doorway, but I caught his attention, his expression softening with worry. I smiled at him, seeing my world, the person who would sacrifice so much in his own life to help mine. He had proven that to me, giving up his dream for another. How would I ever repay him?

Matteo started again. "Do you really think that you can hold one press conference, and everyone is going to believe you—"

"I don't need everyone to believe me," I interrupted, shaking my head. Whether people listened was out of my control. But I was done living behind a lie, behind fear. Telling the truth had set me free. "That's not what that was about. If I can stop just one person from working with you, then I've saved them from your cruelty."

"I'll still be here," he taunted, trying desperately to get a rise out of me. And before, I would've gotten so angry that he'd never truly be gone. I'd run from everything because I'd been so desperate to escape him. I'd let him take my life from me, but not again.

I looked at him, my lips pressed together in an uncaring line, resolve beating at me, keeping me standing strong. "And so will I."

Matteo didn't get a chance to reply as Nico stepped forward, his body in front of mine as if to form a wall of protection. I didn't need it, but I appreciated it nonetheless.

"You need to leave," Nico said through gritted teeth. He almost snarled as he continued. "Now."

Matteo shifted slightly before pausing. His hand landed on the doorframe as he needlessly began to remind me, "I'll always be your dad, Scottie. You can't outrun that."

"I know." I tried to keep my voice clear. "But I also know you still think you did it all for me. You can't see it was all for you. Only for you. You didn't treat me like your daughter or even an equal, and I can't forgive you for that. I became the player that I am today because of you and despite of you, and I won't run from that. Not anymore. But I want nothing to do with you, so please, stay out of my life."

Then, with a deep breath, I stepped past Nico, caught the door in my hand, and shut it in Matteo's face.

CHAPTER FORTY-SEVEN

Scottie

I Know The End – Phoebe Bridgers

A knock sounded through the locker room as Jon appeared in the doorway. "Hey, lovebirds," he said, his tone serious. "It's time."

My stomach lurched again, nerves getting the best of me as Nico released me from his grasp. Without another word, we both grabbed our prepared kit bags and followed Jon out into the hallway.

Nico's hand slipped effortlessly into mine, the movement almost instinctual for him now. I tried to focus on his calloused skin, how his fingers felt interlocked with mine, instead of the steady drum-beat pounding in my chest, the roar of the crowd outside as we finally emerged onto the court. Sunlight beamed down, blinding me temporarily before my eyes adjusted, and I took in the vast court.

I hadn't been here in two years, but it felt like only yesterday when I'd stepped onto the grass, a naïve twenty-two-year-old, completely unaware of how her life was about to fall apart.

I'd fought my way back and earned this spot. And now, I'd play fair and square for the title.

Beside us, our competitors and defending champions, Wilson and Carter, walked out, both of them seemingly cool and collected under the pressure of the final. I nodded at them, trying to maintain my own confident façade as they strolled past, heading to the benches on the opposite side of the court.

Dropping my own kit beside my chair, I pulled out my bottle of water and took a long gulp, all the while trying to ignore the thousands of eyes from the crowd stalking my every movement. Anticipation was quickly building as the clock ticked closer to the start of the game, uncertainty beginning to prick at my skin.

This was what it had come down to. One last match. Take a single misstep, and the entire thing could unravel before me. Or I could keep my nerve, hold that breath, and win. Finally win.

I pulled out my racket, the black ELITE-branded metal gleaming in the sunlight, before turning to Nico. "Ready for this?" I looked to him expecting confidence, that predator-like focus to be ready and in place.

But there was a frown to his lips, an unfocused look in his eyes, like he was moments from vomiting into his kit bag.

My eyebrows creased together as I turned fully to him, closing the space and keeping my voice low. "Is it your knee?

He shook his head, his focus pointed down, his large hands turning his racket over and over, feeling the weight of it, assessing its grip. "I need a moment."

My hand went to his shoulder, squeezing gently, feeling the tight muscles beneath my fingertips as I tried to soothe his anxiety.

"Hey, we got this." I reached up to his chin, slowly redirecting his gaze, so it met mine. I kept my eyes sharp and fixed, lips pressed into a serious line. "Just play like we do in practice."

Any trace of doubt slowly faded as the storm in his grey eyes turned to a determined steel. I watched as the lines on his face flattened, a steadiness locking in his jaw as if sculpted by the sheer force of belief.

"Just like we practised," Nico repeated.

In turn, his confidence fuelled my own, the nerves in my

stomach now settled, and instead I was finally ready for this fight. There was no option for defeat. I fucking hated that feeling too much to accept it now. I was hungry for the win, starved for the glory, and I refused to let us walk off this court empty-handed.

A coin toss determined who served first: us, and we took our places. Me at the net, Nico at the baseline, serving. I stared straight ahead, my eyes stuck on our competitors, both waiting and ready for the first game to finally begin.

We were here. At the final. Centre Court. I'd thought revenge would be getting here alone, without him. Proving to myself that I could do it. But peace was far more rewarding than revenge could ever be.

And Nico Kotas, he was my peace.

The clap of strings meeting the ball cracked through the silence of the area, the powerful serve flying past me and beginning the first game. Wilson and Carter jumped into motion, Carter easily returning the ball as the rally began.

We had our game plan, our positions and tactics were second nature to us, and we had each other. I sprinted across, easily meeting the ball as we swapped positions, covering for each other, every step we took calculated to ensure we didn't leave ourselves undefended.

I glanced quickly over my shoulder as we secured our third point, meeting Nico's confident smile. We were assured in our own skill as singles players, but confident and assertive as a doubles team.

They took the next two games, followed by a stupidly mistimed step from me, which allowed Wilson to level the game score, reminding us of what kind of opponents they were. I'd known Carter off the court, and she was friendly, but on grass she was a killer with the forehand.

3 – 3

With the set score tied, the pressure intensified. I served with precision, forcing Wilson to make a desperate return. We clawed our way back. Nico seized any opportunity that allowed him to unleash his forehand volley and left our opponents scrambling. The crowd erupted in cheers as we clinched the crucial break. The set was ours. One down, one to go.

I couldn't help but take a moment to celebrate, turning to Nico. "Keep it up, old man."

He smirked. "Let me show you how it's done, *katsarída*."

I twirled my racket in my hands, my lips twisting into a playful, teasing expression, feeling a little lighter, more confident, and ready for the second set.

Carter opened with a serve, their tactics becoming increasingly unpredictable, testing our adaptability. We just about kept up, sensing the new gameplay, and between points, we were forced to strategize, finding new ways to exploit the small gaps in our opponents' game. Yet Wilson and Carter fought back fiercely, and the set teetered on a knife's edge, each point a battle for supremacy.

4 – 3

Two more games and the set would be theirs. I could see the frustration building in Nico. He had begun to hesitate when judging each return of the ball. Our opponents were showing their teeth, proving to us what a danger they could be.

We fought on, returning their powerful serves, both Nico and I battling for every single point. Carter angled a volley over the net, almost catching us off guard. I sprinted, the top of my racket just managing to find the ball in time. The rally continued, and they were determined to win this point, Wilson powering the ball over the net, down the middle of the court. It was too fast for me, flying past me.

I followed the ball, sure the point was over, only to find Nico charging for it. He swung, slamming the ball back over, but he didn't stop, gliding across the court and falling forward with a hard hit.

The ball hopped over the net, catching our competitors out and winning us the point, but my attention was firmly on Nico, who wearily got to his feet.

40 – 30

"You okay?" I asked.

He nodded, barely looking at me before carrying on. We crawled back, claiming another point as ours, but I could see Nico slowing down. I wasn't much better. Wilson and Carter were tough, making us fight for every point.

Wilson finally secured the second set with a wide kick serve to Nico's forehand, taking advantage of his hurt knee. He limped, head down, after attempting to reach the ball. My heart sank. It would come down to a final third set.

We were allowed a short break to refresh and hydrate. It was all I could do to not collapse onto our bench. My legs were tired after so many hours on court. It had been two long weeks. I downed almost an entire bottle of cool water, the ball boys quickly replacing it while handing out a fresh towel that I gladly accepted.

"This is going to shit," Nico stated plainly as he sat down on the bench, a towel draped over his head. "We made that second set too easy for them."

I shook my head, not willing to accept defeat yet. My fingers pressed into the plastic of the bottle, crushing it with frustration. "We did not come all this way to give up now."

Nico finished off his own bottle of water. "I agree. What are we going to do about it?"

"They are weakest with cross-court shots," I noted. I looked to the other bench. Carter and Wilson were likely having a similar discussion. "I think we need to put more pressure on the second serve too. Get aggressive with it. Force the play to be faster. It might gain us some momentum."

"That will also tire us out."

"Good thing there's only one set left," I said before taking in his posture. He had his bad leg outstretched, a cold water bottle held to it. "How's the knee holding up?"

"I'm fine," he said through gritted teeth, jaw clenched with frustration.

I paused for a moment, keeping my voice soft as I pressed again. We had no chance of winning if he couldn't be open with me. "Tell me the truth."

"I hurt it halfway through the set. It's getting . . . awkward to run on."

My lips pressed firmly together, anxiety rising. I couldn't lose him mid-match because of too aggressive tactics. It could put the entire game at risk, especially if we had to stop. There was no second chance here.

"Okay," I said with a nod. "You take the shots that come your way, but leave the rest to me."

He shook his head, frustration etched on his face. "Scottie, I can do it."

A quick glance across told me our competitors were almost ready to go, and I looked back at Nico.

"You do what you can," I said, trying to calm him. The last thing we needed was him really hurting his knee. We had to make it through this set. We had to win. And if that meant I had to compensate for us, I'd do it. "But we can't wear you out. We need to get through this final set, and win."

"Are you sure?" he asked, eyes set on me. I held my breath, looking out onto the vast court. It was intimidating, the history here. But to be a part of it with him by my side, could anything be better?

I smiled reassuringly at him. "I'm sure."

He looked resistant, the strong line of his jaw setting, but I pushed. "Let me do this for us. Isn't this what Jon said when we first got together? Strategy is what you're best at. I was to compensate with my bountiful youth and original knee."

"You know, one of these days those old man jokes will have to go into retirement, *katsarída*."

"Too bad today isn't that day." I smiled, watching his own lips curve as his attention dipped to his feet, the racket nervously spinning in his hands. "So? What's the plan? How do we take them down?"

It took him a moment, the time on our break running out as he began to fill me in, and when he did, I was almost certain it would work . . . as long as I could pull it off. It was time to show them who we were, or go home empty-handed.

I took his hand in mine and squeezed it tightly. Just once was enough.

"I love you." His words pulled my heart into a vice tight grip, squeezing and warming inside. "And I can't wait to watch you win this for us."

We stood, taking up our positions on the court. I took the serve, feeling the fuzz of the ball in my hand, inspecting the green surface, before looking ahead to my partner, finding his attention on me, his brows pressed together in question.

I kept my eyes on him, a mask of confidence falling into place.

"Let's do this," I mouthed his way, watching as he mirrored my assurance back at me. A nod of his head indicated he was ready for this fight.

The arena turned silent as I rhythmically bounced the small green ball against the grass, counting each bounce.

One. Two. Three. Just like I'd always done.

I looked to the crowd, saw the box, found my mum and Jon watching us in anticipation. I knew if Dylan could've made it, she'd be up there too. I refocused ahead, finding our opponents, shifting from foot to foot. Ready to pounce, ready to play, ready to win. They were fierce, and just as bloodthirsty for this trophy as we were. But we were not out, not yet. Everything was on the line for this, and I was ready to give my entire body and soul to this court to make it happen.

To take this from them because I fucking wanted it. We wanted this win, and I would not let it slip through our fingers.

Everything that had happened—Matteo, Nico's knee, the last few years of my life—it had brought me back, full circle. Centre Court. Because this was where I belonged. Where we both belonged. My feet on this grass. This racket in my hand. Nico Kotas by my side.

I took a deep breath in, filling deep into my lungs, as I waited for a cool opposite breeze of wind to die down. I threw the ball high in the air, the rest of the moment a second instinct, my body knowing exactly what to do. All I had to do was trust it.

On my exhale, I unleashed my full power, rocketing the ball over the net. With that, the comeback had truly begun.

And this time, we didn't fail.

DREAM TEAM KOTAS AND SINCLAIR
SCORE AT WIMBLEDON

In a surprising turn of events this week at Wimbledon, the singles competition was sidelined by the dreamy duo of Scottie Sinclair and Nico Kotas, who clinched the mixed doubles title in spectacular fashion.

Linked romantically since early April, Sinclair and Kotas put an end to months of speculation with a triumphant display of affection following their victory on Centre Court. Sinclair's stellar performance, particularly in rallying to secure the third set after Kotas suffered a fall, undoubtedly played a pivotal role in their success. After Sinclair won the final set, Kotas swept Sinclair off her feet in a show of sheer romance that is destined to etch itself into Wimbledon history.

However, amidst the celebrations, the tennis world finds itself embroiled in a moment of introspection. Sinclair's courageous decision to speak out against her own father, Matteo Rossi, accusing him of abuse, has cast a sobering light on the sport. Her bravery in confronting such deeply personal trauma in the face of intrusive tabloid scrutiny serves as a stark reminder of the ongoing struggle against sexism in media portrayal. Sinclair's story underscores the pressing need for systemic change within the sports industry, challenging long-standing narratives and demanding accountability at every level.

CHAPTER FORTY-EIGHT

Scottie

The Alchemy – Taylor Swift

A glass of champagne in one hand, a trophy in the other, and Nico Kotas's arms wrapped around my waist. The July sunset with an explosion of pink and orange across a London skyline. I could barely remember a life before him. A lonely life falling out of clubs and burning down yachts and two hot men in red suits.

"You doing okay?" Nico broke the silence, his head nuzzled into my shoulder, a soft breeze blowing in the garden. We had been at my mum's house, a small party to celebrate our win, and the end of another Wimbledon. Inside, the house was full of friends, both Nico's and mine, the loud buzz of the party filled the evening air as we hid in the temporary escape.

"I'm good." I turned in his arms, placing the champagne down on the table to free one hand up. The trophy was glued to me. But still, I pushed slightly up on my toes, my lips easily reaching his. "You taste like champagne."

"That might have something to do with all the Laurent-Perrier your mom has been serving all night." He grinned, his face barely pulled back from mine. I'd never seen his eyes so clear, so bright.

We have everything.

"Are you going to put that trophy down anytime soon?" His gaze dipped momentarily to the left, the piece of silverware still tucked safely under my arm.

I grinned wildly, my limb pulling tighter. "Absolutely not."

"Afraid somebody's going to steal it?" The sound of his laugh warmed my blood.

I somehow managed to tear myself from him for a second, stealing a peek inside the kitchen to the packed crowd, loud music and conversation mixing in the air. "Dylan *is* just inside."

It was easy to spot her, cornered by Inés, wearing her usual scowl, her arms folded. I couldn't blame her. I hadn't expected her to stop by. She'd lost yesterday, another final. I'd still be recovering, but it was a good surprise when Inés had shown up with her in tow.

"It was nice of you to invite her," he hummed, his lips pressing against the right side of my forehead.

So much had changed in the last few days. Starting with a knock on my hotel door and ending with a press conference where we put everything on the line. The ITIA had announced it was investigating Matteo, and the other coaches that had faced similar allegations from fellow players who'd come forward since.

There was a weird ease that came with the news. I'd convinced myself for two years nobody would believe me, and now that it was happening, I hadn't quite let myself trust it. Not just yet. But I wasn't on edge, waiting to turn around a corner and run into *him*. He didn't have that power anymore.

"I have this weird feeling like we might be friends now," I admitted.

"Is she aware?"

"I like to call it trauma bonding." I met his gaze again. "You know, I couldn't have done this without you."

"You mean, you couldn't have won doubles without your mixed partner?" he teased, his arms tightening around my waist, holding me close to his body.

"You know what I mean." I rolled my eyes at him, only for a moment, before I was back on him. Nico, the grumpy player who'd refused to shake my hand the first time we'd met. Who'd played and trained with me on the court from sunrise to sunset. Who'd always had my back.

The one who had stolen my heart completely.

"Are you two just going to spend the rest of the evening out here?" I looked over Nico's shoulder, finding my mum hanging out of the open patio door. "You're missing all the canapés."

I smiled back, grateful that she had been there with me every step of the way.

"In a minute."

She tapped her wrist playfully in response, leaving the door open as she disappeared back inside.

When I turned back to Nico, his hand found the side of my face, gliding up the line of my jaw, and led me back to his lips. The pressure of him gliding against me, the stubble along his jaw dragging against mine.

"You still don't see it, do you?" he mumbled, his lips barely leaving mine. "I couldn't do this without you. I've been trying for years, and this trophy—*our trophy*—is the closest I've ever gotten, and I will forever be thankful for that." His head leaned to the side, his mouth leaving a trail of kisses along my jaw, leading up to my ear, where he stopped. "But you, Scottie Sinclair, never needed me. You are strong and ruthless and so fucking unstoppable, and I can't wait for a lifetime of watching and loudly cheering you on."

The only logical reply was a kiss, one strong enough that I was sure he could feel the ache in my heart at his words, my gratitude for all of him, his attention and love. He might not have seen it, might not have realised how key he was to everything we had achieved together, but I knew, and I'd never forget it.

"I love you," I said.

"I love you too." The words were just as easy for him as they were for me, I could tell. "But we should head inside before everyone starts to think we've abandoned them."

My free hand found his, squeezing in answer for him to lead us inside, to our friends and family, to everyone who had supported us on our way here. Inés and Dylan were tucked amongst the crowd talking to Oliver, who had also made it along. I found Jon hiding in the back, my mum beside him, probably discussing the benefits of preventive Botox.

I'd been alone for so long. No roots, no purpose, and so painfully wounded, the truth like a shard of glass grazing against my heart. It had taken all of them to get here and to heal. To trust again.

All along, I'd just needed Nico, his heart, and a baseball cap to steal.

EPILOGUE

Nico
Clean – Taylor Swift

Scottie jogged on the spot in front of me, peppy and bursting full of energy. Her black tennis skirt fluttered around her thighs. I was almost certain she had only worn it as a distraction, the low cut of her sports bra showing more skin than she normally would.

"Come on, you can't keep putting this off forever," she taunted, smiling brightly. We'd settled at my home in Tampa. She had a month off from the touring and travelling of the tennis season, and I had her all to myself. Four blissful weeks that would've been peaceful, if it wasn't for her competitive edge I loved so much.

"I was stretching." I groaned as I pushed up from the bench to continue with my warm-up. Lengthening my arm across my body into a deep pull, I muttered under my breath, "I can't believe you're making me do this again."

Since we'd won together, the two silver challenge cups from Wimbledon sitting side by side inside the house, I'd relaxed my competition schedule, only competing when it made sense for me, and for Scottie. My knee was a problem, there was no getting around that, but I could handle the strain with a reduced schedule. Competing and playing was its own reward. I still had that hunger

in my bones. But it wasn't an insatiable need to win, more a satisfied grumble, with all four Grand Slam titles under my belt, and
my girl on my arm. Being around to support her was a reward in
itself.

"We made a deal," she reminded me, but I just shook my head.

"We made a deal to stop this madness with the last match."

One night, at the start of the break, after a few too many beers,
we'd made a bet. Every time we played against each other, we'd
keep a running score, and by the end, we'd have the true winner. The best tennis player. I'd been sure she'd win, but to my
surprise, I'd kept up the pace, and in the final week we were neck
and neck.

So then came our next bright idea. Five rounds. Me vs her. No
holding back, no letting the other win. Pure competition. A fight
for the title. It made sense.

The first match had gone well into the night, with neither of us
able to win a tie break before we'd called it. But then the next day,
she argued that there were no "ties" in tennis and made us replay
the point. Over and over, until with some sort of miracle, I'd won.
But one of us had turned out to be a bit of a sore loser.

"But then I lost, so I demanded a rematch." She stuck out her
tongue playfully, her blonde hair tied up in a ponytail, my cap keeping the rest from her face. The sight of her wearing it was enough
to bring me to my knees. "Last time, you got lucky. Beat me by one
point. That's hard for a woman of my—"

"Arrogance?" I argued, interrupting her with one brow pushed up.

"I was going to say talent." Her eyes narrowed on me. "That's
hard for a woman of my *talent* to take."

I couldn't help the smile that broke out across my face, so instead
I turned around, busying myself by pulling my racket out of the
bag, filling my pocket with a few balls until it was under control.

"The last match was supposed to be the final one. You said you'd learn to live with the loss."

I knew it was useless to remind her. I'd been doing it for days, trying to avoid this final game so we could enjoy the last of our time here. But she was relentless, the athlete inside of her unable to cope with the itch of the simple loss. That, and she probably didn't want me holding it over her head.

"I lied." I turned around to find a playful smug look on her face, her pink lips in a smirk. "Come on. Five rounds. Let's go all the way. See who really is the best." Her eyes narrowed on me, a competitive curve pulling at the edge of her lips. I had learned the hard way that when I got *this* look, I should expect devious things from her. I relented, knowing it was useless to put it off anymore. It was either now, or I'd hear about this for the rest of my life. Because that's how long I was planning on keeping her.

"Fine. Let's get on with it." I threw a couple balls her way, watching as she pocketed them in the stretchy hidden pocket of her skirt, my eyes lingering on the tops of her thighs.

She definitely picked that skirt to distract me.

"Personally, I think we're equals," I said over my shoulder, as we began to make our way to opposite sides of the private court, the warm Florida air perfect weather for tennis.

"Personally," she shouted back, spinning around for dramatic effect, "I think you're scared to get your ass handed to you."

"Says the person who's already been beaten twice!"

"The first was a tie!"

I stifled a laugh, shaking my head as we both got into position on the baseline. I watched as she discarded a few balls to the side of the court, taking her time before she picked one. She bounced the ball a few times against the hard surface, counting in her head.

One. Two. Three. Just like she always does.

"Let's just get this over with," I shouted, distracting her back. "We've got a reservation for dinner at seven." My heart pounded with the reminder of what I had planned. A private dinner, in my favourite part of town. A small, romantic Greek restaurant, tucked away in a private corner to remind us of our beginning.

"Too bad I'm about to beat you, old man." She smiled. It wasn't often she still called me that, but whenever she did, I knew she was trying to get under my skin. Instead, all she did was remind me of sandy spring days spent just like this one, standing on the opposite side of the court, watching her serve.

Before that villa, I'd been convinced my life was over. The only thing I'd ever cared about, done. But she'd given me something I didn't know I needed—hope, and a new start.

Now, with a ring hidden in my tennis bag, waiting for the moment when she finally beat me, I knew I'd never been surer about anything. Scottie Sinclair was the love of my life, my best friend. And if every day of the rest of my life was spent here, looking at her from across the court, then I was in the exact place I wanted to be.

"Just keep hittin', Sinclair," I shouted as she threw the ball up in the air, the racket slamming into the ball, sending it flying across the net, landing right at my feet.

I smiled as I realised I'd never stood a chance against Scottie Sinclair.

15 – Love.

DICKTIONARY

For whatever purposes it may serve to the dear reader, this author wishes to inform you that explicit content can be found in the following chapters:

- Chapter Twenty-Seven
- Chapter Thirty-Two
- Chapter Thirty-Six
- Chapter Forty-Four

Happy Reading!

ACKNOWLEDGEMENTS

Whenever I have to write one of these, I like to imagine I've won an Oscar and am battling the clock and the foreboding exit music playing. So here we go!

Hailey and Lisina, you saved me last minute with this book. I owe you my firstborn for your polishing efforts.

To my beautiful, enthusiastic alpha reader Anna P, and my beta readers: Kaity, Jos, Leila, Berty, Michelle, Sefanie, Erin, Gabriela, Hunter, Molly, Iqra, Sascha, Sarah, Ariel, Shandy, Georgia, Kelly, Brooke, Courtney, Jules and Zairn. You are the best group of readers this writer could ever ask for. Thank you for your unhinged comments.

My cover designer, Katie Pridige (@katiecreatescovers). You took my Frankenstein concept drawing and made it beautiful. I still have a screenshot of our conversation where you pitched working together on a cover, and I'll treasure it forever. Thank you for bringing Scottie and Nico to life, and for giving our book the cover of my dreams. I adore you!

My editors, Kourney Spak (@kourtisediting), who took my non-science gameplay and made it shine, and Amy (@Amyedits), I truly don't know how to write a book without your dev edits. Thank you for always seeing what my book needs.

Thank you to Jessie Cunniffe (@bookblurbmagic), who helped me write the blurb of my dreams!

Elliot Fletcher, the real MVP who got me in contact with my agent. I know authors support authors but this is another level. I owe you for life!

Katie Fulford, thank you for seeing something in draft two of the manuscript. For your incredible notes that injected life into this book, and for working so hard to find it a home with my publishers. I can't wait to do amazing things with you.

My publishers, for putting up with my demanding diva antics and for allowing this book to reach a much larger audience!

Mum (J***e B******y—she insisted on the government name being printed), Matt, Dad, Kirsty, Nanny, all my friends and family. Thank you for being so supportive and for not embarrassing me too much.

To my future in-laws . . . I'm sorry for writing this. Please, let's never speak of this.

Sophie, you unrelenting supportive queen. It's a pleasure to be best friends with you. I know you'll dispute this but I'm the one who can put it in print and publish the words: I love you more.

Vicky, thank you for obsessing over Serena Williams for so long that I had no choice but to stan. And then for putting up with all my tennis questions as I tumbled my way through the first draft.

HAILEY DICKERT: QUEEN OF MY HEART. WRITING WIFE AND BESTIE WHO MADE SURE I DIDN'T JUST DROP THIS BOOK BEYONCÉ STYLE WITH NO PROMO. Please never leave me. You've made me entirely dependent on our friendship. I can't survive without you.

Euan, thank you for being cool about me immortalising some of our life in these pages (the Lindos trip. Reader, get your head out of the gutter!). The best parts of my day are spent with you. Sorry for forcing you to watch so many tennis clips as I try to get you interested in the sport. Love you so much.

ABOUT THE AUTHOR

Meg Jones is a Scottish romance author who took beginners tennis lessons (two entire blocks and was still the worst in her class) twelve years ago before putting down the racket and picking up a book instead.

Meg is passionate about female representation in both fictional and non-fictional sports, and was constantly distracted by the idea of a tennis romance for two years before finally putting pen to paper. *Clean Point* is Meg's second book.

You can find Meg spending far too much time over on Instagram @megjoneswrites, or follow her newsletter for updates.